THE MODERN LIBRARY

OF THE WORLD'S BEST BOOKS

Great Spanish Stories

Great Spanish Stories

EDITED WITH
AN INTRODUCTION BY
ANGEL FLORES
Queens College

THE MODERN LIBRARY · *New York*

Acknowledgments

Acknowledgment to reprint copyrighted material in this volume is made as follows:

The Three-Cornered Hat, Copyright, 1928, by Martin Armstrong, reprinted by permission of Simon and Schuster, Inc., and John Lane The Bodley Head Limited; *Torquemada in the Flames,* translated by Willard R. Trask, Copyright 1954 by Hearst Magazines, Inc.; *Sonata of Autumn* from *The Pleasant Memoirs of the Marquis of Bradomín* by Ramón María del Valle-Inclán, Copyright, 1924, by Harcourt, Brace and Company, Inc.; *Prometheus* by Ramón Pérez de Ayala, Copyright, 1920, renewed, 1948, E. P. Dutton and Co., Inc.; *Saint Manuel Bueno, Martyr,* in the translation by Anthony Kerrigan, is used by special permission of the copyright owners, the Henry Regnery Company.

I am also indebted to Anthony Kerrigan, Willard Trask, Zenia da Silva, Leonore Crary and Jess Stein for all kinds of assistance in the preparation of this volume.

A.F.

Contents

Contents

Introduction BY ANGEL FLORES

Spain was the first country in Europe to cultivate prose fiction. This priority may be attributed to the fact that Spain was the only European nation under Arabic domination (from 711 to 1492) and that Arabic cultural forms, such as the short story, found their way into the conquered people. Although calling himself "serf of Christ," the twelfth-century Pedro Alfonso evidenced no embarrassment in adapting the Oriental climate to his piously Christian *Disciplina Clericalis*. On the contrary, he felt its value enhanced because of the prestige then enjoyed by Islamic culture. Six of the stories in his book deal with woman's lechery and unfaithfulness, a theme taken over by Arabian writers from Hindu literature which ultimately entered the mainstream of medieval and Renaissance letters. A century after *Disciplina Clericalis,* a collection entitled *Calila e Dimna* (1251), translated from the Arabic by order of Alfonso the Wise, showed once more the tendency to appropriate Hindu literary traditions, this time from the classic *Panchatantra*. Other works, the *Sendebar o Libro de los engaños e asayamientos de las mujeres* (1253), twenty-six apologues dealing mostly with the trickery of women, and *Barlaam y Josaphat,* a Christian adaptation of a legend attributed to Buddha, continue this trend so popular throughout the Middle Ages and pave the way for the first European writer of prose fiction: Don Juan Manuel (1282-1349?). His masterpiece, *El Conde Lucanor* (1335), deriving to a considerable extent from the sources and works mentioned above, is a series of *exempla* or cautionary tales intended to shed light on life's perplexities. The fictional elements seem often to subserve the practical aim: Don Juan Manuel merely presents *cases* in order *to teach* the reader how to win friends and influence people and so advance his position in life. This strong emphasis on the ethical is a Spanish characteristic that has been highlighted in modern treatises dealing with "the soul of Spain," from Havelock Ellis and Waldo Frank to Mario Praz and Salvador de Madariaga. From these one gathers that Spain, since the days of the Cordoban Seneca, and perhaps even earlier, has been a nation inclined to asceticism and to the stoic way of life. Indeed, the most authentically Spanish fiction —from *El Conde Lucanor,* Fernando de Rojas' *La Celestina* (1499), *Lazarillo de Tormes* (1554) and other picaresque masterpieces by Mateo Alemán and Quevedo, through Cervantes (*Don Quixote* and *The Exemplary Novels*), all the way into our own century with Miguel de Unamuno (*Three Exemplary Novels*) has been eminently cautionary and didactic in intention. Significantly enough, the two greatest novels of nineteenth-century Spain—*La Regenta* (1884) by Leopoldo Alas and *Fortunata y Jacinta* (1887) by Benito Pérez Galdós —fall under this classification.

It would, however, be rather confining to force all of Spain's fiction into such a religio-moral-sociological category. As early as the fourteenth century, Spain was reading *Amadís de Gaula,* the first chivalric novel and a book which seems to open up the sluices of imaginative creativeness. Although there is no lack of moral and religious aims in the book, the world of fantasy, with superhuman action and incredible monsters, imposes itself from the very beginning. In short, materials which the rest of Europe had poured into *fabliaux* and epic poems, had been brought over in Spain into prose fiction. This type of imaginative writing reigned supreme in Spain until Cervantes' *Don Quixote* (1605, 1615) which despite the author's claim that he had written his book to ridicule and destroy the chivalric novel, may be considered, paradoxically enough, the greatest of them all.

Almost contemporaneous with these romances about doughty knights-errant were the pastoral novels, highly artificial tales about make-believe shepherds in impossible love quandaries. The most influential of these was Jorge de Montemayor's *Diana* (1559) which had widespread influence (Sir Philip Sidney and Shakespeare read it in the English translation) and inspired two literary masters of Spain's Golden Age to cultivate the genre: Cervantes in his *Galatea* (1585) and Lope de Vega in his *Arcadia* (1598).

Other novelistic forms flourished but they were generally short-lived: the "sentimental novel," which is represented by Diego de San Pedro's *Cárcel de amor* (1492), and the "novela morisca," depicting the relationships, especially in matters of love, between the Christians and Moors. Of the latter type the best known example is the fourteenth-century anonymous *El Abencerraje*.

We see, then, that for about three centuries, Spanish writers practiced multiple forms of fiction, but of the countless works we still read with great pleasure only one short picaresque tale (the anonymous *Lazarillo de Tormes*), and two long novels (*Don Quixote* and the less known *La Celestina*, which was written in dialogue form and combined picaresque elements with the emotional torments of the sentimental novel). Throughout the second half of the seventeenth, the entire eighteenth century and the opening of the nineteenth, prose fiction remained dormant.

The present anthology presents specimens of the best prose fiction produced during the last eighty years or so, a period of intensive and often felicitous novel and short-story writing.

The last of the Romantics—the Spanish Heine as he is frequently called—Gustavo Adolfo Bécquer (1836-1870) intro-

duced into Spanish literature new elements of the mysterious
and uncanny which he derived from Hoffmann and Poe. One
of his tales, "Master Pérez the Organist," included here, illus-
trates this tendency. The folkloric or "costumbrista" is splendidly represented by the charming "Three-Cornered Hat"
(1874) by Pedro Antonio de Alarcón (1833-1891), a most
engaging regionalist writer, witty, piquant, truculent, whose
little masterpiece inspired Manuel de Falla's ballet by the
same name. This light, ironic vein also runs through the work
of Juan Valera (1824-1905), especially in his facetious *Juanita
la Larga* (1895). More sober and realistic than either of
these writers was the ultra-conservative José María de Pereda
(1833-1906) who staunchly advocated a return to the old
virtues of rural life and the preservation of religious values.
Although a consummate stylist, Pereda failed as a narrator.
Even the novels which brought him fame, *Sotileza* and *Peñas
arriba* (1895), are heavy-footed and unconvincing. Such accu-
sation certainly cannot be leveled at his contemporaries,
Leopoldo Alas (1852-1901) and Benito Pérez Galdós (1845-
1920), who were also keen, critical observers of Spanish life
but whose viewpoints were opposed to his. Alas' "Doña Berta"
(1893), included here, is a finely-drawn portrait by a powerful writer, who in the two-volume *La Regenta* (1884) gave
Spanish literature one of its masterpieces. Comparable to "Doña
Berta" in evocative power is Galdós' "Torquemada in the
Flames" (1899), a poignant picture of life in Madrid. Both
of these Spanish masters, Alas and Galdós, provide illuminating commentaries on their social milieu, exposing those unbearable human relationships caused by deeply-set national
aberrations. Soon thereafter, as the sun set over the Spanish
dominions, the men of the so-called Generation of 1898 began
to dwell in earnest on Spain's dismal future. Miguel de
Unamuno (1864-1936) was one of these men, although the

story included in this anthology, "Saint Manuel Bueno, Martyr," belongs to a more recent date (1930) and is a psychological study of the problem of faith. Another writer of the Generation of 1898, Ramón María del Valle-Inclán (1869-1936) is represented by "Sonata of Autumn" (1902), the finest novel of his early period, when he was cultivating the decadent gardens so familiar to readers of D'Annunzio, Oscar Wilde and Barbey d'Aurevilly. During the latter part of his life Valle-Inclán became keenly aware of Spain's political chaos and through his caricaturelike "esperpentos," a kind of Swiftian satire, he spoke his mind. A much younger writer, Ramón Pérez de Ayala (b. 1890), endeavors in a facetious and at times ferocious tone, to ridicule the pretentiousness, hypocrisy and fanaticism of his fellow countrymen. Each tale, each novel explores some vice. Often, as in "Prometheus" (1916), a corrosive misanthropy flows beneath his verve and tomfoolery.

At the outbreak of the Civil War (1935), Spanish fiction was sharply divided between "proletarian," or, more broadly, socially-conscious, writers (César Arconada, Joaquín Arderíus, Ramón Sender, José Díaz Fernández, Carranque del Río) and the highly dehumanized art-for-art's-sake exponents (Benjamín Jarnés, Rosa Chacel, Francisco Ayala, Antonio Espina, Antonio de Obregón, Valentín Andrés Alvárez, Corpus Barga, Juan Chabás). This latter tendency is illustrated by the story "Saint Alexis" (1928) of Benjamín Jarnés (1888-1950), a poetical evocation of an artificial atmosphere, reminiscent of the preciosity found in the works of Jean Giraudoux.

During the Civil War the sharp lines of demarcation separating social from esoteric art became untenable, for at the crucial hour even the most recalcitrant art-for-art's-sakists found themselves in the trenches or in the barracks editing books and newspapers for the soldiers. The blood bath ended, like all wars, in havoc, indescribable pain, irreparable loss. In order to give a fairly rounded picture of present-day Spanish writing, this anthology includes writers living in Spain now as well as some living in exile: Camilo José Cela (b. 1916), who in a dozen brilliant works, two of which are available in English (*The Family of Pascual Duarte* (1942) and *The Hive* (1951)), has proved himself to be Spain's outstanding prose artist; Carmen Laforet (b. 1921), who won the most coveted literary prize in Spain with her novel *Nada* (1944); Rosa Chacel (b. 1898), a kind of Virginia Woolf, extremely subjective, even cryptic, but always exciting in her myth-making creativeness; Francisco Ayala (b. 1906), a sociologist who writes in his spare time in a vein akin to Kafka's but with a most delightfully sardonic humor; Rafael Dieste (b. 1900), playwright and short-story writer endowed with an unusual fantasy and verve; Antonio Sánchez Barbudo (b. 1910), the perceptive critic of Antonio Machado and Unamuno, author of the novel *Sueños de grandeza* (1946) and poignant storyteller; Max Aub (b. 1903), playwright and novelist of outstanding dynamism who has completed a trilogy set against the background of the Civil War (*Campo cerrado* (1944), *Campo de sangre* (1945) and *Campo abierto* (1951)) and who in his more relaxed moments produces lovely fantasies, like "The Launch" included here; and, finally, José María Gironella (b. 1917), represented here with a poignant allegory, who has shown amazing promise, especially in *The Cypresses Believe in God* (1953), a long novel about the outbreak of the Civil War.

Great Spanish Stories

Master Pérez the Organist

GUSTAVO ADOLFO BÉCQUER

It was there in the portico of the Church of Santa Inés in Seville, while waiting for midnight Mass to begin on Christmas Eve, that I heard the tale from the portress of the convent.

Naturally, after Mass, I waited impatiently for the ceremony to begin, for I was anxious to witness a miracle.

But there was nothing miraculous about the organ at Santa Inés, and nothing more commonplace than the uninspired sounds produced by the organist that night.

As we were leaving the church, I could not refrain from asking the portress rather teasingly:

"How is it that Master Pérez's organ sounds so bad now?"

"Why, because the one in there is not his," the old woman answered.

"Not his? But what happened to it?"

"It was so old that it just fell apart, years ago."

"And what about the organist's ghost?"

"It has never appeared again since they installed that new organ."

And so, if, after reading this story, any of my readers should want to ask me the same question, that is the explanation of why the miraculous occurrence has not continued down to our times.

I

"Do you see that man in the scarlet cape, with the white plume in his hat, and a doublet that seems weighed down by all the gold brought by our galleys from the New World? He is getting out of his sedan chair to offer his hand to that lady there who, after alighting from her own chair, is coming this way, preceded by four pages bearing torches. Well, that is the Marquis of Moscoso, suitor to the widowed Countess of Villapineda. They say that before falling in love with her, he had sought the hand of a very rich man's daughter. The girl's father, however, is said to be rather a miser . . . but hush, speaking of the devil . . . do you see that man coming out from under the Arch of San Felipe on foot, muffled in a dark cape, and preceded only by one servant carrying a lantern? Now he has stopped before the shrine.

"Did you notice the decoration on his chest as he threw open his cloak to genuflect? If it weren't for that mark of distinction, one might take him for a shopkeeper from Culebras Street. Well, that is the father of the girl I was talking about; look how people make way for him, how they bow to him. All Seville knows of his enormous fortune. That one man has more gold ducats in his coffers than His Majesty King Philip has soldiers in his army, and enough galleons to fight the Grand Turk.

"Look over there, at that group of solemn gentlemen; they are the twenty-four city magistrates. Well, well, there is the big Fleming whom the gentlemen of the Inquisition have not been able to arrest, because of his influence with the bigwigs in Madrid. He comes to church simply for the music. . . . Well, if Master Pérez cannot coax tears as big as fists from his eyes, then his soul is not in its right place but already boiling in Satan's pots.

"Ah, neighbor, things look bad, very bad. . . . I fear there is going to be a brawl; I am going to get into the church, for from what I can make out, sword blows are likely to be more abundant than paternosters. . . . Look, look; the Duke of Alcalá's attendants are coming around the corner of San Pedro Square, and I think I espy the Duke of Medina Sidonia's men coming out of Dueñas Alley. Didn't I tell you?

"They've caught sight of each other and stopped. They don't move from their positions. . . . People scurry away and even the police officers make themselves scarce, for on such occasions they get it from both sides. . . . Even the chief constable with his staff and all takes refuge in the portico. . . .

"And this is what they call law and order! That's only for the poor.

"Bucklers shine in the dark. May our Lord of Might protect us! They've begun to fight. Neighbor, neighbor, come, before they shut the door! But hush! What is this? It's over before they've begun! What is that blinding light? Torches! Sedan chairs! It is my lord the archbishop.

"He has been sent to succor us by the Holy Virgin of Mercy in answer to my silent prayers. . . . Ah, if only you knew how much I owe Our Lady! How well she repays me for all the candles I light to Her every Saturday! . . . How handsome he is in his purple robes and red cap! May God keep him in his office for as many centuries as I myself wish to live! If it were not for him, half of Seville would have been destroyed in these quarrels between the dukes. Just look at them, the big hypocrites, crowding around the bishop's chair to kiss his ring. How they follow him, mingling with his attendants! How friendly they are to each other now, yet in half an hour, if they come upon each other in a dark street . . . May the Lord forgive me, I do not mean to say that they are cowards, for many a time have they fought valiantly against the enemies of Our Lord. . . . But the truth is the truth; if they really wanted to come to some understanding, they would find a way of putting an end to these everlasting skirmishes, in which those who really bear the brunt are their kinsmen, their allies and their servants.

"But come, neighbor, come, let us enter the church before it becomes too crowded . . . for on a night like this, it gets so crammed there is no room for a grain of wheat. . . . What a prize those nuns have in their organist! When have you ever seen the convent so favored as now? Other religious communities have made Master Pérez magnificent offers; but of course there is nothing strange about that, for even the lord archbishop has offered him enormous sums to play at the cathedral. . . . But nothing tempts him. He would rather die than give up his favorite instrument. . . .

"You do not know Master Pérez? Of course, you are new to our neighborhood. Well, he is a very saintly man; poor, of course, but the most charitable man alive. He has no other family but his daughter and no friends but his organ, and he devotes his entire life to watching over the innocence of the one and repairing the stops of the other. . . . And, dear me, the organ is so old! But that makes no difference: he takes such good care of it that its tone is unbelievable. . . . He knows it so perfectly that simply by touch . . . I do not know whether I have mentioned it, but the poor gentleman has been blind since birth. . . . With what fortitude he bears his misfortune! When people ask him what he would give to be able to see, he answers: 'A great deal, but not as much as you think, for I have hopes.' 'Hopes of seeing?' 'Yes, very soon,' he adds, smiling like an angel, 'I am already seventy-six, and it will not be too long before I see God. . . .'

"Poor thing! Indeed, it will not be long before he looks upon the Lord . . . for he is as humble as the stones of the street which let everyone trample on them. He says that he is only a poor convent organist, yet he could give lessons to the choirmaster at the cathedral, for he cut his teeth on music. . . . His father was of the same profession; I did not know him, but my mother—may she rest in peace!—said that he always used to take the boy with him to pump the bellows. And the lad showed such talent that he took over his father's post when the old man died. Oh, what hands he has! May God bless them! They should be taken to the Street of the Jewelers and encased in gold. . . . He always plays beautifully, but on a night like this, he is miraculous. . . . He has a special love for the ceremony of midnight Mass, and when they raise the Host at the stroke of twelve when Our Lord Jesus Christ came into the world, the tones of his organ are like angels' voices. . . .

"But why should I praise to you what you will have a chance to hear for yourself tonight? Just look around you and you will see that the cream of Seville society, even the archbishop, has come to hear him; but do not think that only learned people who know all about music appreciate him. Ordinary people do so, also. You see those crowds with lighted torches, bellowing Christmas carols to the beat of tambourines, rattles and drums; they, who usually create disturbances in church, are as silent as the dead when Master Pérez puts his hands to the organ. . . . And when the Host is raised, you can hear a pin drop. Copious tears fall and at the end a deep sigh can be heard, which means that the people who have held their breath all during the music suddenly relax. But it is time; the bells have stopped ringing, and Mass is about to begin; let us go in.

"All over the world this is Holy Night, but for us fortunate ones it is even holier."

As she said this, the good woman who had served as guide to her neighbor crossed the portico of the convent of Santa Inés, and, by pushing and shoving, fought her way into the church and was lost from sight among the crowds pressing through the doorway.

II

The church was magnificently illuminated. The flood of light that spread from the altars to fill every nook and cranny broke on the rich jewels of noble ladies who, kneeling on velvet cushions laid by their pages and taking their prayer books from duennas' hands, formed a brilliant circle around the railing of the choir. Standing near the railing were the twenty-four magistrates and many of Seville's proudest noblemen in richly hued cloaks garnished with gold, under which, with studied carelessness, they let their red and green decorations be seen. In one hand they held hats with plumes so long they swept the ground, and with the other they grasped burnished rapier hilts, or caressed the handles of chiseled daggers. Like a wall they protected their wives and daughters from contact with the rabble. The common folk, at the rear of the nave, were as restless and noisy as a stormy sea; they burst forth into a shout of joy accompanied by the discordant sounds of drums and tambourines at the appearance of the archbishop who, after taking his seat near the high altar under a scarlet canopy surrounded by his attendants, blessed the assemblage three times.

It was time for Mass to begin.

And yet some minutes went by before the celebrant made his appearance. The crowd became impatient and stirred uneasily; distinguished gentlemen exchanged some words in a whisper, while the archbishop dispatched one of his attendants to the sacristy to inquire after the cause of the delay.

"Master Pérez has been taken ill, very ill, and it will be impossible for him to come to midnight Mass."

This was the attendant's report.

The news spread among the crowd instantly. It would be impossible to depict the dismay it produced in everyone; suffice it to say that there was so much excitement that the chief constable rose to his feet and the bailiffs rushed into the crowd in an attempt to establish order.

At that moment, an ill-favored, emaciated, cross-eyed man made his way forward to the prelate's chair.

"Master Pérez is ill," he said, "and services cannot begin. If it is your pleasure, I will play the organ in his absence; for Master Pérez is not the greatest organist in the world and there are others capable of playing this instrument in the event of his death."

The archbishop nodded his head in consent, but several of the faithful, who recognized in that strange individual the envious rival of the organist of Santa Inés, were breaking into expressions of displeasure when suddenly a terrible noise was heard in the portico.

"Master Pérez is here! Master Pérez is here!"

Everyone turned around at the shouts of those pressed together in the doorway.

Master Pérez, pale and drawn, was in fact being carried into church in a chair, and everyone was fighting for the honor of carrying it on their shoulders.

Neither his physicians' protests nor his daughter's tears had been able to keep him in his bed.

"No," he had said, "this is the last time, I know it, and I do not wish to die without visiting my organ, especially on this night, Christmas Eve. Come, it is my wish, it is my order; let us go to church."

His wishes were obeyed. Those about him carried him in their arms to the organ loft and Mass began.

At that moment, the cathedral clock struck twelve.

After the Introit, the Gospel and the Offertory, the solemn moment arrived when the priest, having consecrated the Host, took it by the tips of his fingers and started to raise it.

A cloud of incense spread in blue waves all through the church; the bells rang out and Master Pérez placed his trembling hands on the keys of the organ.

The hundred voices imprisoned in its metal pipes rang out in a prolonged majestic chord which slowly faded as if a gust of air had carried off its last echoes.

This first chord, like a voice rising from earth to heaven, was followed by another, soft and distant, but swelling into a torrent of thunderous harmonies.

It was the voice of angels which had coursed through vast spaces down to earth.

Then there began to be heard faraway hymns intoned by the hierarchies of seraphim; a thousand hymns at once, merging into one which was nevertheless only the accompaniment of a strange melody floating over that ocean of mysterious echoes like a strip of mist over the waves of the sea.

One after another, the parts died away; the harmony was becoming simpler. Just two voices were left, their echoes mingling; then there was just one, all by itself, holding a note as brilliant as a shaft of light. . . . The priest bowed his head, and, over his gray hair through the blue veil of the incense smoke, the Host appeared before the eyes of the faithful. At that moment the note which Master Pérez had been holding opened wide and a burst of mighty harmony shook the church: the imprisoned air vibrated in every corner and the stained-glass windows trembled in their wide arched frames.

Each one of the notes making up that magnificent chord developed into a theme; some were near, others far away, some sharp, others muffled; it was as if the seas and birds, breezes and leaves, men and angels, heaven and earth, were all using their powers to chant a hymn to the birth of the Saviour.

The multitude listened in hushed amazement. Every eye held a tear, every spirit was deeply reverent.

The officiating priest felt his hands tremble, for What he held and What men and archangels worshipped was his God; it was his God and he felt the heavens were opening and the Host was transfigured.

The organ continued playing; but its voice was slowly sinking, dropping from echo to echo, growing faint and distant, when suddenly there was a shriek in the organ loft, a sharp piercing shriek uttered by a woman.

The organ exhaled a strange discordant sound, like a sob, and fell silent.

The crowd surged forward to the stairway leading up to the loft; startled from their religious ecstasy, all the faithful turned anxious countenances in that direction.

"What has happened? What is the matter?" they asked one another. No one could answer although they all ventured guesses; the confusion grew and threatened to upset the tranquillity and decorum that should prevail in church.

"What has happened?" the ladies asked the chief constable, who, preceded by his officers, had been one of the first to mount to the loft and who now, pale and grief-stricken, made his way to the archbishop. He, like everyone else, was anxiously awaiting an explanation for the disorder.

"What is it?"

"Master Pérez has just died."

And, in truth, when the first among the faithful pushed up the stairway to the loft, they found the poor organist fallen face down on the keys of his ancient instrument, which still vibrated dully, while his daughter, racked by sobs and deep sighs, knelt at his feet and called to him in vain.

III

"Good evening, Doña Baltasara. So you too have come to midnight Mass tonight? I really had intended to go to my parish church; but you know how it is: everyone follows the crowd. To tell you the truth, since Master Pérez died, my heart sinks whenever I enter Santa Inés. . . . Poor man! Such a saint! . . . I have a piece of his doublet which I venerate as a relic . . . ; and he deserves it, for, Heaven knows, if only the archbishop would do something about it, our grandchildren would worship him as one of the saints. But that's how it is, the dead and departed are soon forgotten. . . . Nowadays people only follow the fashion. You know what I mean. . . . What, you don't know what is going on? We are completely alike in that regard: all we do is make our way from home to church and then back home, and we pay no attention to gossip. But, you know, one can't help picking up a word here, a word there.

"Well, it seems that the organist of San Román church, that cross-eyed wretch who says nothing but the vilest things about all other organists . . . that sloven who looks more like a butcher than a music teacher, is going to play the organ this Christmas Eve in place of Master Pérez.

"Now you know—it is common knowledge in Seville—that no one had dared to attempt such a thing. Not even his daughter, who is a music teacher and, after her father's death, entered the convent as a novice. That is easy to understand; accustomed as we were to listening to wonders, any other music would have struck us as poor, however much we tried to avoid making comparisons. And so, when, out of respect for the memory of the deceased, the community had decided that the organ would be silent tonight, that awful person turned up and brazenly declared that he would play it. Only fools can be that cheeky. . . .

"Of course, he is not at fault; we should blame those who allow such profanation. . . . But that is the way of the world, and the crowd on hand is tremendous. . . . You'd think that nothing had changed from one year to the next. . . . The same bigwigs, the same ostentation, the same pushing at the door, the same commotion in the portico, the same crowds inside the church. . . . The poor man would turn over in his grave if he knew that his organ were going to be touched by unworthy hands. But if what I hear is true, they have prepared quite a reception for the intruder. When he is about to place his hands on the keys, they'll start banging their drums, their tambourines and rattles. . . .

"But hush, the hero of the day is coming in. Look at the airs he puts on; look at the colors he wears, the pleated ruff and all. . . . Let us go in; the archbishop arrived some time ago, and Mass will soon begin. My dear, it seems to me that what happens tonight will not be soon forgotten."

As she spoke, the good woman, whom our readers will have recognized from her loquacious outbursts, pushed her way in, as was her wont, by dint of shoving and elbowing.

The service had already begun. The church was as brilliantly lighted as the previous year.

The new organist had made his way through the throngs of the faithful in the naves; he had kissed the prelate's ring and

gone up to the organ loft where he tried all the stops of the
organ, one after another, with a dignity that was as ridiculous
as it was affected.

A muffled, indistinct noise could be heard from among the
common people below, a prelude to the storm that was brew-
ing and would soon burst.

"What an incompetent wretch; he can't even look straight!"
said some.

"He's an ignoramus; he made the organ at his parish church
sound like a rattle and now he's come to profane Master
Pérez's instrument," said the others.

And while one fellow took off his cloak to be able to beat his
tambourine more freely, and another made his rattles ready,
and everyone else was keying himself up to make as much din
as possible, here and there an isolated individual dared utter
some lukewarm words in defense of the unwelcome organist
whose pompous pedantic behavior contrasted so strongly with
the modest appearance and kindly manner of the late Master
Pérez.

And finally the moment arrived, the solemn moment when
the priest genuflects, murmurs the sacred words and takes the
Host in his hands. . . . The bells rang out and the sound was
like a shower of crystal notes; diaphanous waves of incense
rose, and the organ sounded.

A frightful uproar filled every corner of the church at that
instant and drowned out the first chord.

Horns, bagpipes, drums, tambourines, every instrument the
populace could muster, raised their discordant voices at once;
but the confusion and clamor lasted only a few moments. Just
as they had begun all together, they fell silent unanimously.

The second chord, full, bold, magnificent, rushed out of the
metal pipes like a sonorous, inexhaustible cascade of harmony.

Heavenly songs like those that caress our ears in moments

of bliss; chants that our spirits perceive but our lips cannot repeat; scattered notes of a distant melody ringing out at intervals as if borne by gusts of wind; the rustle of leaves kissing each other in the trees with a murmur like rain; the trills of larks which rise warbling from among the flowers like arrows aimed at the clouds; rare sounds as overwhelming as the roar of a storm; choruses of seraphim without rhythm or cadence; unknown music of heaven that only the imagination can apprehend; winged hymns which seemed to mount to the throne of the Lord like a whirlwind of light and sound . . . all this was expressed by the hundred voices of the organ with greater power, more mysterious poetry, eerier color, than ever before. . . .

When the organist descended from the gallery, the crowd milling around the staircase was so great and so eager to see and admire him, that the chief constable, fearing, not without reason, that they would suffocate him, ordered some of his officers to use their staves and open a path for him to the high altar where the prelate waited.

"You see," the archbishop said when they had brought the organist to him, "I came from my palace just to listen to you. Will you then be as adamant as Master Pérez, who never spared me the trip, and refuse to play in the cathedral at Christmas Eve Mass?"

"Next year," replied the organist, "I promise to obey you, for not for all the gold in the world would I play this organ again."

"But why?" the prelate broke in.

"Because," the organist went on, trying to control the emotion that betrayed itself in the pallor of his face, ". . . because it is old and out of order and cannot express everything I would wish it to."

The archbishop retired, followed by his attendants. One after

another, the sedan chairs filed out and were lost in the twists
and turns of the neighboring streets; the groups standing in
the portico dispersed in different directions; and the portress
was making ready to shut the doors leading into the portico
when two women were seen to cross themselves and murmur
a prayer before the shrine in the Arch of San Felipe, then
continue their way, turning into Dueñas Alley.

"What would you have, my dear Doña Baltasara?" said one.
"That's the way I am. Each person has his own strange ideas.
If the barefoot Capuchins themselves had said so, I wouldn't
have believed it. That man can't have played what we have
just heard. Why, I've heard him play a thousand times at his
parish church of San Bartolomé where the priest had to dismiss
him for being so bad; we had to stuff our ears with cotton. . . . But then, you've only to look at his face, which,
they say, is the mirror of the soul. . . . How well I remember
poor Master Pérez's face when on a night like this he came
down from the organ loft after having entranced the congregation with his wonderful playing! What a kindly smile, what a
happy glow on his face! Old as he was, he looked like an angel.
Not like this one who stumbled down the stairs as if he were
being chased by a mad dog, and as pale as a corpse. . . . My
dear Doña Baltasara, believe me when I tell you there is something very strange about all this. . . ."

Elaborating on these last words, the women turned the
corner and disappeared.

We hardly think it necessary to tell our readers who one of
them was.

IV

Another year had gone by. The abbess of the convent of Santa
Inés and Master Pérez's daughter were conversing in low tones,
half-hidden among the shadows of the church choir. In a

cracked voice, the bell was calling to the faithful from the tower, and now and then a figure crossed the silent, deserted portico, and, after dipping his fingers in the holy water at the entrance, chose a seat in a corner of the nave where a few people from the vicinity were quietly waiting for midnight Mass to begin.

"You see," said the Mother Superior, "how childish your fears are; there is no one in the church; all of Seville is rushing to the cathedral tonight. Play the organ without any misgivings; only our sisterhood will be here. . . . But you say nothing and keep on sighing. What is the matter? What is wrong with you?"

"I am . . . afraid," the young woman exclaimed, her voice shaking with emotion.

"Afraid! Of what?"

"I don't know . . . of something supernatural. . . . Last night I heard you say that you insisted upon my playing the organ during Mass, and, proud of this honor, I thought of trying the stops and tuning it so that I might surprise you. . . . I came to the choir . . . alone. . . . I opened the door leading to the organ loft. . . . At that moment the cathedral clock struck the hour . . . but what hour, I do not know. . . . The peals were very sad and many . . . many. . . . They kept on ringing while I stood there rooted to the threshold for what seemed a century.

"The church was dark and deserted. . . . At the very back, a flickering light burned like a star lost in the dark heavens. . . . It was the light of the lamp burning on the high altar. . . . Its weak rays only made the horror of the darkness more dreadful, and I saw . . . Mother, believe me, I saw a man, silent and with his back towards me, running one hand over the keys of the organ while with the other he tried the stops. . . . And the organ rang out, but in a manner that I cannot describe. Each note seemed like a sob smothered within the metal pipe, which vibrated with the air compressed in its cavity, and brought forth its tone low, almost imperceptible, but true.

"And the cathedral clock went on ringing out the hour while the man continued running over the keys. I could even hear his breathing.

"Horror had frozen the blood in my veins; I felt my body turn to ice, and there was fire in my temples. . . . I wanted to cry out, but I could not. The man had turned around and was looking at me. . . . No, I am wrong: he was not looking at me, for he was blind. . . . It was my father!"

"Bah, Sister, throw off these fancies with which the evil one tries to disturb weak imaginations. Say an Our Father and a Hail Mary to the Archangel Saint Michael, captain of the hosts of heaven, that he may help you against evil spirits. Around your neck wear a scapulary that has touched the relic of San Pacomio, intercessor against temptations, and go take your seat in the organ loft; Mass will begin soon and the faithful are waiting impatiently. Your father is in heaven; instead of frightening his daughter, he will come down to inspire her in this solemn service which he so loved."

The prioress went to take her seat in the choir, surrounded by the entire sisterhood. With trembling hand, Master Pérez's daughter opened the door to the organ loft and sat down on the bench before the organ. And the Mass began.

The Mass began and it continued without any unusual occurrence until the Consecration. At that moment the organ rang out and with it a shriek from Master Pérez's daughter. . . .

The Mother Superior, the nuns, and some of the congregation ran up to the organ loft.

"Look, look, there he is!" the young woman was saying as

she stared at the bench with terrified eyes starting from their sockets, and seized the railing of the loft with shaking hands.

They all fixed their eyes on that spot. No one was at the organ, yet it kept on playing, making sounds that only archangels might make in mystic rapture. . . .

"Didn't I tell you over and over again, Doña Baltasara, didn't I tell you that there was something very queer about all that? What, you were not at midnight Mass last night? But you certainly must know what happened. They talk of nothing else all over Seville. His Excellency the archbishop is furious, and no wonder. . . . Not to have attended Mass at Santa Inés; not to have witnessed the miracle. . . . And for what? To hear a tin-pan serenade! That's just what that stupid organist of San Bartolomé produced at the cathedral, I am told by persons who heard him. But I said so all the time: that cross-eyed one could never have played that glorious music last year! There was something very queer about the entire business and the queerness was created by Master Pérez's ghost."

The
Three-Cornered Hat

*The True History of an Affair
Current in Certain Tales and
Ballads, Here Written Down
As and How It Befell*

DON PEDRO ANTONIO
DE ALARCÓN

The Author's Preface

Few Spaniards, even among those who have no scholarship or book-learning, can be ignorant of the popular story which serves as basis for the present little work.

A rough goatherd, who had never wandered beyond the remote Farm on which he was born, was the first that we heard relate it. He was one of those country folk, quite unlettered but with a natural wisdom and humor, who play so large a part in our national literature under the title of *picaros*. Whenever there was any festivity at the Farm, a wedding or a christening, or the solemn visit of the landlord, it was his business to arrange the games and pantomimes, to act as clown and juggler, and to recite tales and ballads; and it was on one of these occasions (now almost a lifetime since; that is to say, more than thirty-five years ago) that it was his task to enchant and dazzle our (comparative) innocence with the story in verse of "The Corregidor and the Miller's Wife," or, if you like, "The Miller and the Corregidor's Wife," which we offer to the public today under the more transcendental and philosophical title (for so does the gravity of these days require) of "The Three-Cornered Hat."

We remember, by the same token, that when the goatherd gave them such good measure, the marriageable girls there assembled turned very red; from which their mothers concluded that the story was a little *free*. Whereupon they, in their turn, came near to turning the goatherd black and blue. But poor Repela (for such was the goatherd's name) did not mince matters and answered that there was no reason for anyone to be so shocked, since there was nothing in his Tale that even nuns and children of four didn't know.

"If you don't believe it, just think a moment," he said. "What do we gather from the story of 'The Corregidor and the Miller's Wife'? That married folk sleep together, and that no husband likes another man to sleep with his wife."

"And that's truth!" said the mothers, hearing the laughter of their daughters.

"The proof that Gaffer Repela is right," remarked the father of the bridegroom at this point, "is that all here present, great and small, know well enough that tonight, after the dance is over, Johnny and Manolilla are going to sleep for the first time in the fine marriage bed which Aunt Gabriela has just shown to the girls so that they could admire the embroideries of the pillows."

"And, what's more," said the bride's grandfather, "in the book of Doctrine and even in Sermons, they speak to children of all these things of nature, so that they should understand the meaning of the long barrenness of our Lady Saint Anne, the chastity of Joseph, Judith's stratagem, and many other miracles that I don't remember at the moment. Consequently . . ."

"It's all right, it's all right, Gaffer Repela!" exclaimed the girls, plucking up courage. "Tell us your Tale again: it's very interesting!"

"And very decent too," continued the grandfather. "For there's nothing recommended in it that's bad; and it doesn't teach folk to *be* bad; and as for those that are, they get their deserts . . ."

"Go on! Tell it again!" decreed the mothers.

And Gaffer Repela set about reciting the Ballad again; and, when all had considered it in the light of that honest criticism, they found there was nothing in it to take exception to; which is equivalent to saying that they granted *the necessary license*.

In the course of years we have heard many different versions of that same adventure of "The Miller and the Corregidor's Wife," always from the lips of the Wag of the farm or village, after the order of the now dead Repela, and we have read it too in print in various *Blind Man's Ballads*, and finally in the famous *Romancero* of the unforgettable Don Agustín Durán.

At bottom the subject is always identical; tragicomical, waggish and terribly epigrammatic, like all the dramatic moral lessons of which our people are so fond; but the form, the accidental mechanism, the casual developments, are different, very different, from the way our goatherd told the tale, so different that he could never have told any of the aforementioned versions at the Farm, nor the printed ones either, unless all decent girls had stopped their ears; and if he had, he would certainly have had his eyes scratched out by their mothers. To such a point have the low-minded clowns of other provinces stretched and twisted the traditional matter which was so savorous, discreet, and comely in the version of the classic Repela.

It is a long time, then, since first we conceived the intention of reasserting the truth of the matter, restoring to the strange history in question its primitive character, which we have never doubted was that in which decency is triumphant. And how could we doubt it? That type of Tales, in passing from hand to hand of the common folk, is never denaturalized into something finer, more delicate and decent; what happens is that it is tarnished and mutilated at the touch of clumsiness and vulgarity.

Such is the history of the present book. And so let us put grist to the mill; I mean, let us make a beginning of the Tale of "The Corregidor and the Miller's Wife," not without the hope that your sane judgment (oh, respectable public!) "after you have read it and crossed yourselves more often than if you had seen the devil," as Estebanillo González said at the beginning of his, "will hold it worthy and deserving of publication."

I

Of When the Thing Happened

It was at the beginning of this long century which is already drawing to a close. The year is not precisely known; it is certain only that it was after 4 and before 8.

There still reigned at that time in Spain Don Carlos IV, of Bourbon, *by the Grace of God* according to the coins, and by oversight or especial grace of Bonaparte according to the French bulletins. The other sovereigns of Europe descended from Louis XIV had already lost their crowns, and the chief of them his head, in the disastrous storm which swept this age-worn quarter of the world after 1789.

Nor was that the only singularity of our country in those

times. The Soldier of the Revolution, son of an obscure Corsican lawyer, victor at Rivoli, the Pyramids, Marengo, and a hundred other battles, had just crowned himself with the crown of Charlemagne and completely transfigured the face of Europe, creating and suppressing nations, blotting out frontiers, inventing dynasties, and compelling the nations through which he moved on his charger like a human earthquake or like Antichrist (as he was styled by the Powers of the North), to change their shapes, names, positions, customs, and even their dress. . . .

None the less our fathers (God keep them in His holy Glory), far from hating or fearing him, delighted in the study of his extraordinary exploits, for all the world as if it were a matter of some hero in a Book of Chivalry or of things which were happening on some other planet, nor for a moment did it cross their minds that he might come hither and attempt the horrors he had wrought in France, Italy, Germany, and other countries. Once a week (twice at best) the post from Madrid arrived in most of the important towns of the Peninsula, bringing a few numbers of the *Gazette* (which was not, any more than the post, a daily event), and from it the select few learned (supposing that the *Gazette* happened to mention it) whether there was a state more or a state less beyond the Pyrenees, or another battle had been fought in which six or eight Kings and Emperors had taken part, or whether Napoleon happened to be in Milan, Brussels, or Warsaw. . . . For the rest, our elders went on living, wrapped up in their moth-eaten habits, in God's Peace and Grace, with their Inquisition and their Friars, with their picturesque inequality before the Law, with their privileges, charters, and personal exemptions, with their total lack of municipal or political liberty, governed conjointly by noble Bishops and potent Corregidors (whose respective powers it was far from easy to define since both intermeddled with the temporal and the eternal), and paying tithes, first fruits, excise, subsidies, compulsory gifts and charities, rents, rates, poll taxes, royal thirds, gavels, civil fruits, and fifty more tributes whose nomenclature is not now to the purpose.

And here ends all that concerns the present history of the matters military and political of that epoch, since our sole object in touching upon what was then happening in the world has been to come to the conclusion that, in the year of which we treat, the Old Order was still in authority in Spain in all spheres of public and private life, as if, in the midst of all these novelties and upheavals, the Pyrenees had grown into another Great Wall of China.

II

Of How Folk Lived in Those Days

In Andalusia, for example (since, in point of fact, it was in a city of Andalusia that what you are about to hear occurred), persons of *position* still rose betimes, visited the Cathedral for Prime Mass, even if it were not a Holiday of Obligation, breakfasting at nine off a fried egg and a cup of chocolate with toast sandwiches; dining, from one to two of the afternoon, off a stew and side dish, if there were any game, and, if not, off a stew alone; taking the siesta after dinner; then walking out in the country; going to Rosary about twilight in their respective parish churches; taking another chocolate at the Angelus (this time with a biscuit); the bigwigs attending the evening party at the Magistrate's, the Dean's or the local Lord's; returning home at the ringing of the Animas; barring the great door before the tolling of the Curfew; supping off a salad and ragout, if fresh anchovies were not yet come in, and incontinently going to bed with their wives (those that had them), but not, during nine months of the year, before ordering the bed to be warmed. . . .

Happy times, in which our land enjoyed quiet and peaceful possession of all the cobwebs, dust, moths, all the observances, beliefs, traditions, all the uses and abuses, sanctified by the ages! Happy times, in which there existed in human society a variety of classes, prejudices and customs! Happy times, I say, especially for the poets, who might find round every corner an interlude, a farce, a comedy, a drama, a mystery, or an epic, instead of this prosaic uniformity and savorless realism which came to us on the heels of the French Revolution! Happy times, indeed!

But here we are, returning on our tracks! Enough of generalities and circumlocutions: let us enter resolutely upon the history of The Three-Cornered Hat.

III
Do Ut Des

In those days, then, there stood near a certain city a famous flour mill (which exists no longer), situate at about a quarter of a league from the town, between the foot of a gentle hill peopled with orchards of mazard and cherry, and a richly fertile plain which served as a margin (and sometimes as bed) to the intermittent and treacherous river.

For various and diverse reasons, that mill had already for some considerable time been the chosen objective and place of recreation for the most distinguished pleasure-makers of the aforementioned city. . . . In the first place, it was approached by a carriage road less impassable than the others of that district. In the second place, there was a little flagged court in front of the mill, covered by an enormous vine under which the visitors could enjoy a pleasant coolness in the summer and the warmth of the sunshine in the winter, thanks to the alternate flourishing and falling of the vine leaves. In the third place, the Miller was a very respectable, discreet, fine fellow, who had what you call "a way with him," and who entertained the worthy gentlemen who honored him with their company of an evening, with whatever the season provided; now green mazagans, now cherries and mazards, now lettuces in the leaf without seasoning (which are excellent when accompanied by sippets of bread and oil—sippets which the gentlemen undertook to send ahead), now melons, now grapes from that same vine that served them as canopy, now popcorn if it was wintertime, and roasted chestnuts, almonds, nuts, and now and then, on very cold evenings, a draught of very decent wine (within doors now and about the fire), to which at Eastertide he would add a few fritters, butter cakes, or a slice or two of an Alpujarras ham.

"Was the Miller, then, so wealthy?" you will interrupt me to exclaim, "or was it that his distinguished visitors so far forgot themselves?"

Neither the one nor the other. The Miller had no more than a competence and the gentlemen were the personification of delicacy and proper pride. But in times in which men paid upwards of fifty different contributions to Church and State, a fellow as knowing as our Miller found it well worth his while to keep a hold on the good will of the Aldermen, Canons, Friars, Clerks, and the other folk who could pull wires. And so it was said by not a few that Miller Lucas (for such was our Miller's name), by giving a kindly welcome to all and sundry, was able to put by a very tidy sum at the end of the year.

"Your Worship will let me have the old door from that house you have pulled down," he would say to one. "Your Lordship," he would ask of another, "will order them to give me a rebatement on the subsidy, the excise, or the civil fruits." "Your Reverence will let me take a few leaves from the Convent garden for my silkworms." "Your Honor will give me a permit to gather a little kindling from Mount *This*." "Your Paternity will write me a line so that they'll allow me to cut a little wood in the pine forest of *That*." "You must give me a little note, Venerable Sir, so that I can get it free of charge." "This year I can't pay the tax." "I trust the suit will be settled in my favor." "Today I gave a man a thrashing and I think he ought to go to jail for provocation." "Does your Worship happen to have such and such a thing to spare?" "Is your Lordship using . . . some other thing?" "Can you lend me the mule?" "Will the cart be in use tomorrow?" "Had I better send for the donkey?"

Our Miller was always finding occasion for little requests of this nature, and the reply was always a generous and impartial "As you wish."

And so you perceive that Miller Lucas was not precisely on the road to ruin.

IV

A Woman Seen from Without

The final and perhaps the most potent reason which the gentry of the City had for frequenting Miller Lucas's Mill of an evening was . . . that (Clergy and Laity alike, beginning with the Lord Bishop and His Honor the Corregidor) they could there contemplate at their ease one of the most lovely, accomplished, and admirable works of art that ever issued from the hands of God (styled at that time by Jovellanos and all the frenchified school of our country, the Supreme Being). . . .

This work of art was entitled "Mistress Frasquita."

I will begin by assuring you that Mistress Frasquita, the

lawful wife of Miller Lucas, was a very proper person, and that the illustrious visitors to the Mill were well aware of it. I say more: not one of them betrayed a disposition to regard her with a lustful eye or unsanctified desires. They admired her, certainly, and on occasions they courted her (in the presence of her husband, I suppose), and not only the gallants but the friars, not only the gownsmen but the canons, as a prodigy of beauty who did honor to her Creator, and as a demon of sprightliness and coquetry who brought innocent delight to the most melancholy spirits. "She's a lovely creature," the most virtuous Prelate was accustomed to say. "She's a statue of ancient Hellas," observed a learned Counsellor, Corresponding Member of the Historical Academy. "She's the image itself of Eve," asserted the Prior of the Franciscans. "She's a grand girl," exclaimed the Colonel of Militia. "She's a serpent, a siren, a demon!" added the Corregidor. "Nay, she's a good soul, an angel, a darling, a little four-year-old," said all in conclusion as they returned from the Mill, stuffed full of grapes or nuts, and sought their own dull and unromantic firesides.

The little four-year-old, that is, Mistress Frasquita, was getting on for thirty. She was above five and a half feet in height, and robust in proportion, perhaps even a trifle heavier than her proud stature warranted. She was like a giant Niobe, though she had borne no children; a Hercules . . . a she-Hercules; a Roman matron such as you may still see in Trastevere. But the most notable thing about her was the quickness of her movements, the lightsomeness, the animation, the grace, of her very ample form. For a statue, as the Academician claimed her to be, she lacked the monumental repose. She could bend like a reed, twirl like a weathercock, dance like a spinning top. Her face was more mobile still, and for that the less sculptural. Its lively charm was made more charming still by no less than five dimples; two on one cheek, another on another, another (a very little one) not far from the left corner of her laughing lips, and the last (a very big one) right in the middle of her rounded chin. Add to that the roguish looks, the playful winks, and the changing poses of her head which brought such a charm to her conversation, and you may be able to form some idea of that face so full of beauty and humor, so radiant always with happiness and health.

Neither Mistress Frasquita nor Miller Lucas was from Andalusia; she was from Navarre, he from Murcia. He had gone to a certain town of that province at the age of fifteen, as half page, half servant, to the Bishop previous to the one that now held that See. His good patron educated him for the church, and it was perhaps with an eye to this and in order that he might not lack the wherewithal, that at his death he bequeathed to him the Mill. But Miller Lucas, who at his Lordship's death had only been ordained to Minor Orders, hung up his surplice there and then and joined for a soldier, being more desirous of adventure and seeing the world than of saying Mass and grinding corn. In 1793 he took part in the campaign of the Western Pyrenees as Orderly to the gallant General Don Ventura Caro; he was present at the attack on Castillo Piñón, and then remained for a long time in the Northern Provinces, where he obtained his discharge. In Estella he made the acquaintance of Mistress Frasquita, who at that time was called simply Frasquita; he fell in love with her, married her, and carried her to Andalusia to the Mill where they were to live in peace and prosperity during the rest of their pilgrimage through this vale of tears and laughter.

Mistress Frasquita, then, transported from Navarre to this secluded spot, had taken on none of the habits of the Andalusians and remained markedly different from the country-women of the district. She dressed with greater simplicity, freedom, and elegance than they, washed herself more frequently, and allowed the sun and air to caress her naked arms and throat. She conformed, up to a certain point, with the dress of the ladies of the period, the dress of Goya's women, the dress of Queen Maria Luisa. The skirt, if not half a pace in width, was no more than a pace, and extremely short, so that it displayed her little feet and the spring of her noble leg. Her bodice she wore cut low and round at the neck in the fashion of Madrid, where she had stayed two months with Miller Lucas on her way from Navarre to Andalusia. Her hair, gathered right up on to the crown of the head, showed off superbly the graceful poise of her head and neck. In her little ears she wore a pair of earrings, and many rings on the slim fingers of her hard but spotless hands. Finally, Mistress Frasquita's voice had the tone and range of some beautiful musical instrument and her laugh was as gay and silvery as a peal of bells on Holy Saturday.

Now for a portrait of Miller Lucas.

V

A Man Seen from Without and Within

Miller Lucas was as ugly as the devil. He had been so all his life, and now he was about forty years old. None the less, God can have brought into the world few men more agreeable and sympathetic. Taken by his liveliness, his quick wit, and his charm, the late Bishop had begged him of his parents, who were shepherds, not of souls but of actual sheep. His Lordship being dead and the boy having exchanged the Seminary for the Barracks, General Caro picked him out of his whole army and made him his personal orderly and his servant in the field. After completing his term of service, Miller Lucas found it as easy to subdue the heart of Mistress Frasquita as it had been to win the regard of the General and the Prelate. The young girl of Navarre, who was at that time twenty Aprils old, the apple of the eye of all the boys in Estella, some of them young men of means, was unable to resist the endless witticisms and gay, sparkling sallies, the monkeyish lovelorn glances, and the continual waggish smile, full of mischief, but full of sweetness too, of this fellow from Murcia. Indeed, such was his effrontery, his gift of the gab, his ready wit, his resourcefulness, his bravery and his charm, that he succeeded in turning the head, not only of the coveted beauty, but of her mother and father as well.

Lucas was at that time, and so continued at the date to which we refer, of little stature (at least as compared with his wife), somewhat round-shouldered, and very dusky. His chin was smooth, his nose and ears large, and he was marked with the smallpox. On the other hand, his mouth was well-shaped and his teeth perfect. You might say that only the husk of the man was uncouth and ugly, that as soon as you penetrated beneath it you began to discover his perfections, and that these perfections began with his teeth. Then came his voice, vibrant, flexible, attractive; at times grave and manly, but sweet and honeyed when he asked a favor, and always difficult to resist. And then came the things spoken by the voice; all he said was in season, discreet, well-found, persuasive. And lastly, in the soul of Miller Lucas there was courage, loyalty, honor, commonsense, desire of knowledge, an understanding natural and acquired of many matters, a profound scorn of fools, whatever their social station, and a certain sense of irony, mockery, and sarcasm which made of him, according to our friend the Academician, a sort of Don Francisco de Quevedo in the rough.

Such, within and without, was Miller Lucas.

VI

The Accomplishments
of Our Couple

Well, Mistress Frasquita loved Miller Lucas to madness and held herself to be the happiest woman in the world because *he* adored *her*. They had no children, as we have already learned, and so they had devoted themselves to pampering and petting one another with indescribable care, though this tender solicitude showed none of the cloying sentimentality of almost all childless couples. On the contrary, they treated one another with the directness, light-heartedness, gaiety and trust of children towards their companions in play, who love each other with all their souls without ever confessing as much or even themselves realizing what they feel.

Never before, surely, had the world seen a Miller so neat in his dress and person, or who kept a better table or a home so replete with every comfort, as Miller Lucas. Never was any miller's wife (or for that matter, any queen) surrounded with such attentions, such deference, such consideration, as Mistress Frasquita. And never, surely, did a mill contain such a store of the necessities, conveniences, amenities, distractions, and even the superfluities of life, as the one which is about to serve as theater for almost all of the present history.

All this was largely due to the fact that Mistress Frasquita, the fair, industrious, healthful woman of Navarre, could, would, and in point of fact did, cook, sew, embroider, make sweets, wash, iron, whitewash the house, scour the copper, knead the dough, weave, knit, sing, dance, play the guitar and the castanets, and whist and cribbage, and a vast number of other things to the telling of which there would be no end. And that same result was due no less to the fact that Miller Lucas, could, would, and in point of fact did, direct the Mill, till his field, hunt, fish, do the work of carpenter, blacksmith, and mason, help his wife in all the business of the house, read, write, and keep accounts, etcetera, etcetera.

Not to mention his extraordinary accomplishments in matters of pleasure and luxury.

For example, Miller Lucas adored flowers (and so did his wife) and such a past master was he in the art of floriculture that he had succeeded, by means of laborious cross-fertilization, in producing new *varieties*. He was something too of a natural engineer, and had proved as much by constructing a dam, a syphon, and a millrace which trebled the supply of water to the Mill. He had taught a dog to dance, tamed a snake, made a parrot strike the hour by means of cries in accordance with the time shown by a sundial which the Miller had contrived upon a wall, with the result that the parrot struck the hours with perfect precision even on cloudy days and throughout the night.

Finally, the Mill had a kitchen garden which produced every kind of fruit and vegetable; a pond enclosed in a sort of kiosk of jasmine, in which, in summertime, Miller Lucas and Mistress Frasquita used to bathe; a flower garden; a hothouse or conservatory for exotic plants; a well of drinking water; two donkeys on which the couple rode into town or to the neighboring villages; a henhouse, a dovecot, an aviary, hatcheries for fish and silkworms, beehives whose bees sucked honey from the jasmines, a winepress or vat with its appropriate cellar, both in miniature; an oven, loom, forge, carpenter's shop, etcetera, etcetera; all reduced to the compass of an eight-room house and three acres of land and assessed at ten thousand reals.

VII

The Foundations of Felicity

Yes, the Miller and his wife adored each other to distraction, and yet it might have been thought that she loved him more than he her, albeit he was so ugly and she so lovely. I say that because Mistress Frasquita was inclined to be jealous and to ask for explanations when Miller Lucas was late in getting back from town or from the villages to which he went for corn, while Miller Lucas himself actually took pleasure in the attentions which Mistress Frasquita received from the gentlemen who frequented the mill. He took a pride and pleasure in the fact that she pleased all as much as she pleased him, and although he realized in the bottom of his heart that some of them envied him, coveting her like simple mortals, and would have given something for her to be less of an honest woman than she was, he left her alone for days together without the least concern, and never asked her afterwards what she had been doing or who had been there during his absence. None the less, this did not signify that the love of Miller Lucas was less keen than that of Mistress Frasquita. It signified that he had a greater faith in her virtue than she in his; it signified that he had the advantage of her in penetration and well knew the degree to which he was loved and how much his wife respected herself; and it signified chiefly that Miller Lucas was in every point a man, a man like Shakespeare's men, of few but fixed emotions, incapable of doubt; a man who must trust or die, love or slay; who admitted no degrees or middle paths between supreme happiness and the total extinction of joy.

He was, in fine, a Murcian Othello in rope sandals and a cap, in the first act of a possible tragedy.

But why these lugubrious notes in a music so merry? Why

these ominous flashes in so serene an atmosphere? Why these melodramatic postures in a plain domestic scene?

You shall hear, without more ado.

VIII

The Man with
the Three-Cornered Hat

It was two o'clock of an October afternoon. The Cathedral bell was ringing to Vespers, which is as much as to say that all the principal persons of the town had already dined.

Canons were making their way to the Choir and Laymen to their bedrooms to take the siesta, especially those who by reason of office (for example, the town Authorities) had spent the whole morning at work.

And so it was a matter for surprise that at such an hour (a most unsuitable one, moreover, for taking a walk, since the day was still excessively hot) there should leave the City on foot and attended only by one Bailiff, its illustrious Corregidor, a man to be confused with no other person either by day or by night, not only because of the enormous size of his three-cornered hat and the splendor of his scarlet cloak, but also because of the peculiarity of his grotesque carriage.

There are people, not a few, still surviving who could speak out of a full knowledge of that scarlet cloak and the three-cornered hat. Ourselves, among the number, as well as all those born in that City during the last days of the reign of Don Fernando VII, can remember to have seen hanging from a nail, the unique adornment of a dismantled wall in the ruined tower of the house once occupied by his Lordship (a tower given over at this time to the innocent games of his grandchildren), those two antiquated articles of apparel, the cape and the hat —the black hat on top, the red cape beneath—forming a kind of bogy of Absolutism, a kind of sacred relic of the Corregidor, a kind of retrospective caricature of his authority, designed in charcoal and sanguine, like so many others, for us little Constitutionalists of 1837, who were in the habit of meeting there; in short, a kind of scarecrow, which in other days had acted as a *scareman*, and which still frightens *me* today when I recall that I myself helped to jeer at the thing, carried in procession through that historic City in Carnival time, at the end of a sweep's brush, or serving as a comic disguise for the idiot who could best make the crowd laugh. Poor Principle of Authority! This is the pass to which we have brought you, we who are never tired of invoking you today!

As for that matter of the Corregidor's grotesque carriage, it consisted (so they say) in the fact that he was heavy in the shoulder, heavier even than Miller Lucas; to put it in a word, almost hunchbacked; in height below the average; a puny figure of a man and of poor health, bowlegged and with a manner of walking which was all his own—a rocking of himself from one side to another and backwards and forwards which can only be described by the absurd formula that he seemed to be lame in both legs at once. On the other hand (tradition adds), his face was regular, though somewhat creased and crinkled by reason of a complete lack of teeth. He was dusky—a greenish olive, like almost all the sons of the Castiles; in his large, dark eyes you might often see a flash of anger, of tyranny, or of lust. His fine shrewd features were expressive not so much of personal bravery as of a crafty malice capable of anything, together with a certain self-satisfied air, half aristocratic, half dissolute, which revealed that the man had been, in his remote youth, very agreeable and attractive to the women, in spite of his legs and his hunch.

Don Eugenio de Zúñiga y Ponce de León (for such was his Honor's name), was born in Madrid of an illustrious family. He was at this time close upon the fifty-fifth year of his age and the fourth of his office of Corregidor of the City of our story, whereof, soon after his first arrival, he had married the principal Lady of whom we shall have more to say hereafter.

Don Eugenio's stockings (the only detail of his clothing besides his shoes that the great scarlet cloak left to view) were white, and the shoes black, with gold buckles. But when the heat of the open country compelled him to unmuffle himself, it became evident that he wore a great cravat of cambric, a dove-colored waistcoat of twilled silk richly brocaded with a raised pattern of green sprigs, short breeches of black silk, an enormous coat of the same stuff as the waistcoat, a sword with a steel guard, a stick with tassels, and a pair of straw-colored chamois gloves which he never put on, but grasped as if they were a symbol of office.

The Bailiff, who followed the Corregidor at twenty paces' distance, had the name of Weasel, and he was the spit and image of his name. Lean and nimble, with eyes that darted backwards and forwards and right and left all the time he was walking, with a long neck, a small, repellent face, hands like a pair of flogging faggots, he seemed to have been created expressly for the punishment of criminals—the ferret to smell them out, the rope to bind them, and the lash to scourge them.

The first Corregidor to set eyes on him had exclaimed without further formalities: "You're the Bailiff for me." And he had been so already for four of them.

He was forty-eight years old and wore a three-cornered hat much smaller than his Master's (since *his*, we must repeat, was of abnormal size). His cape was black, as were his stockings and the rest of his dress; he carried a stick without tassels and had a kind of skewer for a sword.

This black scarecrow appeared to be the shadow of his resplendent Master.

IX
Gee Up, Donkey!

Everywhere, when the great man and his pendant passed, the laborers left their work, raised their hats, and bowed, from fear rather than respect; after which they said among themselves, *sotto voce:*

"The Corregidor's going early today to see Mistress Frasquita!"

"Early . . . and alone!" added some of the others who had always been accustomed to see him take that walk in company with various other persons.

"Hark you, Manuel!" a village woman asked of her husband who was carrying her on the crupper of his beast. "Why is the Corregidor going alone this afternoon to see that Navarrese woman?" And at the same time she tickled him in the ribs by way of emphasis.

"Now don't go getting wrong ideas, Josefa," cried the good man. "Mistress Frasquita wouldn't *think*——"

"I don't say she would. But that doesn't mean that the Corregidor wouldn't think of falling in love with her. I've heard say that one of the folk that go to those randies at the mill is up to no good, and *that* one is this gentleman from Madrid who is so partial to a petticoat."

"And how do you know he's partial to a petticoat?" enquired the husband.

"I don't speak for myself . . . ! Corregidor though he is, he would think twice before he tried his flatteries on me!"

Now the good woman, as it happened, was as ugly as she could be.

"Now look here, my girl; you let them alone!" answered he whom we have called Manuel. "Miller Lucas is not the sort of man to stand it. He can show a pretty spirit, can Miller Lucas, when he gets angry."

"Still, be that as it may, he doesn't seem to mind!" remarked Josefa, twitching her snout.

"Miller Lucas is the proper sort," answered the villager, "and the proper sort doesn't hold with a certain sort of goings-on."

"Well, have it your own way! Let them be! But if I was Mistress Frasquita——!"

"Gee up, donkey!" shouted the husband, by way of changing the conversation.

And the donkey set off at a trot and drowned the rest of the conversation.

X
Heard in the Arbor

While this discussion was going on among the laborers who had saluted the Corregidor, Mistress Frasquita was carefully sprinkling and sweeping the little flagged court which served as porch or precinct to the Mill, and was setting out half-a-dozen chairs under the thickest part of the vine arbor into which Miller Lucas had climbed and where he was now gathering the finest bunches and arranging them artistically in a basket.

"Yes, Frasquita," came Miller Lucas's voice from up in the arbor. "The Corregidor is in love with you in a very evil fashion."

"I told you so some time ago!" answered Frasquita. "Well, let him love! Look out, Lucas; don't you fall."

"Never worry; I've got a good hold. . . . And there's another of them——"

"Look here, say no more about it," she broke in. "I know

well enough who's fond of me and who is not. I only wish I knew as well why you're not fond of me."

"Because you're so ugly, of course!" answered Miller Lucas.

"Ugly and all, I could climb up there and pitch you down head first."

"More likely you wouldn't get down again till I'd eaten you alive."

"That's it! And when my young men came up and saw us up there, they'd say we were a couple of monkeys."

"Well, they'd be quite right. Don't I look like a monkey with this hump of mine; and you're a saucy little monkey yourself."

"It's a very nice hump!"

"Then the Corregidor's must be a nicer one still, because it's bigger than mine."

"Come, come, Mr. Lucas! Not so much jealousy, please!"

"I jealous of that old skunk? Nothing of the kind. I'm very glad he loves you."

"And why, pray?"

"Because where there's sin there's penance. You don't have to love him at all, and meanwhile I'm the real Corregidor of the City."

"I like your conceit! Well, you'd better remember that I might come to love him. Stranger things have happened in the world."

"That wouldn't trouble me much, either."

"And why not?"

"Because then you wouldn't be you any longer; and if you stopped being what you are, or what I think you are, damn me if I'd care if the Devil himself ran away with you."

"Well, what would you do then?"

"Me? How am I to know? Because then, you see, I should

be different—not the same man as I am now; and so how can I tell what I should think about it?"

"Why would you be different?" Mistress Frasquita insisted boldly, stopping her sweeping, and standing, hands on hips, to gaze up into the vine.

Miller Lucas scratched his head as if he hoped to scratch some profounder thought out of it. When at last he spoke it was with a greater seriousness than usual:

"I should be different, because now I am a man who trusts you as he trusts himself, and whose whole life is in that faith. Consequently, if I ceased to trust you, I should either die or change into a new man; I should live in a different way; it would be as if I had just been born; I should have a different mind. I have no idea what I should do with you. Perhaps I should burst out laughing and turn my back on you. Perhaps I shouldn't even know you. Perhaps . . . ! But Lord, what a funny way of amusing ourselves, getting into a state over nothing. What do we care if all the Corregidors fall in love with you? Aren't you my Frasquita?"

"Of course I am, you great heathen," she answered, laughing heartily. "I'm your Frasquita and you're my own ugly Lucas, cleverer than everyone else put together, better than good bread-and-butter, dearer . . . well, you'll see how dear when you come down from that vine. Yes, you'll get more pinches and punches than you've got hairs on your head. But hush! What's this? There's the Corregidor coming all by himself. And how early! There's something in this. You were right, seemingly!"

"Well, don't check him, and don't tell him I'm up here. He thinks you're alone. He thinks he's caught me at my siesta and he's going to pop the question. What a joke! I'm going to hear what he's got to say."

So saying, Miller Lucas reached down the basket to his wife.

"Not a bad idea!" she exclaimed, bursting out laughing again. "The old devil! Fancy me catching a Corregidor! But here he comes. Weasel will have followed him; not a doubt of it; and now he'll be sitting in the shade in the gully. What a nonsensical business, to be sure! Mind you keep well hidden in those vine leaves; we're going to have the laugh of our lives."

And so saying, the lovely creature started singing the Fandango which by this time came as natural to her as the songs of her own land.

XI

The Bombardment of Pampeluna

"God guard you, Frasquita," said the Corregidor, dropping his voice, as he appeared on tiptoe under the arbor.

"You're very good, my Lord!" she replied in the most natural voice in the world and made him a thousand curtsies. "How is it you're here so soon, and on a hot day like this too? Come, let your Honor take a seat! It's nice and fresh here. How is it your Honor hasn't waited for the other gentlemen? This evening we are expecting my Lord Bishop in person. He promised my Lucas to come and try the first grapes from the vine here. And how does your Honor? And how is your Honor's Lady?"

The Corregidor felt himself somewhat confused. It seemed to him a dream that his hopes should have been realized and that he should have found Mistress Frasquita alone; a dream, or perhaps a trap set for him by an envious fate to hurl him into the pit of disappointment.

And so he contented himself with replying: "It is not so early as you think. It must be half-past three."

At that moment the parrot gave a scream.

"It is a quarter past two," said Frasquita, gazing fixedly at the old man.

The culprit held his peace and made no further attempt to defend himself.

"What about Lucas? Is he asleep?" he asked after a moment. (We must here remark that the Corregidor, like all who have lost their teeth, spoke with a loose, whistling utterance as if he were in the act of eating his own lips.)

"He is, indeed," answered Mistress Frasquita. "At this time of day he sleeps wherever it happens to take him, even if it's on the edge of a precipice."

"Well, look here! Let him sleep!" exclaimed the old man, turning even paler than before. "And you, my dear Frasquita, listen to me . . . hark ye . . . come here. . . . Sit you down here, beside me. I have much to say to you."

"Certainly, my Lord," replied the Miller's wife, grasping a low chair and placing it in front of the Corregidor, at a polite distance from his own. And having seated herself, Frasquita threw one leg over the other, leaned forward, propped an elbow upon her crossed knee and her fresh, lovely face in one of her hands; and thus, with her head a little on one side, a smile on her lips, the five dimples in action, and her serene eyes fixed on the Corregidor, she awaited his Honor's declaration. She might have been compared to Pampeluna expecting a bombardment.

The poor man tried to speak, but remained open-mouthed, dazzled by that superb loveliness, by the brilliance of those charms; yes, dazzled by the whole awe-inspiring woman, with her alabaster skin, her luscious body, her clean and laughing mouth, her blue unfathomable eyes—a creation, it seemed, of the brush of Rubens.

"Frasquita," murmured at last the King's delegate in fainting accents, while, bathed in perspiration, his withered face, standing out against his hunched shoulders, expressed an intense anguish. "Frasquita!"

"That is my name," she answered. "What then?"

"What you wish . . ." replied the old man with extreme tenderness.

"What I wish," said the Miller's wife, "your Honor knows already. I wish you to nominate as secretary of the Municipal Council a nephew of mine in Estella, so that he can come away from those mountains, where he is in a very bad way."

"I have told you, Frasquita, that it is out of the question. The present secretary——"

"Is a thief, a drunkard, and a beast!"

"I know. But he happens to be in the good books of the Perpetual Aldermen and I cannot nominate another without the concurrence of the Corporation. On the contrary, I should risk——"

"Risk! Risk! And what is there that we of this house, down to the very cats, would not risk to please your Honor?"

"Is that the price of your love?" stammered the Corregidor.

"No, Sir. I love your Honor free of charge."

"Don't call me *your Honor*, woman. Call me plain *you*, or whatever you like. . . . Then you promise to love me! Eh?"

"Haven't I told you that I love you already?"

"But——!"

"There's no *but* about it. You'll see what a fine, honest fellow my nephew is."

"Ah, Frasquita! It's you, my dear, that are fine."

"So you like me?"

"I like you? There's not a woman to compare with you."

"Look, then! There's nothing sham about me," answered Mistress Frasquita, rolling up the sleeve of her bodice and showing the rest of her arm, an arm worthy of a caryatid and whiter than a white lily.

"Like you?" pursued the Corregidor. "By day, by night, at every moment, wherever I am, I think of nothing but you."

"What? Don't you like her Ladyship, then?" asked Mistress Frasquita with a mock sympathy that would have made a hypochondriac laugh. "What a pity! My Lucas told me that it was a pleasure to see her and speak to her when he went to mend the clock in the bedroom for you, she is such a fine lady, so good, so affable in her manner."

"Not altogether! Not altogether!" murmured the Corregidor with a touch of bitterness.

"On the other hand, some folk have told me," proceeded the Miller's wife, "that she is very ill-humored and jealous, and rules you with a rod of iron."

"Not altogether, woman," repeated Don Eugenio de Zúñiga y Ponce de León, turning somewhat red. "Not altogether, and yet perhaps a little! My Lady has her tantrums, no doubt; but there's some difference between tantrums and ruling me with a rod of iron. After all, I am the Corregidor."

"Anyhow, do you love her, or do you not?"

"I'll tell you. I love her much, or, to put it better, I did love her till I met you. But since I saw you, I don't know what has come over me . . . she herself sees that something has come over me. All I can tell you is that nowadays if I pat my wife's cheek, for instance, it gives me the same feelings as if I patted my own. But to touch your hand, your arm, your chin, your waist, I would give all I have in the world."

And so saying, the Corregidor tried to possess himself of the bare arm which Mistress Frasquita in actual fact was stroking under his very eyes. But she, without disturbing herself, reached out her hand, touched his Honor's breast with the peaceful violence and irresistible firmness of an elephant's trunk, and pushed him over, chair and all.

"Holy Virgin," cried the wicked creature, laughing consumedly. "The chair must have been broken."

"What's all this?" cried Miller Lucas at the same moment, pushing his ugly face out of the vine leaves.

The Corregidor, still sprawling on the ground, face upwards, gazed in unspeakable terror at this man hovering in the air above him, face downwards.

You might have said that his Honor was the Devil, defeated, not by St. Michael, but by another devil from Hell.

"What is it? Why his Honor tipped up his chair, tried to rock himself, and tumbled over."

"Jesus, Mary and Joseph," cried the Miller in his turn. "And has your Honor hurt himself? Shall I fetch some water and vinegar?"

"It's nothing! It's nothing!" said the Corregidor, scrambling up as well as he could. And he added, under his breath but so that Mistress Frasquita could hear: "I'll pay you out for this."

"Anyhow, his Honor has saved my life," replied Miller Lucas, who was still up in the top of the arbor. "Just fancy, wife; I was sitting up here looking over the grapes, when I fell asleep just as I was, on this crisscross of posts and branches full of holes as big as my body. So you see, if his Honor's tumble hadn't woken me in time, I should have cracked my crown on the flags down there this very afternoon."

"Eh? What?" replied the Corregidor. "Why then, I'm glad, man; I tell you I'm glad that I tumbled over.

"Yes, I'll pay you out for this," he concluded, turning to the Miller's wife. And he uttered the words with such an expression of concentrated fury that Mistress Frasquita began to look serious.

She saw clearly that at first, believing that the Miller had heard everything, the Corregidor was afraid, but that, being soon convinced that he had heard nothing (for the calm cunning of Miller Lucas might well have deceived the sharpest), he began to indulge his anger to the full and to imagine schemes of vengeance.

"Now, down you come from there, and help me to tidy up his Honor. He's covered with dust," she cried to her husband.

And while Miller Lucas was climbing down, she said to the Corregidor, as she beat his coat and more than once his ears with her apron: "The poor dear has heard nothing. He was sleeping like a log."

More than the phrases themselves, the fact that Frasquita had dropped her voice to say them produced a miraculous effect.

"You wicked creature! You hussy!" babbled Don Eugenio de Zúñiga y Ponce de León, growling still, but with a watering mouth.

"Your Honor won't remember this against me?" coaxed Mistress Frasquita.

The Corregidor, observing that severity paid, did his best to look furious; but, meeting her seductive laugh and her divine eyes shining with supplication, he melted on the spot.

"It depends on you, my love!" he slobbered, and the total lack of teeth was more than ever noticeable in his whistling utterance.

At that moment Miller Lucas dropped to the ground out of the arbor.

XII
Tithes and First Fruits

When the Corregidor had been restored to his chair, the Miller's wife shot a rapid glance at her husband, and found him not merely as undisturbed as usual but ready to burst with suppressed laughter. She threw him a kiss, snatching the first moment when Don Eugenio was not looking; and to Don Eugenio she said, in a siren voice that Cleopatra herself might have envied:

"Now your Honor's going to try my grapes."

Then the lovely creature might have been seen (and so would I paint her, if I had the brush of a Titian) standing before the dazzled Corregidor, fresh, superb, provocative, with her noble figure, her fine height, her naked arms raised above her head and a translucent grape bunch in either hand. Then, between an irresistible smile and a beseeching glance in which there was a flicker of fear, she said to him:

"My Lord the Bishop has not tasted them yet. They're the first to be gathered this year."

She stood there like a great Pomona offering fruits to a country deity—to a Satyr, in fact.

Thereupon, at the far end of the flagged court, there came into view the venerable Bishop of the diocese, accompanied by the Counsellor Academician and two Canons of advanced years, and followed by his Secretary, two body servants and two pages.

His Lordship paused for a moment before a picture at once so comical and so lovely; finally he remarked, speaking with the leisured utterance proper to Prelates of the time:

"Fifthly . . . to pay tithes and first fruits to the Church of God, so Christian doctrine teaches us; but you, my Lord Corregidor, are not content to administer the tithes, but are trying, it seems, to devour the first fruits."

"My Lord the Bishop!" exclaimed the Miller and his wife, leaving the Corregidor and running to kiss the Prelate's ring.

"God reward your Lordship for deigning to honor this poor hovel," said Miller Lucas in accents of sincere veneration as he gave the first kiss.

"My most gracious Lord," exclaimed Mistress Frasquita as

she kissed after him, "God bless you and preserve you to me longer than He preserved my Lucas's master to him."

"What can I do, when you give me your blessing instead of asking me for mine?" replied the kindly Bishop, laughing heartily. And raising two fingers he blessed Mistress Frasquita and then the rest of the Company.

"Here are the first fruits, my Lord," said the Corregidor, taking a bunch of grapes from the hands of the Miller's wife and presenting it courteously to the Bishop. "I had not yet tried them."

As he pronounced these words the Corregidor shot a quick, cynical glance at the superb beauty of the Miller's wife.

"Not, however, because they were green like those in the fable!" observed the Academician.

"Those in the fable," remarked the Bishop, "were not green, my Learned Friend, but out of reach of the fox."

Perhaps neither had intended to allude to the Corregidor, but both remarks, as it happened, were so applicable to what had just happened there, that Don Eugenio de Zúñiga turned livid with anger. "Which is to call me a fox," he said, as he kissed the Prelate's ring.

"*Tu dixisti!*" replied the latter, with the courteous severity of a saint, which, in effect, they say he was. "*Excusatio non petita, accusatio manifesta. Qualis vir, talis oratio.* But *satis iam dictum, nullus ultra sit sermo;* or, what amounts to the same thing, let us leave Latin and inspect these famous grapes."

And he took one grape only from the bunch which the Corregidor was offering him.

"They are very good!" he exclaimed, holding up the grape to the light and then handing it to his Secretary. "I am sorry that they don't agree with me."

The Secretary likewise studied the grape, made a gesture of

courteous admiration and handed it to one of the body servants.

The body servant repeated the action of the Bishop and the
gesture of the Secretary, going so far as to smell the grape,
and then . . . placed it in the basket with scrupulous care,
at the same time remarking to the company in a low voice:

"His Lordship is fasting."

Miller Lucas, who had watched the progress of the grape,
stealthily took it, and, when nobody was looking, ate it.

After this, everyone sat down. They spoke of the season,
which was very dry, although the first storm of autumn (the
scourge of Saint Francis, as they call it) had already occurred.
For a while they discussed the probability of a new war between Napoleon and Austria, and expressed the firm belief that
the Imperial troops would never invade Spanish territory. The
Counsellor complained of the restless and calamitous epoch in
which they lived and envied the tranquil times of their parents
(as their parents had envied those of their grandparents). The
parrot struck five, and, at a sign from the Reverend Bishop,
the smaller of the pages went off to the episcopal coach (which
was waiting in the same gully as the Bailiff), and returned with
a magnificent pastry cake, sprinkled with salt, which had come
out of the oven hardly an hour ago. A table was set in the
middle of the company; the cake was quartered; Miller Lucas
and Mistress Frasquita were given their appropriate share,
despite their energetic resistance, and a truly democratic equal-
ity reigned for half an hour beneath those vine leaves which
filtered the last splendors of the setting sun.

XIII
Said the Jackdaw to the Crow

An hour and a half later all the illustrious company was back
again in the City.

The Lord Bishop and his *family* had arrived some time ahead of the rest, thanks to the coach, and were already *in residence,* where we will leave them to their devotions.

The distinguished Counsellor (who was very lean) and the two Canons (each more plump and dignified than the other), accompanied the Corregidor as far as the door of the Town Hall (where his Honor said that he had some work to do) and then made their way towards their respective homes, steering by the stars like navigators or groping round corners like blind men; since the night had already closed in, the moon was not yet risen, and the public lighting (like that other Enlightenment of the period) existed only in the divine mind.

On the other hand, it was not uncommon to see a lantern or torch flitting now and then along the street, borne by some respectful servant who was lighting his stately master and mistress to the customary party or to pay a call on certain of their relatives.

At the bars of almost every low window was to be seen (or, to speak more accurately, to be scented) a black and silent shape. It was a lover who, hearing footsteps, had paused for a moment in his love-making.

"We're a lot of tomfools," said the Counsellor and the Canons as they passed. "What will they think at home when they see us returning at such hours?"

"And what will the folk say who meet us in the street, like this, after seven of the night, slinking along like brigands under cover of darkness?"

"We shall have to turn over a new leaf."

"We shall! And yet, that delightful Mill!"

"My wife can't stomach the Mill," said the Academician in a tone that betrayed considerable fear of the forthcoming conjugal skirmish.

"And what about my niece?" exclaimed one of the Canons,

who was clearly a penitentiary. "My niece says that priests have no business to pay visits to gossips . . ."

"And yet," interrupted his companion, who was a Prebend, "nothing could be more innocent than what goes on there."

"I should think so when the very Lord Bishop himself is one of the party."

"And then, gentlemen, at our age . . ." replied the Penitentiary. "Yesterday I turned seventy-five."

"The thing's obvious," answered the Prebendary. "But let us talk of something else. How fine Mistress Frasquita was this evening!"

"Oh, as for that, she's a fine woman as fineness goes!" said the Counsellor, affecting a certain impartiality.

"A very fine woman," reiterated the Penitentiary into his muffler.

"And if you don't think so," added the Prebendary, "ask the Corregidor."

"The poor man's in love with her."

"I verily believe he is," exclaimed the Penitentiary.

"Not a doubt of it," added the Corresponding Academician. "Well, gentlemen, this is my best way home. A very good night to you!"

"Good night!" answered the Capitulars, and they continued a few steps in silence.

Then the Prebendary dug the Penitentiary in the ribs. "He's in love with the Miller's wife too," he murmured.

"So it would appear," replied the latter, stopping at the door of his house. "And what a gross fellow he is! Well, till tomorrow, friend! I trust the grapes will agree with you."

"Till tomorrow, if God wills. A very good night to you!"

"God send us a good night," prayed the Penitentiary, already in his porch, which, by the same token, held a lantern and a figure of Our Lady.

He raised the knocker.

Once alone in the street, the other Canon (who was broader than he was long and rolled in his walk) went slowly on his way towards his house . . . and remarked, thinking no doubt of his colleague:

"And you too are in love with Mistress Frasquita! And the truth is," he added after a moment, "that, as fineness goes, she's a fine woman."

XIV

Weasel's Advice

Meanwhile the Corregidor had gone up into the Town Hall, accompanied by Weasel, with whom, in the Council Chamber, he was for some time engaged in a conversation somewhat more familiar than sorted with a person of his quality and office.

"Let your Honor trust a dog that knows the sport," the Bailiff was saying. "Mistress Frasquita is crazy about your Honor, and all that your Honor has just told me shows me as much, clearer than that light . . ." and he pointed to a lamp which hardly illuminated an eighth of the room.

"I am not as sure as you, Weasel," answered Don Eugenio, sighing languidly.

"Then I don't know why! But, if you're not, let us speak frankly. Your Honor (may I be pardoned for saying so) has a certain blemish . . . haven't you?"

"Well, yes," answered the Corregidor. "But Miller Lucas has one too. He is more hunchbacked than I."

"Much more! Very much more! Out of all comparison! But on the other hand (and this is what I was coming to) your Honor has a face of very good appearance, what you call a handsome face, while Miller Lucas is fit to burst with ugliness."

The Corregidor smiled with a certain loftiness.

"Besides," pursued the Bailiff, "Mistress Frasquita is ready to throw herself out of the window to get that nomination for her nephew."

"As to that, I agree. That nomination is my one hope."

"Then get to work, your Honor! I have told you my plan already. The only thing left to do is to set it going this very night."

"I have often told you that I am not in need of advice," cried Don Eugenio, suddenly remembering that he was talking with an inferior.

"I thought your Honor asked me for it," stammered Weasel.

"Don't answer back."

Weasel touched his hat.

"So you were saying," pursued Don Eugenio, mild once more, "that all this might be arranged this very night? Well, look here, my boy; I like the idea of it. What the devil! It's the quickest way of escaping from this cruel uncertainty."

Weasel kept silence.

The Corregidor went to the writing table and wrote a few lines on a sheet of stamped paper, set his own stamp on it, and then put it away in his pocket.

"The nephew's nomination is complete," he said, taking a pinch of snuff. "Tomorrow I will put myself right with the Aldermen . . . and either they will confirm it or there will be another siege of St. Quentin. Isn't that the way to do it?"

"That's the way! That's the way!" exclaimed the delighted Weasel, putting a claw into the Corregidor's snuffbox and snatching a pinch. "That's the way! Your Honor's predecessor didn't beat about the bush either. I remember once——"

"Stop your chattering," said the Corregidor, giving a smack to the thieving hand. "My predecessor was an ass if he had you for a Bailiff. To business! You told me just now that

Miller Lucas's Mill comes within the boundary of the next village and not of this town. Now, are you sure of that?"

"Quite sure! The City boundary ends at the gully where I sat this afternoon waiting till your Honor . . . Devil take me! If *I'd* been in your place——"

"Enough, saucy fellow!" cried Don Eugenio; and, taking a half-sheet of paper, he wrote a note, sealed it, folded it, and handed it to Weasel. "Here is the letter," he said, "which you asked me for, to the Mayor of the Village. You will explain to him by word of mouth everything that he must do. You see, I am following your plan precisely. And woe betide you if you land me in a blind alley."

"Never fear," answered Weasel. "Master Juan López has cause to be heedful, and, as soon as he sees your Honor's signature, he'll do everything I tell him. He owes at least fifteen hundred bushels of grain to the State Granary and another fifteen hundred to the Charity Store; this last against all law, for it's not as if he was a widow or a poor laborer to receive corn without paying interest in kind. He's nothing but a gambler, a drunkard, a brazen-faced villain, always after a petticoat, the scandal of the village. And that man's a person in authority! Well, such is life!"

"I've told you to be quiet. You're disturbing me," blustered the Corregidor. "Well," he added, changing his tone, "to business! It is a quarter past seven. The first thing you must do is to go to the house and tell her Ladyship not to wait for me either for supper or after. Tell her I shall be working here tonight till Curfew and shall then be going on patrol with you, to see if we can catch certain miscreants. . . . In short, tell her something that will make her go peacefully to bed. On your way, tell the other Bailiff to bring me some supper. I won't venture myself into her Ladyship's presence this evening, because she knows me so well that she's quite capable of reading my thoughts. Order the cook to give me some of those fritters that were made today, and tell Johnny to get me from the tavern, when no one is looking, half a pint of white wine. Then off you go to the Village, where you can very well be by half-past eight."

"I'll be there at eight prompt," exclaimed Weasel.

"Don't contradict me," growled the Corregidor, remembering once again who he was.

Weasel touched his hat.

"We have said," continued the other, human once more, "that you will be at the Village promptly at eight. From the Village to the Mill will be . . . it will be, I suppose, half a league."

"A short one!"

"Don't interrupt me."

The Bailiff touched his hat again.

"A short one," pursued the Corregidor. "In consequence, at ten. . . . Shall we say at ten?"

"Before ten! At half-past nine your Honor will be quite safe in calling at the Mill."

"Fellow! Don't tell *me* what I have to do. Now as to *your* place . . . Suppose you are——"

"I shall be everywhere. But my headquarters will be the gully. Ah! I'd almost forgotten! Let your Honor go on foot, and don't take a lantern."

"Again! What the devil do I want with your advice, man? Do you imagine it's the first time I have done this sort of thing?"

"Pardon, your Honor. Ah! Another thing. Don't let your Honor call at the great door which gives on the court where the arbor is, but at the little door there is above the mill-race——"

"There is another door above the millrace? Why, look you, that's a thing that never occurred to me."

"Yes, my Lord. The little door by the millrace leads straight into the couple's bedroom, and Miller Lucas never goes in or out by it. So that, although he came back unexpectedly——"

"I follow. I follow. Don't deafen me, man."

"Lastly, be sure your Honor slips away before dawn. Dawn now is at six o'clock."

"More useless advice. At five I shall be back home. But we have talked too much already. . . . Out of my presence."

"Then, good luck, my Lord," exclaimed the Bailiff, reaching out a hand to the Corregidor and at the same time gazing at the ceiling.

The Corregidor placed in the hand one peseta and Weasel vanished as if by magic.

"S'life," muttered the old man after a moment, "if I haven't forgotten to tell that chatterer that they must bring me a pack of cards as well! With a pack of cards I could have amused myself till half-past nine trying to get that solitaire to come out."

XV

Prosaic Farewell

It would be nine of the same night when Miller Lucas and Mistress Frasquita, having despatched all the business of the Mill and the house, sat down to sup off a bowl of chicory salad, a pound of meat garnished with tomatoes, and a few of the grapes which remained in the aforementioned basket; the whole washed down with a drop of wine and a flood of laughter at the expense of the Corregidor. After which the pair glanced smilingly at one another as if well content with God and themselves, and exclaimed between a couple of yawns which revealed all the peace and tranquillity of their hearts:

"Well, to bed, Sir. There's another day tomorrow."

At that very moment two loud and vigorous knocks rang upon the great door of the Mill.

Husband and wife stared at each other thunderstruck. Never before had there come a knocking at their door at such an hour.

"I'll go and see," said the fearless wife, moving towards the court.

"Stop! This is my job," exclaimed Miller Lucas with such dignity that Mistress Frasquita let him pass. "I've told you not to go," he added sternly, seeing that the obstinate creature wished to follow him.

She obeyed and remained indoors.

"Who is it?" called Miller Lucas from halfway across the court.

"The Law," answered a voice through the great door.

"What Law?"

"The Law of the Village. Open, Sir, to the Mayor."

Miller Lucas had meanwhile applied an eye to a certain peephole cunningly contrived in the door, and had recognized by the light of the moon the clownish Bailiff of the neighboring village.

"Why don't you say 'Open to this drunkard of a Bailiff'?" answered the Miller, drawing the bolt.

"It's all the same," replied the voice outside. "Haven't I his Honor's written order? Good evening to you, Miller Lucas," added the Bailiff as he came in. His voice was less official now, deeper and thicker, as if he already felt himself another man.

"God keep you, Tony!" replied the Miller. "Let's see what this order is! Señor Juan López might have chosen a more suitable hour for business with honest folk. But I expect it's your fault. You've had a drink or two on the way, seemingly. Will you take another?"

"No, Sir: there's no time for anything. You've got to follow me at once. Read the Order."

"Follow you?" exclaimed Miller Lucas, going into the Mill when he had taken the paper. "Here, Frasquita! A light!"

Mistress Frasquita put down something she was holding and unhooked the oil lamp. Miller Lucas cast a rapid glance at the object that his wife had put down and recognized his bellmouth, to wit, an enormous blunderbuss which carried bullets up to half a pound. Then the Miller turned on his wife a look full of gratitude and affection.

"You're a wonder," he said to her, taking her face in his hands.

Mistress Frasquita, pale and calm as a marble statue, lifted the lamp which she held in two fingers, without the least tremor of her pulse.

"Come! Read it!" she answered coldly.

The Order ran as follows: .

"For the better service of His Majesty the King Our Lord (Q.D.G.), I give notice to Lucas Fernández, miller, of this neighborhood, that, as soon as he shall receive this order, he shall present himself before my authority without excuse or pretext; warning him that, the matter being confidential, he communicate it to no one; all this subject to the proper penalties in case of disobedience.

"Juan López, Mayor."

And there was a cross in place of the signature.

"Look here! What's this?" Miller Lucas asked the Bailiff. "What's the meaning of this order?"

"I don't know," replied the rustic, a man of some thirty

years, whose face (a sharp, crooked one it was, like a thief's or a cutthroat's) spoke ill for his sincerity. "I think it's about investigating something to do with witchcraft or false money. But the thing doesn't concern you. They're simply calling you as a witness or an expert. In fact, I haven't gone into the particulars. Señor Juan López will tell you the ins and outs of it."

"Right!" exclaimed the Miller. "Tell him I'll come tomorrow."

"Oh no, Sir! You've got to come now, without losing a minute. Those are the orders I had from the Mayor."

There was a moment's silence. Mistress Frasquita's eyes were flashing; Miller Lucas kept his on the ground as if he were seeking something.

"At least you'll give me the time to go to the stable and saddle a donkey," he exclaimed at last, raising his head.

"Donkey? The devil I will!" replied the Bailiff. "Surely a man can go half a league on foot! It's a beautiful night; there's a moon!"

"Yes, the moon's risen, I know. But I suffer from swollen feet."

"Very well, then, don't let us waste time. I'll help you to saddle the beast."

"Hollo! Hollo! Are you frightened that I'll escape?"

"I'm frightened of nothing, Miller Lucas," answered Tony, as cool as a corpse. "I am the Law."

So saying, he *ordered arms,* and by so doing revealed the musket which he carried under his cloak.

"Look here, Tony," said the Miller's wife. "As you're going to the stable, in the exercise of your duty, do me the favor to saddle the other donkey too."

"Why?" asked the Miller.

"For me. I'm going with you."

"You can't, Mistress Frasquita," objected the Bailiff. "My orders are to fetch your husband, nothing more, and to prevent you following him. It's as much as my neck's worth to do otherwise. Señor Juan López told me as much. And so . . . come along, Miller Lucas." And he turned towards the door.

"Well, anything stranger——!" said the Miller in a low voice.

"Very strange!" answered Mistress Frasquita.

"There's something . . . I can see . . ." Miller Lucas went on, murmuring so low that Tony could not hear.

"Would you like me to go to the City," whispered his wife, "and let the Corregidor know what's happening?"

"No!" replied Miller Lucas aloud. "No! Not that."

"Then what would you like me to do?" said the Miller's wife, ready for anything.

"I'd like you to look at me," answered the ex-soldier.

The couple gazed at one another in silence and drew such satisfaction from the tranquillity, the resolution, and the energy that each poured into the other's soul that they had to grasp each other by the shoulders and laugh.

This done, Miller Lucas lighted another lamp and went off to the stable, calling slyly to Tony on the way:

"Come on, man! Come and help me, if you'll be so obliging."

Tony followed him, humming a tune through his teeth.

A few minutes later Miller Lucas left the Mill mounted on a fine jenny and followed by the Bailiff.

The farewell of husband and wife was no more than as follows:

"Lock up the house," said Miller Lucas.

"Wrap yourself up, it's cold," said Mistress Frasquita, locking up with bolt, bar, and key.

That was all. No more good-byes, no more kisses, no more embraces, no more glances.

Why?

XVI

A Bird of Evil Omen

For our part, let us follow Miller Lucas.

They had already covered a quarter of a league without a word, the Miller mounted on his she-ass and the Bailiff driving her from behind with his staff of office, when they observed in front of them, at the top of a rise in the road, an enormous bird which was coming towards them.

The thing stood out sharply against the moonlit sky, depicted upon it with such precision that the Miller exclaimed at once: "Tony, that is Weasel, with his three-cornered hat and his long spindleshanks."

But before Tony could reply, the shape, anxious doubtless to avoid that encounter, had left the road and set off at a run across country with the speed of a real weasel.

Then Tony replied. "I see no one," he said, in the most natural way in the world.

Miller Lucas swallowed his words. "Neither do I," he answered. And the suspicion which had already occurred to him at the Mill began to take on body and consistency in the distrustful soul of the hunchback.

"This journey of mine," he said to himself, "is a plot of the Corregidor's. What I heard yesterday afternoon from the top of the arbor shows well enough that this old fool from Madrid can't wait any longer. Without a doubt, he's going back to the Mill tonight, and so he has begun by clearing me out of the way. But what does it matter? Frasquita is Frasquita! Even if they set the house on fire she won't open the door. I'd go further! Even if she did open it, even if the Corregidor managed by some trick to get at my dear girl, the old rogue would soon come out again with his tail between his legs. Frasquita is Frasquita! Still," he added after a moment, "it will be as well for me to get back home tonight as soon as I possibly can."

Hereupon Miller Lucas and the Bailiff reached the Village and made their way to the house of the Mayor.

XVII

A Rustic Mayor

Señor Juan López, who, as man and Mayor, was tyranny, ferocity, and pride personified when dealing with his inferiors, condescended none the less at that time of day, after having despatched his official duties and those of his farm and having given his wife her daily beating, to drink a jug of wine in company with the Secretary and the Sacristan, an operation which was about half completed tonight when the Miller appeared before him.

"Hollo! Miller Lucas," he said, and he scratched his head so as to set his bump of mendacity working. "How are you? Now, Mr. Secretary, a glass of wine for Miller Lucas! And Mistress Frasquita? As fine as ever, I suppose? It's a long time since I've seen her. Ah, man; milling's a fine job nowadays. Rye bread nowadays is as good as the best white. Well, come, sit you down and rest. God be thanked, we're in no hurry."

"Devil a bit, as far as I'm concerned," answered Miller Lucas, who till now had not opened his mouth, but whose suspicions were growing stronger every moment at the friendly reception he was receiving after so formidable and pressing a summons.

"Well then, Miller Lucas," continued the Mayor, "as you're in no great hurry, you'll sleep the night here and early tomorrow we'll despatch our little business."

"Good!" replied Miller Lucas with an irony and dissimulation which were more than a match for the diplomacy of Señor Juan López. "As the thing is not urgent, I don't mind spending the night away from home."

"Neither urgent nor involving any risk for you," added the Mayor, tricked by the man he thought he himself was tricking. "You can set your mind at rest about that. Here, Tony, hand over that bushel, so that Miller Lucas can sit down."

"More drinks then," cried Miller Lucas, seating himself.

"Help yourself," replied the Mayor, handing him the full glass.

"After you, Sir! After you!"

"Well, here's your very good health," said Señor Juan López, half emptying the glass.

"The same to you, Mr. Mayor!" replied Miller Lucas, draining the second half.

"Hi! Manuela!" called the Mayor. "Tell your mistress that Miller Lucas is staying the night here. Tell her to put him a bolster in the granary."

"No! No! Nothing of the kind. I shall sleep like a king in the hayloft."

"But we have plenty of bolsters."

"I'm sure you have! But why should you trouble the family? I have my cloak."

"Well, as you like, Sir. Manuela! Tell your mistress not to trouble about the bolster."

"I've only one favor to ask," continued Miller Lucas, yawning atrociously, "and that is that I may go to bed at once. Last night I had a lot of stuff to grind and I haven't had a wink of sleep yet."

"By all means!" replied the Mayor, majestically. "Retire when you feel inclined."

"I think it's time for us to retire as well," said the Sacristan, gazing into the jug to gauge how much wine was left. "It must be ten already, or very near it."

"A quarter to ten," announced the Secretary after sharing among the glasses the rest of the night's allowance of wine.

"Well, to bed, gentlemen," said the host, swallowing his share.

"Good night, Sirs!" added the Miller, drinking his.

"Wait till we get you a light! Tony, take Miller Lucas to the hayloft."

"This way, Miller Lucas," said Tony, taking the jug with him in case there were a few drops left.

"We meet tomorrow, if God wills," said the Sacristan, finishing the last drop out of each glass. And off he went, staggering as he went and gaily singing the *De Profundis*. . . .

"Well, Sir," said the Mayor to the Secretary when they were alone, "Miller Lucas has suspected nothing. We can safely go to bed and . . . good luck to the Corregidor."

XVIII

In Which It Is Seen That Miller Lucas Was a Very Light Sleeper

Five minutes later, a man dropped from the window of the Mayor's hayloft, a window which gave on a yard and was hardly twelve feet from the ground. In the yard was a shed covering a row of mangers to which were tied six or eight horses, mules and donkeys, all of them mares. The stallions were stabled apart in a place near by.

The man untied a jenny, which was in fact already saddled,

and went off, leading her by the bridle, towards the gate of the yard. He undid the bar and loosed the bolt which secured it, opened it cautiously, and found himself in the open country.

Once there, he mounted the jenny, drove his heels into her, and was off like an arrow in the direction of the City, not however by the ordinary cartway, but over field and dale, as one who keeps clear of some untoward meeting.

It was Miller Lucas making for his Mill.

XIX

Voces Clamantes in Deserto

"That's the way we treat Mayors where I come from!" said the Miller to himself as he cantered along. "Tomorrow morning I shall go and see my Lord the Bishop, by way of precaution, and tell him all that has happened tonight. Sending for me with such hurry and secrecy at that time of night! Telling me to come alone! Talking to me of the Service of the King, false money, witches, spooks! And all to hand me a couple of glasses of wine and send me to bed! The thing's as clear as clear can be! Weasel brought those instructions to the Village from the Corregidor, and now the Corregidor will be setting his springes for my wife. Who knows if I shall not find him knocking at the door of the Mill? Who knows if I shall not find him inside already? Who knows? But what am I saying? Suspect my good girl? Oh, that's an offense against God! It's impossible that she . . . ! It's impossible that my Frasquita . . . ! It's impossible . . . ! What am I talking about? Is there anything in the world impossible? Didn't she marry me, beautiful as she is, and me so ugly?" And at the thought of that the poor hunchback began to weep.

Then he reined in his jenny so as to calm himself a little,

wiped his tears, sighed deeply, drew out his pouch and rolled himself a cigarette, took his flint, tinder, and steel, and after striking once or twice, succeeded in getting a light.

At that moment he heard a sound of footsteps on the road, which was about three hundred yards away from where he had stopped.

"I'm a silly fool," he said. "Suppose they're after me already! I shall have given myself away by striking that light."

So saying, he put out the light, dismounted, and took cover behind the jenny.

But the jenny understood the situation differently and let out a bray of satisfaction.

"Confound the beast!" exclaimed Miller Lucas, trying to shut her mouth with his hands.

Just then another bray rang out from the road, by way of gallant reply.

"We're done for!" thought the Miller to himself. "The song's right:

> "Woes are fiftyfold increased
> For the man that trusts a beast."

And reflecting thus, he mounted again, clapped heels to his jenny and set off headlong in the direction opposite to that of the answering bray.

And the strange thing was that the person who rode the other ass must have taken fright at Miller Lucas just as Miller Lucas had taken fright at him. I say so because he too left the road, doubtless suspecting that it was a bailiff or some rascal in the pay of Don Eugenio, and went off at a gallop across the fields at the other side of the road.

The Miller, meanwhile, thus continued his reflections:

"What a night! What a world! What a life I've led during the last hour! Bailiffs turned into pimps! Mayors plotting against my honor, donkeys braying when they ought not; and here, in my breast, a wretched heart which has dared to suspect the noblest wife that God ever created! Oh! My God, my God! Grant that I may come quickly home and find my Frasquita safe."

Miller Lucas went on his way over field and thicket, until at last, about eleven of the night, he came without further adventure to the great door of the Mill.

Damnation! The door of the Mill was open!

XX
Suspicion and Reality

It was open! Yet when he set out from home he had heard his wife fasten it with bolt, bar, and key.

Consequently, none but his wife herself could have opened it.

But how? When? Why? Because of a trick? In obedience to an order? Or of her own free will and resolve, in virtue of a previous understanding with the Corregidor?

What was he going to see? What was he going to discover? What awaited him in his home? Could Frasquita have flown? Had they kidnapped her? Was she dead? Or was she in the arms of his rival?

"The Corregidor reckoned that I could not get back all night," said Miller Lucas to himself gloomily. "The Mayor of the Village must have had orders to put me under lock and key rather than let me return. Did Frasquita know all that? Was she in the plot? Or has she been the victim of a trick, of violence, of infamy?"

Over these cruel reflections the unlucky fellow spent no more time than it took him to cross the little court of the arbor.

The house door too was open. The first room (as in all country dwellings) was the kitchen.

In the kitchen there was nobody.

None the less, an enormous fire was blazing in the fireplace, though there had been no fire when he went out nor did they ever light one there until well on in December.

Lastly, from one of the hooks of the rack hung a lighted lamp.

What could it all mean? How reconcile these signs of wakefulness and company with the deathly silence that reigned throughout the house?

What had become of his wife?

Then, and then only, Miller Lucas caught sight of certain clothes hung over the backs of two or three chairs set round the fire.

On those clothes he fixed his eyes and let out a growl so deep that it stuck in his throat, and changed into a dumb and suffocating sob.

The wretched man felt himself choking and raised his hands to his neck while, livid, convulsed, his eyes starting out of his head, he stared at that clothing with the horror of a criminal at the point of death when they hold out for him the sack of execution.

For what he saw before him was the scarlet cape, the three-cornered hat, the dove-colored coat and waistcoat, the black silk breeches, the white stockings, the buckled shoes, down to the very stick, sword and gloves of the execrable Corregidor. What he saw before him was the death-sack of his shame, the shroud of his murdered honor, the extinction of his happiness.

The terrible blunderbuss stood in the same corner where, two hours before, his wife had left it. Miller Lucas sprang on it like a tiger and seized it in his hands. He tried the barrel with the ramrod and found that it was loaded. He examined the flint and saw that it was in place. Then he turned to the staircase which led to the room in which for so many years he had slept with Mistress Frasquita, and murmured dully:

"They are there!"

He took one step in that direction; but next moment he paused to look round him and see if anyone was watching.

"Nobody!" he said to himself. "Only God, and He . . . has willed this!"

Having thus confirmed the sentence, he was just going to take another step when his wandering gaze detected a folded paper lying on the table.

To see it, to hurl himself upon it, to hold it in his clutch, was the work of a second.

That paper was the nomination of Mistress Frasquita's nephew, signed by Don Eugenio de Zúñiga y Ponce de León!

"This," thought Miller Lucas, "is the price. She has sold herself," and he crammed the paper into his mouth to stifle his cries and give nourishment to his fury. "I always suspected that she loved her family more than me. Ah! We never had children! That's what caused it all."

And the unhappy man was on the point of bursting into tears again. But at that moment fury came upon him once more and with a terrible gesture rather than by word of mouth he exclaimed:

"Upstairs! Upstairs!"

And he began to climb the stairs like a beast, one hand on the floor, the other grasping the blunderbuss, with the infamous paper between his teeth.

In corroboration of his suspicions, on arriving at the bedroom door, which was locked, he saw a light through the keyhole and at the joins in the woodwork.

"Here they are!" he muttered again. And he stood for a moment as if to drain this new cup of bitterness.

Not a sound came from within.

"Suppose there's no one there," whispered the timid voice

of hope. But at that very instant the unhappy man heard someone cough in the room.

It was the asthmatical cough of the Corregidor.

Not a doubt remained; not a plank of salvation in his immense shipwreck!

In the darkness the Miller smiled horribly. How can darkness be dark before such flashes of the soul? What are all the fires of torture compared with that which sometimes burns in the heart of man?

None the less, no sooner had he heard his enemy's cough, than Miller Lucas (for such was his soul, as we have already said elsewhere) began to grow calm. The reality hurt him less than the suspicion. As he himself had said that evening to Mistress Frasquita, from the moment in which he had lost the one faith which was the life of his soul, he began to change into a new man.

Like the Moor of Venice (with whom we have already compared him in describing his character), disillusionment slew all his love at a single blow, transforming at once the nature of his spirit and forcing him to look upon the world as a strange land in which he had just arrived. The one difference was that by temperament Miller Lucas was less tragic, less austere, and more of an egoist than the insensate sacrificer of Desdemona.

Strange but true of such situations—doubt, or rather hope (which in this case is the same) came back again and subdued him for a moment!

"What if I were mistaken!" he thought. "What if the cough were Frasquita's!"

In the agony of his mischance he forgot that he had seen the clothes of the Corregidor round the kitchen fire, that he had found the door of the Mill open, that he had read the proof of his disgrace.

He stooped and looked through the keyhole, trembling with doubt and anguish.

His glance could only discover a little triangle of bed, up beside the head. But precisely in that little triangle appeared one end of the pillows, and on the pillows the head of the Corregidor.

Once more a diabolical laugh distorted the face of the Miller. It was almost as if he were happy once again.

"Now I know the truth," he murmured, straightening himself calmly. "Let me think."

And he went downstairs again with the same precautions with which he had gone up.

"It's a ticklish subject. I must reflect. I have plenty of time for *everything*," he thought as he descended.

When he had reached the kitchen he sat down in the middle of the room and covered his face with his hands.

So he remained for a long while, until he was roused from his meditation by a light blow on one foot. It was the blunderbuss which had slipped from his knees and had chosen that way of attracting his attention.

"No! I tell you, no!" murmured Miller Lucas, face to face with the weapon. "You are not what I want. Everyone would pity *them,* and they'd hang *me.* We are dealing with a Corregidor, and in Spain it is still an unforgivable sin to kill a Corregidor. They would say that I killed him from unfounded jealousy and then undressed him and put him in my bed. They would say too, that I killed my wife simply on suspicion . . . and they'd hang me. Most certainly they'd hang me! Besides, I should have shown myself very small-souled, very little-witted, if in the ending of my life I had earned nothing but pity. Everyone would laugh at me. They would say that my ill-luck was very natural, when I was a hunchback and Frasquita so beautiful. No! Nothing of the sort! What I want is to revenge myself, and, after that, to triumph, scorn, laugh, laugh hugely, laugh at everybody, so that no one will ever be able to make fun of this hump which I have made almost enviable, and which would look so grotesque on a gallows."

So reasoned Miller Lucas, without perhaps taking account of it word by word; and in virtue of some such reasoning he put back the weapon in its place and began to pace to and fro with his hands behind him and his head bowed, as if seeking for his revenge on the ground, in the earth, in all that is base in life, in some ridiculous and ignominious joke against his wife and the Corregidor, far from seeking that same revenge in the law, in a challenge, in forgiveness, or in Heaven, as any other man of a condition less rebellious against all the dictates of human nature, society, or his own feelings, would have done in his place.

Suddenly his gaze came to rest on the clothes of the Corregidor. He stood still.

And then, little by little, there spread over his face an indefinable look of joy, of glee, of triumph, until at last he burst out laughing, hugely, in great guffaws, but without making a sound (for fear they should hear him upstairs), clutching his hands to his sides to stop himself bursting, the whole man shuddering like an epileptic, forced at last to drop into a chair until that convulsion of sarcastic merriment had left him.

It was the laugh of Mephistopheles himself.

The moment he was calm again, he set about stripping himself with feverish haste, laid all his clothes on the chairs formerly occupied by those of the Corregidor, dressed himself in the latter, from the buckled shoes to the three-cornered hat; girt on the sword; wrapped himself up in the scarlet cape; snatched up the stick and the gloves, and left the mill and set off for the City, waddling just as Don Eugenio de Zúñiga waddled, and now and then muttering to himself this phrase, which very aptly summed the thought that possessed him:

"Well, the Corregidor's lady is a fine woman too!"

XXI

On Guard, My Lord!

And now let us leave Miller Lucas and take a look at what had happened at the Mill from the time that we left Mistress Frasquita alone there until her husband returned to make these astounding discoveries.

An hour had gone by since Miller Lucas went off with Tony, when his distressed wife, who had resolved not to go to bed until her husband returned and now sat knitting in her bedroom, which was on the upper floor, heard pitiful cries outside the house in the direction of the millrace, which was close to that part of the building.

"Help! I'm drowning! Frasquita! Frasquita!" It was a man's voice and its accent was the melancholy accent of despair.

"Can it be Lucas?" she thought, filled with a terror that we hardly need describe.

In the bedroom was a little door, of which Weasel has told us already, which gave on the upper part of the millrace. Without a moment's hesitation, Mistress Frasquita opened it, although she had not recognized the voice that called for help, and to her amazement found herself face to face with the Corregidor who at that very moment was emerging, his clothes streaming with water, from the headlong rush of the channel.

"God forgive me! God forgive me!" babbled the infamous old man. "I thought I was drowning!"

"Why! It's your Honor! What's the meaning of this? How dare you? What do you want to come here for at this time of day?" cried the Miller's wife, more indignant than afraid, though mechanically she retreated.

"Hush! Hush, woman!" stammered the Corregidor, slipping into the room behind her. "I will tell you all. I was within an ace of drowning. The water was on the point of sweeping me away like a feather. Look, look at the state I'm in!"

"Out you go from here," replied Mistress Frasquita with growing vehemence. "You need explain nothing! I understand it all too well! What do I care whether you drown or not? Did I ask you to come? Ah, the infamy of it! That's why you sent for my husband!"

"Woman, listen——!"

"I won't listen! Off you go at once, Sir! Off you go, or I won't answer for your life!"

"What are you saying?"

"I'm saying what I mean. My husband's not at home, but I'm quite capable of protecting our home myself. Off you go, to where you come from, unless you want me to take you and throw you back into the water!"

"My dear, my dear, don't shout so! I'm not deaf!" exclaimed the old rake. "If I'm here, it's for a good reason. I have come to free Miller Lucas, whom a village Mayor has arrested by mistake. But, first of all, you must dry these clothes for me. I'm soaked to the skin."

"Off you go, I tell you."

"Be quiet, foolish creature! What do you know about it? Look, I've brought you your nephew's nomination. Light the lamp and we'll talk about it. And while these clothes are drying, I'll get into this bed here."

"Ah! So you confess you've come to see *me?* You confess that's why you sent and had Lucas arrested? So you were bringing the nomination and all? Saints of Heaven! What sort of an idea has this old figure of fun got of me?"

"Frasquita! I am the Corregidor!"

"If you were the King himself, what has it got to do with

me? I'm the wife of my husband and the mistress of my house! Do you think I'm frightened of Corregidors? I'll go to Madrid, I'd go to the world's end, for justice against the insolent old rogue who drags his authority in the mud like this. And, what's more, tomorrow morning I'll put on my mantilla and go and see her Ladyship!"

"You'll do nothing of the sort!" replied the Corregidor, losing patience, or changing his tactics. "You'll do nothing of the sort; because, if I see that you're not going to listen to reason, I'll put a bullet through you."

"A bullet?" exclaimed Mistress Frasquita in a low voice.

"Yes, a bullet! And it will do me no damage, either. As it happens, I've left word in the City that I was coming out tonight after certain miscreants. And so don't be silly, but love me . . . as I adore you!"

"A bullet, Sir?" repeated the Miller's wife, putting her arms behind her and throwing her body forward as if to spring upon her opponent.

"If you give me trouble, I shall shoot you, and then I shall be free of your threats and your beauty," answered the terrified Corregidor, taking out a pair of pocket pistols.

"Pistols too! And my nephew's nomination in the other pocket!" said Mistress Frasquita, nodding her head up and down. "Then, Sir, I have no choice. Wait a moment, I'm going to light the light."

So saying, she ran to the stairs and in three leaps was down them.

The Corregidor snatched up the light and went after her, fearing she would escape; but he had to take the stairs much more slowly, with the result that, when he reached the kitchen, he ran into Frasquita who was already coming back in search of him.

"So, you were saying, you would put a bullet through me?"

cried the indomitable woman, taking a pace backwards. "Then, on guard, my Lord! I'm ready for you!"

So saying, she raised to her cheek the formidable blunder-buss which plays so important a part in this history.

"Stop, wretched creature! What are you about?" shouted the Corregidor, half dead with fright. "My bullet was a joke. Look, the pistols are unloaded. On the other hand it's true about the nomination. Here it is! Take it! I give it you! It's yours . . . for nothing . . . free, gratis, and for nothing!"

He placed it, trembling, upon the table.

"Good!" replied Frasquita. "I'll light the fire with it tomor-row when I cook my husband's breakfast. I wouldn't take salvation itself from you now; and if sometime my nephew comes from Estella, it will be to stamp his foot on the foul hand that wrote his name on that filthy paper. There now! So off you go out of my house! Quick, now: quick! I'm be-ginning to lose my temper!"

The Corregidor made no reply to this outburst. He had grown livid, almost blue; his eyes were distorted, his whole body was shaken by a tremor like ague. Then his teeth began to chatter and he fell to the ground in the grip of a horrible convulsion.

The shock of the millrace, the drenched state of his cloth-ing, the violent scene in the bedroom, his terror of the blunder-buss which Frasquita held to his head, had sapped the strength of the feeble old man.

"I'm dying!" he babbled. "Call Weasel! Call Weasel! he's there in the gully. I must not die in this house!" He could say no more. He closed his eyes and lay as if dead.

"And if he dies, as he says," broke out Mistress Frasquita, "that would be the worst job of all. What am I doing with this man in my house? What will they say about me, if he dies? What will Lucas say? How can I clear myself, when it was I myself who opened the door? Oh, no! I can't stay here with him. I must go and find my husband; rather than folk should think ill of me I'll disgrace the lot of them."

Having so resolved, she put by the blunderbuss, ran to the yard, took the remaining jenny, saddled it anyhow, mounted it at a bound, despite her goodly size, and made for the gully.

"Weasel! Weasel!" she shouted, as she approached the spot.

"Here!" replied the Bailiff, appearing behind a fence. "Is it you, Mistress Frasquita?"

"Yes, it's me! Go to the Mill and look after your master, who's at death's door!"

"What? You're joking."

"It's the plain truth, Weasel!"

"And you, my good soul; where are you off to at this time of night?"

"Me! Mind your own business! I'm going . . . to the City to fetch a doctor," answered Mistress Frasquita with a kick to the donkey and another to Weasel, and off she went. But she took, not the road to the City as she had just said, but the one to the neighboring village.

Weasel did not notice this last circumstance, for he was striding already on his long shanks towards the Mill, his mind busy with some such thoughts as these:

"Going for the doctor! What else could the woman do? But *he's* a poor sort of man! A nice time to be ill! Well, God gives all the plums to them that can't eat them!"

XXII

Weasel Excels Himself

When Weasel reached the Mill, the Corregidor was beginning to come round, and was trying to get up off the floor. On the floor too, just beside him, stood the lighted lamp which his Honor had brought down from the bedroom.

"Has it gone?" was Don Eugenio's first remark.

"Has what gone?"

"The devil, I mean the Miller-woman!"

"Yes, my Lord, she's gone. And not in the best of tempers, I think!"

"Ah, Weasel! I'm dying!"

"But what's the matter with your Honor? Man alive——!"

"I fell into the millrace and I'm sopped to the skin. I'm perished to the very bones!"

"Well, I never! And it's come to this!"

"Weasel, mind what you say!"

"I'm saying nothing, my Lord!"

"Very well! Help me out of this!"

"This very minute! Your Honor'll see, I'll put everything right at once."

No sooner said than done. The Bailiff took the lamp in one hand and with the other tucked the Corregidor under his arm and carried him up to the bedroom, stripped him stark naked, put him to bed, ran to the shed, snatched up an armful of wood, ran back to the kitchen, made a great fire, took down all his master's clothes, hung them on the backs of two or three chairs, lighted a stable lamp, hung it on the rack, and went up to the bedroom again.

"How are we now?" he asked Don Eugenio, holding the lamp high to get a better view of his face.

"Admirable! I shall be sweating soon! Tomorrow, Weasel, you'll hang for this!"

"But why, my Lord!"

"And you dare to ask why? Do you think, when I followed your precious plan, that I expected to end up alone in this bed, after receiving the sacrament of baptism for the second time? Yes, you shall hang tomorrow."

"But tell me something about it. Mistress Frasquita——?"

"Mistress Frasquita tried to murder me. That's all I've got out of your advice. Tomorrow morning, I tell you, you shall hang."

"It won't be as bad as that, my Lord!" answered the Bailiff.

"Why not, you saucy fellow? Because you've got me here on my back?"

"No, my Lord! Because Mistress Frasquita can't have been quite so cruel as you say, when she's gone to the City to fetch a doctor for you!"

"Good God! Are you sure she's gone to the City?" cried Don Eugenio, more terrified than ever.

"She told me so, anyhow!"

"Run, run, Weasel! Oh, I'm done for, hopelessly done for! Do you know why Mistress Frasquita has gone to the City? To tell the whole business to my wife! To tell her that I'm here! My God, my God! I never thought of that. I thought she had gone to the Village to find her husband; and as I've got him safe and snug she was free to go there, for all I cared. But if she's gone to the City——! Run, Weasel, run . . . you're a good runner . . . and save me from perdition! Stop that wild Miller-woman from getting into my house!"

"And if I do, your Honor'll let me off the hanging?" asked the Bailiff ironically.

"Instead of a hanging, I'll give you a good pair of boots which are too big for me. I'll give you anything you like."

"Then I'll be off. Let your Honor sleep in peace. In half an hour I'll be back and Frasquita will be in jail. I can be quicker than a donkey when I like."

So saying, Weasel disappeared down the stairs.

It so fell out that precisely when the Bailiff was away, the Miller came back to his Mill and saw signs and wonders through the keyhole.

So let us leave the Corregidor sweating in a strange bed and

Weasel running to the City (whither Miller Lucas with the
three-cornered hat and the scarlet cloak was to follow hard
on his heels), and, ourselves too becoming runners, let us fly
towards the village in the train of the valiant Mistress Frasquita.

XXIII

Again the Desert and
the Aforementioned Voices

The only adventure which befell the Miller's wife on her journey from the Mill to the hamlet was to be somewhat startled
at observing someone striking a light in the middle of a field.

"Suppose it's some ruffian of the Corregidor's! I shall be
stopped," she thought to herself.

At that moment there came from the same direction a loud
bray.

"Donkeys loose at this time of night!" thought Mistress
Frasquita, "when there's no orchard or farm hereabouts! God
bless us if ghosts aren't up to their games tonight. Surely my
husband's jenny couldn't be . . . ! Nay, what would Lucas
be doing at midnight, halting, away off the road? No! No!
Without doubt, it's a spy!"

The jenny which Mistress Frasquita was riding thought fit,
at that moment, to bray too.

"Be quiet, you she-devil!" said the Miller's wife, sticking
a two-inch pin into her withers.

And, fearing some untoward encounter, she too turned her
beast off the road and trotted away across the fields at the
other side.

Without further mischance she reached the gates of the village at eleven of the night or thereabouts.

XXIV

A Monarch of That Time

The mayor was sleeping off the effects of his evening's pota-
tions, his back turned to the back of his wife (thus assuming
with her the form of the two-headed Austrian Eagle, as the
immortal Quevedo has remarked), when Tony knocked at the
door of the nuptial chamber and informed Señor Juan López
that "Mistress Frasquita from the Mill" wished to speak with
him.

It is not for us to record all the snarling and swearing
which accompanied the waking and dressing of the Mayor,
and so we transport ourselves to the moment when he appeared before the Miller's wife, stretching himself like a gym-
nast exercising his muscles, and exclaiming in the middle of
an endless yawn:

"How d'you do, Mistress Frasquita! What brings you here?
Didn't Tony tell you that you must stay at the Mill? Is this
the way you obey the Authorities?"

"I must see Lucas!" answered the Miller's wife. "I must see
him at once! Please tell them to let him know that his wife
is here!"

"*I must! I must!* You forget, Ma'am, that you're talking
to the King!"

"Leave Kings alone, Señor Juan; I'm in no mood for jokes!
You know well enough what's happened to me! You know
well enough why you've arrested my husband!"

"I know nothing, Mistress Frasquita. And as for your husband, he's not been arrested: he's sleeping peacefully in this
house, treated as well as I always treat visitors. Here, Tony!
Tony! Go to the hayloft and tell Miller Lucas to get up and
come here at once. Well now, Mistress Frasquita, tell me
what's happened. Were you afraid to sleep alone?"

"Think shame of yourself, Señor Juan. You know well enough that it's no good your trying to deceive me. What's happened is soon told. You and the Corregidor have done your best to ruin me, but you've made a mess of it. Here I am without a stain on my character, and the Corregidor is at the Mill, dying."

"The Corregidor dying!" exclaimed his underling. "Madam, do you know what you're saying?"

"Yes, it's the truth. He fell into the millrace and nearly drowned himself, and now he's got pneumonia or Heaven knows what . . . That's her Ladyship's concern. I've come to find my husband, and even when I've found him it won't prevent me starting for Madrid tomorrow to inform the King."

"The devil! The devil!" murmured Señor Juan López. "Here, Manuela! Girl! Go and saddle me the little mule. Mistress Frasquita, I'm off to the Mill and woe betide you if you've done any harm to the Corregidor!"

At that moment Tony came in, more dead than alive.

"Mr. Mayor! Mr. Mayor!" he exclaimed. "Miller Lucas is not in the hayloft. And his jenny is not in the stables either, and the yard door is open. Your bird's flown!"

"What are you talking about?" cried Señor Juan López.

"Holy Virgin! Then what will be happening at home!" exclaimed Mistress Frasquita. "Come, let us hurry, Mr. Mayor; we must lose no time. My husband will murder the Corregidor when he finds him there at this time of night."

"Then you think Miller Lucas is at the Mill?"

"Well, haven't I good reason to? I'll say more . . . On my way here I passed him without knowing him. Without a doubt it was he who was striking a light in the middle of a field. Good Lord! To think that animals have more sense than human souls! For I may tell you, Señor Juan, that undoubtedly our two donkeys recognized each another and wished each other good evening, while Lucas and I did neither. Far from it; we ran for our lives, each thinking the other was a spy."

"Your Lucas will land himself in a pretty pickle," replied the Mayor. "Come, let us be off, and we'll see what's to be done with the lot of you. You can't play tricks with me. I'm the King; and not a King like the one we have now in Madrid, or out at El Prado, but like the one they had in Seville that they called Don Pedro the Cruel. Here, Manuela! Bring me my stick, and tell your Mistress that I'm going out."

The servant obeyed (she was a better girl, certainly, than the Mayor's wife and the reputation of his house deserved), and, as Señor Juan López's little mule was ready saddled, Mistress Frasquita and he set off for the Mill, followed by the indispensable Tony.

XXV

Weasel's Star

We ourselves, who enjoy the privilege of travelling faster than anyone else, will precede them.

Weasel had already got back to the Mill, after having ransacked every street in the City for Mistress Frasquita.

The wily Bailiff had looked in, on his way, at Headquarters, where he found everything perfectly quiet. The doors were still open as in daytime, as is the custom when the Authority is out in the town exercising its sacred functions. Other bailiffs and petty officers were dozing on the landing of the staircase and in the hall, peacefully awaiting their master; but when they heard Weasel arrive, two or three of them stretched themselves and asked their immediate senior and chief:

"Is the Master coming?"

"Not he! Don't disturb yourselves! I looked in to see if anything had happened——"

"Nothing!"

"And her Ladyship?"

"Her Ladyship has retired to her own apartments."

"Did no woman come, a short time ago?"

"No one has been here all night."

"Then don't let anyone in, whoever he is and whatever he says. Arrest him instead. If the morning star itself comes to ask after the Master and her Ladyship, arrest it and put it in the jail."

"Then you're after rare birds tonight?" asked one of the officers.

"Big-game hunting!" added another.

"Yes, the biggest!" answered Weasel solemnly. "You can imagine it's something rather delicate when the Corregidor and I are doing the hunting ourselves. Well, good-bye, boys; and mind, keep a sharp eye on things!"

"Good luck to you, Señor Bastian!" answered all, saluting Weasel.

"My star's on the wane!" he murmured as he went out of Headquarters. "Even the women fool me! The Miller's wife went to the village to seek her husband instead of coming to the City. Poor old Weasel! What's become of your scent?"

Thus ruminating he took the turn to the Mill.

The Bailiff's doubts of his ancient powers were not ill-founded, for he failed to scent a man who at that moment was hiding behind some willows, not far from the gully, and who muttered in his sleeve, or rather in his scarlet cloak:

"Look out, my boy! Here comes Weasel! He mustn't catch me here!"

It was Miller Lucas, dressed as the Corregidor, who was on his way to the City, every now and then repeating his diabolical phrase:

"Well, her Ladyship's a fine woman too!"

Weasel went by without seeing him and the false Corregidor left his hiding place and made his way into the town.

Shortly afterwards, the Bailiff reached the Mill, as we have already recorded.

XXVI
Reaction

The Corregidor was still in bed, exactly as Miller Lucas had just seen him through the keyhole.

"I'm sweating finely, Weasel! I've saved myself from a dangerous illness!" he exclaimed as the Bailiff entered the room. "What about Mistress Frasquita? Did you come across her? Is she with you? Has she seen my Lady?"

"The Miller's wife, my Lord," answered Weasel in agonized tones, "has fooled me properly. She didn't go to the City; she went to the village . . . to find her husband. Let your Honor forgive my stupidity!"

"Better! Far better!" cried the old man of Madrid, his eyes sparkling with iniquity. "Then all's well again! Before dawn the pair of them will be on their way to the jail of the Inquisition, and there they can rot. They'll find no one there to whom they can tell tonight's adventures. Bring me my clothes, Weasel; they must be dry by now! Bring them up and help me to dress! The lover is going to change into the Corregidor!"

Weasel went down to the kitchen for the clothes.

XXVII
In the King's Name!

Meanwhile, Mistress Frasquita, Señor Juan López and Tony advanced upon the Mill, which they reached a few minutes later.

"I'll go first!" exclaimed the village Mayor. "I'm not the

Authority for nothing! Follow me, Tony; and you, Mistress Frasquita, wait at the door till I call you."

Then Señor Juan López went in under the vine arbor, where by the light of the moon he saw a man, almost hunchbacked, dressed like the Miller, in a waistcoat and breeches of gray cloth, black sash, blue stockings, a plush Murcian cap, and a cape on his shoulder.

"It's him!" cried the Mayor. "In the King's name! Give yourself up, Miller Lucas!"

The figure in the cap tried to get back into the Mill.

"Surrender!" cried Tony in turn, leaping on the man, seizing him by the neck, thrusting a knee into his back, and sending him rolling on the ground.

At the same moment another kind of beast sprang upon Tony, and, clutching him by the belt, flung him down on the pavement and began to drub him soundly.

It was Mistress Frasquita.

"Villain!" she cried. "Leave my Lucas alone!"

Thereupon another person who had come on the scene, leading a donkey, threw himself resolutely between the two, and tried to rescue Tony.

It was Weasel, who had mistaken the village Mayor for Don Eugenio de Zúñiga.

"Madam," he shouted to the Miller's wife, "kindly respect my Master!" and he knocked her down on the top of Tony.

Mistress Frasquita, finding herself between two fires, gave Weasel such a backhander in the middle of the stomach that he measured his length on the pavement.

There were now, including Weasel, four people rolling on the ground.

Meanwhile Señor Juan López was preventing the supposed Miller Lucas from getting on to his feet by planting one foot on the small of his back.

"Weasel! Help! In the King's name! I'm the Corregidor!" cried Don Eugenio, who was almost bursting under the pressure of the Mayor's hoof, which was shod with a bull's-hide clog.

"The Corregidor! So it is!" said Señor Juan López, cold with consternation.

"The Corregidor!" repeated everybody.

And soon all four sprawlers were on their feet again.

"To jail with the lot of them!" cried Don Eugenio de Zúñiga. "To the gallows with the whole pack!"

"But, my Lord——!" observed Señor Juan López, falling on his knees, "your Honor must forgive me for ill-treating you! How was I to know your Honor in common clothes like these?"

"Ruffian!" replied the Corregidor. "I had to put something on, hadn't I? Don't you know that they've stolen mine? Don't you know that a gang of thieves, sent by Miller Lucas——"

"You lie!" cried the Miller's wife.

"Listen to me, Mistress Frasquita!" said Weasel, calling her aside—"By your leave, my Lord Corregidor and company!— If you don't put this right, Ma'am, they'll hang the lot of us, beginning with your Lucas."

"But what's happening?" asked Mistress Frasquita.

"Miller Lucas is, at this very moment, on his way to the City disguised as the Corregidor . . . and God alone knows if he hasn't got into her Ladyship's very bedroom by this time."

And the Bailiff told her in four words what we know already.

"Holy Jesus!" cried the Miller's wife. "Then my husband believes I'm disgraced! He's gone to the City to have his revenge! Come, let us be off at once to the City and prove to Lucas that I'm innocent!"

"To the City at once! We'll stop this fellow seeing my wife

and telling her all this stuff and nonsense that he's got into his head!" said the Corregidor, making for one of the donkeys. "Give me a leg up, Mr. Mayor!"

"Yes, to the City!" added Weasel. "And Heaven grant Sir, that Miller Lucas, in your clothes, has contented himself with talking to her Ladyship!"

"Miserable creature, what are you talking about?" burst out Don Eugenio de Zúñiga. "Do you imagine the villain is capable——?"

"He's capable of everything!" answered Mistress Frasquita.

XXVIII
Half-past Twelve and a
Fine Night!

Thus was the watch crying through the streets of the City when the Miller's wife, the Corregidor, each on one of the Mill donkeys, Señor Juan López on his mule, and the two Bailiffs on foot, came to the door of Headquarters.

The door was shut. For Governors and Governed alike, it seemed, everything was over for that day.

"This looks bad!" thought Weasel. And he beat two or three times on the great knocker.

Time passed, and nobody opened or answered.

Mistress Frasquita's face was yellower than wax.

The Corregidor had already gnawed away all the nails of both hands.

No one spoke a word.

Poom! Poom! Poom! Knocks and knocks again on the door of Headquarters! The Bailiffs and Señor Juan López took turns with the great knocker. And nothing! Nobody replied! Nobody opened! Not a mouse stirred!

Only there came the clear ripple of a fountain from the court within.

And so the minutes ran by, long as eternities.

At last, about one o'clock, a little window opened on the second floor and a woman's voice called:

"Who's there?"

"That's the Wet Nurse's voice!" muttered Weasel.

"It's I!" answered Don Eugenio de Zúñiga. "Open the door!"

There was a moment's silence.

Then came the Wet Nurse's voice again. "And who are you?"

"Can't you hear who I am? I'm the Master! The Corregidor!"

There was another pause.

"Off you go, and good night to you!" answered the good woman. "My Master came in an hour ago and went straight to bed. You had best go to bed, too, and sleep off some of that drink you've been filling your stomachs with!"

Again the window was slammed to.

Mistress Frasquita covered her face with her hands.

"Nurse!" thundered the Corregidor, beside himself with rage. "Open the door; don't you hear me? Can't you hear it's me! Do you want me to hang you too?"

The window opened once more.

"Come, let's see! Who are you to be shouting like that?" hazarded the Nurse.

"I'm the Corregidor!"

"Get along with you, you humbug! Aren't I telling you that my Lord the Corregidor came in before twelve, and I saw him with my own eyes lock himself into her Ladyship's apartments? But if you must have your joke, then wait a minute! You'll see!"

At the same moment the door opened suddenly and a whole

host of servants and understrappers, armed with sticks, threw themselves on the party outside, shouting furiously:

"Let's see him! Where's this fellow who says he's the Corregidor? Where is he; the wag, the drunkard?"

And then there broke out in the darkness the Devil's own shindy; nobody knew where he was, and the Corregidor, Weasel, Señor Juan López, and Tony all came in for their share of whacks.

That was the second drubbing that the night's adventure had cost Don Eugenio, to say nothing of the soaking he had given himself in the millrace.

Mistress Frasquita, who had managed to keep out of the tangle, was, for the first time in her life, weeping bitterly.

"Lucas! Lucas!" she cried. "How could you suspect me! How could you clasp another in your arms! Ah! There's no remedy now for our misfortune!"

XXIX

Post Nubila . . . Diana

"What is this disturbance?" The calm, dignified voice, with its pleasant tone, sounded across the hurly-burly.

All raised their faces and saw that a woman dressed in black stood looking down from the chief balcony of the building.

"Her Ladyship!" said the servants, and they paused in their beating of those human drums.

"My wife!" stammered Don Eugenio.

"Let them come in. The Corregidor says that they are to be admitted," added her Ladyship.

The servants made way and Don Eugenio and his companions entered the porch and began to climb the staircase.

Never did criminal approach the gibbet with step so uncertain and countenance so altered as those of the Corregidor when he mounted the stairs of his own home. None the less, the idea of his dishonor was already beginning to surpass, in his mind's noble egoism, all the misfortunes which he had brought on others and himself, and the absurdities of the situation in which he now found himself.

"Before all," he thought, as he climbed the stair, "I am a Zúñiga and a Ponce de León! And woe betide those who have forgotten it! Woe betide my wife if she has sullied my name!"

XXX

A Great Lady

Her Ladyship received her spouse and the rustic company in the principal saloon.

She was alone, and stood waiting for them, her eyes fastened on the door.

She was a lady of great distinction, still tolerably young, of a calm and severe beauty more suited to the Christian painter than the Classic sculptor, and she was dressed with all the stateliness and sobriety conformable with the taste of the period. Her dress—the short, narrow skirt and the high, puffed sleeves—was of black bombazine; a shawl of blond lace of a yellowish tinge veiled her admirable shoulders, and long mittens of black tulle almost entirely covered her arms, which were white as alabaster. One hand wafted with slow dignity a huge fan, brought from the Philippine Islands; in the other she held a lace handkerchief whose four corners hung down symmetrically with an orderliness to be compared only with that of her attitude and minor movements.

This beautiful woman inspired all who beheld her with reverence and fear, for she had about her something of the queen and much of the abbess. For the rest, the punctiliousness of her dress at such an hour, the gravity of her bearing, and the fact that the saloon was brilliantly lighted, showed that her Ladyship had taken some pains to impart to that scene a dramatic solemnity, a touch of ceremony, which contrasted strikingly with the coarse and vulgar character of her husband's adventure.

Finally, let us remark that this Lady was named Doña Mercedes Carillo de Albornoz y Espinosa de los Monteros, and that she was a daughter, granddaughter, great-granddaughter, great-great-granddaughter, and all the way to twentieth granddaughter of the City, being a descendant of its illustrious Conquistadors. Her family, for reasons of worldly vanity, had persuaded her to marry the wealthy old Corregidor, and she, who would otherwise have been a nun, since her natural vocation drew her to the cloister, had consented to this grievous sacrifice.

At this time she had already borne two children to that gay old dog from Madrid, and it was whispered that there was yet another on the way.

And so let us return to our story.

XXXI

The Pains of Retribution

"Mercedes!" exclaimed the Corregidor as he entered the presence of his spouse. "I must be told at once——"

"Ah, Miller Lucas! You here?" her Ladyship interrupted. "Is there anything the matter at the Mill?"

"I'm in no humor for jokes, Ma'am!" replied the Corregidor, wild with rage. "Before entering upon any explanations of my own, I must know how my honor stands——"

"That is not my affair! Did you leave it in my keeping?"

"Yes, Ma'am! In your keeping!" replied Don Eugenio. "Wives are the keepers of their husbands' honor."

"Then, my good Miller Lucas, ask your wife. There she is, listening to us!"

Mistress Frasquita, who had remained at the door of the saloon, gave a kind of growl.

"Come in, Mistress, and sit down," added her Ladyship, addressing the Miller's wife with superb dignity; and she herself went over to the sofa.

Mistress Frasquita, noble creature that she was, saw and appreciated from that moment the true greatness of the attitude of that injured, and perhaps doubly injured, wife. And so, rising at once to an equal height, she controlled her natural impulses and preserved a dignified silence. Nor had that silence anything to do with the fact that Mistress Frasquita, secure in her strength and her innocence, was in no hurry to defend herself. For she was in a hurry, a great hurry, to accuse; though certainly not to accuse her Ladyship. No, it was with Miller Lucas that she wished to settle her account, and Miller Lucas was not there!

"Mistress Frasquita," repeated the noble lady, seeing that the Miller's wife had not moved from her place, "I have told you that you can come in and sit down."

This second intimation was made in a voice kinder and more indulgent than the former. You would have said that her Ladyship, on observing the restrained bearing and the robust beauty of the woman before her, had in her turn instinctively divined that she had to do, here, with no low and contemptible being, but rather perhaps with another unhappy creature like herself —unhappy in the single fact of having known the Corregidor!

Then those two women, who supposed themselves doubly rivals, looked at each other with calm and indulgent eyes and discovered, to their surprise, that their souls took pleasure in one another, like two strangers who meet and know themselves for brothers.

Not otherwise do the pure snows of lofty mountains behold and hail each other from afar.

Tasting these sweet emotions, the Miller's wife advanced with dignified carriage into the saloon and seated herself on the edge of a chair.

On her brief return to the Mill, foreseeing that she would have to pay some important calls in the City, she had taken the opportunity to set herself somewhat in order and had put on a black woolen mantilla with a plush fringe, which suited her divinely. She looked every inch a lady.

As for the Corregidor, it is said that throughout that episode he remained completely silent. The growl of Mistress Frasquita and her appearance on the scene had, of course, startled him extremely. That woman inspired in him a greater terror than his own wife.

"Now, Miller Lucas," pursued Doña Mercedes, turning to her husband, "here is Mistress Frasquita. You can now put your question again. You can ask her of this business about your honor."

"Mercedes! By Christ's nails!" cried the Corregidor. "You don't know, it seems, what I am capable of. Again I solemnly conjure you to leave joking and tell me all that has happened here during my absence. Where is this fellow?"

"Who? My husband? My husband is getting up and cannot be much longer in coming."

"Getting up!" roared Don Eugenio.

"You are surprised? Then where would you have an honest man be, at this time of night, but at home, in bed, and asleep with his lawful wife, as God commands?"

"My dear Mercedes! Watch your words! Remember that others hear us! Remember that I am the Corregidor!"

"Don't shout at *me*, Miller Lucas, or I shall send for the Bailiffs to take you to jail!" replied her Ladyship, rising to her feet.

"Me to jail? Me? The Corregidor of the City!"

"The Corregidor of the City, the representative of the Law, the King's proxy," replied the great lady with a sternness and energy that drowned the voice of the pretended Miller, "arrived home at the proper hour, to rest from the noble labors of his office, to continue tomorrow his task of defending the honor and lives of the citizens, the sanctity of the hearth and the modesty of women, thus providing that no one, dressed up as a Corregidor or any other thing, shall enter the bedrooms of other men's wives; that no one shall surprise virtue in its unguarded moments of repose, that no one shall abuse its innocent sleep."

"Mercedes! Of what are you speaking?" exclaimed the Corregidor, and his lips and gums whistled the words. "If such a thing has happened in my house, then, I say, you are nothing but a wicked, perfidious, and licentious creature."

"To whom is this fellow speaking?" her Ladyship broke out disdainfully, casting her eyes over those that stood about her. "Who is this madman? Who is this tipsy rascal? I cannot even believe now that it is an honest miller like Miller Lucas, although this rustic suit is his. Señor Juan López, believe what I say," she continued, turning to the village Mayor who stood there appalled. "My husband, the Corregidor of the City, came home two hours ago, with his three-cornered hat, his scarlet cloak, his knightly sword, and his staff of authority. The servants and bailiffs who are here listening to me, rose up and saluted when they saw him pass through the porch, up the staircase, and across the hall. After that they locked all the doors, and since then no one has got into the house until you all arrived. Is this so? Answer, all!"

"It's true! It's quite true!" answered the Wet Nurse, the servants, and the underlings, all of whom, grouped about the door of the saloon, were assisting at this singular scene.

"Out of here, everybody!" roared Don Eugenio, foaming

with rage. "Weasel! Weasel! Arrest all these vile creatures who don't know how to respect me! To jail with the lot of them! To the gallows with the whole crew!"

Weasel was nowhere to be seen.

"For the rest, Sir," continued Doña Mercedes, changing her tone and deigning now to look at her husband and to treat him as such, for she began to fear that the jest might go too far, "we will suppose that you are my husband. We will suppose that you are Don Eugenio de Zúñiga y Ponce de León."

"And so I am!"

"We will suppose, too, that I am somewhat to blame for having mistaken for you a man who came into my bedroom dressed as a Corregidor——"

"Infamous rogues!" cried the old man, clapping his hand to his side and finding himself left in the lurch with the Miller's sash in place of a sword.

The Miller's wife covered her face with one side of her mantilla to hide her jealous tears.

"Let us assume whatever you wish," continued Doña Mercedes with indescribable calm. "But tell me now, my Lord; what right have you to complain? Can you stand up as counsel for the prosecution and accuse me? Can you sentence me, as judge? Have you, by chance, just returned from the Sermon, or from Confession, or from hearing Mass? Or what is it that you are returning from in this dress and with this lady? Where have you been passing half the night?"

"Allow me——" exclaimed Mistress Frasquita, rising to her feet as if lifted by a spring and throwing herself proudly between her Ladyship and her husband.

The latter, who was just about to speak, stood openmouthed on seeing that the Miller's wife was entering the fray.

But her Ladyship anticipated her.

"I will not trouble you, Ma'am," she said, "to waste explanations on *me*. I demand none; far from it! But here comes one who has a right to demand them! Settle your affairs with *him!*"

At that moment a door that led into a closet was thrown open and there stood Miller Lucas, dressed from top to toe as a Corregidor, with staff, gloves, and sword, as if in the very act of entering the Council Chamber of the Corporation.

XXXII

Faith Moves Mountains

"A very good evening to you all!" The new arrival, doffing his three-cornered hat, pronounced his greeting with the mouthing utterance peculiar to Don Eugenio de Zúñiga. And thereupon he stepped into the saloon, swaying in all directions, and went to kiss her Ladyship's hand.

The whole party was thunderstruck. Miller Lucas's resemblance to the real Corregidor was astounding. The servants, and even Señor Juan López himself, could not restrain a guffaw of laughter.

Under this new affront Don Eugenio flung himself upon Miller Lucas with the eyes of a basilisk.

But Mistress Frasquita blocked his way. She put the Corregidor aside with that arm of which he had had more than enough experience already, and his Honor, to avoid another somersault and the consequent humiliation, gave in without a murmur. Evidently the woman was born to be the master of the poor old man.

At the sight of his wife standing before him, Miller Lucas turned pale as death; but he controlled himself and, with a laugh so horrible that it forced him to clap his hand to his heart lest it should burst, he said to her, still imitating the Corregidor:

"God bless you, Frasquita! Have you sent your nephew his nomination yet?"

Then you should have seen the Miller's wife. She threw back her mantilla, raised her head with the majesty of a lioness, and fixing on the false Corregidor two eyes like two daggers, she flung her answer in his face:

"Lucas, I despise you!"

All believed that she had spat at him; such violence did her gesture, her attitude, and the tone of her voice impart to the phrase.

When he heard his wife's voice, the Miller's face was transfigured. A kind of heavenly inspiration had pierced his soul, flooding it with light and gladness: so that, forgetting for the moment all that he had seen and thought he had seen at the Mill, he cried out, with tears in his eyes and sincerity on his lips:

"Then you are my own Frasquita?"

"No!" answered the Miller's wife, beside herself with anger, "I am not your Frasquita! I am——! Ask all your fine doings of tonight, they'll tell you what you have made of the heart that loved you so!"

And she fell a-weeping like an ice mountain that collapses and slowly turns to water.

Her Ladyship, who could contain herself no longer, went towards her and gathered her in her arms with great tenderness. And then Mistress Frasquita fell to kissing her, hardly knowing what she did, murmuring to her between her sobs, like a child that seeks refuge in its mother:

"My Lady! My Lady! How unhappy I am!"

"Not so unhappy as you think!" answered her Ladyship, her generous heart touched to tears.

"And how unhappy am I!" groaned Miller Lucas at the

same time, struggling against the tears that he was ashamed to shed.

"And what about me?" Don Eugenio broke out at last, softened by the contagious grief of the others, or hoping, himself too, to escape by the watery way: I mean, by the vale of tears. "Ah! I'm a sinful man, a monster, a worthless rogue who has only got his deserts!"

And he began to bellow mournfully as he clasped the paunch of Señor Juan López.

And the latter and all the servants wept similarly, and it seemed that all was concluded without a soul having made any explanation whatsoever.

XXXIII

Well? and What About You?

Miller Lucas was the first to rise above that sea of tears. The fact was, he was beginning to remember all that he had seen through the keyhole.

"Ladies and Gentlemen," he said. "Let us explain ourselves!"

"Where is the use, Miller Lucas?" exclaimed her Ladyship. "Your wife is an angel."

"Good . . . yes . . . ; but——"

"I will have no buts. Let her speak; you will see how soon she proves her innocence. From the moment I first saw her, my heart told me she was a saint, in spite of all you had told me."

"Good; then let her speak!" said Miller Lucas.

"I will not speak!" answered the Miller's wife. "It's you that will have to speak, because the truth is that you——"

And Mistress Frasquita said no more, for she was silenced by her invincible respect for her Ladyship.

"Well? And what about you?" replied Miller Lucas, again losing all faith.

"It's not a question of her, now!" shouted the Corregidor, once more in the grip of his jealousy. "It's a question of you and this Lady! Ah, Mercedes! Who would have believed that you——!"

"Well? And what about you?" replied her Ladyship, and she measured him with her eye.

And for some moments the two couples repeated a hundred times the same phrase:

"What about you?"

"Well? and what about you?"

"Come, you!"

"No, you!"

"But how could *you*——?"

Etcetera, etcetera, etcetera!

The thing would have gone on forever, had not her Ladyship, resuming her dignity, at last addressed Don Eugenio thus:

"Look you here, Sir; you keep quiet for the present. We can air our particular grievances later on. What is urgent now is to restore peace to the heart of Miller Lucas; a very simple matter, in my judgment, for I see there Señor Juan López and Tony, who are dying to prove Mistress Frasquita's innocence."

"I have no need of men to prove my innocence," replied the latter. "I have two more credible witnesses, witnesses whom no one can say that I have bribed or corrupted."

"And where are they?" asked the Miller.

"They are downstairs at the door."

"Then tell them to come up, with her Ladyship's permission."

"The poor things couldn't come up."

"Ah, two old women, I suppose! Fine, trustworthy witnesses, and no mistake!"

"No, not women! Just two females!"

"Worse and worse! Two children, then! Perhaps you'll tell me their names."

"One is called Hazel and the other Frolic."

"Our two donkeys! Frasquita, you're making fun of me."

"No, I'm speaking quite seriously. I can prove to you, with our two donkeys as witnesses, that I was not at the Mill when you saw the Corregidor there."

"In God's name, explain!"

"Listen, Lucas! and think shame of yourself for having doubted my honor! While you were riding tonight from the village to our house I was on my way from our house to the village, and so we passed on the road. But you were riding off the road, or rather you had stopped to strike a light in the middle of a field——"

"Yes, it's true that I stopped! Continue!"

"At that moment your jenny brayed."

"Yes, so she did! Ah, how happy I am! Go on! Go on! Every word gives me back a year of my life!"

"And another bray on the road answered that one."

"Ah, yes! Yes! God bless you! It's as if I heard it still!"

"It was Hazel and Frolic, who had recognized each other and, like good friends, wished each other good evening, while we did neither."

"Say no more! Say no more!"

"You and I recognized each other so little that the two of us took fright and went tearing off in opposite directions. And so you see that I was not at the Mill. If you want to know now why you found the Corregidor in our bed, feel those clothes that you have on, which must still be wet, and they'll tell you better than I can. His Honor fell into the millrace and Weasel stripped him and put him to bed. If you want to know why I opened the door, it was because I thought it was you who were drowning and shouting for me. And, lastly, if you want to know about the nomination . . . But I've no more to say at present. When we're alone, I'll tell you about that and other little things . . . which I must not mention before her Ladyship."

"All that Mistress Frasquita has said is the pure truth," cried Señor Juan López, who was anxious to curry favor with her Ladyship, seeing she was the real power at Headquarters.

"Every word of it!" added Tony, following his master's lead.

"Every word of it, so far!" added the Corregidor, much relieved that Mistress Frasquita's explanations had gone no further.

"So you're innocent!" cried Miller Lucas, submitting to the evidence. "My Frasquita! My own Frasquita! Forgive the wrong I did you and let me give you a kiss!"

"Oh, that's another sack of wheat," said the Miller's wife, recoiling from him. "Before I give you a kiss I must hear *your* explanations."

"I will give all explanations both for him and myself," said Doña Mercedes.

"I've been waiting for them for the last hour!" vouchsafed the Corregidor, trying to recover his position.

"But I shall not give them," went on her Ladyship, turning her back scornfully on her husband, "until these two gentlemen have changed back into their own clothes; and, even then, I shall give them only to the one who deserves to hear them."

"Come! Come, let us change!" said the Miller to Don Eugenio, very glad now that he had not murdered him, but still eying him with a truly Moorish hatred. "Your Honor's dress chokes me! I have been thoroughly miserable ever since I put it on."

"Because you don't understand how to wear it!" replied the Corregidor. "I, on the other hand, am eager to get back into it, so as to hang you and half creation with you, if my wife does not exonerate herself to my complete satisfaction."

Her Ladyship, who heard this, reassured the company with the gentle smile that belongs to those patient angels whose ministry is to watch over men.

XXXIV
Her Ladyship's
a Fine Woman Too!

When the Corregidor and Miller Lucas had left the saloon, her Ladyship seated herself once more on the sofa, placed Mistress Frasquita at her side, and, turning to the servants and underlings who crowded the doorway, said to them with kindly simplicity:

"Now, my men: tell this excellent woman all the evil that you know of me."

The servants came forward and ten eager voices all tried to speak at once, but the Wet Nurse, as the person of most weight in the household, imposed silence on the rest, and spoke as follows:

"You must know, Mistress Frasquita, that I and my Lady were looking after the children tonight, waiting for the Master to return and reciting the third Rosary to pass the time (since the message brought by Weasel had been that my Lord the Corregidor was going out after certain very terrible criminals, and there was no question of going to bed till we had him safe home again), when we heard the sound of someone in the next room, which is my Lord's and my Lady's bedroom. We snatched up the lamp, half dead with fright, and went to see who was in the room; when, Holy Virgin, on going in, we saw that a man dressed like my Lord, but who was not him (since it was your husband!), was trying to hide under the bed. 'Thieves!' we started shouting at the top of our voices, and a minute later the room was full of people and the bailiffs were dragging the sham Corregidor from his hiding place. My Lady, who, like all of us, had recognized Miller Lucas, was afraid, seeing him in those clothes, that he had killed the Master, and began to make lamentations fit to melt a stone; while the rest of us shouted: 'To jail! To jail with him!' 'Thief! Murderer!' was the best thing that Miller Lucas heard of himself; and the truth is, he stood there like a corpse, up against the wall, not fit to say Boo to a goose. But, when he saw they were going to take him to jail, he said . . . what I'm just going to repeat, though in truth it would be better left unspoken: 'My Lady,' he said, 'I am neither a thief nor a murderer; the thief and the murderer . . . of my honor is in my house, in bed with my wife.' "

"Poor Lucas!" sighed Mistress Frasquita.

"Poor me!" murmured her Ladyship quietly.

"So we all said: 'Poor Brother Lucas and our poor Lady!' Because, to tell the truth, Mistress Frasquita, we had a notion that my Lord had fixed his eye on you; and, although nobody imagined that you——"

"Nurse!" exclaimed her Ladyship severely. "No more of that!"

"I'll go on!" said a Bailiff, seizing the opportunity to put his word in. "Miller Lucas (who fooled us properly with his clothes and his way of walking when he came in, so that we all took him for my Lord the Corregidor) had not come with the best of intentions as you might say, and if her Ladyship had been in bed, you can imagine what would have happened——"

"Here! That'll do for you as well!" interrupted the Cook. "You're talking nothing but nonsense. Well, yes, Mistress Frasquita: Miller Lucas, so as to explain why he was in my Mistress's bedroom, had to confess why he had come . . . ! Well, of course, my Lady couldn't contain herself when she heard that, and she caught him a smack on the mouth that pushed half the words down his throat. I myself, I'm bound to say, called him a lot of bad names and was ready to scratch his eyes out. . . . Because you know, Mistress Frasquita, although he's your husband; to come poaching like that on other people's preserves——"

"You're nothing but a chatterbox!" shouted the Porter, getting in front of the oratress. "What else would you have had? . . . Finally, Mistress Frasquita, listen to me and we'll get to the point. . . . Her Ladyship did and said what was worthy of her. Then, when she had got over her annoyance, she felt sorry for Miller Lucas and began to turn her mind to the bad behavior of my Lord the Corregidor, after which she spoke these words, or something like them: 'Infamous though your thought has been, Miller Lucas, and although I can never pardon such insolence, it is necessary that your wife and my husband should believe for some hours that they have been caught in their own trap, and that you, helped by this disguise, have paid them tit for tat. The best revenge we can take on them is to play them this trick, which we can easily explain away when it suits us.' Having hit on this happy thought, her Ladyship and Miller Lucas lessoned us all in what we had to do and say when his Honor came home; and, to be sure, I caught Sebastian Weasel such a whack on the backside, that I don't think he'll forget St. Simon and Judas's day for a bit."

When the Porter stopped talking, her Ladyship and Mistress Frasquita had been whispering together for some time, hugging and kissing each other every moment, and sometimes unable to contain their laughter.

It's a pity that what they said could not be heard! But the reader can imagine it for himself without great trouble; and if not the reader, the readeress.

XXXV
Imperial Decree

Upon that, the Corregidor and Miller Lucas came back into the saloon, each in his own clothes.

"Now it's my turn!" said the illustrious Don Eugenio de Zúñiga as he entered.

And, after giving two blows on the floor with his staff as if to recover his energy (like an official Anteus, who did not feel strong until his Malacca cane had touched Earth), he said to her Ladyship, with an emphasis and a coolness that cannot be described:

"Mercedes! I am waiting for your explanations!"

Meanwhile the Miller's wife had risen to her feet and had given Miller Lucas a pinch of peace that made him skip to the ceiling, while she gazed at him with reconciled and bewitching eyes.

The Corregidor, who observed this pantomime, was dumbfounded at the spectacle of so unaccountable a reconciliation.

Then he addressed himself again to his wife.

"Madam!" he said to her, as sour as vinegar, "all have reached an understanding except us! Put me out of my doubts! I order you both as husband and as Corregidor!"

And again he beat his staff on the floor.

"So you are going?" exclaimed Doña Mercedes, going over to Mistress Frasquita and paying not the slightest attention to Don Eugenio. "Then go with your mind at rest, for this scandal shall have no consequences. Rosa! Light this lady and gentleman, who tell me that they are going. Good-bye, Miller Lucas!"

"Oh, no!" shouted Don Eugenio, throwing himself in the way. "Miller Lucas cannot go! Miller Lucas is under arrest until I know the whole truth. Ho, Bailiffs! In the King's name!"

Not a single officer obeyed Don Eugenio. All fixed their eyes on her Ladyship.

"Come, Sir! Move out of the way!" she added, passing almost over her husband and bidding everyone good-bye with the greatest courtesy; that is to say, with her head on one side, holding her skirt with the tips of her fingers, bending gracefully to execute the bow which was the fashion at that time, and which was called the *pompa*.

"But I . . . But you . . . But we . . . But they——" the wretched old man went on mumbling, taking his wife by the dress and disturbing her in the process of her social duties.

But in vain! Nobody paid the least attention to his Honor.

When all had gone and only the discordant couple were left in the saloon, her Ladyship at last deigned to speak to her husband with such an accent as the Tsarina of all the Russias might have used to fulminate upon a fallen Minister the order of perpetual exile to Siberia:

"If you live to be a thousand, you shall never know what happened tonight in my bedroom. If you had been there, as you ought to have been, you would not be under the necessity of asking. For my part, there is not now, and there never will be, any reason for me to satisfy you; since I despise you so much that, if you were not the father of my children, I would throw you this very moment from that balcony, as I banish you forever from my bedroom. And so, good night, my Lord!"

Having pronounced those words, which Don Eugenio heard without so much as winking (since his courage left him when he was face to face with his wife), her Ladyship entered the closet and from there passed to her bedroom, locking the doors behind her; and the poor man was left high and dry in the middle of the saloon, murmuring between his gums (not between his teeth) with a surely unparalleled cynicism:

"Well, Sir, I did not expect to get off so easily! Weasel must find me accommodation!"

XXXVI

Conclusion, Moral, and Epilogue

The little birds were chirping their greetings to the dawn when Miller Lucas and Mistress Frasquita left the City and turned in the direction of their Mill.

The couple travelled on foot; in front of them, side by side, walked the two donkeys.

"On Sunday you'll have to go to Confession," said the Miller's wife to her husband, "to wash yourself clean of all your evil thoughts and wicked designs of last night."

"You're quite right!" replied the Miller. "But, meanwhile, you must do me another favor, and that is to give away our bedclothes and mattress to the poor and renew the whole lot. I don't sleep where that poisonous old beast has been sweating!"

"Don't speak of him, Lucas!" answered Mistress Frasquita. "Let's talk of something else. I want another favor from you."

"You've only got to ask."

"This summer you must take me to the baths at Solán de Cabras."

"But why?"

"To see if we can't have children."

"A very good idea! I'll take you, if God gives us life."

And thereupon they reached the Mill, at the moment when the sun, though it had not yet risen, was gilding the summits of the mountains.

In the afternoon, to the great surprise of the Miller and his wife, who expected no more visits from high personages after a scandal like that of the preceding night, there came to the Mill more gentry than ever. The venerable Bishop, several Canons, the Counsellor, two Priors, and sundry other persons (who, as afterwards appeared, had been summoned thither by the noble Prelate) quite filled the little court under the vine arbor.

The Corregidor alone was missing.

As soon as the party was complete, the Lord Bishop spoke to the following effect: that, whereas certain events had happened in that house, his Canons and himself would continue to come there as before, so that neither the honest Miller and his wife nor the other persons there present should have any share in the public censure, incurred only by him who had profaned with his foul conduct so temperate and virtuous a gathering. He exhorted Mistress Frasquita paternally to be, for the future, less provocative and enticing in her speech and manners and to cover her arms somewhat more and wear a higher neck to her bodice. He recommended Miller Lucas to be more circumspect, less self-seeking, and less free in his intercourse with his superiors, and ended by giving his blessing to all and announcing that, as he was not fasting that day, he would eat with much pleasure a couple of bunches of grapes.

All were of the same opinion, at least as regards this last particular, and that afternoon the arbor was shaken indeed.

The Miller reckoned the consumption of grapes at no less than four stones' weight.

Those delightful gatherings continued for about three years, until, contrary to everybody's expectations, the armies of Napoleon entered Spain and the War of Independence began.

The Lord Bishop, the Prebendary, and the Penitentiary died in the year 8, and the Counsellor and the other cronies in the years 9, 10, 11, and 12, unable to endure the sight of the Frenchmen, Poles, and other vermin that invaded the land and smoked their pipes in the very sanctuaries of the churches during Mass.

The Corregidor, who never again went back to the Mill, was deprived of his office by a French Marshal and died in the State Prison, because (be it said to his honor) he would not for a moment truckle to the foreign domination.

Doña Mercedes did not marry again. She brought up her children admirably, and retired in old age to a convent where she ended her days in the odor of sanctity.

Weasel went over to the French.

Señor Juan López became a guerrilla, commanded a band, and died, as did his Bailiff, in the famous battle of Baza, after killing a great number of Frenchmen.

Lastly, Miller Lucas and Mistress Frasquita (although they never succeeded in having children, in spite of vows and prayers and the visit to Solán de Cabras), went on loving each other in their own way and lived to a great age. They saw the end of Absolutism in 1812 and 1820, and its return in 1814 and 1823, and, at last, the establishment of the Constitutional System in good earnest at the death of the Absolute King; and they passed to a better life just at the outbreak of the Seven Years Civil War. But the tall hats which by this time everyone was wearing never made them forget the good old times symbolized by The Three-Cornered Hat.

Torquemada in the Flames

BENITO PÉREZ GALDÓS

In 1868, the year of the Revolution, Don Francisco Torquemada bought a tenement house in the calle de San Blas—a
very useful piece of property with twenty-four small flats,
which, not counting the inevitable bankruptcies, repairs, taxes,
etc., brought him in thirteen hundred reals a month, equivalent
to between seven and seven-and-a-half per cent on his invest-
ment. Every Sunday, Don Francisco appeared in person to
collect the rents, the receipts in one hand, his staghorn-handled
walking stick in the other. By 1874, the year of the Restoration, he had doubled his capital, and the radical political
change brought him very pretty opportunities to place it in
advances and loans. The brand-new dignitaries, who had to get
together wardrobes, and the functionaries, who emerged from
obscurity ravenous, made him a good harvest. When, in 1881,

the Liberals, who had so long been out of it, got into the government, Torquemada was again on the crest of the wave: good loans, good payments and here we go! In short, he soon found himself eying another house—not a tenement this time, but a house in a good neighborhood, almost new, fit for decent tenants, and which, if it brought in only three-and-a-half per cent all told, would be much less of a headache, so far as running it and collecting the rents went, than the troublesome object of his Sunday excursions.

Everything was going as smooth as silk for this ferocious ant when heaven suddenly visited a terrible calamity upon him: his wife died. She died of intestinal colic, and it must be said in Torquemada's behalf that he spared no expense to save the poor woman's life. The loss was a cruel blow to Don Francisco, for the couple had lived in virtuous and industrious peace for over twenty years. With Doña Silvia guarding every penny in the house so that it should not get out, and Don Francisco combing the outside so that nothing that passed by should escape, they had made a couple which could serve as a model for all ants, whether above or below ground.

During the first days of his widowhood, Torquemada the Worse, as certain unpublished historians call him, hardly knew what was going on around him. He turned even yellower than usual, and some white appeared in his hair and beard. But time did what it always does, sweetening the bitter, gnawing with unfeeling tooth at the asperities of life; and by the time two years had passed Torquemada seemed to have become consoled—though, to his honor be it said and repeated, he had no desire to marry again.

Two children remained to him: Rufina and Valentín. At the time of my narrative, Rufina had passed twenty-two, Valentín was just twelve. And—to show you what a lucky star this beast of a Don Francisco had—both of his children were, in their different ways, real jewels, almost like divine blessings showered upon him to console him in his loneliness. Rufina had copied all of her mother's domestic virtues and managed the house almost as well. To be sure, she possessed neither the high business sense nor the consummate acumen nor the other half-moral, half-olfactory aptitudes which had characterized that remarkable matron; but in manners, behavior and seemly presence, no girl of her age could outdo her.

If we turn from Rufina to Torquemada's male offspring, we shall find a still better explanation for the vanity which his children caused in him, because (I say it sincerely) I never knew a more beguiling boy than Valentín, nor such extraordinary precocity as his. Despite his resemblance to his father, the lad was as attractive as could be, with such an expression of intelligence that you were stupefied to find it in such a face; with such charms of person and character, and touches of behavior so far beyond his years, that to see him, talk with him, and love him dearly were one and the same thing. And what an enchanting seriousness he had—yet not incompatible with the restlessness that is characteristic of childhood! Tall and lanky, he had thin but well-shaped legs; a head bigger than normal, with some slight malformation in the bony structure. As for his aptitude for study, it was literally prodigious—the terror of his school and the pride and joy of his masters. All I can say is that our Torquemada never deserved such a jewel, and that if he had been a man capable of praising God for the benefits bestowed upon him, he had reason to stand hour after hour, like Moses, with his arms raised to heaven. He did not raise them, because he knew that none of the joys he delighted in would come to him from that direction.

Torquemada was not one of those usurers who spend their lives multiplying money for the Platonic pleasure of possessing it. No. Don Francisco could not escape the influence of this second half of the nineteenth century, which has almost made a religion of the decorously material side of life. Misers of the old stamp, who laboriously gathered wealth and lived like beggars and died like dogs on a pallet full of fleas, with bank notes stuffed among the straw, were the mystics or metaphysicians of usury; their egoism concentrated and sublimated itself in the pure idea of business; living in a period which began with the expropriation of monasteries, Torquemada, without comprehending it, underwent the metamorphosis which has changed the nature of usury from metaphysical to positivistic; and if it is true, as history affirms, that from 1851 to 1868, which was his real period of apprenticeship, he went about shabbily dressed and with an affectation of poverty, his face and hands unwashed, constantly scratching his legs and arms as if he had lice, his hat greasy and his coat threadbare; if, again, the neighborhood chronicle states that in his house there was fast-day food all year round and that his wife went out on her errands in a torn kerchief and old shoes that had belonged to her husband, it is equally certain that by 1870, or thereabouts, he was living on quite another footing; that Doña Silvia dressed very well on particular occasions; that Don Francisco changed his shirt more often than once a fortnight; that they ate less mutton and more beef, and on Sundays some chicken giblets were added to the soup; that beans at every meal, with dry bread and sausages now and again, were becoming a thing of the past; that, in short—and lest this enumeration become boring—the whole family began to live as God intended that human beings should.

Well, sir: Doña Silvia ups and dies, Rufina takes over the reins of household government—and the metamorphosis becomes even more marked. New monarchs, new principles. Torquemada—what else could he do?—submitted to the logic of the times. He put up with a clean shirt twice a week; without much protest, he accepted a clean tablecloth in the middle of the week, wine at meals, lamb with peas (in season), and turkey at Christmas; he tolerated a braided jacket, which in him was a refinement of etiquette, and said nothing about the carpet in the drawing room, nor the many other improvements which were gradually smuggled into the house.

And very soon Don Francisco saw that these innovations were good and that his daughter was really very clever, because—it seemed extraordinary, but there it was!—he would go out into the street and feel, in his good clothes, more of a personage than ever before. He walked more vigorously, coughed more vehemently, talked more loudly and spoke up in the discussions at his café, even finding courage to defend his own opinions; whereas before—no doubt as the result of his shabby exterior and his habitual affectation of poverty—he had always been of everyone else's opinion. Little by little he became aware of his vigorous social and financial possibilities; he tapped himself, and the sound told him that he was a landlord with a comfortable income. But vanity never blinded him.

In his character there was something that resisted change. His mannerisms even increased; he was still forever saying that the times were very bad, very bad indeed; forever complaining that his hard work was out of all proportion to his miserable profits; his tones were as honeyed as ever; he kept his habit of making a wry face to show what he thought of life. Except for his clothes, which were improved in quality if not in his manner of wearing them, he was the same: his face the same strange mixture of the soldier and the ecclesiastic, his complexion bilious, his eyes black and a little dreary, his gestures and manners expressing hypocrisy and effeminacy in equal degree—

the same unctuous, treacherous and repulsive person, always very quick when anyone greeted him to hold out a hand that was sure to be sweaty.

He was so proud of Valentín's precocious intelligence that he could hardly contain himself. To the honor of our usurer be it said that if he thought of himself as physically reproduced in this offspring of his own body, he felt his son's superiority and rejoiced in it more than in having given him life. For little Valentín was the prodigy of prodigies, a sublime fragment of the Divine Being fallen to earth.

Let no one think that there is the least exaggeration in what I say of the boy's unexampled intellectual gifts. Once his infancy was over, he never had to be punished or even scolded. He learned to read miraculously, in a few days, as if he had brought the art with him from his mother's womb. At five he knew many things which other boys can hardly learn at twelve.

Grammar he knew by heart; but geography he mastered like a grown man. Outside of schoolwork, it was amazing to see the assurance of his answers and observations, yet with no trace of childish arrogance. Shy and discreet, he seemed not to realize that there was any value in the talents he revealed, and he was astonished to see them evoke so much attention and applause. No boy outdid him in obedience and modesty, and, that not a perfection should be lacking, he was even as careful as possible not to wear out his clothes.

But his most extraordinary aptitudes had not yet shown themselves: it began when he studied arithmetic. No sooner had he imbibed the first notions of the science of quantities than he added and subtracted two- and even three-digit numbers in his head. His arithmetical sense was infallible, and even his father, who in the course of his reveries had become a wizard at calculating interest due, would often consult him. But it was when he began to study mathematics in secondary school that the full measure of his arithmetical genius was revealed. He did not learn, he already knew; the textbook simply awakened his ideas, made them open, if I may say so, like buds which the warmth of spring brings to flower. One day his teacher called on his father and said: "The boy is beyond explaining, Señor Torquemada. Before long I'll have nothing left to teach him. He is Newton come back to earth."

How Torquemada felt when he heard this, it is easy to understand. From that day on, he was beside himself with pride: he not only loved his son, he even treated him with a certain superstitious respect. He took care of him as if he were a supernatural being, placed in his hands as a special privilege. He watched his diet and became terrified if he showed a lack of appetite; when he saw him studying, he shut the windows to keep out drafts; informed himself of the temperature outside before letting him go out, to determine whether he should wear a muffler, or his greatcoat, or his rubbers; walked on tiptoe when he was asleep; took him out for a stroll, or to the theater, on Sundays, and if the little angel had shown any desire for strange and expensive playthings, Torquemada would have conquered his stinginess to buy them for him. But this prodigy of a boy manifested no liking for anything but books: he read fast and as if it were by magic, mastering the contents of each page as quick as a wink.

At the suggestion of the teacher who had praised him, Valentín was put into the hands of a professor who prepared students for special careers and who, as soon as he sampled the boy's colossal intelligence, was flabbergasted. One day, putting his hands to his head in stupefaction, and running out in search of other professors of higher mathematics, he announced: "I am going to show you the phenomenon of our times." And he exhibited him, and the others were amazed, for the boy went to the blackboard and solved the most difficult problems like someone scribbling to amuse himself and waste chalk.

It really made an interesting picture, and one worthy to figure in the annals of science: four dignified gentlemen in their fifties, bald and half blind from study, silent and perplexed in front of a boy who had to do his figuring on the bottom of the blackboard. One said he was the Antichrist; another picked him up and set him on his shoulder; and all quarreled over which of them should have the honor of finishing the education of this mathematical genius. Valentín looked at them, neither proud nor shy—innocent and master of himself, like the boy Christ among the doctors.

Torquemada was still living in his house in the calle de Tudescos; and there every evening a certain Don José Bailón would call on him to play a game of draughts or cards. This Señor Bailón was a priest who abandoned the cassock in '69, in Málaga, and applied himself to revolution and religious freedom with such furious ardor that he could no longer return to the flock. The first thing the scoundrel did was to let his beard grow, talk nonsense at clubs, write tremendous invectives against those of his profession, and, finally, following the principle of *verbo et gladio,* fling himself on the barricades with a blunderbuss whose mouth was as big as a trumpet.

Defeated and left to his own devices, a few years later our man was to be found living in Chamberí, and, according to the gossip of the quarter, sharing bed and board with a rich widow who owned a flock of goats and a herd of milch asses. What is public knowledge is that the widow died, and that soon after Bailón appeared with money. The dairy and the goats and asses belonged to him. He rented the whole thing out and moved to the center of Madrid, where he set up as a moneylender—and

I need say no more for my reader to understand how his acquaintance and dealings with Torquemada originated, because it is obvious that the latter was his teacher.

Bailón was very tall, athletic, robust in limb, with strong features—a real live anatomical study by virtue of his muscular development. He had gone back to shaving, but he looked neither a priest nor a monk nor a bullfighter. He was more like a degenerate Dante. At the time of my narrative he was fifty.

Torquemada thought highly of him because in his business relations Bailón made a great show of formality and even of a certain delicacy. And since the renegade had such a colorful history and knew how to tell it well, embellishing it with lies, Don Francisco was ravished when he listened to him and regarded him as an oracle on all subjects of an elevated nature. Don José was one of those people who with four ideas and not many more words put them together in a way which dazzles the innocent and ignorant—no one more dazzled than Don Francisco.

On certain evenings the two sharpers would go walking together, conversing endlessly. And if Torquemada was the sibyl in business, in other branches of knowledge there was no greater sibyl than Señor Bailón. In politics especially the renegade priest made a great show of being an expert. They talked a good deal about urban reforms. Public hygiene preoccupied them both; the cleric put the blame for everything on noxious effluvia, and formulated certain biological theories which were something to hear.

But his encyclopedic knowledge nowhere showed to better advantage than in matters of religion. His meditations and studies had enabled him to plumb the great and venturesome problem of our entire destiny.

"What will happen to us when we die? Why, we shall be born again—it's as clear as water. I remember," he said, looking hard at his friend and dismaying him by the solemn tone which he gave to his words, "I remember having lived before. As a boy I had a vague recollection of my former life, and now, as the result of meditation, I can see it clearly. I was a priest in Egypt, back I don't know how many years ago . . . yes, Don Francisco, a priest in Egypt. I seem to see myself in a cassock or vestment the color of saffron. They burned me alive, because in the church—I mean the temple—there was a priestess who attracted me. . . . In short, the thing got going, and the goddess Isis and Apis the bull took it in very bad part. . . . What I tell you is as true as that the sun is shining.

"Concentrate, my friend; search your memory; and you too will know that you lived in another age. That boy of yours, prodigy that he is, must once have been Newton or Galileo or Euclid. As for the rest of it, my ideas are perfectly clear. Hell and heaven do not exist—they are sheer symbolic pap. Hell and heaven are here. Here, sooner or later, we pay for whatever we have done; here, if not today then tomorrow, we get our reward. . . . God—oh, the idea of God is very mysterious . . . and to understand it you have to beat your brains as I have beaten mine, read, and then meditate.

"God . . . " (he looked very reverent and spread both his hands in a gesture indicating that he was taking in an immense space) "is Humanity, Humanity—do you understand me?— which does not mean that He ceases to be personal. Mark me well. Personal is what one is. And the great Totality, my dear Don Francisco, is One because there is nothing else, and possesses the attributes of a being infinitely infinite . . . do you understand . . . ?"

Torquemada had not understood a word; but the other had involved himself in a maze from which there was no escape except to stop talking. The only thing Don Francisco got out of the whole rigmarole was that "God is Humanity" and that

Humanity is what makes us pay for our skulduggeries and rewards us for our good works. He'd be hanged if he understood the rest.

To tell the truth, none of these theological considerations long occupied our scoundrel's imagination, which was always intent on the base reality of his business. But a day came—or rather a night—when they were to take possession of his mind with a certain tenacity, for a reason which I shall now set forth. One late afternoon in February, Don Francisco returned home, planning what steps he should take the next day, when his daughter, who opened the door for him, addressed him as follows: "Don't be alarmed, Papa, it is nothing. . . . Valentín came home from school sick."

The prodigy's indispositions always upset Don Francisco. This one might be unimportant, as others had been. Yet in Rufina's voice there was a tremor, a strange tone, which left Torquemada cold with anxiety.

"I put him right to bed and sent a note to Dr. Quevedo to come as quickly as possible."

Rousing from his stupor as if he had been slapped, Don Francisco ran to the boy's room and found him in bed, with so many covers over him that he appeared to be suffocating. His face was flushed, his eyes vague. The father put his hand to the innocent prodigy's temples, which were burning.

"That useless Quevedo! May he burst. . . . What is the fool thinking of? Better send for a doctor who knows something."

His daughter tried to calm him but he refused to be comforted. His son was not an ordinary boy, and he could not be sick without the order of the universe changing. The grieving father would not eat; all he did was to pace through the house, waiting for the accursed doctor, going again and again from his own room to his son's and from there to the dining room, where each time his heart would be wrenched by the sight of the slate on which Valentín wrote his mathematical problems with chalk.

The problem he had set down that morning was still there, symbols which Torquemada did not understand but which almost made him weep, like sad music: the square-root sign, with letters above and below, and somewhere else a network of lines forming a sort of many-pointed star with little figures at the points.

Finally—God be praised!—the fortune-favored Quevedo appeared. After examining the boy, the doctor did not look very cheerful. Putting both his hands on Torquemada's shoulders, he said: "I don't like this at all; but we must wait until tomorrow to see if some eruption doesn't break out. He has a high fever. I warned you you'd have trouble with your prodigy. So much studying, so much knowledge, an extravagant intellectual development! What you should do with Valentín is put a bell around his neck, turn him loose in the country with a herd of cattle, and not bring him back to Madrid until he is really strong."

Torquemada hated the country and could not conceive that there was anything good about it. But he made up his mind, if the boy recovered, to take him to a dairy farm where he could drink plenty of milk and breathe fresh air. Ah, it was those accursed effluvia Bailón talked about which were to blame for what had happened! Don Francisco was so distraught that if he could have laid hands on an effluvium just then, he would have torn it limb from limb.

The children's room, where Valentín's bed was, adjoined his own bedroom; the boy passed a very restless night; he choked, his skin was on fire, his eyes sparkled, yet seemed not to see, his speech was uncertain, his ideas disconnected, like the beads of a rosary when the string breaks.

The following day was a day of shocks and anguish. Quevedo concluded that the disease was "inflammation of the meninges" and that the boy was in danger of death. He did not tell this to the father, but to Bailón, who was to try to prepare him. Torquemada had to go out on various errands in connection with his laborious profession, but he kept returning to the house every few minutes, panting, his tongue hanging out, his hat on the back of his head. He came in, took a look, and went out again. He brought in the medicines himself, and told the whole story at the apothecary's . . . "a sudden giddiness at school; a terrible fever ever since . . . what good are doctors?"

The night of the second day, Torquemada, overcome with fatigue, planted himself in an armchair in the sitting room, and there he stayed, turning over a sly idea which had come into his head. "I have sinned against Humanity, and the damned so-and-so is making me pay up now. . . . No: because if God, or whoever it is, takes my son from me, I'll turn even worse! . . . That'll show them! Nobody can play with me.

"But what nonsense am I talking? . . . This saying that I have never done anyone any good is a lie. Let them prove it . . . saying it is not enough. What about all the people I have gotten out of tight corners? Because if they have gone running to Humanity with stories about me . . . I've had too much of this. . . . If I have never done good, I'll do it now—now, because there must be something in the saying that it is never too late to do good. Let me see . . . if I started praying now, what would they say up there? Bailón must be mistaken, I think; Humanity can't be God, it must be the Virgin. . . . No, no, no . . . Humanity is God, the Virgin and all the saints. . . . Hold on, man, hold on, you're going mad. . . . All I can be certain of is that without good works everything is, so to speak, dung. . . . Oh God, oh God how I suffer! If You make my son well for me, I don't know what I won't do! Things so magnificent, so . . . But who has the impudence to say that I have never done any good works? It's because they want to undo me, want to take away my son, who was born to teach all the scholars and leave them pigmies. And they envy me because I am his father, because that glory of the world came from these bones and this blood. . . . Envy . . . but that hog Humanity is nothing but envy! No, I don't mean Humanity, because that is God . . . I mean men, all of us, we're all scoundrels."

Then he remembered that the next day was Sunday and that he had not written out the receipts for the rents from his tenement house. The following morning, between nine and ten, he went to make the Sunday collection.

He began with the ground floor, and the bricklayer and the two cigarette girls paid without a murmur, only wanting to see the last of the hated Don Francisco. They noticed something unusual and abnormal about him, for he took the money mechanically and without examining it and gloating over it as usual—as if his thoughts were a hundred miles from the important act he was performing.

When he reached the room of the widow Rumalda, the ironing woman—with her mother lying sick on a miserable pallet and three little boys running around the patio with their skin showing through the holes in their clothes—the poor woman, her voice shaking as if she were confessing a terrible crime in court, brought out the regulation phrase: "I can't today, Don Francisco. I'll make it up later." I cannot convey the stupor which descended upon the widow and her two neighbors, who happened to be present, when they heard the usurer say, in the most lachrymose of voices: "No, my dear, if I don't press you . . . if it hasn't entered my head to scold you . . . how can I put it? The thing is that you are all convinced that I am a man who . . . Where did you get the idea that there is no compassion in me . . . no . . . no charity? Instead of being grateful to me for what I do for you, you slander me. When times are bad, my dears, what can we do but help one another?"

On reaching the next floor, he ran into another tenant, a woman who was always in arrears but who had the courage to stand up to the lion. Seeing him coming, and judging from his face that he was in a worse humor than ever, she took the offensive with these arrogant words:

"Listen, you—don't you come worrying me. You know I haven't got it. My man is out of work. Do you want me to take to the streets? Can't you see that our place is as bare as a poorhouse?"

"And who told you, you foulmouthed so-and-so, that I have come to squeeze you? I'd like to see any of you ill-conditioned hags maintain that I have no humanity. Just any of you dare to say it to my face. . . ."

In the crowd which had collected, nothing was to be seen but open mouths and expressions of stupefaction.

"I tell you—and I tell all of you—that it doesn't matter a peppercorn to me if you pay me today or not! I'd like to know how to put it so that you can understand it! . . . And don't go believing that I'm doing this so that you'll call down blessings on me. Just bear witness that I am not grinding you down; and, so that you can see how goodhearted I am . . . "

He stopped and thought for a moment, putting his hand in his pocket and looking at the floor.

"No—that's all, that's all. Good-bye and God bless you."

At the next three doors, he collected without difficulty.

"Oh, Don Francisco," said the woman in No. 14, "here is your damned fifty reals. To scrape it together, all we've had to eat is two pennyworth of tripe, with dry bread."

"But this is an insult, an injustice; because if I have been hard on you, it was not for the money, but because I like to see people keep their promises . . . so that no one can say . . . Here, you can keep your money. Or better, so that you won't take it too lightly, we'll divide it and you can keep twenty-five reals. You can give them to me some other day. . . . You are all the same—when you ought to admit that I treat you like a father, you accuse me of being inhuman and I don't know what else! No, I assure you one and all that I respect humanity, that I esteem and regard it . . ."

The group followed him, whispering: "Something bad must have happened to him. . . . He's not right in the head. Look at that gallows face of his. Don Francisco showing humanity!"

All the women watched him as he went down the stairs, and across the patio, and out the door, with gestures that made him look like the very Devil crossing himself.

He hastened homeward and, contrary to his habit, took a cab to get there sooner. His heart began telling him that he would find good news, the sick boy better, Rufina smiling when she opened the door; in his insane impatience, the carriage seemed not to be moving, the horse to be stumbling, the coachman not flogging the poor creature enough. "Give him the whip, man!" he screamed. "Can't you see I'm in a hurry!"

As he panted up the stairs, he was justifying his hopes to himself. What a bitter blow to find Rufina's face so sad and to hear the "just the same, Papa," which sounded in his ears like a death bell! He approached his son's bed on tiptoe and looked at him. The poor boy was drowsing, so Don Francisco could observe him with comparative calm. But when he moaned in delirium, Torquemada felt a desire to start running and hide himself and his grief in the farthest corner of the world.

That afternoon Bailón, the butcher from the ground floor, the tailor from the second and the photographer from upstairs, sat with him for a time, all trying to console him with the conventional phrases; but Torquemada, unable to continue talking on so sad a theme, thanked them curtly. All he could do was sigh volubly, stride up and down, gulp mouthfuls of water, and occasionally beat the wall with his fists. . . .

The flower of the world cut down! It was enough to drive anyone mad. A pretty piece of work God, or Humanity, or whoever the big so-and-so was, had done when he invented the world and put us in it! To take that boy, that light of science, and leave all these fools here! Did it make any sense? And what a blow for the father! Because imagine what Don Francisco would be when his son had grown up and begun to shine and confound all the scholars and turn science upside down!

Up there, in the invisible depths of the sky, someone had taken it into his head to hurt Torquemada. But . . . if it were not envy, but punishment? If it had all been arranged to humble the cruel usurer, the tyrannical landlord? Ah, when that idea had its turn, Torquemada was seized by an impulse to run against the nearest wall and smash himself to pieces. But he had an instant reaction. No, it could not be a punishment because he was not wicked, and if he had been, he would reform. He was enviable; they hated him for being the father of such supreme eminence. They wanted to kill his future and take away the joy and opulence of his declining years . . . because his son, if he lived, was bound to make a lot of money, a very great deal of money, and hence the celestial intrigue. But he (he thought it sincerely) would renounce all claim to his son's pecuniary gains. After all, his own business was a competence.

When Bailón was left alone with him, he told him that he must be philosophical, and since Torquemada did not quite understand the meaning and application of the word, the sibyl explained his idea as follows: "We must resign ourselves, considering our littleness before these great evolutions of matter

. . . or vital substance. We are atoms, my dear Don Francisco, nothing but inane atoms. Let us respect the dispositions of the great All to which we belong, and let trouble come. That is what philosophy is for, or, if you prefer, religion: to give us courage in adversity."

At nightfall Quevedo and the other doctor talked to Torquemada in disconsolate terms. They had little or no hope, though they were afraid to say that they had entirely lost it.

Grief-stricken, Don Francisco went to the half-open door of his son's room and looked timidly in; with the boy's labored breathing, he thought he heard something like the sizzling of his flesh as it grilled in the fire of fever. He listened to the delirious lad's incoherent expressions and heard him say: "x square, minus 1, divided by 2, plus 5 x minus 2, divided by 4, equals x times x plus 2, divided by 12 . . . Papa, Papa, the characteristic of the logarithm of a whole number contains as many units minus 1 as . . ." No torture of the Inquisition equaled what Torquemada suffered as he heard these words. He fled to the living room and flung himself on the sofa, where he lay for half an hour, holding his head in his hands as if it were trying to get away. Suddenly he rose, frenzied by an idea; he went to his desk, took out a roll of coins, which must have been coppers, and emptying them into his trouser pocket, put on his cape and hat, took the door key, and went out.

After walking for a long time, he stopped at a corner, looked uneasily in all directions, then hurried along the street again with the step of a moneylender tracking down his prey. Each time his right leg swung forward, the coins in his pocket jingled. Great were his impatience and disgust at not finding, on that night, what, on other nights, turned up at every step to annoy and bore him. At last—praise be to God!—a beggar approached. "Here, take it, man! Where on earth have you all been hiding tonight? When nobody wants you, you're out like flies, and when somebody looks for you to help you—not a trace. . . ."

Farther on, an apparition emerged from an alley. It was a woman who begs in the lower part of the calle de la Salud, dressed in black, with a heavy veil shrouding her face. "Here, take it, take it. And now let anyone say that I have never given an alms! Can you imagine what a calumny! Go now, you must have scraped together enough coppers for tonight. Because there are people who say that, begging as you do, and with that veil over your face, you have gotten together a nice little capital. Go now, it's turning very cold . . . and pray to God for me."

"Hey lad, are you begging or what are you doing there like a fool?" This was addressed to a boy who stood leaning against the wall with his hands on his shoulders. He held out a hand stiff with cold. "Here, take that. . . . Didn't your heart tell you that I would come along and help you? Take more, and go home, if you have a home. I am here to get you out of your difficulties; I mean, to share a loaf of bread with you, because I am poor too, and more unfortunate than you are—if you only knew it. . . ." He walked quickly away without looking into the mocking face of his protégé, and went on giving, giving, until there were only a few coins left in his pocket.

Hurrying back home, he stared up at the sky—an action very much out of his normal behavior, because if he had occasionally looked at it to see what the weather promised, never until that night had he contemplated it. What a multitude of stars! And an idea came into the eminent moneylender's head: "When he gets well, he must solve this problem for me: If we turned all the stars in the sky into coins, how much would they produce at five per cent compound interest since the time when all this began to exist?"

He reached home about one o'clock, feeling some relief in his torment; he slept without undressing; and the next morning Valentín's fever had gone down considerably. Was there hope?

"Papa," said Rufina, weeping, "pray to the Virgin of Carmen, and forget your Humanities."

"You think I should? I'm willing. But I warn you that without good works there is no use putting faith in the Virgin. And there shall be Christian deeds, cost what it may: that I assure you. I will clothe the naked, visit the sick, console the afflicted. . . . God knows that such is my intention, indeed He knows it. . . . Let us not hear anything later about His not knowing it . . . He knows it, I say. . . ."

The poor boy's legs were on fire with poultices, his head a pitiful sight from the embrocations which had been applied to induce an artificial eruption. More ice had to be bought for the ice bag on his head; then iodoform was needed—errands which Torquemada performed with feverish activity, going in and out every few minutes. Returning home again at nightfall, he encountered an old, tattered beggar wearing army trousers, hatless, with a rag of a jacket over his shoulders, exposing his bare chest. A more venerable face could be found nowhere but among the illustrations of *The Christian Year*. His beard was tangled, his forehead full of wrinkles, like St. Peter's. "Señor, Señor," he said, with the tremor of intense cold, "look at what I have come to!" Torquemada avoided him, then stopped at a little distance; he looked back, hesitated for a moment, and finally went on. An idea had flashed into his mind: "If only I had on my old cape instead of this new one . . ."

And, entering the house:

"Curse me! I should not have let that Christian act escape me."

He left the medicine he was bringing, and, changing his cape, hurried back into the street. A little while later, Rufina, seeing him come in capeless, said in amazement:

"But Papa, your wits are wandering! . . . Where did you leave your cape?"

"My dear child," the sharper answered, lowering his voice and assuming an expression of great compunction, "you have no conception of what a real act of charity, of humanity, is. . . . My cape? Why, I gave it to a poor old half-naked man who was almost dead with cold. That's how I am; I stop at nothing when I take pity on the poor. . . . I see you are surprised. What is a miserable piece of cloth worth?"

"Was it your new cape?"

"No, the old one."

Nothing more was said on the subject, because graver matters demanded their attention.

Don Francisco felt that he bore his trouble best alone. He sat down in the dining room, his hands on the table, his burning forehead resting on his hands. There he had remained for I do not know how long, when his friend Bailón made him sit up by slapping him on the back and saying: "There is no reason to despair. We must keep a stiff upper lip and never let trouble get us down. . . . In the face of Nature, of the sublime Totality, we are ignorant fragments of atoms."

"Go to the devil with your Totalities and your drivel!" said Torquemada, his eyes flashing.

Bailón did not insist; and, judging that the best thing was to distract his friend from his grief, he began to talk to him about a certain piece of business he had in mind. The lessee of his flocks of asses and goats having voided his contract, Bailón had decided to exploit the business on a large scale, putting up a big modern dairy, with regular home deliveries, moderate prices, an elegant office, telephone, and so on. . . . He had gone into it, and . . . "Believe me, my dear Don Francisco, it is a sure thing, especially if we go into cow's milk too, because in Madrid milk . . ."

"Leave me in peace with your milk and your . . . What have I to do with asses or cows?" shouted Torquemada, jumping up and looking at him scornfully. "You see the state I am in—by thunder!—half dead with grief, and you come and talk to me about milk, damn it. . . . Talk to me about how we can get God to pay attention when we ask Him for what we need."

At that moment, Valentín screamed—a harsh, strident scream which left them both tense with terror. It was the "meningeal scream," which resembles the scream of the peacock. This strange encephalic symptom had begun that day, and showed the dangerous and terrifying progress of the poor boy-mathematician's disease. Torquemada would have hidden himself in the center of the earth to avoid hearing that scream: he retired to his office, disregarding Bailón's exhortations and slamming the door in his Dantesque face. From the threshold he was heard to open the drawer of his table, and soon afterward he appeared, carrying something in the inside pocket of his coat. He took his hat and went out without a word.

I will explain what this meant and where the unfortunate Don Francisco was bound that afternoon. The day on which Valentín had been taken ill, his father received a letter from an old and well-plucked client of his, asking for a loan on his household furniture. The relations between the victim and the inquisitor were longstanding, and the latter's profits had been enormous, because the client was in delicate health, a weakling who allowed himself to be skinned, fried and pickled as if he had been born for it. There are such people. Day in and day out, Torquemada went after him, harassed him, put the screws on him and screwed them tight, without succeeding in getting even the past interest. It is easy to imagine the usurer's wrath when he received the letter asking for a new loan. What atrocious insolence!

But now time and occasion had come—precipitated by Valentín's peacock scream. And the sharper had felt a wild impulse. A fiery inspiration had kindled in the sharper's brain, he had taken his hat—and here he is, on the way to see his unfortunate client. The latter was a decent enough man, but with limited abilities, an unlimited family and a wife who aspired to elegance. I don't know what devils possessed the money in that house, to make it be drawn like iron filings to the magnet of the accursed moneylender. The worst of it was that even with the family in hot water up to their necks, the slut of a wife kept charging Paris dresses, inviting her friends to teas or thinking up some other fashionable nonsense in the same style.

Well, sir, here is Don Francisco, off to the house of the gentleman I have described. Suddenly he felt a tug at his cape. He turned . . .

"Isadora!" he exclaimed, looking delighted (a thing which he very seldom did). "Where are you going with that weary body of yours?"

"I was on my way to see you. Have pity on us, Señor Don Francisco. . . . Haven't you even a drop of humanity?"

"My dear child, you misjudge me. What if I told you that I was thinking of you just now . . . that I was remembering the letter you sent me by the concierge's son yesterday?"

"But you don't realize our situation!" said the woman, bursting into tears. "Martín dying, in that freezing garret . . . no bed, no medicines, nothing to make even a miserable stew to give him a cup of something hot! Don Francisco, show some Christianity and do not forsake us. I know we have no credit left, but Martín still has half a dozen very pretty sketches."

"Eh, eh . . . stop crying, woman. . . . I am on tenterhooks myself. . . . I have such a grief in my soul, Isadora, that . . . Go home and wait for me there. I'll come in a little while. . . . What—do you doubt my word? You might hold something else against me; but that . . . Go home and stop worrying . . . and until I get there, pray to God for me with all the fervor you have."

He soon reached his client's house. While he waited, Torquemada looked at the handsome coat stand and at the splendid living-room curtains, which could be seen through the half-open door, and such magnificence suggested the following reflections: "So far as the furniture goes, it is good enough . . . yes, very good." His friend received him in his office. Torquemada had scarcely asked after the family before he sank into a chair with an appearance of great consternation.

"But what is the matter?" asked the other.

"Don't speak of it, don't speak of it, Señor Don Juan. My soul is hanging on a thread. . . . My son . . . !"

"Poor boy! I heard he is very ill. . . . But have you no hope?"

"No . . . I mean, no real hope . . . I don't know; I am going mad; my head is a volcano!"

"I know what it is," the other remarked sadly. "I lost two sons. They were the joy of my life—one four, the other eleven."

"But your grief cannot be like mine. As a father, I am not like other fathers, because my boy is not like other boys. . . . You'll see, my dear Don Juan. . . . When I received your letter, I couldn't attend to it. . . . My grief would not let me think. . . . But today, although I'm half dead with grief, I remembered you and I said to myself: 'Poor Don Juan! What he must be going through! Being the man I am, I can't leave him in this fix. We must help each other in our afflictions.' And here I am to tell you that, although you owe me seventy-odd thousand reals, which come to more than ninety with the unpaid interest, I have made up my mind to make you the loan you ask on your furniture."

"It is all taken care of," said Don Juan, coldly. "I don't need the loan any longer."

"You don't need it! Consider one thing, Don Juan. I'll do it for you . . . at twelve per cent."

And seeing the other shaking his head, he rose and readjusting his cape, which was slipping off, took a few steps toward Don Juan, laid his hand on his shoulder, and said:

"It seems you don't want to deal with me because people say I'm hard. I think that twelve per cent . . . Have you ever heard of better terms?"

"I consider the interest very reasonable; but, I repeat, I no longer need the money."

"I take it you have won the grand prize, then," exclaimed Torquemada with crude sarcasm. "Don Juan, don't waste time trying to joke with me. . . . Because, so far as your not needing it goes—you!—who, to say nothing of a trifle like this, could eat up the Mint all by yourself. . . . Don Juan, Don Juan, let me tell you that I have my humanity too, just like anyone else, that I even do favors for those who loathe me. You hate me, Don Juan, you detest me—don't deny it—because you cannot pay me; that is clear. Very well: to show you what I am capable of, I'll give it to you at five . . . at five!"

And as the other began shaking his head again, Torquemada became even more disturbed and raising his arms—at which, of course, his cape fell off—he delivered this tirade:

"Not even at five! But less than five is unheard of! Do you want me to throw in the shirt I have on? How can the fellow suppose . . . If I do it, I am mad. But so that you may see how far my generosity goes: I'll give it to you without interest!"

"Thank you very much, my dear Don Francisco. But the matter is settled. When you did not answer my letter, I went to see a relative of mine, and found the courage to tell him my sad situation. Would that I had done it sooner!"

"Then your relative has got what he deserves! He can say he has thrown his money down the sink. If he does much more of that kind of business. . . . In short, you didn't want to take it from me. You'll be sorry. . . . And now try saying that I haven't a good heart; it is you who haven't a good heart."

"I? You must be out of your head!"

"Yes, you, you!" he said indignantly. "Well, I must be off: I am expected somewhere else where I am very much wanted, where they are waiting for me like manna from heaven. . . ."

He soon reached the other house, where Isadora heard his footsteps and opened the door. Don Francisco found himself in a room whose sloping ceiling descended to the floor on the side opposite the door; overhead, a skylight, with several of its panes broken and stuffed with rags and paper. On the bed, in a confusion of blankets and clothing, lay a man of about thirty —handsome, with a pointed beard, large eyes, and a fine forehead, but wasted by illness, his upper face slightly flushed, greenish hollows in his cheeks, and his ears as transparent as the wax of a votive candle. Torquemada looked at him without answering his greeting, and thought: poor fellow, he is more consumptive than Traviata. What a pity! Such a good painter and such a fool. . . . He could have made a lot of money!

"Well, you see the state I am in, Don Francisco . . . with this damned catarrh. How grateful I am to you."

"There's nothing to be grateful for. . . . What next? Does not God command us to clothe the sick, feed the afflicted, visit the naked? . . . Oh, I've mixed it all up. . . . What a head!"

He looked at the walls, which were almost covered by studies of landscapes, some of them upside down, fastened to the wall or leaning against it.

"Very pretty things, these!"

"As soon as my cold gets better, I shall go to the country," said the sick man, his eyes bright with fever. "I have an idea —what an idea! I think I shall be well in a week, Don Francisco, if you will help me—and then, off to the country . . ."

The graveyard is where you will go, and very soon, my friend, thought Torquemada; and then, aloud: "Yes, it is a matter of days, that's all. Then you can leave here . . . in a carriage. Do you know this attic is very chilly? Do you mind if I wrap up in my cape?"

"And put on your hat—don't stand there bareheaded," said the sick man, sitting up. He was taken with a violent fit of coughing; Isadora ran to support him and piled pillows behind him. The wretched man's eyes seemed to be bursting, his exhausted lungs labored like a broken pair of bellows.

"Talk as little as possible, dear," Isadora advised him. "I will settle matters with Don Francisco; he and I will come to terms—you'll see."

Her smile showed her beautiful teeth, one of the few charms that remained to her. Torquemada, playing the kindly friend, made her sit down beside him and put his hand on her shoulder, saying: "Of course we'll come to terms."

"Don Francisco, have you realized our situation? Martín's studio was attached. Our debts were so heavy that all we were able to save is what you see here. For Martín to get well and be able to go to the country, we need three thousand reals . . . and I do not say four to keep from frightening you."

"Three thousand reals!" said the usurer, assuming the expression of doubtful reflection which he kept for cases of benevolence. "My dear child, consider . . ." And, making a

perfect circle with his thumb and forefinger, he presented it for
Isadora's contemplation, and continued: "I don't know if I
can spare three thousand reals at the moment. In any case, it
seems to me that you could do with less. Think it over carefully, and review your accounts. I have made up my mind to
look after you until things get better. I will even go so far as
to sacrifice myself, to take the bread out of my own mouth, so
that you shall not go hungry; but . . . but bear in mind that
I must also consider my own interests."

"Make it any interest you please," the sick man said emphatically; it was obvious that he wanted to get it over with.

"I am not alluding to the materialism of a return on the
money, but to my interests, my interests. Of course I expect
you to give me some sort of security too. . . . I have it. . . ."

"Yes indeed. My studies. Take as many as you please."

Casting a practiced look around, Torquemada explained himself as follows:

"Very well, my friends; I am going to tell you something
that will astound you. Ah! the idea that you have of me! Because once upon a time you owed me a small sum and I kept
after you tooth and nail, you think I am made of marble? You
don't know me, I assure you, you don't know me. . . . I am so
good, so good, that I am obliged to praise myself and be grateful to myself for the good that I do. Now see here . . ."

Again the perfect circle appeared, accompanied by these
solemn words: "I shall give you the three thousand reals, and I
shall give them to you here and now. . . . But that is not the
best of it—I shall give them to you without interest. . . . Now
what do you say—is that something, or isn't it something?"

"Don Francisco!" Isadora exclaimed effusively. "Let me give
you a kiss!"

"I'll give you another if you will come over here," cried the
sick man, trying to get out of bed.

"All the caresses you please," said the usurer, letting them both embrace him. "But don't praise me, because such actions are the duty of everyone who respects Humanity."

Taking the paper which Isadora offered him, he looked at his debtors paternally: "My dear children, no doubt you think that I am going to keep this I O U. . . . You couldn't be more mistaken. I am not lending you three thousand reals, I am giving them to you, just because I like you. Look here . . ."

And he tore up the paper. Isadora and Martín believed it because they saw it.

"Only a great man could have done this," said Isadora, deeply moved.

"The most I will do," said Don Francisco, rising and examining the pictures, "is to accept a few of your studies as a souvenir. . . . This one of the snow-covered mountains, and that one of the donkeys at pasture. And I think, Martín, that, if I may, I will also take this little seascape and the ivy-covered bridge there . . ."

Martín's coughing fit had developed and he was choking. Isadora, hurrying to help him, cast a furtive glance at the selection which the diligent moneylender was making.

"I accept them as a souvenir," he said, setting them aside. "And, if you don't mind, I'll take this other one too. And I'd like to tell you this: if you are afraid these pictures will suffer from being moved around, bring them to my house—I'll keep them there and you can have them back whenever you wish. . . . Isn't that damned cough ever going to stop? Never mind, by next week you won't be coughing at all, not at all. You'll be off to the country. . . . But what am I thinking of—here I am, almost forgetting the three thousand reals. Come here, Isadorita, and pay attention. A hundred-peso bill and another and another . . ." (As he counted them out, he moistened his finger with saliva for each bill so that they should not stick together.) "Seven hundred pesos. I haven't got a fifty-peso bill on me, my child. I'll give it to you another day. There you are —exactly two thousand eight hundred reals . . ."

Night was falling, the unhappy usurer's bedroom had grown dark, when, clear and distinct, he heard the peacock scream which Valentín gave in the paroxysm of his fever. "And they said he was better! Oh, my dear son. . . . They've taken us in. We've been sold!"

Rufina entered the lion's den weeping. "Oh, Papa, he is so much worse, so much worse!"

"That bungler Quevedo!" cried Torquemada, raising his fist to his mouth and biting it furiously. "I'll tear his guts out. . . . He has killed him."

"Papa, for God's sake. You must not rebel against the will of God. . . ."

"I am not rebelling, thunder and lightning! I am not rebelling. It is only that I cannot, I cannot give my son, because he is mine, blood of my blood and bone of my bones."

"Resign yourself, resign yourself, and we will submit together," exclaimed his daughter, weeping unrestrainedly.

"I cannot, I do not want to resign myself. It is sheer robbery. Envy, pure envy. What is there for Valentín in heaven? Nothing, let them say what they please; nothing. . . . God, what a lie, what a fraud! Who can still say there's a heaven, a hell, a purgatory, a God, a Devil, a . . . stuff and nonsense! And Death! A fine fool Death is, forgetting all the scoundrels, all the quacks, all the fools, and wanting my boy, because he is the finest boy in the world! . . . Everything is evil, and the world is a stinking shambles."

Rufina went away, and Bailón entered, wearing an expression of great compunction. He had just visited the sick boy, who was now in his death agony, surrounded by a few neighbors and intimate friends of the household. The pious renegade prepared to comfort the afflicted father, and began by embracing him and saying in muffled tones:

"Courage, my friend, courage! The strong soul rises to such occasions. Remember the great philosopher who died on a cross, consecrating the principles of Humanity."

"Get out of here with your principles and your . . . Will you get out of here, you louse! You are the stupidest, dullest, most nauseating creature I ever saw! Every time I am in trouble, you plague me with your drivel!"

"My dear friend, calm yourself. Before the designs of Nature, of Humanity, of the Supreme All, what can man do? Man! That ant, or even less, that flea . . . and still less again."

"That bugbear . . . or even less, that . . ." Torquemada added with horrible sarcasm, imitating the sibyl's voice and then shaking his fist at him. "Thunder and lightning! If you don't shut up, I'll smash your face in. . . . I care as much about the Supreme All as I do about the Supreme Nothing . . . and the supreme louse who invented it. Get out, leave me alone, or . . ."

Rufina came in again, supported by two women who had taken her away from the agonizing spectacle in the dying boy's room. The poor girl could not stand up. She fell to her knees, sobbing, and seeing her father struggling with Bailón, she said:

"Papa, for God's sake, stop. Resign yourself. . . . I am resigned—can't you see? . . . My poor little brother . . . when I went in . . . for a moment, he recovered consciousness. He spoke in a clear voice, and said that he saw the angels calling him."

"Oh my son, oh my dearest son!" Torquemada shouted with

all the power of his lungs, in a savage frenzy. "Don't go, don't listen to them; they are trying to put one over on you. . . . Stay here with us . . ."

Then he fell flat on the floor; one leg stretched out stiff, the other, and the corresponding arm, contracted. Bailón, with all his strength, could not control him. At the same time, his tense mouth gave a terrible roar and spat foam.

Valentín had expired. His sister was summoned and went to the room. She gave him countless kisses and then, assisted by her friends, prepared to perform the last duties owed to the unfortunate boy. She was brave, far braver than her father, who, when he came out of his terrifying faint and was able to realize the utter extinction of all his hopes, fell into a profound physical and moral depression. He wept silently and exhaled sighs which could be heard all over the house. After a considerable time, he asked for coffee and half a slice of toast, because he felt horribly weak. The complete loss of hope calmed his nerves and brought an urgent need to repair his exhausted organism. At midnight he had to have a substantial potion, which the sister of the photographer and the wife of the butcher made for him from eggs, sherry and broth.

"I don't know what is happening to me," said Torquemada the Worse, "but I feel as if life were trying to leave me." His deep sighs and silent sobbing continued until almost dawn, when he was attacked by a new paroxysm of grief, crying out that he must see his son, must "bring him back to life, at any cost," and tried to get out of bed against the combined efforts of Bailón, the butcher, and the other friends who tried to hold him down. At last they succeeded in quieting him, a result in no small degree due to the renegade cleric's philosophical admonitions and the wise things which fell from the lips of the butcher, a man of small education but a good Christian.

"You are right," said Don Francisco, exhausted and breathless. "What is left but to submit? Submit! Advice is the cheapest thing in the world! Just see what anyone gets for being as good as an angel and sacrificing himself for the afflicted, and doing good to those who can't bear the sight of us. . . . In short, what I intended to use to help a bunch of scoundrels—wasted money, sure to find its way to pothouses and gambling houses and pawnshops!—I say that I'm going to take it and spend it on giving my son the most magnificent funeral Madrid has ever seen! Oh, what a son, what a prodigy! And I have lost him! He was no son; he was a little god, engendered half by me, half by the Eternal Father. . . . Don't you think I should give him a splendid funeral? It is morning already. Bring me pictures of hearses . . . and black-bordered cards for invitations to all the professors."

Excited by these vainglorious plans, our man was up and dressed by nine o'clock, making arrangements efficiently and serenely. He ate a good breakfast and received the many friends who came to visit him.

And the splendid funeral took place and was attended by a great crowd of eminent personages—all of which induced in Torquemada a satisfaction and pride which were the only balm for his profound torment.

The following morning, Torquemada had no sooner opened his eyes than the fever of business took possession of him. Since Rufina was so broken by sleeplessness and grief that she could not attend to her household duties, the maid and the indefatigable old-clothes woman who called at the house, Tia Roma, took her place as far as possible. And behold—when Tia Roma came in to bring the Grand Inquisitor his morning chocolate, he was already up and sitting at the desk in his office, writing a great many things with feverish hand. And since the old woman was perfectly at ease with the master of the house, and permitted herself to treat him as an equal, she went to him, laid her cold, scrawny hand on his shoulder, and said: "You never learn. . . . Here you are, getting your executioner's tools ready again. You will die an evil death, you God-forsaken fiend, if you don't reform."

Torquemada gave her a look which was absolutely yellow, because in his case, yellow was the color of what, in the majority of human eyes, is white, and he said: "I do exactly as I damn well please, you old gargoyle. A fine thing it would be if I had to ask an ignoramus like you what to do!" For a moment his eyes fell on Valentín's slate and he gave a sigh; then he went on: "If I am getting my tools ready, it is none of your business nor anybody's business, because I know all that is to be known on earth and even in heaven—thunder and lightning! I know you are going to come back at me with the materialism of works of mercy. . . . And I answer you that I tried doing my best and what I got for it was a kick in the jaw. All the mercy I have, they are welcome to bash in my skull with!"

Doña Berta

LEOPOLDO ALAS

I

There is a certain spot in northern Spain that neither the
Romans nor the Moors ever reached; and if Doña Berta de
Rondaliego, proprietress of this hushed green hideaway, knew
a little more about history, she would swear that never did
bold Agrippa, Augustus, Musa, or Tariq set foot on this soil
forever soft with lush, fresh grass, juicy-crisp, dark, velvety,
and glistening; her soil, the earth of her own private haven,
deaf, like her, to the noises of the world, wrapped in the thick
verdure of infinite trees and fertile fields, just as she herself is
always wrapped in yellow flannel because of her chronic little
ailments.

Doña Berta's minute empire of foliage and greens belongs
to the parish of Pie del Oro, in the township of Carreño, judi-
cial district of Gijón; and within the parish itself, Doña Berta's
immediate vicinity is referred to as Zaornín, and there, the
luxuriant valley, in the middle of which lies an extensive
meadow named Aren, is called Susacasa. Along the extreme

northwest of the meadow runs a brook bordered with tall pop-
lars, birches, and cone-shaped, dark-leaved *humeros,* and the
waters spiral about the trunks along the ground, encroaching
upon the grass and flowers on the banks.

The stream does not have any name at all there; nor does
it deserve one, for it barely has enough water for a christening.
But the geographical vanity of the owners of Susacasa has
designated it for centuries "the river," and the residents of
other parts of that area, just out of malice toward the distinguished Rondaliego clan, call the aforementioned river "the
drip," and humiliate it in any way they can, scrupulously main-
taining insidious rights of way that traverse the current of the
Aren's and the cornfields' elusive crystalline visitor; and they
cross it, oh! the irony of it all!, without need of any bridges—
not Roman bridges, naturally, for it is understood that the
Romans never set foot on that ground, but not even bridges
made of hollow, half-rotted tree trunks green again from touching the moist earth of the banks. These tyrannical easements
of unknown and suspicious origin, fruit of time-sanctioned
democratic victories, are the object of Doña Berta's bitter com-
plaints, not so much because they humiliate the river, crossing
it without a bridge (and with only a large rock in the middle
of its bed, a little island of quartz worn down by the friction
of bare feet and nailed shoes for centuries on end), but because they crush the loveliest wild flowers and kill the sprouting new grass of the fecund Aren, marking up its immaculate
green with scars that cross it like cordons across a chest; scars
made by gross footsteps.

But leaving such unhappy subjects for another time, I
should like to add that beyond and above the meadow (above,
because a hill begins there), beyond the "river" that one can
jump over without bridges or fords, lies what we call *la llosa,*
a generic name for a certain kind of corn-producing lowland

that needs no further specification here; and when the tall stalks grow, and their leaves, like flexible spears, sway above the stems, bowing in graceful curvature, the field looks like a green sea blown by the breezes. Well, on the other side of that sea is the "mansion," a not very large white house, the ancestral home of the Rondaliegos; this house, with its surrounding lands, and its appurtenances, namely: the chapel, attached to the main house, the wine press (now converted into a hayloft), a granary made of chestnut wood and with stone posts known as *pegollos,* and a square white pigeon roost, all this together, plus a little hut that serves as a farmhouse and hugs the same slope as the "mansion," but at a distance of some thirty yards from it—all this, I repeat, is Posadorio.

II

Doña Berta and Sabelona live alone in the "mansion." They and "the cat," which, like the stream that courses the Aren, has no name because it is the only one of its species thereabouts. The farmhouse is inhabited by the "caretaker," an old man, deaf like Doña Berta, and, with him, his almost imbecilic daughter who, nevertheless, helps him in his chores like a brawny plowboy, and a servant, always rather brutish and always a different one every few days, because the old man is ill-tempered and fires people for the slightest provocation.

The manor is considerably rundown. But even if it were maintained at best, it would not be worth much; for that green, fresh-looking land is not first-class, and produces practically nothing; which is why Doña Berta is poor, though genteel, and the dignity of her almost imaginary eminence consists in part of the beauty that emanates from the soul. Doña Berta combines and confuses in her mind the idea of purity with that of solitude, isolation. With perfect equanimity she

lives the life of an ascetic, who spins and washes the linens,
great quantities of it, and kneads bread at home, too. At Doña
Berta's house, they make their bread every five or six days;
and in this task, which requires more muscle than she and her
fading Sabel possess together, the caretaker's imbecile daughter helps them; but their spinning the two old women do
themselves, and taking care of the wash, as soon as it comes
back from the river, is also their exclusive province. The garden is white from end to end with the clothes set out to dry
on the grass, and from the little house on the hill, overlooking
everything, Doña Berta, unhearing and silent, thanks God as
she contemplates happily the snowfall of immaculate linen that
is spread below, and the scrubbed-looking greenery that frames
the laundry, stretching from the grove of trees around the
house down to the cornfields and even to the Aren, which, in
turn, looks as if it were mown by a very fine barber and almost
has the air of a closely shaven, well-soaped, fragrant-smelling
man. Yes, it seems as though the grass is cut with shears and
then washed with soap and trimmed; the land is not completely flat, but rather convex, and sinks away mysteriously
out there near the *humeros* as it kisses the stream. And a
thousand times Doña Berta wished she had the hands of a
giant, a mile long each, so that she could stroke the Aren's
back, just as she caresses her cat's. If she is in a bad mood
as she gazes across the meadow, her eyes rest on the two paths
that cross it, on those unspeakable blotches, mark of the common hordes, of those blamed clodhoppers who, just out of envy,
meanness, and pure malice needlessly and without any why or
wherefore maintain those public easements, stain on the Rondaliego escutcheon.

Zaornín is not on the way to anywhere; the world ends
there. No hunter, no army or bandit or rogue, ever went
through Susacasa. Highways and railroads stop far from it,

and even the local roads bypass it, making a respectful detour around the limits of that dwelling embroidered with grass and foliage. You can hear the creaking of carts, but always in the distance—Doña Berta does not hear it at all—and still those dreadful people insist upon disturbing such perfect peace, on sullying those smooth carpets with paths that look like a blight on the fresh green, paths that wear the prints of their coarse shoes and dirty bare feet, like the vulgar stamp of their trespass on the absolute dominion of the Rondaliegos. Since when has the riffraff been able to pass through there? "Since time immemorial," witnesses have said a hundred times. "It's a lie!" retorts Doña Berta. "You can just imagine the old Rondaliegos allowing that rabble to trample the grass of the Aren with their filthy hoofs!" The Rondaliegos did not want any truck with anybody. They always intermarried within the family and never mixed their blood or their heritage; *they* wouldn't let their lineage or their lands be defiled. Of course, Doña Berta herself could not remember since when there were public paths crossing her property; but her heart told her that it must be since about the time of the fall of the old regime, when there were liberals and things like that in the world.

"This place isn't on the way to anywhere. This is the tip end of the world," says Doña Berta, who has some rather capricious notions of geography, a Homeric map of the world as she pictures it; and she believes that the earth comes to a point and that that point is Zaornín, with Susacasa, the meadow Aren, and Posadorio.

"Neither the Moors nor the Romans ever trod on the grass of the Aren," she says day in and day out to her ever-faithful Sabelona (big Isabel), who has been a servant of the Rondaliego family from the age of ten, and over whom neither Moors nor Christians ever passed, for she is as virgin today as the day she was born, and that was seventy years ago.

"Neither the Moors nor the Romans!" Doña Berta repeats
at night, as she sits in the candle glow near the hot embers
of the kitchen hearth, which is on the floor. And Sabelona nods
her head in assent, with the same blind belief with which she
kneels shortly thereafter repeating the "acts of faith" that her
mistress recites before her. Neither Doña Berta nor Isabel
knows anything that matters about the Romans and Moors,
except for the negative fact that they never passed through
there. Perhaps they are not wholly certain of the total decline
of the Roman Empire nor of the conquest of Granada, which
Doña Berta, on the whole better versed in the humanities,
tends to confuse with the glorious war in Africa, and, especially, with the taking of Tetuán. At any rate, neither believes
that the respective periods of Moslem and Roman domination
were as long ago as they really were; and, in short, Romans
and Moors have come to stand for both of them as a symbol
of everything strange, everything foreign, everything enemy.
And so, when some person once dared to tell them that the
French never reached Susacasa either, nor was there any reason for them to do so, they just shrugged their shoulders, as if
to say, "Well, that's all included in the Moors and Romans."
And the fact is that this hereditary obsession of the Rondaliegos
was passed on to Doña Berta from a tradition prior to the
French invasion.

III

Oh! the Liberals! They indeed had arrived in Posadorio. We
have already spoken of Sabelona's intact virginity. The reader
may have assumed that Doña Berta was a widow, or that her
virtue had been passed over in silence. Virtuous she was . . . ,
but a virgin she was not; single, yes. If Sabelona had been in
the same situation as her mistress, she would not have been
so pure either. This she understood perfectly, and therefore

affected no attitude of moral superiority with respect to her employer. It had been a misfortune, and dearly had she paid for it, misfortune and all.

The Rondaliego family consisted of four brothers and one sister, Berta, all orphaned since childhood. The eldest, Don Claudio, acted as father to the rest. Purity of the blood was a sacred cult among them. All good, affable people, like Berta, who was a walking smile, they did their works of charity—from afar. They feared the common people, whom they loved as brothers in Christ, but not in the Rondaliego fellowship; and their aristocratic aloofness had as much gentle, resigned asceticism about it as preoccupation with pedigree. The library of their house was symbolic of those tendencies; it contained hardly anything but religious books of simple, unworldly devotions, and books on heraldry; everywhere there were crosses; everywhere gold, silver, and the reds of the crests stamped on parchment.

Several generations back, a Rondaliego had been found dead in a forest, called the Matiella, half a league from Posadorio, and it was strongly suspected that he had been murdered by a local resident. Since then the whole family has been ever on guard, even when distributing alms. The greatest sin of the Rondaliegos was to think ill of the villagers they protected. For their part, the townsfolk, who perhaps were once vassals of Posadorio, received their benefactions with a gesture of servile humility, and then joked behind their backs about the decadence of that noble house, and whenever they could do so without showing their faces, manifested their lack of respect in every possible way. In this they were abetted somewhat by certain new laws, and a great deal by the recent political climate. For the residents of Pie del Oro, the symbol of public liberties (of course, they didn't call it that) was the growing contempt for the Rondaliegos, and they were encouraged in this attitude by legal sanction, through such devices as assessing the Rondaliegos unduly in the apportionment of local taxes, imposing upon them disproportionate and obligatory duties in public projects, discontinuing rural police protection within the limits of Zaornín and particularly of Susacasa, and a hundred other such underhanded jabs, for which the Village Board, the law, modern practices, and these terrible times were uniformly held to account.

As for the theft of fruit, hay, firewood, etc., the law could not be blamed directly, since it did not actually authorize people to enter and burglarize the Rondaliegos' property; but if the law was not responsible, its representatives, the mayor, the judge, or their underlings, according to the case at hand, helped the townsfolk through their inertia and apathy, which made it impossible for them ever to apprehend the guilty parties. All this had happened many years back. The Rondaliegos' good fortune was the topographical roughness of their domain: if the family's innate disposition alienated its members from the multitude, so did the location of their home seem a refuge from society. The folds of the land and the thick brush that surrounded it, plus the fact that it was not on the way to anywhere, effected a near oblivion which, although it implied scorn, brought too the peace they longed for. "Fine," the owners of Posadorio would say to themselves. "The people, the common villagers, don't like us, and we don't like them; so be it." Nevertheless, the Rondaliegos gave charitably to the residents of that vicinity at every possible occasion.

All the brothers of the family were bachelors; they were cold and impassive, although kindly and pleasant. Their idol was their unblemished honor, their noble blood preserved immaculate. And the sanctuary of that purity was to rest in Berta, their only sister. But, although Berta resembled her brothers outwardly—she, too, was fair, heavy set, amiable, and mild of gesture, voice, and ways—she had within her depths of tenderness that her brothers lacked. The second eldest brother, who was something of a literary man, would bring home current novels translated from the French. The whole family read them. On the men they left not the least impression; but on Berta they wrought inner cataclysms. Romanticism, which for so many men and women of city and town was just something to talk about, or at most an excuse for the libertine, had a veritable high priestess in Posadorio, even though by the time it arrived there, in woefully abridged serials, it was but the echo of an echo. Never could the brothers have suspected that there dwelt such a roaring flame of fantasy and emotion right there in Posadorio. Not even after the "misfortune" did they think of romanticism as its real cause; instead, they attributed it to chance, to the moment, to treachery, all of which were partially to blame. Perhaps the most evil-minded of them all went so far as to lay it to sensuality, of which Berta was innocent; but nobody ever thought of idyllic love, of a heart that melts when it nears the fire it adores. Berta let herself succumb with all the eagerness of her soul. The story was quite simple, like the plots of her books. Everything happened the same way. Along came "the Captain," a captain of Queen Cristina's armies; he was wounded; a fugitive; he collapsed right at the gate of the manor; the dog barked; Berta came out; she saw the blood, the pallor, the uniform, and a pair of gentle blue eyes that seemed to beg for mercy, maybe even for love. She took the poor fellow in, hid him in the chapel of her home, all by herself, until she could decide whether or not it would be wise to tell her brothers about it; because they were Carlists, like her, and might turn the fugitive over to their own side if some of them should happen through there looking for him. After all, he was a Liberal, an enemy "Black." She thought it over well and hit upon the solution. She revealed her secret; her brothers approved of what she had done; the wounded man was moved from his cot in the chapel to the finest feather bed in the house; and everyone kept the matter quiet. The Carlist troops that passed through those parts later never found out that their enemy, the captain who had been the particular scourge of the "Whites," lay hidden so nearby. For two months Berta took care of the Liberal all by herself, solicitous of his every want, and smitten since the very first day. Her brothers let her nurse him and fall in love with him; they let her care for him as a devoted wife ministers to a dying husband; and they expected—naturally!—that the day her charge was well enough to leave Posadorio, all affection would disappear, and that the young lady of the Rondaliego family would be just a stranger to the handsome captain, who wept with gratitude every night, while the brothers snored and their sister kept vigil near his bed, accompanied by an old woman and by Sabel, who was then an attractive young girl.

When the Captain was well enough to get up and stroll around the garden, two of the brothers, who were in Posadorio at the time (the other two, the oldest and the youngest, had gone to the city for a few days) saw in the enemy "Black" an excellent companion, one capable of distracting them from their resigned boredom. The friendship between the Carlists and the Liberal grew day by day. The Captain was expansive, warm, and had a vivid, fertile imagination; he liked people and was likable himself; and, aside from that, he induced the phlegmatic Rondaliegos to join in innocent diversions, such as fencing bouts, which he directed without taking a very active part in them himself; he organized chess matches and card games, and he read to them aloud, in a beautifully modulated, smooth, rhythmic voice that gently put them to sleep after supper, in the light of the ancient brass lamp of Posadorio's great hall, which echoed with words and with footsteps.

I V

The day came when the Liberal felt himself morally obliged to announce his departure, for, having recuperated fully, he was in a position to rejoin his comrades at the front. His heart would remain behind, with Berta, but he really had to leave. The brothers would not hear of it. They indicated to him in a thousand oblique ways that the longer he delayed returning to fight against the Carlists, the better would he repay the Rondaliegos for their hospitality and for the life he claimed to owe them. Besides, and this was the main reason, they enjoyed his company so much! They were all living together in a perfectly delightful interlude, oblivious of political differences and of everything that existed beyond the woods that formed a green frame for the idyllic portrait of Susacasa.

The Captain let himself be persuaded. He remained in Posadorio longer than he should have; and one day, when the strength of his body and the force of his love had reached a degree of intensity that produced a delicious and very dangerous harmony within him, he threw himself impetuously at Berta's feet on the first tempting occasion he found to be alone with her. And she, who knew nothing about such things, burst into tears; so when his flaming kiss seared her lips and her heart, all she could do was cry, cry with turbulent, mingled love and fear. She didn't lose her virtue that day, but later on, in the garden, under a majestic laurel that smelled like paradise. It was at twilight. The brothers, blind to what was happening, had left her and the Captain home alone. They had gone hunting, which still was too arduous an exertion for the convalescent who wanted to go back to the wars before he was ready.

A lonely nightingale was singing in the nearby oak grove, a nightingale like the one that sang to immortal Saint Dulceline, sister of the venerable Bishop Hugues de Dignes, and transported her with love. "Oh, what a strange, marvelous tune that bird sings!" said the Saint, and thereupon she remained in ecstasy, absorbed in God through the song of the bird. So relates Salimbeno. And that is what happened to Berta. The nightingale made her weaken and all her stern, cold powers of resistance disappeared. A sublime poetry that permeates everything with love flooded her soul; she lost all sense of right and wrong; and, rapt in the song of the bird, she fell into the arms of the Captain, who there became a guileless Don Juan. Perhaps if the Liberal, the man who owed his life to her, had not been around, Berta, listening to the lonely nightingale that evening, would have vowed to become another Dulceline, to love God and only God, with the sweet name of Jesus, in the solitude of the cloister, or, like Saint Dulceline, in society, in the world, but in that world of Susacasa, which was more secluded than a convent. At any rate, on that day, at that hour, under that laurel, with that music, Berta most assuredly would have wept with devotion overwhelming, and would have consecrated her life to its cult. When circumstances permitted the Captain to think about the legal aspect of their supreme happiness, he volunteered, as a lover and a gentleman, to return as soon as possible to Posadorio, to resign his commission, and ask her brothers for her hand in marriage, since they would never consent to her marrying an active Liberal officer. Berta, who was completely innocent, realized that something serious had happened, but not that it was anything irreparable. She kept the incident to herself, more from the sweet warmth of its mystery than from fear of the consequences of her revelation. The Captain promised to come back and marry her. That was fine. It was the proper thing to do. But as for happiness, she already had it locked in her heart. She would wait a hundred years if she had to. The Captain would flee the danger of death like a coward; he was returning to his colors just as a formality, to fulfill his obligation, but actually he was determined to save his own skin and request his discharge; for he felt that his life was no longer his own—it belonged to Berta's honor.

But man proposes and the hero disposes. One evening, at the very hour when Berta's and Saint Dulceline's nightingale had sung, the Liberal Captain heard the clarion call of war's hymn. Glorious death, like a supreme love, beckoned him from his trench. His soldiers awaited his example, and he gave it to them; and, in a rapture of sublime courage, the valiant who had been happy only twice in his life, and who on those two occasions had caused a misfortune and engendered a luckless life, surrendered his body to the bullets and his soul to God. All this, translated into the only language that the Rondaliego brothers would understand, meant that a despicable Liberal, defiling hospitality, gratitude, friendship, trust, law, virtue, and everything sacred, had ravished their honor and had fled.

They never heard from him again. Neither did Berta. She didn't know that her heart's choice had been unable to come back to her to comply with the mandate of Church and state because an irrepressible instinct had forced him to answer the call of his flag. The Captain had left Zaornín the day after the consummation of his bliss; and nobody suspected the shame he left behind him until, to the astonishment and fear of the brothers, and to the astonishment but not fear of Berta, the unlucky girl was stricken with an ailment that ended in a mysterious, carefully concealed baptism, as was befitting in such a shameful case.

Berta began to realize her transgression through its punishment. Her son was snatched from her, and her brothers, the snatchers, left her alone in Posadorio with Isabel and some other servants. Their inheritance, which had not yet been distributed, was divided up, and Berta was allotted, aside from the small share that was due her, the usufruct of all of Susacasa, including Posadorio. Since she had besmirched the ancestral home by sinning there, she was given the site of her dishonor, where she would be more isolated than in any other place. When she gave up hope of her Captain's return, then did the disgraced girl fully understand that henceforth her world would be that little lost nook, hidden by the verdure that surrounded and nearly submerged it.

Many years passed before the Rondaliegos began, if not to forgive, at least to forget. Two died with their grievances, one in the war, into which he plunged in desperation, the other in the Carlist withdrawal, months later. Both had spent their entire patrimony on behalf of the cause for which they fought. The other two also contributed part of their estate to Don Carlos' forces, but they did not expose their persons to the bullets. They lived to be old men, and these were the two who would occasionally revisit the "theater of their dishonor." They no longer called it that. The secrecy with which they had hidden their disgrace had taken away much of its bitterness; and later the passing years had veiled Berta's lapse with the prescription that time offers, like a cloak of indulgence made of layers of dust, above all the conventional. Approaching death turned the Rondaliegos to more positive, serious thoughts. Old age tacitly forgave youth for those long-past transgressions, of which, unfortunately, it was no longer capable itself. Berta had forgiven herself too, almost without thinking about it. But she remained in the imposed retirement which she had accepted willingly, out of habit, like the bird in Lope's sonnet that turned away so that it would not see a woman cry.

Berta came to the point where she could not grasp life outside of Posadorio. Her preoccupation with her gradually forgotten exploit, in its aspects of shame and sin, not as the poetic memory that persisted and acquired a new acuteness and sublimation in her old age, was succeeded by family difficulties and her alienation from society as a whole and from all contact with the masses. But if Berta had succeeded in excusing her own error, in the bottom of her heart she never forgave her brothers for the "theft" of her son, which, although it wounded her deeply, had seemed justifiable to her when she was young. But when mature judgment made her view with forbearance the horrible sin for which she had hitherto reproved herself, her maternal instincts returned in force, and she could pardon neither her brothers nor herself. "Yes," she would say to herself, "I should have protested; I should have demanded the fruit of my love; I should have gone afterwards to seek him out at any cost, and not have believed my brothers when they assured me that he had died."

When it finally occurred to Berta to rebel, to ascertain the whereabouts of her son, to find out whether they were deceiving her with the announcement of his death, it was already too late. Either he had really died, or, at least, he had disappeared. The Rondaliegos had conducted themselves in that matter with the especial cruelty of fanatics who sacrifice the soul's most intimate realities for the sake of absolute abstractions. Those good men, those kindly, sweet, mild-mannered, blameless gentlemen, were four Herods against one poor infant, whom they regarded as an affront to their lineage. He was the son of the Liberal, of the traitor, of the scoundrel. To keep him nearby, to take care of him and expose themselves by these attentions to the discovery of their connection with the "bastard nephew," seemed to the Rondaliegos as insane as casting a bell out of the metal of the scandal and hanging it from a roof of Posadorio, so that day and night it would ring forth the ignominy of their race, the eternal, irreparable shame of their family. Absurd! The "accursed child" was handed over to some friars of Mercy, hastily, without any guarantees of safety, without any precautions other than those necessary to allay any suspicions about the baby's origin. The only thing they did try to do was to surround him with money, to make sure that he would not starve. And this contributed to his total disappearance. He vanished from sight. Carefully eradicating every trace of him, some, on the one hand, in order to maintain their family honor, and others out of selfishness and greed, they eliminated all possible means of locating him. When conscience began to torment the surviving Rondaliegos and urged them to look for the lost boy, they could no longer do anything about it. The self-interest, the egoism, of these good people rejoiced in having thought up long ago the fable about the poor child's death. At first, they lied in order to punish the wretched girl who presumed to beg for the fruit of her enormous sin. Afterwards, they lied so that she would not grow despondent with grief, cursing the assassins of her maternal felicity. The last two Rondaliegos died in Posadorio two years apart. Berta did not dare to ask the first one, her eldest brother, about it at the time of his death. As he lay dying, Berta stood near his bed, her mind clear, her lips ready to speak, looking at him intently, questioning him not even with her eyes, but thinking about her son. The dying brother also looked in Berta's eyes now and then, but he did not offer the least hint of the answer that he should have given without being asked. He said nothing with his lips or with his eyes. And still, Berta felt that he too was thinking about the child who was dead or lost. And shortly afterwards, she herself, drenched with tears, closed those eyes that held her secret. When her only remaining brother was breathing his last, Berta, who was about to be left alone in the world, threw herself upon the thin chest of the dying man, and, pitying only her own anguish, asked him in desperation, invoking God and the memory of their parents, whom neither he nor she had ever known; she asked him about her son. "Did he die? Did he really die? Are you absolutely certain? Swear to me, Agustín, swear by Our Lord, whom you are going to meet face to face!" And Agustín, the youngest of the Rondaliegos, looked at his sister, no longer seeing her, and let fall the last tear with which souls are wont to depart this world.

Berta was left alone with Sabel and the cat, and began to age rapidly until she turned to parchment and lived the life of a dried-up oak tree's bark. She was becoming parchment inside as well; but two sentiments, like two crystallizing diamonds, still glowed amid all that desiccation, and there they acquired the automatism of an obsession that sways in the soul with the tick-tock of a pendulum. The solitude, the isolation, the purity and cleanliness of Posadorio, of Susacasa, of the Aren . . . here the pendulum swung upwards to the scurrying activity of that skinny, yellowed old woman (she, who was once so fair and round), who, hard of hearing and light of foot, came and went up and down the cornfield, giving orders to sow the lands, trim the trees, or clean out the hedges. But in the midst of all this bustle, she would contemplate the unsoiled green of her lands, the loneliness and seclusion of Susacasa, and then the memory of the Liberal, of her Captain, traitor or not, the thought of her son who had died or vanished, would overtake her. And the poor old woman now in her seventies would cry for her child, whom she had always loved with a rather abstract emotion, without sufficient imaginative powers to visualize him. She wept for her son and loved him with the tepid affection of a grandmother; tepid, but obstinate. And there the pendulum of her involuntary thoughts swung down to the wretchedness of despair, to the shadows and chills of the heart, and she blamed the world, destiny, her brothers, and herself. Sabelona was aware of only half of this up-and-down existence, the overt, the active, the material half. Just as during her brothers' lifetime, the more delicate and poetic, the subtler, sadder side of her soul still doomed Berta to absolute solitude. As they spun in the candlelight of the chimneyed kitchen whose hearth was in the floor, the two old women looked like two mummies, and so they were. But one, Sabel, was resting in peace, while the other, Berta, had a flitting mouse, a restless spirit, under her skin. At times, after talking about the wash for an hour, Berta would be quiet for a while, not even replying to Sabel's observations. And then, amid the silence, she would look at her servant with eyes that burst with the torment of her thoughts . . . and she imagined that that other woman, who knew nothing of her anguish, of the stream of painful thoughts that flowed through her head, was not a woman at all . . . ; she was a spinner carved of old ivory.

V

One afternoon in August, when the sun ceased to burn and its slanting rays brought a gleam to the white clothes spread out on the sloping land, and lighted a diamond on the•tip of each blade of grass, which, cut close by the scythe, looked like a steel point, Doña Berta, after gazing from the house above at the whites and greens of her domain, swayed by an impulsive breeze of joy, began to hum one of those romantic ballads that she had learned in her innocent youth, and which she liked to recall when she wasn't too sad and when Sabel was neither with her nor anywhere around. In the presence of her servant, she was ashamed of her inveterate sentimentality. But when she was completely alone, the deaf lady, hearing herself only from within, and in tones as consistently out of tune as they were melancholy, would sing a kind of air that could be called the manifest voice of romanticism in music. The words, which were barely pronounced, were no less sentimental than the music, and always dealt with great thwarted passions or with the idyllic tranquillity of an innocent pastoral love.

Having glanced through the boughs of the pear trees and apple trees to see whether Sabel was wandering below, and made sure that there was no such impediment thereabouts, Doña Berta gave forth the pearls of her repertoire. And while she bent over, sprinkler in hand, watering her pepper plants and removing snails from her trees and bushes (she loved to do several things at the same time), her shaky voice was saying:

> *"Come, O shepherdess, to my cabin,*
> *Leave the mountain, leave the lea,*
> *Leave behind thy lambs that gambol,*
> *And come and join me by the sea. . . ."*

When she reached the far end of her garden, near the gate that gives on the woods, a forest of oaks, firs, and chestnut trees, she stood and thought. She had gotten an urge to go out through it, to wander up the hill among the ferns and brambles. Such an idea had not occurred to her for years, but at that moment she felt a ray of winter's sun in her soul, and her body craved adventure, daring. How many times when she was young had she stood before that gate hidden among dark foliage, and dreamed that her happiness, that something unexpected, something poetic, ideal and extraordinary, would

come to her through it. Later, when she was waiting for her
flesh and blood dream, for her Captain who never returned,
she watched for him through that gate. She turned the key in
the lock, lifted the latch, and went out into the brush. After a
few steps, she had to sit down on the untouched ground to pick
the thorns out with her hand. The incline was difficult for her,
and, besides, the tall ferns and the prickly plants blocked her
way. Seated in the shade, she continued singing:

"And together in my little boat . . ."

A noise in the thicket, which she finally heard when it was
already very close, made her hush, like a bird surprised in its
sanctuary. She rose to her feet, looked up, and saw before her
a handsome young man of about thirty to thirty-five, dark,
strong, and heavily bearded, and, although he was dressed
casually—a sport jacket, slouch hat, and trousers that were
too wide—his clothes appeared to be fine and costly. In short,
he seemed to be a young gentleman of the Court, despite his
disarray. He was carrying a box that hung from a strap around
his shoulder. The two stood there looking at each other in
silence. Doña Berta realized that at last the stranger was
greeting her, and without hearing him, she answered by bow-
'ng her head. She wasn't afraid. Why should she be? But she
was taken aback and a little annoyed. Such a gentlemanly
gentleman, how had he come to stop in the woods of Susacasa,
so far from his usual surroundings? After all, Susacasa wasn't
on the way to anywhere; this was the dropping-off place . . . !
It offended her somewhat that a traveler should cross her domain. They got around to explanations. She told him bluntly
that she was hard of hearing and the mistress of everything
he saw there. And what about him? Who was he? What was
he doing in those parts? Although the initial reception was not

very courteous, each felt a growing affinity toward the other. She felt even more—that that gentleman was admiring her. After the first few words, they were talking like good friends. The charming affability of both overcame the gruffness of suspicion, and a few minutes later, when they were going through the gate into the grounds, Doña Berta already knew who the man was. He was a famous painter, and while his latest master-work hung in Madrid, where half of Spain was admiring it, and the critics were busy singing the praises of his palette, he sought refuge from the incense and the clamor; and alone with his muse, solitude, he was wandering through the valleys and bypaths of Asturias, of which he was especially fond in the summer, in search of effects of light, shades of the green of the earth and the grays of the sky. He knew inch by inch all the secrets of the natural beauty of those folds of the coast; and finally, by being more daring or more fortunate than either the Romans or Moors, and after breaking through thickets and all kinds of dense underbrush, he had reached the very forest of Zaornín and the woodlands of Susacasa itself, which was like penetrating the heart of the heart of the mystery.

"Do you like it here?" Doña Berta asked the painter, smiling at him, as they sat together on a sofa of the great hall, which echoed their words and their steps.

"Yes, madam, very, very much," answered the painter with voice and gesture so that she could understand him better.

And he added under his breath:

"And I like you, too, you wonderful old woman, you living antique."

And, in truth, the distinguished artist was delighted. His meeting with Doña Berta had made him understand the special interest that one who lives there can give to the physical setting. Susacasa, which, when he discovered its close woods and greenery, had made him sing out, recalling Gayarre:

Oh, paradise . . .
You are mine . . .

suddenly acquired a dramatic meaning, a spiritual sense when
that slight figure, "full of outlines" in her thinness, and whose
"colors" could be summarized by saying wax, tobacco and
ashes, appeared amid those wilds. Her skin was wax, her head,
ashes, her eyes and clothing, tobacco. Little by little, and without realizing it, Doña Berta had been choosing dresses and
shawls of the color of dead leaves; and her hair, which was
rather curly, had turned as it dried out to a certain shade that
was not the white of silver, but the faded remains of its former
color, more melancholy than pure white, like the obstinate rose
pink of dusk on long days, which cannot quite decide to yield
the horizon to the black of night. To the painter, that woman
with those colors and that "ogival" contour seemed to be the
copy of a miniature in ivory. She struck him as something
escaped from the background of a precious antique fan. He
imagined that she must smell of sandalwood.

The artist accepted most gratefully the chocolate and the
preserves that Doña Berta offered him. They ate in the garden,
under a majestic laurel, a son or grandson of that other one.
They had spoken a great deal. Although he had tried to keep
the conversation away from himself, in order to observe better,
and to cast the light exclusively on the story of the old woman
and on her domain, Doña Berta's curiosity, and finally the
pleasure that we always derive from communicating our sorrows and hopes to others who seem "intelligent" of heart, made
even the painter forget his "study" at times and think about
himself. He also told his life story, which amounted to a series
of dreams and a series of pictures. Into his works he put his
own character. A rich, pleasant nature, but with something

mysterious, almost sacred about it, and sweet, heart-warming figures, sad or heroic, always modest, circumspect . . . and wholesome.

He had painted a girl he had loved in the setting of a fountain. The public too had fallen in love with his lady of Colunga; but when the painter returned in the spring, intending perhaps to marry her, he had found her dying of consumption. Since this memory was very painful to him, the artist turned away once again from thoughts of his personal life, in order to spare himself any further grief. By association of ideas, and piqued with curiosity, he took the liberty of asking the gentle lady, as tactfully as he could, if she had ever had a love affair, and if so, how it had turned out. In the face of such sweetness, of the candor reflected in the smile of that dark-haired, bearded "genius," and the sorrow of a lover who had been true, Doña Berta felt her heart fill up with her dead youth, as if the presence of a ghost, of her own dear love, had flooded it with a mysterious light. And impelled by the whimsical, adventurous spirit that had moved her a short while before to sing and to go out into the woods, she decided to tell about her love affair, omitting the dishonorable incident; but this she did with such lack of dexterity that the painter, who was a man of the world, was able, by tying up loose ends and clarifying certain obscurities that he had noted in her previous accounts of the Rondaliegos, to assume something very close to the hidden truth—in fact, the truth itself, in substance. So when she asked him if, in his opinion, the Captain had been a traitor or had died in the war, he could appreciate fully the kind of treachery in which the Liberal must have been involved, and he was inclined to believe, in view of what Doña Berta had said about his character, that her lover had not returned . . . because he could not.

Doña Berta thought: "It seems incredible, but this is the first time in my life that I have spoken to anyone else about these things!" And such was the case. Never before had those words, which represented the whole history of her soul, reached her lips. The painter, emerging suddenly from his meditation, then said something to this effect:

"I think I can see at this very moment the cause of your Captain's eternal absence, dear lady. A noble spirit like his, a gentleman of the quality that you depict, would certainly have returned from the wars to fulfill his promise to his beloved . . . unless a glorious death had first granted him its favors. Your Captain, as I understand it, did not return . . . because, when he went to request his discharge, he found himself inwardly compelled instead to discharge his duty. That very Liberal, who was fortunate enough to meet you and be loved by you, my worthy friend, because of the blood of his wounds, that Captain, I say, lost the fulfillment of his love because of the noble blood that coursed his veins. It is as if I could see it now, madam: he did not return because he died like a hero." . . .

Doña Berta, whose small eyes were shining with a kind of mystical madness, was about to speak; but the artist put out his hand, and continued:

"Here is where our stories meet, and when I tell you about the inspiration of my latest painting—the one that has been acclaimed so, both here and abroad, without its really deserving such praise—then you will understand why I presume, why I feel intuitively, that your Captain acted just as mine did. I also have 'my' Captain. He was a very dear friend . . . ; that is, we knew each other for a long time; but his death, his glorious, beautiful death, made him the incarnation of my visions as a painter who attempts to portray a heart in a face. My latest painting, madam, the one that even you, who have no contact with the outside world, knew something about through the newspapers that your peas and sugar come wrapped in, is . . . certainly the least bad of all my efforts. And do you know why? Because I envisioned it suddenly, and I saw it in reality first. Some years ago, during the second civil war, although I was already fairly well-known and recognized, I had not achieved what you might call fame; and, because it suited my purse and my plans, I accepted a correspondent's job that an illustrated foreign newspaper offered me to make current sketches of Spanish life, and especially of the war. With this commission, plus my great passion for strong emotions, and my desire to gather accurate material for a major portrait of military heroism that I had in mind, I went off to the wars in the North, determined to see actual combat at first hand, so that my own physical danger might afford me the insight I desired. I looked for danger, then, not because I wanted to risk my life, but in order to be *close to* heroic death. People say, and even certain famous writers have said, that each individual sees nothing great, nothing poetic in a war. This is not true—for a painter. At least, for a painter like me. Well, during that war I met 'my' Captain. He allowed me to do certain things that military discipline probably did not authorize, like being at times where only a soldier was permitted. My Captain was a brave fellow and a gambler; but he played so well and was so honorable in his dealings that gambling seemed almost a virtue in him, since it gave him the opportunity to display so many of his good qualities. One day I spoke to him about his foolhardy daring, and he frowned. 'I am not foolhardy, or even brave,' he said peevishly. 'I am obliged to be almost a coward. . . . At least, I have to be careful about risking my life. My life is not mine . . . ; it belongs to a creditor. Recently, a friend of mine, a fellow officer, prevented me from killing myself because, for the first time in my life,

I had gambled more than I owned, and had lost a sum that I could not pay back to my opponent. My friend, who surprised me in the moment of desperation that was leading me to suicide, came to my aid. I paid my debt with his money . . . , and now I owe him my money, my life, and my gratitude. But my friend warned me, after it was already too late for me to return it to him, that with that sum he had placed his honor in my hands. "Live," he said, "so that you can pay me back by working and saving as much as you can. Some day I shall have to give back that amount that I had available today and that I used to save your life; and if I don't give it back, I shall lose my reputation. Stay alive so that you can help me recoup that small fortune and save my honor." The honor of two people, his honor and mine, depend, then, on my life. And so, Mr. Artist, I try to avoid, or at least I should try to avoid, combat. But I have two addictions: war and gambling, and since I am obliged neither to gamble nor to die, I shall request my discharge, as soon as I can do so honorably. And in the meantime, I shall be very cautious.' That, madam, is more or less what my Captain told me; and I noticed that, on the following day, he did not take any unnecessary chances during an encounter with the enemy. But the weeks passed, there was more combat, and he began again to be foolhardy. This time I didn't tell him how his conduct struck me. Until, at last, there came 'the day of my picture' " . . .

The painter stopped. He paused for breath, reflected a moment as he was wont to; that is, he recomposed in his mind the picture, not as it appeared in his masterpiece, but as it had happened in reality.

Doña Berta, thanking the artist for shouting so that she would not miss a single word, listened in astonishment to the story of the famous painting, and learned that on a certain gray, cold day, a decisive battle had brought the Captain's men to the extreme of despair that ends either in a shameful rout or in heroism. They were all about to retreat, when the gambler, who owed his life to a creditor, hurled himself into a sure death, just as he would wager his whole fortune on a single card. And death surrounded him like a halo of fire and blood. He took many of his men with him into death and glory. But first there was a moment, the one that had become inscribed on the artist's memory as with a flash of lightning, filling his imagination; a moment when the gambler captain, standing atop a battlement, shone alone, as in sublime exaltation, while below him and in the distance the soldiers hesitated, fear and doubt painted on their faces.

"That man's gesture, which, miraculously, I was able to preserve exactly and incorporate into my general idea, was of such extraordinary expressiveness that it removed it from all classical and conventional depiction. There were no 'canonical' lines in it to show the fervor of war, the rapture of patriotism. It was something very different . . . ; there was pain, there was regret, there was blind passion and overwhelming impulse in those eyes, in that forehead, in that mouth, in those arms. It was obvious that that soldier was plunging into heroic death as into the abyss of a fascinating temptation that one is powerless to resist. The public and the critics have fallen in love with my Captain. Everyone has interpreted in his own way the special ideality of the face and of the whole attitude, but all of them have seen in it the best part of the painting, my major accomplishment: They see a mysterious spiritual conflict of intense force, which they admire without understanding, try as they will to divine the reason for their admiration. But *I* know the secret of my triumph; it is this, madam; it is what I saw that day in that man who disappeared amid the smoke, the blood, and the panic that soon blotted everything from view. The rest of us had to retreat finally; his heroism was wasted . . . ; but my painting will preserve his memory. What the world will not know is that my Captain died violating his pledged word not to seek out danger." . . .

"That's how *mine* died," exclaimed Doña Berta ecstatically, standing up and extending one hand as if enraptured. "Yes, my heart shouts to me that he also abandoned me for a death of glory!"

And Doña Berta, who never had spoken or gestured like a sibyl in all her life, dropped into her chair and wept, wept with such despair that the painter was really taken aback, and it struck him that there before him was a statue of History shedding tears over the anonymous dust of forgotten acts of heroism, of great virtues ignored, and great sorrows unrecorded.

A cold breeze blew by; the old woman shivered, stood up, and indicated to the painter with a gesture that he should follow her. They returned to the great hall, and Doña Berta, reclining on the sofa, kept on sobbing.

VI

Sabelona came in quietly and lit all the lights on the silver candelabras that adorned a console table. She felt that her idea of illuminating the dig dark hall without anyone's telling her to do so was quite an inspiration. Night was falling, but neither the painter nor Doña Berta noticed it. While Berta hid her face in her hands, so that Sabel would not see that she had been crying, the artist began to walk up and down the long room, his head bowed, his heart flooded with deep, intense emotions. But when he reached the console, the light attracted his attention, he raised his head, looked around, and saw on the wall directly in front of him the portrait of a young woman dressed and groomed in the fashion of some forty or more years before. It took him some time to make out her features; but when at last he could grasp the full image clearly, he felt a chill sweep across his body like a whiplash. He asked Sabelona by signs who the lady of the portrait was; and Sabel, with another gesture, serenely pointed out the old woman, who still sat there with her face hidden between her hands. Sabelona tiptoed out of the room, for that was her way of respecting the troubles of the "masters" when she did not understand them; and as the painter, pale and almost afraid, continued contemplating the portrait, he did not realize that two tears had welled in his eyes. And when he started to pace again on those creaking chestnut boards, he thought to himself: "Things like this don't belong in painting; besides, because of their accidental, implausible character, they don't really belong in poetry either: they belong only in life itself . . . and in hearts that can understand them." And he paused to look at Doña Berta, who was somewhat calmer now and had stopped crying; but, with her hands crossed over her skinny knees, she sat there staring at the floor with lifeless eyes. Like a ghost, her dead love was passing once again through that wrinkled, rigid heart, just as the perfumed breeze leaves a garden to kiss the marble slabs of the tomb.

"My friend," said the old woman, standing up and wiping away the last tears with her thin, rootlike fingers, "time has sped by while we were talking about my life, and now it is too late for you to find some place else to stay. Night is falling, and"—she added with a smile—"although I'm afraid that people may gossip, you will have to have dinner and spend the night in Posadorio."

The painter accepted gladly and without any coaxing.

"I intend to pay for my lodgings," he said.

"How?"

"By making a copy of that portrait tomorrow. I'll make a

few sketches so that I can paint another canvas later on at home—a portrait like that one, in so far as it resembles the original—that is, if it really does."

"They say it does," Doña Berta broke in, shrugging her shoulders with a false modesty that was amusing amid her sad indifference. "They say," she continued, "that it is a perfect resemblance of a certain Berta Rondaliego, whom I scarcely remember."

"Well then, my copy, I may say without boasting—will be slightly less bad than that one, in technique . . . ; and absolutely faithful as a likeness."

And he did what he promised. On the following morning, the painter, who had slept in the walnut bed in which the last Rondaliego had died, got up very early. He had the portrait brought out to the garden, and there, in the open air, he began his task. He ate with Doña Berta, studying her intently when she wasn't watching, and, after his coffee, went back to work. In the middle of the afternoon, when he finished his sketches, he packed up his effects, took leave of his new friend with a warm embrace, and, walking across the Aren, disappeared among the brush, waving his last good-bye from afar with a white handkerchief that shimmered like a flag.

Once again Doña Berta was left alone with her thoughts; but how different her thoughts were! Her Captain, most assuredly, had not returned because he hadn't been able to; he had not been a scoundrel, as her brothers used to say; he had been a hero. . . . Yes, indeed, just like the other one, the painter's Captain, the gambler who gambled even his honor to win glory. . . . Doña Berta's regrets, which were more nostalgia than remorse, became increasingly poignant from that day when her heart told her, and she believed it truly, that her lover had been a hero, that he had died in the war, and that

that was why he had not come back for her. Such being the
case, wouldn't he have the right to demand an account of their
son? What had she done to find the "fruit of their love"?
Almost nothing; she had let herself be terrorized, and she remembered with horror the days when she herself had come to
believe that to undertake secret investigations in search of her
son would be the height of foolishness. And now . . . how late
it was for all that! . . . Either her son had really died, or
he was lost forever. It was impossible even to dream of locating him. She herself had lost the maternity within her . . . ;
now she was but a grandmother. A vague twinge of conscience
told her that she could not feel as strongly as she used to long
ago; the minutiae of daily life, the prose of her chores, distracted her constantly from her grief, from her meditations.
Her thoughts would return, it is true, but they flitted in and
out of her mind, and that perpetual rhythm of forgetting and
remembering was making her ill. She herself began to think:
I must be getting senile. This is a mania, not a sentiment.
And still, she thought at times, particularly after dinner, before
going to bed, as she walked through the spacious kitchen in
the light of Sabelona's candle—she thought that she had within
her a hidden energy that would lead her to great self-sacrifice,
to total abnegation . . . if there were a reason for it. "Oh!
where wouldn't I go for my son . . . dead or alive! What
wouldn't I give—the years of my life, if I had any left to
offer, or my years in heaven, and I would gladly spend them
in purgatory, just to be able to kiss his fleshless bones! I don't
know whether it is because I am like the grave itself, a soul
that is already disintegrating, or because I have a premonition
of death, but whenever I imagine that I look for him and find
him, involuntarily I always seem to find his remains, not his
open arms waiting to embrace me."

While Doña Berta was immersed in these and other such bitter thoughts, she was surprised to receive a note that the painter sent her by messenger a week after his departure. A villager, who disappeared immediately without waiting for a tip or refreshment, delivered to Doña Berta a large package that contained the painter's card and two portraits in oil. One was of Berta Rondaliego, an exact copy of the picture that hung over the console in Posadorio's great hall, but an idealized copy full of expression and life, thanks to the artist's great skill. Doña Berta, who hardly recognized herself in the portrait in her living room, saw herself suddenly—in a mirror of more than forty years back, when she looked at the new one. The other portrait that the painter sent had at the bottom a caption that said in small red letters: "My Captain." It was only a head. But when Doña Berta saw it, she gasped and let out a cry of astonishment. That captain of his was also hers —hers, fused with her very being, with the Berta of forty years ago, with the Berta of that other picture. She put the canvases together, compared them, and saw the marked resemblance that the painter had noted between the picture in the living room and the Captain of his memories, and of his masterpiece. But aside from that, and even more important, she saw another likeness that was even more pronounced, between certain features, in fact the whole expression of that face, and the features and expression that she recalled from the image that was engraved in her mind, indelibly chiseled there, just as a drop of water carves its path through stone. Her only love, her dead love, had forged in her imagination a fixed, indestructible image, resembling in its way granite polished by the kisses of many generations of the faithful, who cry and wait at the feet of a stone Virgin or saint. The painter's "Captain" was like a restoration of the portrait of another Captain that she still saw in her mind's eye, somewhat dimmed by time, with the dark film of her hidden, prolonged devotion; smoky from the holocaust of old love, the way church pictures are blurry from wax and incense. And so, when Sabelona came to call Doña Berta, she found her pale, her face distraught, and almost in a faint. All she said was "I don't feel well," and she let her servant put her to bed. On the following day, the local doctor came and he shrugged his shoulders. He didn't prescribe any medication. "It's just old age," he said. Within three days, Doña Berta was running about the house again, more active than ever, and with a feverish glow in her eyes. Sabelona was amazed to see a messenger leaving Posadorio with a sealed letter early the next morning. To whom could she be writing? What could there be way out there in the outside world, that might concern her? Her mistress had written to the painter; she knew his name and the name of the county in which he was accustomed to spend his summers; but she knew nothing else—not the name of the village in which the artist had his country abode, nor whether he was home at the time or far away, on one of his frequent excursions.

The messenger returned in four days, without a reply and without Doña Berta's letter. After a great many difficulties and endless inquiries, he had gotten them to accept the letter at an inn in the county seat, where they assured him they would deliver it to the painter when he returned there, probably within a week. It was useless to look for him immediately. He could be very near, or twenty leagues away. Day after day slipped by, and Doña Berta, almost out of her mind with impatience, waited in vain for news of the painter. In the meantime, her letter, which revealed the secret of her honor in veiled terms, was traveling about in God knows whose hands. Several unhappy weeks passed, and the poor old woman, whose memory was very feeble, began to forget exactly what she had written to the painter. Now all she remembered was, vaguely, that she had told him by implication the story of her "sin," and she begged him, by everything he held most dear, for information about "his Captain": What was his name? Who was he? Where did he come from? What about his family? And she also wanted to know who had given the money to the poor hero who had died without repaying it; and how would it be possible to locate the creditor. . . . . And finally—oh! what a mad thing to do!—she asked him about his painting, about his masterpiece. Did he still own it or was it already sold? How much would it cost? Would she have enough money left to buy the painting if she sold everything she owned and first paid off the Captain's creditor? Yes, she had spoken about all that in her letter, though she no longer remembered how she phrased it. But of one thing she was absolutely sure—that she would not turn back. While she lay in her bed, during the few days in which she was confined to it, she had made up her mind to go through with that "madness," and she was not the least bit sorry. Yes, indeed, she was determined; she *wanted* to pay her "son's" debt, she *wanted* to buy the picture that portrayed her son's heroic death and that contained her son's *whole body* at the very moment when he was surrendering his life.

She had no idea of the approximate sale value of Susacasa, Posadorio and the Aren; nor even the remotest notion about the amount of her son's debt and the price of the painting. But it didn't make any difference. That is why she wanted to find out, that is why she had written to the artist. Her reasons for her "madness" were quite simple. She had never given her son anything while the poor fellow was alive; now she had "found" him dead, and she wanted to give him everything; her son's honor was her honor; what he owed, she owed, and she wanted to repay it, if she had to beg for charity afterwards. And if she still had enough money to buy the painting after paying off the debt, she would buy it if she starved to death. Because it would be like having the grave of the two captains; it would mean restoring their honor, and besides she would have the faithful likeness of her beloved son and the reflection of that other beloved image. Doña Berta felt that her unshakable, absolute, irrevocable determination was due to an extraordinary invisible impulse that had gotten into her head like something from without and was dominating her completely.

"I certainly must have gone crazy," she thought. "But so much the better; I'm happier, I'm less uneasy; this decision is something I can hold on to. I would rather suffer the material loss that may come from it than endure the unbearable *tick-tock* of my old regrets, the flitting back and forth of the same ideas. . . ."

In order to encourage her own heroic resolution, in order to make her sacrifice without duress, but from her own desire and pleasure, and not because of that irresistible impulse that didn't seem really her own, Doña Berta tried to stir up her mother love, to awaken her maternal instincts . . . but she couldn't. She wore out her spirit in vain; the images that might fill her with tenderness wouldn't come to her mind; she didn't know how to be a mother. She tried to imagine her son as a child, abandoned . . . left without a lap to cry on. . . . She couldn't; the son that she saw was a brave captain standing on a battlement, amid fire and smoke . . . : it was the head that the painter had sent her. And she would tell herself, "This is just as though I wanted to fall in love at my age . . . and couldn't."

Nevertheless, her determination was absolute. With the painter's help or without it, she would look for the picture, she would see it, oh yes!, she would see it before she died!, and she would seek out the creditor or his heirs and she would pay them her son's debt. "It seems that we have two souls," she would say to herself at times, "one that dries up with the body, and that is the one that dreams, that feels strongly, picturesquely; and another deeper, purer soul, that cries without tears, that loves without memory and even without sensation . . . and that is the soul that God must take with him to Heaven."

When a few months went by without any word from the painter, Doña Berta decided to act on her own: There was no reason to tell Sabelona about it until the final moment, the moment of parting. Good-bye, Zaornín, good-bye, Susacasa, good-bye Aren, good-bye, Posadorio! Her mistress received a visit that surprised Sabel and made her shudder.

Mr. Pumariega, Don Casto Pumariega, a retired notary and an actively practicing usurer, a field rat, a sponge on the area, a great collector of productive lands and of all kinds of real estate, presented himself in Posadorio and, with that perpetual smile that had made so many destitute villagers shed tears of blood, he asked for Miss Rondaliego. This gentleman lived in the county seat, several kilometers from Zaornín. He arrived on horseback, dismounted and, ever smiling, ordered that his mare be given some fodder, but not from the new batch; and then, thinking better of it, he went himself to the stable and, with his own hands, filled the manger with hay.

He still had some pieces of straw in his beard and stuck to the lenses of his eyeglasses when Doña Berta, pale, her voice quivering, but resolved upon her sacrifice, received him in the living room. She got right down to business. It would have been absurd, even shameful, to let Mr. Pumariega know the sentimental reasons for her strange decision. Don Casto did not know *why*, but the fact was that Doña Berta needed, in cold cash that she could carry away in her pocket, all the money she could get from the fair sale of Susacasa, including the Aren and Posadorio. The house, its appurtenances, the cornfield, the woods, the meadow, everything—but in cash. If he preferred to lend her the money, with a mortgage on the aforementioned properties, that would be all right, too; she probably would not make many interest payments, because she expected to die soon, and Mr. Pumariega could have everything; if he did not want such a deal, she would sell it, sell it outright.

Mr. Pumariega was on the point of being shocked by the almost uncanny determination of the Rondaliego woman, but he remembered that it would be much more practical to consider forthwith the advantages of the transaction, without letting surprise enter into it at all. Amazement ill befit the matter at hand, especially when he was being offered a profitable deal. And so, just as if it involved the sale of some barrels of cider or the hay crop of that autumn season, Don Casto plunged into the negotiations, without any manifestation of surprise, or even curiosity.

And as was his custom, when he gave his arguments to show the advantages of a mortgage loan, he called the contractual parties A and B. "The mortgagee B, the mortgage M, the chattel C . . ." That is the way Don Casto spoke, for he hated anything personal and never saw in the "party of the other part" a human being, a fellow man, but a letter, an element of a formula that had to be eliminated. Doña Berta, who had acquired certain experience and even shrewdness as a result of administering her estate for many years, realized that she was caught like a fly in a spider web; but she didn't really care. Don Casto insisted on trying to fool her, on making her see that she would not necessarily lose Susacasa under the plans that he proposed to her, and she pretended to fall into the trap. She understood that Pumariega would come out of that venture as owner of all the Rondaliego properties, but that, precisely, was the essence of her sacrifice. That was what she wanted—she wanted the scoundrel to crucify her. When the transaction was settled, Doña Berta hung anxiously on the obsequious, fawning, cringing moneylender's every word, waiting to find out the exact amount, how many thousands of *duros* the "field rat" was going to give her. When Don Casto told her, Doña Berta felt her heart jump with joy. The usurer was offering her more than she had expected; she hadn't thought that her run-down, impoverished lands could be worth so many thousands of *duros*.

When Pumariega was leaving Posadorio, Sabelona and the caretaker, who watched him out of the corner of their eyes as they helped him mount, saw him smiling as usual; but, besides, his little eyes were sparkling right through the crystals of his glasses. Shortly afterwards, Don Casto stopped on a hill that overlooked Zaornín and turned his horse around so that he could contemplate the boundaries and the fine appearance of his "new possessions." Out of false modesty, he always called a "possession" those properties that he knew how to make his own with all the hooks and claws of legal sanction that the stamped documents and the books of the Town Registry afforded him.

Three days later, Pumariega was in Posadorio again, accompanied by the new notary, whom he controlled, and by several witnesses and experts, all of them his debtors. Being fleeced by the cold shears of Mr. Pumariega was not as brief and simple an affair as Doña Berta wished, and had imagined it to be. Pumariega wanted all kinds of guarantees and tried to bewilder the party of the other part completely with legal formalities and complications. The only thing that Doña Berta objected to energetically was appearing personally in the county seat. That she would not do; she would not budge from

Susacasa . . . until the day she left to take the train for Madrid. Everything was settled, finally, and Doña Berta was able to put into the little box that held her old secrets the thousands of *duros* that the usurer was "lending" her. She understood fully that she was saying good-bye forever to Posadorio, to the Aren, to everything. . . . How could she ever repay that large sum she was being lent? How could she pay even the interest, if she did live a few more years? A miracle might happen. That would be the only way. If the miracle did come along, Susacasa would continue to be hers, and this hope was always an encouragement, or at least, a consolation. Yes, she would lose everything. But she was going to pay her son's debts, buy the painting . . . and then die of hunger, if necessary.

And what about Sabelona? Don Casto had given her to understand clearly that in order to guarantee the security of his mortgage, he would have to entrust the administration of said mortgaged properties to a completely reliable overseer; he had no objection to the overseer's remaining in his lodge for the time being, but as for the keys to Posadorio and the care of the "mansion" and its appurtenances . . . he preferred to take charge of those himself. So Sabelona could not remain in Posadorio. Her mistress hesitated before asking her to go along with her. It was a question of the expense; she had to economize, to reduce her capital as little as possible, for she did not know whether even the whole amount would cover both the debt and the price of the painting; so any expense that could be eliminated would have to be forgone. Sabelona meant another mouth to feed, another lodger to house, another person to transport. Practically a double expense. Nevertheless, Doña Berta, promising herself to make up the extra cost by cutting down on her own personal comforts, offered to take her servant to Madrid with her.

Sabelona did not have the courage to accept. She had not gone crazy like her mistress, and she saw the dangers. Too many misfortunes had already befallen her without looking for another, greater disaster, sure death. She go to Madrid! She had always thought about those faraway things vaguely, as if they were in the other world. She wasn't sure that there really were places so distant from Susacasa. . . . Madrid! The train . . . so many people . . . so many streets . . . Impossible! She hoped her mistress would forgive her, but Sabel's affection and loyalty did not go to that extreme. She was being asked to perform an act of heroism, and she just did not have it in her. Sabelona, like St. Peter, refused her mistress, deserted her in her deed of sublime madness, abandoned her in a moment of danger, at the foot of the cross. Just as, if Doña Berta were dying, Sabelona would be terribly sorry, but she would not accompany her to the grave, so now she was abandoning her by the side of the road to Madrid. The maid had some distant relatives in a nearby county, and there she would go, much to her sorrow, during her mistress's absence, now that Mr. Pumariega wanted to carry off the keys of Posadorio, against all laws divine and human, according to Sabel.

"But, aren't you the mistress? What right does he have to give orders here?"

"Please leave me alone about that, Isabel; he can give all the orders he wants to, because he is the one who is giving me the money. All this is practically his already."

Doña Berta was deeply hurt that her companion for so many years, the companion of her whole life, should desert her in the supreme peril to which she was exposing herself. But she forgave her servant's weakness, because she herself needed all her courage, all her unshakable determination, to leave her home and plunge into that labyrinth of roads, towns, noises, and strange people—"enemies." The poor woman sighed and said to herself: "Since Sabel isn't coming . . . I'll take the cat." When the maid found out that the cat was going too, she looked at him aghast, as if consulting him. To tell the truth, it did not seem right to her to take advantage of the poor animal because he could not say "no," as she did. But if the cat knew what he was in for, she was sure that he too would refuse to accompany his mistress. Sabel did not dare, however, to object, even though it was she who had brought the little animal into the house, and he was rightfully hers. But she couldn't take him to the home of her distant relatives: two more mouths to feed would be too much. And he couldn't remain alone in Posadorio, and much less with Don Casto, who would starve him to death. So it was decided that the cat should go to Madrid with Doña Berta.

VII

One morning Sabelona arose from her chaste bed, looked out of a kitchen window, peered at the sky with one hand placed over her eyes as a shade, and with a sour gesture and an even sourer tone of voice, exclaimed, speaking to herself for a change:

. "What a day for traveling!"

And thereupon she thought to herself, without saying it: "The last day!" She lit the fire, swept up a little, went to get fresh water, made her own coffee, and then her mistress's chocolate. And as though nothing extraordinary were about to take place, she gave her customary knocks on Doña Berta's bedroom door, her usual way of informing her that breakfast was ready; and just as if everything were not coming to an end that very morning, as if what was going to happen within an hour were not like the end of the world to her, she, Sabel, plunged into the routine order of her domestic duties, most of which were unnecessary then, because from that night on nobody would be sleeping in Posadorio any more.

While she was scouring a bucket, the cat, covered with dew, and with the mist of that dull, dank morning sticking to his shiny white body, came in through the garden gate, which was at the level of the kitchen. Sabelona looked at him with affection, envy, and pity. And she said to herself: "Poor animal! He doesn't know what's waiting for him." The cat had made absolutely no preparations for his trip; the life he lived, as far as he knew, since time immemorial, surely seemed eternal to him. The possibility of a change was not dreamt of in his philosophy. He began licking the plates of the previous evening's supper, just as any good epicurean would have done in his situation.

Doña Berta entered quietly; she saw the chocolate on the kneading board, and there, as always, she went to drink it. The preparations for the journey had been made, down to the last detail, many days before. All there remained to do was to leave, and, before that, to say good-bye. Mistress and servant hardly spoke during that last scene of their life together. An hour went by, and Don Casto Pumariega, who had "taken charge of everything" with an affability that no one had the heart to thank him for, arrived. He would take Doña Berta right to the station, the nearest one to Zaornín; he would check her baggage; he would put her in a second-class coach (Doña Berta had not wanted first class, in order to save some money), and all set! In Madrid, the owner of a cheap boarding-house was expecting her. Don Casto had written to him, so that the proprietor should be indebted to him for sending a lodger. This is where he himself used to stop when he went to Madrid, even though he was so rich.

With Don Casto there came into the kitchen a young fellow

from whom Pumariega had rented the donkey that Doña Berta was to ride to the station, which was two leagues from Posadorio. Mistress and servant, who had been so quiet, who had seemed even hostile to each other that morning, as if they were silently blaming each other for that separation, felt an overwhelming tenderness, a swooning weakness, in the presence of those "who had come to fetch them." They burst into tears and cried for a long time in each other's arms.

The cat stopped licking plates and looked at them dumbfounded.

That was something new in that house, where affection was never expressed. They all loved each other, but they made no open manifestation of it. He himself was treated very well, but no kisses or petting. Just in case they needed him, he brushed against his old ladies' skirts and scowled at Mr. Pumariega.

Doña Berta asked Don Casto to wait a moment, and she went out through the garden gate. She climbed the hill, reached the top, and paused there to contemplate her domain. The dense woods were swaying gently, all shiny with the mist, and they seemed to be softly complaining. Some sparrows were chirping. Doña Berta did not have even the consolation of poetizing the solemn scene of her farewell. To her lifeless, preoccupied imagination, Nature was not kind enough to offer the personal note that usually gives such comfort to melancholy dreamers. Neither the Aren, nor the cornfield, nor the woods, nor the "mansion," said anything to her. They merely stood there, indifferent, unaware of her going away; their egoism was the same as Sabel's, though theirs was more frank: the kind that the cat would have shown if they had consulted his wishes about the trip. It didn't matter. Doña Berta did not feel that she was loved by her lands, but just the same she loved them infinitely. Yes, indeed. In this world, one loves not only people, but things. The Aren, the cornfield, the vegetable garden,

Posadorio, were part of her soul, for themselves, without any need for linking them with memories of human loves. One must know how to love Nature the way that true lovers love, in spite of being rebuffed. To adore the idol, to adore the stone, something that neither feels nor can reciprocate, is the supreme adoration. The greatest believer is the one who remains prostrate before the altar that bears no image. The sparrows were chirping. They seemed to be saying: "What do you have to say to us? You are going away, we are staying; you are crazy, we are not; you are going off to look for the portrait of your son . . . and you are not sure that he is your son. Good-bye and good luck." But Doña Berta forgave the birds, which, after all, were very little, and even the green Aren itself, which, still crueler, just kept quiet. The woods were moaning, yes, they were; but slightly, like a child who, tired of crying, converts his wail into a rhythm and amuses himself with his grief. And Doña Berta realized, with the clairvoyance of those supreme moments with Nature, realized that the woods were not moaning because she was leaving—they always complained like that; that dull, dank morning cold was one of the thousand forms of boredom that can be read so often in Nature. The woods were grumbling, as usual, with the boredom of everything that lives stuck to the earth and of everything that moves through space in the world, bound by gravity as by a chain. All the things she saw seemed to her then like prisoners who bemoan their shackles but nevertheless love their jail. She, who was free, could break the chain, and she had broken it . . . ; but caught on the chain remained half of her soul.

"Good-bye, good-bye," said Doña Berta, wanting to go down quickly; but she didn't move. In her heart was the pain of many generations of Rondaliegos who were saying good-bye to their land. Her father, her brothers, her grandparents . . . , all of them there, in her chest and in her throat, choking with pain along with her. . . .

"But Doña Berta, we are going to miss the train!" shouted Pumariega down there below; and to her it sounded as if he were saying: "You are going to miss the gallows."

Don Casto and his lackey were already in the patio; the executioner and his assistant, and also the donkey on which Doña Berta was to ride to the "scaffold."

The cat was going in a basket.

VIII

Dawn was breaking, and the snow that fell in heaps, with that feline silence that has the treacherous air of a cat's walk, was spreading shovelfuls of ermine, layer by layer, over the entire breadth of the Puerta del Sol, and had already erased hours ago the tracks of the early morning passersby. All the doors were closed. There was only one ajar, that of the Café Principal; a cruller stand that someone had attempted to pull out into the open air had been dragged into the doorway of the Government Building.

Doña Berta, who was contemplating the spectacle from a corner of Carmen Street, did not understand why they let people fry crullers, or, at least, sell them, in the doorway of the Ministry; but the truth was that the stand had disappeared from there, and with it two officers and another man who looked like a telegraph operator. And the square remained empty; empty except for Doña Berta and the snow. The old lady stood there motionless, her feet shod in overshoes sunk in the softness of it, her open umbrella looking as if it were faced with white cloth. "Just like back home," she thought. "That's the way the Aren must be."

She was going to early morning Mass. The Church was her

refuge; only there did she find something that resembled home. She felt herself linked to her "fellow human beings" of the Court only through the bond of religion. "After all," she would say to herself, "all Catholics, all brothers." And this thought took away some of the fear that all strangers inspired in her, not so much as individuals, but considered as a whole, as a multitude, as "people." The Mass was like the one she used to hear in Zaornín, on the crossroad of Pie del Oro. The priest said the same things and did the same things. That was always a consolation. That was the reason for her hearing Mass every day; but her getting up so early was for another reason. Contemplating Madrid when it was deserted reconciled her somewhat with it. The streets seemed less hostile, more like the small, narrow lanes she knew; the trees, more like the "real trees." She had wanted to stroll through the outskirts . . . but they were so far away! Her legs were so skinny, and the coaches were so expensive and so dangerous! . . . Finally, once or twice, she reached the limits of that seemingly endless conglomeration of houses . . . ; but she gave up such discoveries, because the "country" was not country; it was a desert. All brown! All dried up! Her heart tightened, and she felt terribly sorry for herself. "I should have died without seeing this, without knowing that there was such desolation in the world; for a poor old woman from Susacasa, that joyful green retreat, it is too painful to be far away from the real world, from the real earth, and to be separated from the freshness, from the grass, from the branches, by these leagues and leagues of stone and dust." Looking at the sad expanses, she had the sensation that she was chewing dust and touching dry earth, and her hands twitched convulsively. She felt so foreign to everything that surrounded her that, at times, in the midst of it all, she had to restrain herself from calling for help, from begging them for pity's sake to take her to her Posadorio. In spite of such sad thoughts, she would walk through the streets smiling, smiling from fear of the throngs, whom she anxiously courted, whom she wished to flatter, to adulate, so that they should not do her any harm. She gave everyone the right of way on the sidewalk. Since she was deaf, she tried to guess with her glance whether the passerby into whom she bumped was saying something to her; and that is why she smiled, and greeted people with expressive nods, and murmured apologies. The people must have liked the poor, neat, lively old lady dressed in tobacco-colored silk. Many of them smiled at her too, and made way for her. Nobody had robbed her or tried to defraud her. Nevertheless, she was still afraid, and anyone who saw her stop and cross herself before leaving the doorway of her house would never suspect that it was an act of heroism for that old woman to go out into the street every day.

She was afraid of the multitude . . . , but most of all, she was afraid of being run down, trampled, crushed by horses, by wheels. Every carriage, every cart, was a loose, wild animal that was about to jump on her. She plunged into crossing the Puerta del Sol the way a Christian martyr would enter the arena of the amphitheater. The trolley looked like a cautious monster, an insidious serpent, to her. She imagined that the guillotine was something like those hidden wheels that slid like a knife along the two iron lines. The noise of wheels, footsteps, bells, whistles and horns reached her brain confused and awful, in her mysterious world of shadow-sound. When the trolley approached from behind and she became aware of its proximity through signs that were almost intuitions, through a kind of reflection of imminent danger in the faces of the other passersby, through a tremor that ran through her, through the noise she could not quite fathom, Doña Berta would move away with a nervous agility that seemed impossible in an old woman. She would let the beast pass, turning her face toward it, and she would also smile at the trolley, and even make it an unconscious bow; pure sycophantism, because in the bottom of her heart she hated it, especially because it was a traitor and a sneak. How it jumped at her! What barbarous, refined cruelty! . . . Many passersby had saved her from serious dangers, pulling her out from between the feet of horses or the wheels of carriages; they caught her in their arms, they pushed her to keep her from being run over. . . . And how grateful she was! How she would turn toward her savior, outdoing herself in gestures and words of praise and indebtedness! "I owe you my life. Sir, if I could do something . . . I am deaf, very deaf, please forgive me; but if there is anything that I could do for you . . ." And those passing arms of providence left her with the words still on her lips. "Why is it that I am so afraid of people, when there are so many good people who pull a person out from the clutches of death?" It would not have surprised her if the indifferent mob let her be trampled by a horse, or cut in two by a wheel, without extending a hand to her, without a shout of warning. What connection did she have with all those strangers? What did she matter in the world outside of Zaornín, rather, of Susacasa? That is why she was so grateful to those who helped her escape from a carriage, or from the trolley. . . . She too wanted to serve her fellow man. Street life, in her opinion, was like a daily battle into which all the residents of Madrid entered impassively, valiantly: the battle of collisions, of accidents. Well, in that journey of endless dangers, she too wanted to help her brethren, for, after all, that is what they were, although they were so different, so strange. And she always walked along, ever on the lookout, compensating with her sight for her hearing, and with her attention fixed on her own steps and on everyone else's. At each intersection, on every cobblestoned crossing, in each square, there were salvos (that is how she thought of it) of horses and carriages, the greatest perils; and when she came to these tremendous crises of crossing the street, she redoubled her attention, and, afraid as she was, she thought about the others just as much as about herself; and great was her satisfaction when she could save a child, an old man, a poor old lady like herself, anyone at all, from one of those misfortunes. One day, as she stood on the sidewalk by the Imperial during the hour of heaviest traffic, she saw a drunkard crossing the Puerta del Sol, making large esses with the thousand circumlocutions and periphrases of his feet; and meanwhile, trolleys, buggies and cabs, public carriages and carts, and horses and loaded-down porters, were coming and going, like arrows that cross in the air. . . . And the drunkard, sober because of his very insobriety, kept walking unperturbed, tracing every line of the most complete treatise on curves, reproducing every kind of orbit and ecliptic, without even dreaming of the danger, of the sure death, in that constant line of fire across which he was stumbling. Doña Berta watched him advance, retreat, miraculously escape every encounter, pursued in vain by the scornful shouts of coachmen and men on horses . . . ; and she, standing on the sidewalk, with the palms of her hands joined, prayed to God for that man, as she might have prayed from the shore for the life of a shipwrecked man who was drowning before her eyes.

And she did not breathe until she saw the drunkard in the safe harbor of the arms of a policeman, who was taking him she knew not where. Undoubtedly, Providence or the Guardian Angel watched over the fate and false steps of the drunkards of the capital!

That constant preoccupation with noise, with traffic, with collisions and accidents, had come to be an obsession, a mania, the immediate, constant, endlessly repeated material impression that, unfortunately, distracted her from her major concerns, from her tormented life as a "quester." Yes, she had to admit it; she was thinking much more about the dangers of these hordes of people, of the coaches and trolleys, than about "her case," her unequal combat with those wealthy people who opposed her fulfilling the desire that had drawn her to Madrid. She did not know how or why it happened, but since she had left Posadorio, her ideas and her heart had undergone an upheaval; she reasoned and felt more egoistically; she was very sorry for herself and thought of death with horror. How horrible it must be to go off to another world no less, when it was already such a great torment to take a few steps out of Susacasa, on this very earth, which, as far as appearances go, already seemed like a different one. Since she had boarded the train, she had been seized with a mad desire to turn back, to get off, to run away and find "her people"—who were Sabelona and the trees, and the meadow and the mansion . . . , all the things she was leaving so far behind. She lost the sense of distance, and it occurred to her that she had traveled through infinite extensions of space; she felt that it was not impossible that it would take centuries at least to retrace her course. . . . And what a headache she had! And how fleeting, it struck her, was the existence of all those other people, of all those indifferent strangers "without history," who went in and out of the second-class coach in which she was riding, who asked her for her tickets, who offered her services, and who took her in a buggy to an inn. She was lost, lost in the big, wide world, in the infinite universe, in a universe peopled with phantoms! It struck her that with so many people on the earth, each one lost some of his value; the life of this one or that one did not matter at all; and that is how everyone else must have thought, to judge from the indifference with which they met, spoke, and parted with each other forever. That hustling-bustling way of life, those confused hordes of people, seemed to her like the swarms of mosquitoes that she used to avoid in the woods and near the river in the summertime.

She spent a few days in Madrid without the least thought of budging, not even dreaming that somehow it might be possible to begin her inquiries to find out what she needed to know, to accomplish what had brought her to the capital. Without a doubt, it had been a crazy thing to do. For the present, she thought only about herself, about how she could keep from dying of disgust at the table, from dying of misery in her inside room that faced a dirty alley they called a "patio," and of cold in the narrow, filthy, hard, miserable bed. She took sick. Eight days in bed gave her some courage; she got up somewhat more disposed to orient herself to that inferno that she had not suspected could exist in this world. Her landlady at the inn became friendly with her; she tended to be a charitable person, but poverty did not let her be so completely. Doña Berta began to question people, to make inquiries . . . ; she left the house. And that is when her feverish obsession about the danger of the streets began. This fever would not go away as the fever of her illness did. But anyway, amidst her fears, amidst her "battles," she succeeded in finding out something: that the painting she was looking for "lay" deposited in a large building that was closed to the public, and the Government was keeping it there until it was decided whether a cabinet member would get it or whether a wealthy Latin American would take it first to his mansion in Madrid, and then, perhaps, to his palace in Havana. So much she knew, but not the price of the painting, which she still had not been able to see. And this is what she was involved in at the moment: in the necessary steps toward fulfilling her ambition to see it.

That cold, snowy morning was the morning of a day that was going to be very important for Doña Berta; through the influence of a fellow boarder, she had been offered as a favor an opportunity to see the famous painting, which was no longer on exhibit to the public, but was just lying, waiting to be wrapped, on the floor of a cold, empty room, way off in the outskirts of the city. What a peculiar coincidence! It was that day or maybe never. She would have to go through a great deal of snow. . . . But that didn't matter. She would take a carriage, something she usually did not do—that is, if the cabs were allowed to move about that day. She was going to see "her son"! In order to be well prepared, to enlist the good will of Heaven so that everything should turn out well in her bold pretensions, first she would go to early Mass at church. The Puerta del Sol, snowy, lonely, and silent, augured well. "This is how it must be back home. What a clean sheet! What lovely, unstained whiteness! No paths, no muddy, frosty tracks, no footprints . . . It looks like the snow of the Aren, that nobody steps on."

IX

In the dark, cold, empty church, she occupied a corner that she already considered her own. The lights of the altar and the lamps brought a familiar warmth, the warmth of a loved home, to the bottom of her soul. The priest's murmurings in Latin, mixed with his asthmatic coughs, sounded perfectly wonderful to her, like something from home. The altar images, that merged vaguely with the shadows, spoke silently of the solidarity of heaven and earth, of the constancy of faith, of the oneness of the world, which concept Doña Berta (without realizing it, of course) was losing in her hours of fear, depression, desperation. She left the church encouraged, brave, ready to fight for her cause. Ready to look for "her son" . . . and her son's creditors.

The appointed time arrived, after she had lunched quickly

and without any appetite. She went outside alone, holding her card of introduction, took a public cab, gave the address of that distant building, and when she heard the driver curse and saw him hesitate, as if looking for an excuse not to go so far, Doña Berta said to him, with a persuasive smile, "By the hour," and soon, step by step, a sad, drooping, yellowish animal was pulling her up the street. Doña Berta, with her pass in her hand, managed to get by the guards at the door; and after walking from room to room, chilled to death, hearing the dry, muffled blows of many hammers that were nailing up boxes, she came into the presence of a fat, poorly dressed man, who seemed to be directing that noisy, confused operation of moving the works of art. The paintings were being taken away; most of them had already gone; hardly any still remained on the walls. One had to walk carefully to avoid stepping on the canvases that carpeted the floor: how many thousands of *duros* that rug was worth! The large paintings, some of which were already famous, lay stretched out on a platform. The fat man read Doña Berta's card of introduction, stared intently at the old woman, and when she indicated to him, by smiling and pointing to one ear, that she was deaf, he scowled. Undoubtedly, he felt that it was too great an effort to raise his voice a little for the sake of such an insignificant being, who had been recommended by one of those nobodies who consider themselves friends and are merely casual acquaintances.

"So you want to see Valencia's painting? Well, you almost missed the boat, Grandma. Within half an hour it will be on its way to its new home."

"Where is it, where is it? Which one is it?" she asked, trembling.

"That one."

And the fat man pointed out with his finger a large sheet of gray, almost dirty-looking, cloth that was lying at his feet.

"That one, that one! But . . . For Heaven's sake! You can't see a thing!"

The other shrugged his shoulders.

"You can't see a thing!" repeated Doña Berta in terror, imploring compassion with her look and her gesture, and her voice quivering.

"Of course not! The canvases weren't made to be seen on the floor. But what do you expect me to do about it! You should have come sooner."

"I didn't have the pass before. The public wasn't admitted. This place was closed. . . ."

The coarse fat man shrugged his shoulders again, and turned to a group of workmen to give them orders and to try to forget that the old lady was still there.

Doña Berta found herself alone, completely alone, with the formless mass of confused, sad smears that lay at her feet.

"And my son is in there! That's what he is . . . , part of that gray, black, white, red, blue, all mixed up thing that looks like a big scab! . . ."

She looked all around as if asking for help.

"Oh, of course! They aren't going to nail it up on the wall again just for my pretty face. . . . It doesn't even have a frame. . . ."

Not noticing the old woman, four men in shirtsleeves came over to the canvas, and in words that Doña Berta could not make out, began to discuss the best way of lifting up the painting and carrying it to a more suitable place for packing.

The poor seventy-year-old looked at them aghast, trying to figure out their purpose. . . . When two of the men bent down to pick up the canvas, Doña Berta let out a cry.

"For God's sake, gentlemen! Wait a moment!" she exclaimed, grabbing the shirt of a blond, pleasant-looking young man with her clawlike fingers. "One moment! . . . I want to see him! . . . One second! . . . Who knows whether I shall ever have him in front of me again!"

The four porters looked in amazement at the old lady, and they all burst out laughing.

"She must be crazy," one of them said.

Then Doña Berta, who did not cry often, in spite of all the reasons she had for crying, felt two tears come into her eyes, like a consolation. Pure, solitary, and sad, they slid down her shrunken cheeks.

The workmen saw them fall, and they stopped laughing.

Maybe she was not crazy. It might be something else. The pleasant blond fellow gave her to understand that they were not in charge there, and that that picture could not be seen any more, because it was being moved: They were taking it to the home of its owner, a very rich Latin American who had bought it.

"Yes, I know. . . . That is why . . . I have to see that figure in the middle of it. . . ."

"The captain?"

"Yes, that's right, the captain. Dear me! . . . I left my town, my home, only for this, to see the captain . . . , and if you take it away, how do I know that I'll be able to get into that gentleman's mansion? And while I am scheming to get inside, who knows whether they won't take the painting off to America?"

The workmen ended up shrugging their shoulders, just like the fat man, who had disappeared from the room.

"Listen," said Doña Berta, "one moment . . . for pity's sake! This stepladder over here will do. . . . Yes; if you will move it a little closer for me . . . I don't have the strength! . . . if you would bring it over here, in front of the painting . . . on this side . . . I could climb up . . . climb up three, four, five rungs . . . holding on tightly . . . Of course I can!

. . . and from up there, I should be able to see something. . . ."

"You'll kill yourself, Grandma."

"No, sir; back home in the garden, I used to climb up like
that to pick fruit and to hang out the wash. . . . I won't fall,
no I won't. Please! Help me! From up there, if I turn my head
around enough, I should see something . . . Please! Help me!"

The blond porter felt sorry for her; the others didn't. Impatiently, they grabbed the canvas, while their companion
quickly brought over the stepladder; and while he held it on
one side to keep it from slipping, he gave his other hand to
Doña Berta, who, hurriedly and trembling, climbed with great
difficulty up those worn, slippery rungs one by one. She went
up five, held onto the wood with all her strength, and, twisting
her neck around, looked upon the famous canvas . . . which
was moving, because the workmen had begun to pick it up.
Like an undulating phantom, like a dream, what she saw amid
smoke, blood, stones, earth, the splashy colors of uniforms, was
a face that looked at her for an instant with eyes of sublime
fear, of heroic terror . . . : the face of "her Captain," the
one she had found, also stained with blood, at the gate of
Posadorio. Yes, it was "her Captain," merged with herself, with
her older brother; he was a Rondaliego grafted onto the mate
of her soul: it was her son! But he passed like a flash of
lightning, moving in a zigzag, supine as if they were taking him
to be buried. . . . He was going with his arms open, a sword
in his hand, stepping on crumbling stones and sand, among
dead bodies and bayonets. She could not fix the image in her
mind; she had seen scarcely more than that face that filled her
heart suddenly, that pale face, swaying and vanishing among
other blurs and shapes. . . . But the expression of that face,
the magical power of that look, remained fixed in her brain
. . . And just when the painting, which was being carried away

by the workmen, was disappearing from view, Doña Berta's vision began to blur, she lost consciousness, collapsed, and fell, sliding down the stepladder into the arms of the compassionate young man who had helped her in her painful ascent.

That too was a picture; it resembled, in its way, a Descent from the Cross.

X

Doña Berta, who came to very quickly, although she had hardly enough strength to walk, was brought home in the same coach that she had hired by the hour, and which was waiting for her at the door. Another two days in bed. Then her nervous, feverish activity revived; new investigations, more hunting of recommendations, in order to find out where the owner of "her Captain" lived, to be admitted into his house, to be able to contemplate the painting . . . and to broach the grand question . . . about its purchase.

Doña Berta did not tell anyone, not even those who were helping her get cards of introduction, about her tremendous aspiration to acquire that masterpiece. She was afraid that talk might get around in the inn that she was rich enough to pay thousands of *duros* for a canvas, and she feared that someone might steal her money, which she always carried with her. She never yielded to the advice to put it in the bank, to deposit it. . . . Such things were foreign to her. They could swindle her; the safest place for it was in her own clutches. The banknotes sewn to her clothes, to her corset: that was best.

Isolated from the world (in spite of walking about the busiest downtown streets of Madrid) because of her deafness and her habits, among which was not that of getting the news through the newspapers—she neither read them, nor believed in them— she still was not aware of a sad occurrence which was to have a decisive influence on her own affairs. She did not find out about it until she had succeeded, at last, in gaining admittance into the mansion of her "rival," the owner of the painting. He was a gentleman of approximately her age, healthy, strong, affable, a man who tried to atone for his riches by distributing benefactions; he lent his aid in misfortune, without understanding it; he did not feel other people's pain, but he alleviated it; through logic he would cure the ravages of poverty, not by opening up his heart, which was completely occupied with himself. Doña Berta amused him. He thought, like those workmen in the building where the paintings had been kept, that she was crazy. But her madness was entertaining, harmless, interesting.

"Imagine"—he would say to his group of banking and political dignitaries—"Imagine! She wants to buy *Valencia's last painting* from me!" Unanimous laughter always greeted these words.

That Latin American magnate had snatched *Valencia's last painting* from the very hands of the Government by dint of money and diplomatic intrigues. There had even been recommendations from abroad that the poor devil of a Secretary of the Interior should yield, in deference to the priority of money. Besides, justice, charity, were on the side of the financier. Valencia's "heirs," which, according to his will, were the hospitals, would end up gaining much more if the Latin American were to get the artistic gem, since the Government had not been able to go beyond the amount fixed as the price of the work during the painter's lifetime, and the millionaire from across the seas was paying its just price in consideration of its being a posthumous sale. The sum to be paid had tripled through the "accident" of the author of the painting's having died that fall, out there in Asturias, in an obscure little harbor town, as a result of a chill, of a terrible drenching. There had been some legal irregularity in the preference accorded to the richer bidder; but the fairest thing, actually, was that the one who had paid most for the painting should get it.

Doña Berta did not know all this during the first few days that she visited the Latin American's private museum. It took some time before she could meet and speak to the millionaire, who had let her enter his mansion on someone's recommendation, without even knowing who she was, or what she wanted. The servants admitted the old woman, who wiped her shoes very carefully before stepping on those rugs, distributed smiles and tips and stood there as at Mass, withdrawn, absorbed, always staring at the same canvas, "the disputed one," as it was called in the house.

The painting, placed in its gilded frame, hanging on the wall in that luxurious room, among many other marvels of art, seemed different to Doña Berta. Now she contemplated it at her pleasure; she read in the features and in the pose of the hero who was dying on that glorious bloody pile of earth and bodies, in a halo of fire and smoke, she read everything the painter had wished to express; but . . . she did not always recognize her son. According to the lighting, according to the state of her own spirits, according to what she had eaten and drunk, so she did or did not see her own son and "her Captain" in that captain of the famous painting. The first time that she felt her faith vacillate, that she knew doubt, she had chills, and a cold, deathlike sweat ran down her spine.

If she lost her inner conviction that the captain of the painting was her son, what would become of her? How could she give up her whole fortune, how could she plunge herself into poverty, to acquire a piece of canvas when she did not know whether or not it was the shroud of her son's "image"! How could she devote herself to seeking out the creditor or his family in order to pay that hero's debt, if he was not her son!

And just to doubt, just to live in fear of being mistaken, she had handed over her Posadorio, her green Aren, to avarice and usury. Just to doubt and fear she had consented to come to Madrid, to throw herself into the inferno of the streets, into the daily battle of the coaches, horses and passersby.

She repeated her visits to the mansion of the Latin American as frequently as she was allowed. There were days when she hurried to her place in front of the painting morning and afternoon. The tips stimulated the servants' tolerance. As soon as she left there, the desire to return became a fever. When she doubted, that was when she desired most to go back to her contemplation, to fortify her belief, immersing herself like an ecstatic in that face, in those eyes from which she wanted to extract the revelation of their secret. Was he or was he not her son? "Yes, yes," her soul would tell her sometimes. "Can it be, ungrateful mother, that even now you don't recognize me?" those parted lips seemed to shout. And at other times, the lips were still and Doña Berta's soul would say: "Who knows, who knows! The likeness may be coincidence, coincidence and overanxiety. What if I am crazy? At least, may I not be senile? But what about the resemblance he bears to 'my Captain' and to me, and all the Rondaliegos? It is he . . . it isn't he! . . ."

She recalled the saints, the mystical saints, whom the devil used to tempt; whom the Lord abandoned from time to time in order to test them, leaving them in the aridness of a spiritual desert.

And the saints were victorious; and even when the sun of their spirits was darkened, clouded . . . they believed and they loved . . . they prayed in the absence of the Lord for Him to return.

Doña Berta came to feel the sublime, austere joy of *faith in doubt*. To sacrifice oneself for something that is evident, what glory was there in that? What triumph? Courage lay in giving one's all, not for one's faith . . . but for *one's doubt*. She loved the faith that lay within doubt, the way mothers love a child more and more when he is sick or when death claims him. "Weak, sickly faith" became greater in her eyes than blind, robust faith.

From the time she began to feel that way, her determination to move Heaven and earth to make the painting hers was firmer than ever.

And this was her state of mind when, for the first time, she met the rich Latin American in the salon of his museum. The first day she did not dare to communicate to him her extraordinary pretension. At their second meeting, which she requested, she spoke to him seriously about her idea, her infinite longing to possess that canvas.

She knew how much the State had been about to give for it a while back. Her means did cover that amount, and there were even thousands of *pesetas* left over to pay "her son's debt," if the creditors were to appear. Doña Berta awaited anxiously the millionaire's reply, paying no heed to the astonishment he showed, and which she had already anticipated. It was then that she found out why her painter friend had not answered the letter she had sent him through a messenger: she learned that "her son's" companion, the amiable, illustrious artist who had changed the life of the last Rondaliego at the end of his career, the stranger who had appeared in the woods . . . had died out there on her earth, on one of those excursions of his in search of Nature's lessons.

And the picture of "her Captain," because of that death, was now worth so many thousands of *duros* that all of Susacasa, even if it were three times its size, would not be enough to pay for those few yards of cloth.

The poor old woman cried, leaning on the shoulder of that

foreign magnate, who was a very plain man, and knew how to
affect all the poses of the charitable. . . . The good woman
was crazy, without any doubt; but not for that was her pain
less real, nor the situation less interesting. He was extremely
kind to the little old lady; he tried to deceive her like a child;
he would do everything he could, except, of course, let the
painting go, not only for what she could offer him, but even
for what it was really worth. That would be a fine thing! What
would the Government say? Besides, even supposing that the
good woman did have the capital that she offered, to yield to
her pleas would mean impoverishing her, ruining her; a case
of wanton prodigality, madness. Impossible!

Doña Berta cried a great deal, begged a great deal, and
finally realized that the possessor of her only claim to happiness was being quite patient in tolerating her, although he was
not soft enough to yield. Nevertheless, she hoped that God
would help her with a miracle; she made up her mind to get
blood out of that stone, tenderness out of that round rock that
the millionaire had in his chest. And so she contented herself
for the time being with being permitted to go there and look
at the painting every day, as long as it was not sent to America. And from time to time she would also have to endure seeing *him,* that rich man, speaking to him and entreating him
on her knees. . . . The man humored her in everything, so
sure was he of never letting himself be won over—of course!
—because it was absurd.

And Doña Berta came and went, braving the dangers of the
coaches' wheels and horses' hoofs; each time more bewildered,
more debilitated . . . and more set on the impossible. She was
already famous, known as a crazy woman in the Latin American's social circle, and very familiar to all the habitual passersby on certain streets.

Half of Madrid knew the image of that smiling, lively yellowish little old woman, who wore a terribly outmoded costume of the color of tobacco, who ran from public vehicles, took refuge in doorways, and spoke affectionately and with a thousand gestures to the crowds of people, who did not stop to listen to her.

One afternoon, when the Rondaliego woman heard that the man from Havana was going away and was taking his "museum" with him, paler than ever, barely keeping herself from crying, her voice firm at first, she requested a last meeting with her tormentor; and when they were alone, in the presence of "her son," a mute, "dead" witness . . . she revealed her secret, the secret that was traveling about in the lost letter to the deceased painter. But even that had no effect. The owner of the painting neither softened nor believed this new "madness." Assuming that it was not all pure fable, pure invention on the part of the crazy woman; supposing, in fact, that the woman had had an illegitimate child, how could she prove that her son was the original of the presumed portrait of the painting? All that Doña Berta could get was permission to be present at the solemn, unhappy act of taking down the painting and packing it for the long trip; she would be allowed to say good-bye forever to her Captain, to her "supposed son." The millionaire offered something else, too; he would keep the secret, of course; but without prejudice toward the initiation of inquiries concerning the identification of the original of that figure, under the presumption that what the old woman told him was not pure fancy. And Doña Berta said good-bye until the following day, the last day, with relative tranquillity, not because she was resigning herself, but because she still hoped to win. Undoubtedly, God wished to try her to the utmost, and he was reserving the miracle for the last moment. "Oh, but there would be a miracle!"

XI

And that night Doña Berta dreamed that from a remote village, far off among the harbor towns of her land, where her painter friend had died, there came as if by enchantment, on the wings of the wind, a small, very small, almost dwarf-sized notary whose voice was like a cricket's and who shouted, waving a yellowish paper in his hand: "Wait, gentlemen! Here is the last will and testament, the real one, the other one is invalid; the artist does not leave 'Doña Berta's painting' to the hospitals; he bequeathes it, as is fitting, to the mother of 'his Captain,' of his friend. . . . So pick up your pictures, Mr. American Millionaire, and hand over the painting . . . ; give it to its legitimate owner, Doña Berta Rondaliego."

She awoke early, remembered the dream, and fell into a bad humor, because that solution, which would have been just perfect for realizing the miracle she had anticipated the previous evening, would now have to be discarded. Alas! She knew too well, through all the sad experience of her life, that dreams do not come true!

She went into the dining room to ask for her chocolate, and there she had an unpleasant experience, which was especially inopportune, because, by making her become irritated, it took away the concentrated fervor she needed in order to make her last attack on the stony-hearted Croesus and to see if a miracle *would* happen.

The trouble was that the landlady, Doña Petronila, was again taking the floor (the dining-room floor) to discuss the eternal question, the only one that divided those two peace-loving women—the question of the cat. She could not stand him, she had already told her so; he seemed undomesticated; the way he had been spoiled as an only cat of two old women of advanced years, with his country animal habits, his inde-

pendent, stubborn, mischievous, unsociable—in short, his savage—nature, she simply could not stand him. Since there was
no garden for him to go out into, he was dirtying up the whole
house, even the parlor; he broke glasses and plates, tore chairs,
curtains, rugs, and clothes; he ate up delicacies and meat.
Something would have to be done. Either the cat and his mistress left the house, or she would have to agree to the horrible
animal's perpetual confinement in a safe place, from which he
could not escape. Doña Berta argued, defended the liberty
of her best friend, but finally gave in, because she did not want
any domestic complications on such an important day for her.
Sabelona's cat was locked up in the attic, in a storeroom, which
was a secure prison because the iron bars of the skylight were
covered with a wire netting. Since nobody lived near there, the
prisoner's cries could not interrupt the neighbors' sleep; nobody would hear him, even if he turned into a tiger to vocifer-
ate his rights to the open air.

Doña Berta left her lodgings sad, crestfallen, angry, and upset about the incident of the cat and the recollection of her
dream, which would have been so good if it had been reality.
It was a holiday; the traffic at those hours horrified the Rondaliego lady. The ground was slippery, dry and polished by
the frost. . . . It was early; she had time to spare. She entered the church, heard two Masses; then she went to a store
to buy a collar for the cat, intending to embroider some initials
on it, so that he could be identified if he got lost. . . . Finally,
the time came. She was in the Carrera de San Jerónimo; she
crossed the street; by dint of apologies and discreet, timid
pushes, she elbowed her way through the crowd that was mob-
bing the entrance of the Imperial. Then came the serious crisis,
that of crossing Alcalá Street. It took her half an hour to get
up her courage. She took advantage of an "opening," as she
used to say, and, lifting her skirt slightly, began to run . . .

and without any untoward event, amid the crowd that swallowed her up like a wave, she reached Montera Street, and went up it slowly, because she was becoming fatigued. She felt more tired than ever. Perhaps it was weakness; she had gulped down her chocolate during the quarrel about the cat. She crossed the intersection of San Luís, thinking: "I should have crossed further down, where the street is narrower." She entered Fuencarral Street, which was one of those she feared most; there the trolley tracks seemed like razor blades shaving her flesh: they ran so 'close to the sidewalk! When she passed in front of a large old house that stood at the head of the street, she forgot for a moment, unlike her wont, about the danger and her precautions to avoid being run over; and she thought: "I believe that is where Mr. Cánovas lives. . . . He could perform the miracle for me. He could give me . . . a Royal order . . . I don't know . . . anyway a note so that the Latin American would be forced to sell me the painting. . . . They say that this Don Antonio has so much power . . . My goodness! This is what such power should be used for, to order things to be done in justice that are not covered by law."

While she was thinking about these things, she had taken some steps without realizing where she was going. At that moment she heard a confused noise as of voices, saw hands reaching out toward her, felt a blow in the back . . . and something stepping on her skirt. "The trolley," she thought. It was too late. Yes, it was the trolley. A horse knocked her down and trampled her; a wheel passed over the middle of her body. The vehicle stopped before leaving its victim behind. She had to be pulled out very carefully from between the wheels. She already looked dead. Within ten minutes she really was dead. She neither spoke, nor sighed, nor anything. She lay on the sidewalk for a few minutes, until the police arrived. The crowd stood all around, staring at the body. Some recognized the little old woman who used to come and go so much and who smiled at everybody. An affable, lively young newspaperman suddenly became sad, remembering, and so he told the people gathered there how that poor old woman had saved him from a similar accident on Mayor Street, near the Council Buildings.

The corpse was not repugnant or horrifying. Doña Berta seemed to be asleep, because when she was asleep she looked dead. Her face the color of yellowish ivory; her wavy hair, the color of ashes; the rest of her, including her shoes, all tobacco. There was only one red stain, a trickle of blood that came out of the corner of her thin white lips. Among the crowd, there was more sympathy than regret. One way or another, that feeble little woman would not have lasted much longer; she would have had to fall apart soon. Within a few minutes the evidence of the accident was removed; traffic was restored, the body disappeared, the trolley disappeared, and the bad news traveled from the street to the Prefecture, to the newspapers. Thus came to an end the last Rondaliego, Doña Berta, of Posadorio.

On Tetuán Street, in a corner of a storeroom, in an attic, there remained a cat, who had no name, who had been happy in Susacasa, who had been a hunter of field mice, a great botanist, and devoted to butterflies and of siestas taken in the shade of century-old trees. Forgotten by the whole world, his mistress dead, the cat lived many days throwing himself against the walls, and finally he perished like an Ugolino, but without even a bare bone to chew on; hearing the mice in the empty neighboring attics, but unable to alleviate his hunger with a single prey. At first, furious, raging, he snorted, jumped, scratched, and chewed on doors and walls and the iron of the grate. Later, with the final resignation of overpowering weakness, he dropped into a corner, and he died, dreaming perhaps of the butterflies that he had been unable to catch, but that had gladdened his days, out there on the Aren, which blossomed in April with fresh grass and delightful shade along its borders, at the edge of the stream that the gentlefolk of Susacasa used to call the "river."

Sonata of Autumn

*These pages are taken from the "Very Pleasant
Memoirs" written in exile in old age by the Marquis
of Bradomín. He was an ideal Don Juan—perhaps
the most admirable of all time.*

He was ugly, a Catholic, and a sentimentalist.

RAMÓN MARÍA DEL VALLE-INCLÁN

I

"Love of my life, I am dying—my one desire is to see you."
It is long now since that letter from poor Concha came to
wring my heart. It was heavy with yearning and sadness, with
the perfume of violets and remote love. I kissed it before reading to the end. Nearly two years were gone since she had
written me, and now she called me to her side, ardently, sor-
rowfully imploring. The three emblazoned sheets bore traces of
tears—piteous marks that eternity cannot obliterate. Withdrawn from the world, in the old Brandeso Palace, poor Concha
was dying and she called to me with an infinite longing. Those
perfect hands, perfumed and pale, the hands that once I had
loved so much, had written to me again. Tears filled my eyes.

The hope that our dead love might live again had remained
with me always; vague, nostalgic, undefined, it breathed into
my life a faint aroma of faith—the sweet chimera of the future, asleep in the depths of the azure lakes that mirror the
stars of destiny. Sad destiny for her and for me! The rose of

our love was to bloom again only to shed compassionate petals over a tomb. Poor Concha was dying.

I received her letter at Viana del Prior where I went every autumn to hunt. The Brandeso Palace lies but a few leagues distant. I felt that, before starting upon my way, I would like to talk with Concha's sisters, María Isabel and María Fernanda, and I went to see them. They were both nuns in the sisterhood of the Comendadoras. They came into the parlor and extended to me through the bars of the grating the chaste, patrician hands of virgin brides of the Church. As children we had played together in the great halls of the old baronial palace, and now they talked to me simply and without formality. Both repeated mournfully that Concha was dying.

I left the sisters with heavy sadness in my heart. The bell for the nuns was ringing; I entered the church, which was still deserted, and knelt down in the shadow of a pillar. The dim stillness was broken by the footsteps of two women who were visiting the altars, austere and solemn in their dress of heavy black. They seemed to be two sisters, mourning a common sorrow, imploring a common grace. From time to time they exchanged a hushed word, sighed and relapsed into silence. Thus they made the rounds of the seven altars, side by side, rigid, disconsolate. The uncertain flame of a dying lamp at moments threw a livid light over the two women and left them once more wrapped in shadow. The murmur of their prayers came to me faintly; in the white hands of the sister who led, I could distinguish the rosary. It was of mother-of-pearl with cross and medals of silver. I remembered that Concha used to pray with such a rosary. She had scruples about permitting me to play with it, for poor Concha was very devout and the belief that our love was a mortal sin caused her poignant grief. On many a night of tryst I have entered Concha's boudoir to find her upon her knees. . . . Without speaking, she raises fervid eyes to mine, beseeching silence; I sink down in a great arm-chair and watch her pray as the beads of the rosary pass slowly and reverently between her pale fingers. Sometimes, not waiting for the prayers to end, I draw near and take her in my arms; she turns still paler and covers her eyes with her hands. I love with a veritable frenzy that sorrowful mouth, the quivering lips held closed and cold as lips in death. Concha nervously frees herself and, rising, replaces the rosary in its casket. Then, her arms flung about my neck, she lays a fainting head upon my shoulder and weeps—weeps from love and the fear of eternal punishment. . . .

When I returned home from my visit to the sisters, night had fallen. I passed the evening alone and sad in my big chair before the fire. I had fallen asleep. Suddenly loud knocks upon the door broke the silence. In the still hours of the night the sound was awesome and sepulchral. I jumped up, startled, and opened the window. It was the servant who had brought Concha's letter, come to tell me that we must start upon our journey.

II

Concha's major-domo, an old countryman wearing the hooded cape of frieze and wooden shoes of the Galician peasant, was stationed before the door astride his mule, holding another by the bridle.

"What is it, Brión?" I called into the darkness.

"Dawn, Señor Marquis."

I descended promptly without stopping to shut the window, which was rattling in the gusty wind, and we started off without delay. A few stars were still shining when Brión called me; as we took the road I heard the cocks of the neighboring hamlet begin to crow. With the best of luck we could not reach the Palace before sundown; though the distance is but nine leagues, the rough road over the mountain is hard on the mules' feet. The old peasant at once took the lead to show the way and we passed through Quintana de San Clodio at a trot, beset by a chorus of barks from the watchdogs tied under the grain cribs on every farm.

Day was breaking when we reached the open country. Far away a line of hills loomed desolately through the fog; beyond them, others and yet others lay stretched under white shrouds of mist; they seemed never-ending, far as the eye could see. In the distance a pack of laden mules filed slowly across La Puente del Prior. The muleteer, riding sidesaddle on his old horse, ambled along behind, singing a song of his native Castile. The sun touched the tops of the hills with gold; flocks of sheep, black and white, climbed the slopes; far off in the valley spread the green lands of a stately palace, and above its ancient towers flights of doves wheeled white against the sky.

As we rode on rain overtook us. We dismounted at the old Gundar mills and, with the air of lords of the domain, knocked authoritatively at the door. Two lean dogs rushed out barking at the major-domo and behind them appeared a woman spinning. The old countryman saluted her piously: *"Ave María Purísima."*

The girl responded: "Immaculate Mother of God."

She seemed a simple creature, full of kindliness. When she saw that we were stiff with cold, saw the mules huddled under the shed and the threatening sky, she threw the door hospitably open. "Enter and sit by the fire," she said humbly. "It's bad weather for travelers. Ah, what weather! With the crops all under water. . . . There's a lean year ahead of us!"

We had scarcely entered when Brión went back for the saddlebags, while I walked to the hearth where a wretched fire was smoldering. The girl poked the embers into life and brought an armful of wet green twigs that hissed and sputtered as they gave out clouds of resinous smoke. At the back of the room a rickety door, the stones of its ancient sill white with flour, creaked incessantly. Tac! tac! tac! The voice of an old man starting a song and the hum of the mill wheel came from the room beyond.

The major-domo returned with the saddlebags hanging over his shoulder. "Here is our luncheon," he said. "The Señora got up from her bed to prepare it with her own hands. Saving Your Excellency, I think we should take advantage of this chance to eat, for if the rain closes in again we shall have no let-up before night."

The miller's daughter approached us, humbly solicitous: "I'll set a trivet by the fire in case you would like to warm the food." As she placed the little iron stand, the major-domo drew out a large damask napkin, spread it over the hearthstone and began to empty the saddlebags. I walked to the doorway and stood for a long time watching the gray curtain of rain undulate in the wind.

After a while Brión approached me with respectful familiarity: "Whenever Your Excellency is ready. . . . We've a fine feast, I tell you!"

I went back into the kitchen and sat down by the fire. I felt no desire to eat, and I ordered Brión to serve me nothing but a cup of wine. The old peasant obeyed in silence. He drew a leathern bottle from one of the saddlebags and poured out the sparkling red wine from the vineyards of the palace, using one of the little cups that our forebears had fashioned from the silver sols of Peru, one cup from a coin. I drank off the wine and, in order to escape from the thick smoke of the kitchen, returned to my place in the doorway. Thence I bade the major-domo eat, and the girl as well. She asked permission to summon the old man who was singing in the next room.

"Father! Father!" she called loudly. He came in, his coat

white with flour, with his cap over one ear, the song still on his lips—a silver-haired old man with a merry eye, as waggish as a book of ballads.

They drew rough, smoke-begrimed stools before the fire and sat down to eat amid a chorus of benedictions, while the two lean dogs circled hungrily around them. It was the loving forethought of poor, sick Concha that had spread the feast; like the anointed hands of a saintly princess of legend, the pale hands that I had loved so much were serving at the table of the lowly.

Before touching his wine the old miller rose to his feet and droned out in a monotone: "To the health of the noble caballero who gives this wine! May we live to celebrate for many a year to come the day we drink it in his noble presence!"

After the old man, the others drank with equal ceremony. They talked in lowered voices as they ate; the miller asked where we were going. The major-domo answered, to the Brandeso Palace; the old man knew that road well; he paid a tithe, dating from ancient times, to the Señora of the Palace . . . a tithe of two ewes, seven quarter-bushels of wheat and seven quarter-bushels of rye; the past year there had been a great drought and her ladyship had remitted all the grain; she was a kind Señora who had sympathy for the poor peasant. . . .

As I stood in the doorway watching the rain fall, I heard their words and was touched and pleased. I turned my head and let my glance stray over the group gathered in the smoke about the fire. Their voices sank still lower and it seemed they were talking of me.

The major-domo rose. "If it please Your Excellency," he said, "I'll go now and see to the mules and we will be on our way."

The miller offered his help and they left the room together. At the back of the kitchen the dogs were growling over a bone.

The girl began to sweep the hearth. As she gathered the ashes, the poor creature mumbled an endless stream of benedictions: "God grant you good health and good fortune! May joy meet you when you reach the Palace! God will that you find the Señora well! With the color of the roses in her cheeks!"

With each sweep of the broom the poor soul repeated monotonously: "God will that you find her blooming like a rose! Like a rose on a rosebush!"

Taking advantage of a clearing in the weather, the majordomo came in for the saddlebags while the miller untied the mules and led them from the shed for us to mount. The girl came and stood in the doorway to watch us: "May the noble caballero go in happiness! And the Lord be with him!"

When we were mounted she came out to the road. She had flung an apron of heavy cloth over her head to shield her from the rain which was beginning to fall again. She came close to me with an air of mystery. The draped figure might have been some spirit of a thousand centuries ago. Her flesh was quivering and her eyes burned hotly beneath the folds of the mantle. She held a bunch of herbs in her hands. With the bearing of a prophetess she reached them out to me, murmuring in a low voice: "When you are with my Lady, place these herbs beneath her pillow. Let her not know of it. They will make her well. Souls are like nightingales—they long to try their wings. Nightingales sing in gardens, but in royal palaces they pine and die."

The old miller came up smiling and pushed the girl aside to make way for the mules. "Give no heed, Señor," he said. "She's just a simpleton, poor child!"

I felt the dark wing of superstition brush across my soul as I silently took the bunch of rain-drenched herbs—sweet-scented, wholesome herbs that can cure alike a longing soul or an ailing sheep, add to the store of homely remedies or swell the harvest. . . . But a little while and they would flower above poor Concha's grave in the fragrant green cemetery of San Clodio de Brandeso.

III

I had a vague remembrance of the Brandeso Palace where as a child I had visited with my mother. I remembered the ancient garden with its green labyrinth that frightened and yet attracted me. I was returning after all these years at the entreaty of the little girl with whom I had so often played in the old flowerless garden.

The sinking sun threw a glow of gold between the black green of the venerable trees—cedars and cypresses, silently attesting the great age of the Palace. The garden had an arched gateway with four escutcheons carved in stone above the cornice, bearing the arms of four different lines. Lineage of the founder of the house, noble on all sides of his ancestry!

As the Palace came in sight our tired mules trotted up briskly to the gate and stopped short, impatiently pawing the ground. A peasant dressed in homespun was waiting at the entrance and hurried forward to hold my stirrup. I dismounted, throwing him the reins of my mule, and with a spirit heavy with memories penetrated the dark, leaf-strewn avenue of chestnut trees. At the far end I distinguished the Palace, all the windows closed, the panes illumined by the sun. All at once I saw a white shadow pass behind the glass, saw it stop and raise both hands to its forehead; the central window slowly opened and the white phantom greeted me with a waving of ghostlike arms. It lasted but an instant, no more—and the branches of the chestnuts crossed again, blocking my vision. As I emerged from the avenue I searched the windows anew. They were all closed, even the one in the center.

With a fast-beating heart I entered the great dark hall. My

footsteps on the broad flagstones resounded through the silence. Some peasants waiting to pay their tithes were seated along the walls on benches of age-polished oak. In the background stood the antique chests that held the wheat, their covers lifted. On seeing me enter the tithe-payers rose, murmured a respectful *"Santas y buenas tardes"* and, slowly seating themselves again, remained motionless in the shadows that almost engulfed them. With a quickened step I went up the broad stairs, with their balustrade of rudely carved granite; before I reached the top a door opened noiselessly and a servant, Concha's old nurse, came down the steps to meet me carrying a lamp in her hand. "Thank God you've come!" she said. "Now you will see the Señorita. Many's the day the poor child has been crying for you. . . . She wouldn't write to you, for she thought that you'd forgotten her. I persuaded her that you had not. I was not wrong, Señor Marquis?"

I could scarcely murmur: "No. Where is she?"

"She's been lying down all the afternoon. She was anxious to be up and dressed when you came . . . like a child . . . the Señor knows. . . . But her impatience was too much for her. She was shaking so that her teeth chattered and I had to put her to bed."

"Is she so ill?"

The old woman wiped her eyes. "Very ill, Señor. Much changed." And indicating a lighted doorway down the length of the hall, she added in a low tone: "In there."

We went on in silence. Then Concha heard my footsteps and called in an anguished voice: "At last! My life! At last!"

I entered. Concha was lying propped against the pillows. She gave a little cry and, instead of holding out her arms to me, covered her face with her hands and began to sob. The old servant placed the light on a small table, sighed and walked out. Trembling with emotion, I went over to Concha. I kissed

the hands she held over her face, then gently drew them down.
Without a word she raised her beautiful sick eyes to mine and
held me in a long look of intense love. Then, languid with the
burden of her happiness, she closed her lids again. I watched
her thus for a moment. How pale she was! Anguish squeezed
at my throat. She softly opened her eyes, and pressing my
temples between her burning hands she gazed long at me again,
a look of mute love drowning in the melancholy of approaching
death.

"I feared you would never come."

"And now?"

Her mouth, a pale flower, trembled. "Now I am happy."

She closed her eyes again in ecstasy as if she would imprison
in her thoughts a beatific vision.

IV

Concha sat up in bed and reached for the bell rope. I seized
her hand: "What do you want?"

"To summon my maid to come and dress me."

"Now?"

"Yes." She leaned her head back and added with a pitiful
smile: "I wish to do you the honors of my Palace."

I tried to persuade her not to get up. Concha insisted. "I
shall order a fire lighted in the dining room. A great big fire!
I am going to have supper with you."

She turned her soft eyes to me with a wonderfully tender
expression on her sweet pale face. "I wanted to stay up till
you arrived but I couldn't. I thought I should die of impatience. I felt ill."

Taking her hand in mine I kissed it and we smiled at one
another.

"You do not ring. Why?" I asked, adding, just above my
breath: "Will you let me be your maid?"

Concha freed her hand: "What a wild idea!"

"I disagree. Where are your clothes?"

Concha smiled as a mother smiles at the whim of a child: "I don't know where they are."

"Come now, tell me."

"But I don't know!" As she spoke a roguish movement of eyes and lips indicated a large oak wardrobe which stood at the foot of the bed. The key was in the lock and I opened it. The faint fragrance of an antique perfume drifted from its depths where hung the garments that Concha was to wear that day.

"Are these what you want?"

"Yes . . . that white gown . . . nothing else."

"You won't be cold?"

"No."

As I lifted down the soft white tunic a perfumed warmth seemed still to cling to it.

"Foolish fancy!" Concha murmured in confusion.

I drew her little feet from under the bedclothes. They were white and fragile as a child's, with blue veins tracing perfect paths for kisses. With an ecstatic shiver Concha thrust her feet into the slippers of soft dark fur. Her voice seemed singularly sweet: "Now open the big chest. Choose a pair of stockings for me."

I selected a pair of black silk, embroidered with lavender clocks. "Will these do?"

"Yes. Any you like."

I dropped to my knees on the tigerskin beside the bed to put them on.

Concha protested: "No, no. Get up. I do not wish to see you so!"

Smiling, I disregarded her. The little feet tried to escape my hand. Sweet little feet, I could do no less than kiss them.

Concha, quivering with rapture, exclaimed: "Always, always the same!"

Over the black silk stockings I slid the garters, white ribbons clasped with silver. I dressed her with the reverent lover's devotion that pious women bring to the adornment of a Holy Image. With trembling hands I tied the cords of her white robe under the sweet round chin, and Concha stood up leaning her weight upon my shoulders. She moved slowly over to her dressing table with the wraithlike air that illness lends to a beautiful woman. She looked at herself in the glass and smoothed her hair.

"How pale I am!" she sighed. "You see what I am—nothing but skin and bone."

"I see nothing of the kind, Concha," I protested.

She smiled wanly: "Tell me truly. How do I look?"

"Once you were the Princess of the Sun and now you are the Princess of the Moon."

"Flatterer!" She turned her back to the mirror and looked at me, at the same time striking a gong by the dressing table.

The old nurse came in immediately: "Did the Señorita ring?"

"Yes. I wish a fire made in the dining room."

"There is a good hot brazier in there now."

"Well, have it taken away and have the fire lighted."

The servant gave me a quick look: "Does the Señorita intend to go to the dining room also? Remember the corridors are very cold."

Concha sat down on the end of the sofa. Voluptuously wrapping the draperies of her nunlike gown about her, she said, with a little shiver: "I can put a shawl around me going through the corridors."

Reluctant to oppose her I was silent. She turned to me now with a sweet submission.

"If it is against your wish I will not go."

"It is not against my wish, Concha," I answered uncomfortably. "I am only afraid it may do you harm."

"But I do not want to leave you all alone," she sighed.

Faithful old Candelaria here made a suggestion: "Naturally you wish to be together. That's why I thought you would have your supper here at the little table. What do you think of that, Señorita Concha? And you, Señor Marquis?"

Concha laid her hand on my shoulder and answered laughingly: "Of course! Of course! You are a genius, Candelaria! Accept our sincere gratitude. You may tell Teresina we will have our supper here."

We were alone. Concha with eyes blinded by tears held out her hand to me and, as in other days, my lips crept tenderly over the fingers and brought pale roses to the tips. A bright fire was burning on the hearth. Seated on the floor before it, with an elbow resting on my knee, Concha poked the logs with the great bronze tongs. As the flame sprang upward it spread a faint rose tint on the eucharistic whiteness of her face—like sunlight on antique Pharos marbles.

V

Concha dropped the tongs and held out her arms for me to lift her from the floor. Our eyes met in a long deep look that held the shining happiness one sees in the eyes of a child who forgets a sorrow and laughs through its tears. The little table was now spread. Still clasping hands, we took our seats in the big chairs that Teresina had just placed for us.

"Do you remember," Concha asked, "how many years it is since you were here with your mother?"

"Yes, I remember. Do you?"

"Twenty-three years ago! I was eight. I fell in love with you then. What I used to suffer when you played with my big

sisters! It seems impossible that a child could suffer so from
jealousy. Later, when I grew up, you caused me many tears
too, but then I had the consolation of upbraiding you."

"Yet how sure you have always been of my love. Your letter
is proof of that."

Concha winked away the tears that trembled on her lashes:
"I was not sure of your love, only of your compassion."

Her mouth curved in a mournful smile and two tears shone
bright in her eyes. I wanted to get up and comfort her, but
she stopped me with a look. Teresina entered. We began to
eat in silence. To dissemble her tears Concha raised her glass
and slowly sipped her wine. As she was replacing it on the
table I took the glass from her hand and touched my lips
where hers had been. Concha turned to the maid: "Tell Candelaria to come and wait upon us."

Teresina left the room. I looked at Concha and we both
smiled.

"Why do you send for Candelaria?"

"Because I am afraid of you, and poor old Candelaria fears
nothing in the world."

"And Candelaria, like a good Jesuit, looks upon our love
with indulgence."

"Let us not begin that . . . let us not begin!" In pretty
annoyance Concha shook her head and touched a finger to her
pale lips: "I will not permit you to pose as another Pietro
Aretino, or as a Cesare Borgia either."

Poor Concha was extremely pious, and the æsthetic admiration which, in my youth, I professed for the son of Pope Alex-
ander VI, inspired her with as much fear as if it had been the
cult of the devil himself. She laughingly exaggerated her fear
now: "Be still . . . be still," she begged, with a roguish side-
wise glance at me. Then, turning her head slightly: "Candelaria, fill my glass with wine. . . ."

Candelaria, who was standing behind the chair with hands crossed on the front of her starched apron, hastened to serve her. Concha's voice, but a moment since sweet with happiness, trailed off in a moan. I saw her eyes close in a spasm of anguish and her mouth, a sick white rose, turned whiter still. I started up terrified: "What is it? What is the matter?"

She was unable to speak. Her head fell dully back against the chair. Candelaria ran to the dressing table and brought a bottle of smelling salts. Concha drew a sighing breath and opened wandering, bewildered eyes as if she were awaking from a dream peopled with chimeras. Fixing her gaze on me, she murmured feebly: "It was nothing. I am sorry you were frightened."

She passed her hand over her forehead, breathing distressfully. I forced her to take a few sips of broth. It seemed to revive her and a faint smile illumined her pallor. She made me sit down again while she continued to take the broth by herself. When it was finished, she reached out slender fingers for the wineglass and sweetly, tremblingly, offered it to me. To please her I touched it to my lips, then Concha drained the glass and drank no more that night.

VI

We were seated upon the sofa and had been talking long together. Poor Concha had been telling me of her life during the two years that we had not seen each other—a life of silent resignation, watching the days pass with a sad smile and weeping through the darkness of the night. I had no need to tell her of my life. Her eyes seemed to have followed it from afar and to know it completely. Poor Concha! Seeing her now, wasted by illness, so changed, so different from her former self, I felt a bitter remorse that I had ever listened to her entreaty on that night when, weeping, upon her knees, she had begged

me to go away and forget her. Her sainted mother, black-robed
and sorrowful, had come to part us.

But neither of us desired to remember the past; we fell silent, she in resignation, I assuming an expression of gloomy
tragedy the memory of which now brings a smile to my lips.
It was a beautiful gesture of a kind that I have rather forgotten, for since lovely woman does not succumb to the seduc-
tions of an old Don Juan the pose is only seemly in a young
one. Ah, yes, if now, with my white locks and fallen cheeks
and senatorial beard, some pure young thing were to love me
—some daughter of the stars arrayed in grace and candor—I
should deem it criminal to adopt any other attitude toward her
than that of the venerable prelate, the confessor of princesses,
versed in naught of love but its theology. But with poor
Concha the pose of Satan repentant stirred her to passion and
made her tremble. She was very good and, in consequence, very
unhappy. The poor child summoned a sorrowful smile, the
ultimate expression of her sick heart.

"How different our lives might have been," she murmured.

"True. I do not understand now how I ever yielded to your
entreaty. It must have been because you cried."

"Don't be untruthful. I expected you would come back. . . .
And my mother always had the fear."

"I didn't come back because I was waiting for you to send
for me. . . . The devil, pride!"

"Ah, no, it was not pride. . . . It was another woman. . . .
You had been unfaithful to me for a long time. When I learned
of it I believed I would die. I felt so desperate that I agreed
to live with my husband again."

She crossed her hands and fixed her intense eyes upon me.
Her pale mouth was quivering. "What agony when I realized
why you did not come!" she sobbed. "But never, not for a
single day, did I feel any bitterness toward you."

I had no courage at the moment to attempt deception, so I maintained a romantic silence. Concha passed her hands over my hair and clasped her fingers about my forehead: "What a wild life you've led these two years!" she sighed. "Your hair is almost white."

I, too, sighed dolefully: "Ah, Concha, that is from grief."

"No, not grief . . . something else. . . . Your grief could never have equaled mine, yet my hair is not white."

I sat up to look and pulled out the gold pin holding the heavy knot. The silky black wave rolled over her shoulders.

"Your forehead burns like a white star under that ebony mass. You are pure and pale as the moon. . . . Do you remember how I used to long to be whipped with those heavy tresses? Concha, cover me with them now."

Tenderly compliant, she spread over me the perfumed veil of hair. With my face buried in the scented mass I drew a breath as from a sacred fountain, and my spirit was rapturously transported to a blossoming garden of memories. Concha's heart was beating violently; with shaking hands I unfastened her loose gown and pressed my lips against the bare flesh, soft with the anointment of love's balm.

"My life!"

"My life!"

Concha closed her eyes for a moment. Then quickly she was on her feet, gathering up the loose coils of her hair: "Go. For God's sake, go."

I looked at her and smiled: "Where would you have me go?"

"Go. . . . Emotion exhausts me. I must rest. I wrote for you to come because there can be nothing between us now but a spiritual love. You surely understand that, ill as I am, nothing else is possible. To die in mortal sin . . . how horrible!"

Paler than ever, she crossed her two arms over her breast, laying her hands upon her shoulders in a characteristic pose of exalted resignation. I moved toward the door: "Good-bye, Concha."

She drew a sighing breath: "Good-bye."

"Will you be good enough to call Candelaria to guide me through the corridors?"

"Ah, it's true you don't know yet . . ."

She walked to the dressing table and touched the gong. We waited in silence. No one came. Concha looked at me uncertainly: "Candelaria must have gone to bed."

"In that case . . ."

She saw my smile and shook her head, gravely sorrowful: "In that case I will be your guide."

"But you shouldn't go out."

"Yes, yes."

She took up one of the candelabra from the dressing table and went swiftly to the door, trailing her long nunlike draperies. On the threshold she turned her head, calling me with her eyes and, white as a phantom, vanished into the dark corridor. I followed, exclaiming as I caught up with her: "Foolish child!"

With a silent little laugh she grasped my arm and leaned close to me.

The crossing of two corridors opened out into a vast circular antechamber, dismantled but for the pictures of saints and ancient chests along the walls. A small oil lamp, burning in a niche, threw a dying circle of light before the torn, discolored feet of Jesus of Nazareth. We stopped as we saw the outline of a woman huddled by a window. It was Candelaria, asleep, with hands crossed in her lap and head sunk upon her breast. At the sound of our footsteps she waked with a start: "Ah! . . . I was waiting here to show the Señor Marquis to his room."

"I thought you had gone to bed," Concha answered.

We went on in silence until we reached an open door where there was a light. Concha let go of my arm and stood still, trembling and very pale. Finally, she went in. It was my bedroom. Candles were burning in silver candelabra, placed on an antique console. Against the far wall stood the bed with coverings of antique damask. Concha's eyes examined the room with maternal solicitude. She stopped to smell the roses standing in a vase and then moved toward the door: "Good-bye till tomorrow."

I lifted her in my arms as if she were a child: "I will not let you go."

"Please, yes."

"No, no."

And my eyes laughed into her eyes and my mouth laughed upon her mouth. The Turkish slippers dropped from her feet. Without letting her touch the ground, I carried her to the bed and, with loverlike care, I put her down. She yielded then to happiness. Her eyes shone and over the pure surface of her cheeks two rose leaves spread. She gently pushed away my hands and began in some confusion to unfasten the soft white gown. As it slid the length of her pale quivering body, she opened the sheets and took refuge between them. Then she began to sob and I sat by the bedside and comforted her. When she seemed to be asleep, I lay down beside her.

VII

All night long fever burned in the frail body at my side, like a sepulchral light burning in a vase of fragile porcelain. The head rested on the pillows framed in waves of dark hair that enhanced the leaden pallor of her face. The colorless mouth, wan cheeks and wasted temples, the waxen eyelids sunk in violet hollows, gave her the spiritualized loveliness of a beautiful saint consumed by fasts and penitence. Her neck flowered from her shoulders like a drooping lily, her breasts were two white roses perfuming an altar, and the slender, graceful arms encircling her head were the handles of the amphora.

The cock had twice crowed; the light of dawn came palely through the closed windows. The candles in their silver candelabra had burned all night and were now almost entirely gone; their dying glimmer rippled amid the shadows on the ceiling. Thrown across a chair by the bed was my hunting cloak, still damp from the rain; scattered over it lay the mysterious herbs whose occult powers were known to none but the poor mad creature of the mill. I rose softly and gathered them up. With an extraordinary feeling of mingled irony and superstition, I hid the sweet green talisman under Concha's pillow. Without awakening her, I lay down again and pressed my lips against the perfumed hair. Insensibly I fell asleep.

For a long time nebulous visions of the day, savoring vaguely of tears and smiles, floated through my dreams. I think that once, still half asleep, I opened my eyes and saw Concha sitting up at my side. I think she kissed my forehead, smiling dreamily, and raised a finger to her lips. My eyes closed again without volition and I floated off once more into the clouds of sleep. When I wakened a luminous ladder of dust stretched from the window to the farthest wall. Concha was no longer there, but presently the door was softly opened and Concha came in on tiptoes carrying fresh sprays of roses in her arms. I pretended to sleep. Without a sound she came close to me, looked at me intently and sighed. She placed the roses in water, then walked to the window and dropped the curtains to soften the light. She was going away, as noiselessly as she had entered, when I called to her, laughing: "Concha, Concha."

She turned: "So you are awake?"

"I was in dreamland with you."

"And now you are with me here."

"How do you feel?"

"Absolutely well."

"Love is a splendid doctor."

"Ah, yes, but we must not abuse his medicine."

We laughed for happiness, again in one another's arms, lips to lips and heads resting on one pillow. Concha was pale with the frail delicate pallor of a Dolorosa and so beautiful in her wan slenderness that my eyes, my lips, my hands found their utter delight in the very things that made me grieve. I confess that I never remember having loved her in the past as madly as I loved her that night.

VIII

I had brought no servant with me, and Concha, who indulged in whims, like the princesses of picaresque romance, had placed a page at my service—the better to do me honor, as she laughingly explained. He was a boy whom Concha had taken into the Palace from her estates at Lantañón where his parents acted as stewards—one of the hundred or so godchildren of her uncle, Don Juan Manuel Montenegro, the eccentric and munificent lord of the ancient Lantañón Palace. I can see the child now as he first appeared at my door, deferentially removing his cap and asking meekly: "Have I the Señor's permission?"

He entered with head bent down, his white cloth cap clasped in both hands: "My mistress begs that you will command me."

"Where is your mistress?"

"In the garden."

He stood in the middle of the room, not daring to take a step. It is a memory that still brings a smile. Concha's favorite, unlike the pages of the old ballads, was neither blond nor melancholy, but his soft black eyes and romantic, sun-kissed cheeks might as easily have enticed the love of princesses.

I bade him open the windows and he ran to obey. A fresh perfumed breeze blew in from the garden and tossed the curtains gaily. The page had left his cap on a chair and picked it up again. I proceeded to question him.

"You are in service in the Palace?"

"Yes, Señor."

"Have you been here long?"

"Nearly two years."

"And what do you do?"

"Well, I do everything I am told, Señor."

"You have no parents?"

"Yes, Señor, I have."

"What do they do?"

"Well, they do nothing. They dig the ground."

He gave his answers with the impassivity of an outcast. With his barbarous accent and rough garments, his timid eyes and hair clipped like a monk's, he might have been the child of an ancient bondman.

"Was it the Señorita who sent you to me?"

"Yes, Señor. I was in the courtyard teaching the *riveirana* to the new blackbird—the old ones know it well already—when the Señorita came and sent me to you."

"So you are Master of Blackbirds here?"

"Yes, Señor."

"A high responsibility."

"Yes, Señor."

"And how old are you?"

"I think . . . I think I am . . ." The page kept his eyes upon his cap as he passed it slowly from one hand to the other, sunk in deep cogitation: "I think I am twelve; I am not sure."

"Where were you before you came to the Palace?"

"I served in the house of Don Juan Manuel."

"What did you do there?"

"There I trained ferrets."

"Another important charge!"

"Yes, Señor."

"How many blackbirds does the Señorita own?"

The page looked disdainful: "Not a single one."

"Whose are they then?"

"They are mine. When I have them well trained I sell them."

"To whom do you sell them?"

"Why, to the Señorita. She buys them all from me. Can't you guess why she wants them?—to set them free. The Señorita likes to hear them singing in the garden, but they fly away. One Sunday, in the month of June, I was walking with the Señorita. Far beyond the meadows of Lantañón we saw a blackbird high up on a branch of a cherry tree. He was singing the *riveirana*. I remember what the Señorita said: 'Just look where our caballero has flown to!'"

This ingenuous tale made me laugh, and the page laughed too. Though he was neither blond nor melancholy he was born to be the page of a princess and the recorder of a kingdom's chronicles.

"Which has the higher importance," I asked, "the teaching of ferrets or the teaching of blackbirds?"

After a moment's meditation the page answered: "They are just alike."

"Why did you leave the service of Don Juan Manuel?"

"Because he has many servants. Don Juan Manuel is a very great gentleman. All the servants in the Palace are afraid of him, I can tell you. Don Juan Manuel is my godfather; it was he who fetched me to the Palace to serve the Señorita."

"And which place do you find the better?"

The page fixed his childish black eyes upon me. With his cap clasped in his hands, he gravely formulated the remark:

"To the humble in heart all places are good." A reply worthy of a Calderón.

This page also knew how to turn a phrase; his destiny could not be doubted. He was born to live in a palace, tame ferrets, teach blackbirds, tutor a prince and make a king.

IX

Concha's mirthful voice called to me from the garden. I went out into the glass-walled loggia, warm and golden in the morning sunlight. The country had the feeling of the southland, yoked oxen, ripe vineyards, fecund fields. Concha was standing below me on the terrace: "Where is Florisel?"

"Is Florisel my page?"

"Yes."

"He must have been baptized by the fairies."

"I am his godmother. Call him for me."

"What do you want?"

"Tell him to come and carry up these roses." And Concha showed me her skirt brimming over with dew-wet roses, like the joyous fruitage of a perfect love brought to blossom with kisses.

"I have stripped the garden. They are all for you."

I had a vague remembrance of that ancient garden where immemorial myrtle clung to the four stone shields and crept around the forsaken fountain. Age had touched garden and Palace with the melancholy of places where, in other days, life has passed in scenes of gallantry and love. Beneath the green of the labyrinth, across the terraces and through the salons, laughter and madrigals had flowered; when the white hands in the old portraits on the walls, barely sustaining a little handkerchief of lace, sought the sweet secrets of the heart from the guileless petals of the marguerites. Beautiful memories of long ago! I too remembered days that were past, that sunlit autumn morning when the garden lay wet and freshly green from the constant rain of the night. Under the pure blue of the limpid sky, the venerable cypresses seemed wrapped in visions of monastic peace. The trembling light caressed the flowers like a golden bird, and the breeze traced fantastic footprints on the velvet grass as if unseen fairies were dancing there. Concha stood at the foot of the stairs arranging a huge bunch of roses. Some of them had dropped their petals in her skirt; smiling, she showed them to me: "See, what a pity!" And she buried her pale cheeks in the velvety freshness. "Oh, how sweet."

"Perfume divine! Essence of yourself!" I said, smiling.

With closed eyes she drew a blissful breath. When she raised her head her face was wet with dew like another rose, a pure white rose. Against the background of soft, dark green, with the sunlight wrapping her in draperies of diaphanous gold, she might have been the madonna in the dreams of some Franciscan monk. As I came down the steps to join her she greeted me with a shower of petals from her skirt. We strolled about the garden together. The paths were covered with dry, yellowed leaves which the wind swept before us with a long-drawn rustle. Snails, motionless as old paralytics, sunned themselves on the stone benches. The flowers in the fretted myrtle-bordered baskets were beginning to fade. They filled the air with an intangible sweetness that held the melancholy of remembrance. In the heart of the labyrinth the fountain murmured amid the cypress trees. The soft crooning of the water seemed to have lulled the garden into the peaceful sleep of age: serene, abstracted, forsaken.

"Let us rest here," Concha said.

We sat down in the shade of the acacias on a stone bench covered with dead leaves. The gateway to the green mysterious labyrinth opened before us; the two carved monsters, embellishing its arch, were stained with moss. A path—a single dark path—wound through the myrtle like a solitary life, silent, unknown.

Florisel passed between the trees in the distance carrying a cage for his blackbirds. Concha pointed: "There he goes."

"Who?"

"Florisel."

"Why do you call him Florisel?"

She answered with a light laugh: "Florisel is the page in the fairy tale with whom the disconsolate princess falls in love."

"Who was the author of that fairy tale?"

"Ah, nobody will ever know who wrote the fairy tales."

Her eyes darkened mysteriously as she gazed into the distance and her laugh sounded so strange to me that I felt chilled —the chill of an understanding of life's perversities. It seemed to me that Concha shivered too. The truth is, it was late October and the sun was beginning to cloud over. We returned to the Palace.

X

The Brandeso Palace, although built in the eighteenth century, is almost pure plateresque in style—an Italian palace with balconies and fountains and gardens, built by the Bishop of Corinto, Don Pedro de Bendaña, Knight of the Order of Santiago, Comisario de Cruzada and Confessor to the Queen, María Amelia of Parma. I believe that my ancestor, Marshal Bendaña, and one of Concha's ancestors, had some litigation over the inheritance of the Palace. I am not certain, because this ancestor of mine engaged in litigation over everything, even over the Crown itself. The history of the noble house of Bendaña is the history of the Court of Chancery of Valladolid, and in consequence I inherited quite a fortune in legal documents.

Since Concha cherished the cult of memories, she was eager

to have me go over the Palace with her and recall the days when I used to visit there with my mother; when she and her sisters were pale little girls who came and kissed me and took me by the hand to play with them. Sometimes we played in the tower, sometimes on the terrace or in the glass-walled loggia that looked on the road and the garden. As we went up the ruined stairs that morning, doves took wing and came to light above the stone escutcheons. The sun threw a blaze of gold against the windowpanes; ageless gillyflowers bloomed in the cracks of the wall; a lizard crawled on the balustrade. Concha smiled languidly: "Do you remember?"

And that faint smile magically brought back all the past, as the pervasive fragrance of fading flowers will bring vague but happy memories. . . . Here it was that a pious, sorrowful lady used to relate to us the histories of the saints. How many times she had sat in the window corner showing me the pictures in the Año Cristiano, open in her lap. I can still remember the ethereal hands as they slowly turned the pages. The lady had a beautiful and ancient name; she was called Agueda. She was the mother of Fernandina, Isabel and Concha, the three pale little girls with whom I used to play. After many years I visited again the formal salons and familiar rooms; silent white rooms, walnut-floored, which preserved throughout the year the smell of the autumn apples placed to ripen above the windows; the salons, draped in antique damask, with clouded mirrors and old portraits—ladies in wide petticoats, stern soldiers, pale abbesses, and prelates with pedantic smiles. Our footsteps resounded through the rooms as through deserted churches. In one room only, where the carpeting was cork, our footsteps made no sound; they were quiet as the tread of phantoms with never an echo. The doors swung slowly open on their ornate iron hinges to emit, from the silent obscurity beyond, a faraway perfume of other lives. Seen in the mirrors, as if reflected in an enchanted lake, the salons seemed to stretch on and on into a dreamland where the people of the portraits, early bishops, mournful maidens, and dark-skinned primogenitors seemed to live forgotten, in secular tranquillity.

Concha stopped where two corridors opened into a huge dismantled antechamber furnished with ancient chests. A faint circle of light came from the small oil lamp that burned day and night before a Christ of livid flesh and disheveled hair.

"Do you remember this antechamber?" Concha asked in a low tone.

"Yes. The circular antechamber?"

"Yes—where we used to play."

An old woman sat spinning in a window corner. Concha drew my attention with a gesture.

"Micaela, my mother's maid. Poor thing, she is blind. Say nothing."

We passed on. Sometimes Concha stopped at the threshold of a door and, pointing to the silent room beyond, asked, with an evanescent smile that seemed itself to vanish into the past: "Do you remember?"

She recalled things farthest away in time. She remembered us, as children, jumping up and down in front of the console tables to see the rose-filled vases shake and the lamps with their branching ornaments—the days when our wild, young laughter shook the lofty abstraction of the Palace, as it trilled through the big bright antechambers and floated down dark corridors and out through the slitted windows where the white doves were cooing.

XI

Toward nightfall Concha felt so cold that she was forced to go to bed. Alarmed at the way she trembled and at her deathlike pallor, I wanted to send to Viana del Prior for a doctor, but she opposed it and at the end of an hour she looked at me with a languid smile of love. Lying motionless on the white pillows, she said softly: "Do you know that now it seems a happiness to be ill?"

"Why?"

"Because you are taking care of me."

I smiled without speaking.

"You don't know how much I love you," she sweetly insisted.

In the dusk of the bedroom Concha's subdued voice had a deeply sensuous charm. My soul felt the contagion.

"I love you even more, Princess."

"No, no. . . . In times gone by I knew I appealed strongly to your senses; for however innocent a woman may be, she always recognizes that, and you remember how innocent I was."

I leaned over and kissed her eyes which were veiled with tears.

"Will you believe it, I don't remember that, Concha," I said to divert her.

She laughed and exclaimed: "What a cynic you are."

"Say, rather, what a bad memory I have. It was so long ago!"

"How long was it? Let me see."

"Don't make me sad remembering the years."

"Well, confess anyway that I was very innocent."

"As innocent as a married woman can be."

"More so, much more so! Ah! you were completely my master."

She breathed the last words as if they were sighs and pressed one of her hands to her eyes. As I watched her I felt voluptuous memories exciting my senses. All the fascination that

Concha held for me in other days existed still, purified by her frailness and her pallor. It was true that I had been completely her master. Wedded as a child and to an old man, she was as guilelessly inexperienced as a virgin. For there are bridal beds as cold as sepulchers and bridegrooms who lie like statues of granite. Poor Concha! Close to her lips, perfumed by prayers, my lips had been the first to sing love's triumphs and its glorious exaltations. I must needs teach her the whole book of verse; line by line, the two-and-thirty sonnets of Pietro Aretino. That white, unfolding flower, a child though married, could scarcely murmur the first word. There are husbands and there are lovers who are useless to serve us even as forerunners —though, God knows, the dark, red rose of evil is a flower that never blossomed in love of mine. I have ever preferred to be the Marquis de Bradomín rather than that supreme disciple of perversity, the Marquis de Sade. That alone may explain why some women have found me disdainful; but Concha was never one of these.

Because we had fallen into silence she asked: "Of what are you thinking?"

"Of the past, Concha."

"I am jealous of it."

"Don't be silly! It was of our love of long ago."

She smiled and closed her eyes as if she too were evoking memories. Then she murmured, with a kind of sweet resignation, perfumed with love and melancholy: "I have begged just one thing from the Virgin of the Conception and I believe she will grant it to me . . . in the hour of my death, to have you near me."

We fell once more into a sad silence. After a time Concha raised herself on the pillows; her eyes were full of tears.

"Xavier," she said in a very low voice, "give me the jewel

box on the dressing table. Open it. I keep your letters with my jewels. . . . We will burn them together. . . . I don't wish them to live after me."

The silver casket, engraved with the decadent sumptuousness of the eighteenth century, exhaled a soft perfume of violets. I breathed it in with closed eyes.

"Have you no letters but mine?"

"None."

"Ah! Your new love does not know how to write."

"My new love? Who is my new love? You have been thinking some atrocity!"

"I believe it."

"What?"

"I won't tell you."

"Suppose I guess."

"You can't guess."

"What enormity have you thought of?"

"Florisel!" I exclaimed, laughing.

A shadow of annoyance passed over Concha's eyes: "Were you capable of thinking such a thing!" She buried her hands in my hair, rumpling it over my head: "What shall I do to you? Kill you?"

I laughed, and she laughed too. Her voice was fresh, sensuous, happy. "It's impossible that you should have thought that."

"Say, rather, it seems impossible."

"But you did think it?"

"Yes."

"I don't believe you. How could you even imagine it?"

"I remembered my own first conquest. I was only eleven years old when a lady fell in love with me. She was a very beautiful lady, too."

"My Aunt Augusta," Concha murmured in a low voice.

"Yes."

"You told me of that before. But were you not more beautiful than Florisel?"

I hesitated an instant. I believe my lips were about to stain themselves with a lie, but I finally had the courage to confess the truth: "No, Concha, I was less beautiful."

She gave me a mocking glance and closed the jewel case. "We will burn your letters some other day—not today. Your jealousy has put me in a good humor."

And throwing herself on the pillow she broke into peals of happy laughter.

The day for us to burn the letters never arrived. I have always shrunk from burning love letters. I adore them as poets adore their verses. When Concha died they were inherited by her daughters together with the jewels in the silver casket.

XII

Souls that are sick and in love are perhaps more prone than others to dream dreams and weave illusions. I had never seen Concha so gay or so happy. This rebirth of our love was like an afternoon of golden clouds in a soft and melancholy autumn, an afternoon and clouds such as I gazed upon from the glass-walled loggia as Concha with romantic weariness leaned upon my shoulder. Beneath the rays of the dying sun the road wound luminous and solitary through the moist green country. Concha's eyes were lost in the distance; she raised a pale hand and pointed to the far-off cypresses of the cemetery.

"That is the road we both must travel," Concha sighed.

Poor Concha talked much of dying but without believing in it.

"Concha, don't sadden me," I mocked. "I am a prince, you

know, that you are holding in your palace under enchantment. If you want the enchantment not to be broken you must make a happy ending for the tale."

Concha smiled, forgetting her twilight sorrows. "It is the road, too, by which you came," she said.

Concha made an effort to seem gay. She had learned that all tears are bitter and that sighs, be they ever so soft and sweet, must last but a breath and be gone. Poor Concha, white and pale as the branching lilies that fill the chapel with a rarer perfume as they fade!

Again she raised her hand, diaphanous as a spirit's, and pointed to the distance: "Do you see a man on horseback over there?"

"No."

"He is passing La Fontela now."

"Oh, yes, I see him."

"It is my uncle, Don Juan Manuel."

"The magnificent hidalgo of Lantañón!"

Concha's look was full of pity. "Poor man. He is coming to see you, I am sure."

Don Juan Manuel halted in the middle of the road, stood up in the stirrups and swept off his wide hat to us. His powerful voice shouted out: "Cousin, cousin! Send a servant to open the garden gate."

An echo in the distance repeated: "Gate."

Concha motioned with her arms that she had already done so; then, laughing, she turned to me: "You tell him they are coming."

Shaping my hands to carry the sound, I shouted: "Coming!"

Don Juan Manuel pretended not to hear me. The privilege of making oneself heard at such a distance belonged exclusively to him. Concha covered her ears: "Stop! Stop! For he will never admit he hears you."

I continued to call: "Coming! Coming!" To no purpose. Don Juan Manuel leaned over and patted his horse's neck. He had made up his mind not to hear me. He stood in the stirrups again: "Cousin, cousin!"

Concha leaned against the window laughing merrily like a child while the old man continued to shout: "Cousin, cousin!"

"Isn't he magnificent!"

Magnificent in sooth was Don Juan Manuel Montenegro. It evidently seemed to him that the gate was not opened with the requisite dispatch. He jabbed his horse with the spurs and galloped off, turning to shout from the distance: "Can't wait. Must go to Viana del Prior. Have to thrash the notary."

Florisel, running to open the gate, stopped to watch how gallantly he rode away, then turned and retraced his steps up the ancient ivy-covered stairs. As he passed in front of us he observed in a heavily solemn tone, without lifting his eyes: "A grand Señor, a very grand Señor is Don Juan Manuel!"

I think it was a reproof, for we were still laughing at the old hidalgo.

"Wait, Florisel!" I called.

He stood trembling. "What are the Señor's orders?"

"Does Don Juan Manuel seem to you a very grand Señor?"

"Even more grand than he who hears me now." And he fixed his childlike eyes on Concha, begging forgiveness. Concha absolved her favorite with the air of an indulgent queen; then spoiled it by a wild burst of laughter. The page went silently away. We kissed each other joyously, and before our lips were separated we heard, far off, the song of the blackbirds, led by Florisel's flute of reeds.

XIII

It was a moonlight night. Deep in the labyrinth the fountain sang like a hidden bird. We were silent, with hands enlaced.

Presently, weary footsteps sounded along the corridor. Candelaria entered with a lighted lamp. Concha cried out as if waking from a dream: "Oh! . . . take that light away!"

"You are not going to sit in the dark? You know, there is danger in the moonlight."

"What danger, Candelaria?"

The old woman lowered her voice: "The Señorita knows— witches!"

Candelaria went away with the lamp, crossing herself repeatedly. We turned again and listened to the fountain's song of complaint, as she told the moon of her dark prison in the labyrinth. The ancient cuckoo clock, which had marked the ancestral hours for generations, struck seven.

"How early it gets dark! Only seven!"

"Winter is almost here."

"When do you have to leave me?"

"I? When you tell me to go."

"Ah! When I tell you to go!" sighed Concha. "That I shall never do."

She silently pressed my hand. We were sitting in the loggia. The garden lay before us bright in the moonlight. The weathered cypresses, crowned with stars, were silhouetted against a churchly blue, and from the black fountain came the gleam of silver water. Concha spoke.

"I received a letter yesterday. I shall have to show it to you."

"A letter from whom?"

"From your cousin Isabel. She is coming with the children."

"Isabel Bendaña?"

"Yes."

"But has Isabel children?"

"No," Concha murmured timidly. "My children."

Something like an April breeze passed over the garden of my

memories. Concha's two little daughters had been fond of me in times gone by, and I had loved them too. I raised my eyes to look at their mother, and I never remember so sad a smile on Concha's lips.

"What is it? What is the matter?"

"Nothing."

"Are the children with their father?"

"No. I am having them educated in the Convent of the Enseñanza."

"They must be almost women now."

"Yes. They are big girls."

"They used to be lovely. Are they now?"

"Like their mother."

"Ah, no. Never like their mother."

Concha's lips curved to their accustomed mournful smile. She sat pensively looking at her hands: "I have a favor to ask of you."

"What is it?"

"We must play a little comedy when Isabel comes with the children. I shall tell them that you are at Lantañón hunting with my uncle. Some afternoon you will come and, either because there is a storm or because we are afraid of robbers or something, you will stay on at the Palace as our protector."

"How many days must my exile endure?"

"Not one . . ." Concha answered eagerly. "The very afternoon they come. . . . You are not offended . . . really?"

"No, my life."

"You make me very happy. I have been worrying over it since yesterday, not daring to tell you."

"Do you think Isabel will be deceived?"

"I am not doing it for Isabel. I am doing it for the children; they are almost women now."

"And Don Juan Manuel?"

"I will tell him. He has no scruples—another descendant of the Borgias. Your own uncle, is he not?"

"I don't know—perhaps the relationship is through you."

"I think not," she answered laughing. "I have an idea that your mother called him cousin."

"Oh! My mother could tell us the history of all the branches of the family, but for the present we shall have to consult Florisel."

"He shall be our king-at-arms," Concha replied, and a smile trembled on the flowerlike lips. She crossed her hands in her lap and gazed pensively into the garden.

Florisel's charges, hanging in a cage of reeds in the doorway, were singing an ancient *riveirana;* the lively rustic rhythm evoked a memory of gay, Celtic dances beneath the ancient oaks. Concha began to sing, too. Her voice was as soft as a caress. She got up and walked idly about the loggia. White in the moonlight against the dark shadows of the room, she began to dance the graceful steps of an idyllic pastoral. She stopped soon and sighed: "Ah! How tired I get! I have learned the *riveirana,* you see."

"Are you too a pupil of Florisel?" I answered laughing.

"Yes."

I went over and put my arms around her. She crossed her hands on my shoulder and, leaning her cheek upon them, looked up at me with beautiful sick eyes. We kissed, and her frail lips devoured mine.

XIV

Poor Concha, so wasted, so pale, had for pleasure the sublime endurance of a goddess. That night the flame of passion, now dying down, now raging, long enwrapped us with its golden tongue. As the birds began their choral in the garden I fell asleep in Concha's arms. When I waked she was sitting up against the pillows with an expression of such intense suffering that a chill went through me. Poor Concha! Seeing that my eyes were open she managed to smile.

"What is it, dear?" I asked, caressing her hands.

"I don't know. I think I am very ill."

"But what is it?"

"I don't know. . . . What a shameful thing it would be if they found me here dead."

Her words kindled in me the desire to keep her close to me, and I seized her in my arms.

"Poor love, you are trembling."

She turned down her eyes with the sweet droop that meant she wanted me to kiss the lids. She still trembled; with ardent lips I tried to warm her entire body. My mouth jealously traveled the arms to the shoulder and placed a collar of roses around her neck. I raised my eyes to look at her. She was holding her pale hands crossed in front of her, contemplating them mournfully. Poor hands, so frail, so bloodless, almost ethereal.

"The hands of the Dolorosa," I whispered.

She smiled: "The hands of a corpse."

"To me they are most beautiful when they are whitest."

A happy light came into her eyes: "Ah, yes, I still please you very much. I can still make you feel."

She threw an arm about my neck and with one hand lifted her breasts to me, roses of snow consumed by fever. I clasped her passionately, my desire heightened by the biting terror that I might see her die. I heard her sigh and thought it was the breath of death. Trembling, I placed a kiss as if administering the sacrament. With an aching voluptuousness never felt before my soul floated off on the perfume of that wasting flower whose beauty my impious fingers reverently profaned. I saw her eyes open, filled with amorous light. But nevertheless I divined that she was suffering intensely. The following day Concha was unable to rise from her bed.

XV

Late in the afternoon there was a heavy shower. I had taken refuge in the library and was reading the *"Florilegio de Nuestra Señora,"* a book of sermons compiled by the founder of the Palace, Don Pedro de Bendaña, Bishop of Corinto. At times I was distracted by the roar of the wind in the garden, the swish of dead leaves whirling along the paths of age-old myrtle and the tapping of bare branches on the leaded windowpanes. Within the library there reigned a monasterial peace, a sleep canonical and doctoral. One felt in the atmosphere the breath of the ancient parchment-bound folios—studies of theology, books on linguistics—in which the Bishop used to delve.

All at once I heard a powerful voice in the corridor calling: "Marquis! Marquis de Bradomín . . . !"

I turned the *"Florilegio"* over on the table to keep the page and stood up. The door opened and Don Juan Manuel appeared on the threshold, shaking the rain from his cloak in a shower of drops.

"A bad day, nephew."

"Very bad, uncle." And our relationship was sealed.

"Shut up in here, reading? . . . Nephew, it's the worst thing in the world for your eyes."

He went up to the fire and stretched his hands to the flame: "There is snow falling."

He turned his back to the fire and puffed himself up proudly in front of me. From the depths of his collar his grandiloquent voice boomed out: "Nephew, I see you have inherited your grandfather's mania for reading. He too spent his time poring

over books . . . and lost his wits as a result. What learned
tome is this?"

His deep-sunk eyes, greenish in hue, directed a glance filled
with scorn at the *"Florilegio de Nuestra Señora."* He left the
fire and paced up and down the library with resounding spurs.
Suddenly he stopped: "Marquis de Bradomín, is there no more
of the Blood of Christ in the Brandeso Palace?"

I understood what he wanted and rose. With a haughty expression Don Juan Manuel extended a detaining arm.

"Do not move. Are there no servants in the Palace?"

From where he stood he began to shout lustily: "Arnelas!
Brión! . . . One of you! Come at once!"

He was rapidly losing patience when Florisel appeared at
the door: "Your command, Master?"

Advancing, he kissed the hand of the old hidalgo who patted
the boy on the head: "Bring up the red wine of La Fontela."
And Don Juan Manuel turned to pace the library once more.

From time to time he stopped before the fire and extended
his hands, white, noble and fleshless as the hands of an ascetic
king. Although the years had whitened his hair completely he
preserved the erect, arrogant carriage of his prime when, in the
Noble Guard, he had served His Majesty the King. It was
many years now since he had retired to his estates of Lantañón,
where he passed his days in the usual pursuits of the noble
landowner—trading at the fairs, gaming in the villages, and
sitting at table with the parish priest on feast days. Since
Concha had come to live in retirement in the Brandeso Palace,
it was a frequent occurrence for him to appear there. He would
tie his horse at the garden gate and enter, shouting at the top
of his voice. He would call for wine and drink till he fell asleep
in his chair. When he awoke, whether it was night or day, he
would call for his horse and ride off to his Palace, swaying
wildly in the saddle.

Don Juan Manuel had a great predilection for the red wine of La Fontela which was kept in an ancient cask dating from the time of the French. Growing impatient at the servant's delay in coming up from the wine cellar, he stopped in the middle of the library: "The wine! The wine! . . . But perhaps they are gathering the grapes."

Florisel appeared, all of a tremble, with a large jug which he set upon the table. Don Juan Manuel divested himself of his raincoat and sat down in a big armchair.

"Marquis de Bradomín, I assure you that this wine of La Fontela is the best in the district. You know the wine of Condado? This is better. If it were made of selected grapes it would be the best in the world."

So saying, he filled his glass, one of those massive antique drinking vessels, with a handle, that recall the refectory of a monastery. It was of crystal, engraved on the bottom with the cross of the Order of Calatrava. Quietly and deeply, Don Juan Manuel drank, draining the wine at a single draught and filling his glass again.

"If my niece Concha had drunk more wine like this she would not be as she is today."

As he spoke, Concha came through the doorway, trailing her nunlike draperies and smiling at me: "My uncle, Don Juan Manuel, would like to have you go back with him to his Palace. Has he told you? Tomorrow is a day of festival in one of his villages, San Rosendo de Lantañón. My uncle tells me that you will be received with the honors accorded to a prince of the Church."

Don Juan Manuel assented haughtily.

"You must know that, for three centuries, it has been the privilege of the Marquises de Bradomín to be so honored in the parishes of San Rosendo de Lantañón, Santa Baya de

Cristamilde and San Miguel de Deiro. The three benefices were
gifts of your house. Am I not right, nephew?"

"Quite right, uncle."

"Oh, you needn't ask him," Concha interrupted, laughing.
"Sad though it be, the last Marquis de Bradomín knows not
one word of these things."

Don Juan Manuel gravely shook his head. "He knows that.
He must know it."

Concha dropped into the chair that I had occupied a moment
before and opened the *"Florilegio de Nuestra Señora"* with a
learned air: "I am positive that he doesn't even know the
origin of the house of Bradomín."

Don Juan Manuel turned to me, nobly conciliatory: "Pay
no heed to your cousin. She is mocking you."

Concha insisted: "Why he hardly knows how the coat-of-
arms of the house of Montenegro is composed."

Don Manuel twisted his rugged white brows into a frown.
"The merest child knows that."

With a smile of delicate irony Concha murmured: "It being
the most illustrious of Spanish houses."

"Spanish and German too, my child. We Montenegros of
Galicia are descended from an Empress of Germany. It is the
only Spanish escutcheon which wears metal upon metal—
spurs of gold upon a silver field. The line of Bradomín is very
ancient, too. But among the many titles of your house—
Marquisate of Bradomín—Marquisate of San Miguel—Earldom
of Barbanzón—Señorío of Padín—the most ancient and the
most illustrious is the Señorío. It dates back to Don Roldán,
one of the twelve Peers of the Realm. You know, Don Roldán
did not, as history states, die at Roncesvalles."

I knew nothing, but Concha assented with a nod. Doubtless
she had been made acquainted with this family secret. Don
Juan Manuel, after draining another glass, continued: "I, like

you, am a descendant of Don Roldán; consequen̄
the facts very well. Don Roldán managed to esc
and reached the Island of Salvora. There he was lured by
siren and was shipwrecked upon the coast. He had a son by
the siren who, being born of Don Roldán, was called Padín—
which afterwards became Paladin. That is why a siren clasps
your shield in the Church of Lantañón."

He rose, walked to the window and looked through the
leaded panes to see if the weather was clearing. The sun was
barely visible through the clouds. Don Juan Manuel stood for
a moment studying the sky. Then he turned toward us: "I
shall now go to my mills, not far from here; I will return for
you. . . . Since you have this mania for reading, nephew, I
will give you an old volume at the Palace, with big clear type,
where all this history is related at length."

Don Juan Manuel emptied his glass and stalked from the
library with clanking spurs. When the echo of his footsteps was
lost down the long corridor, Concha, leaning on her chair, got
up and, white as a phantom, came toward me.

XVI

In the depths of the labyrinth the fountain sang like a hidden
bird; the air was warm and sweet. The setting sun gilded the
panes of the loggia where we waited; delicate arches of stained
glass formed the walls, the workmanship of the *grand siècle*
which invented the pavan and the gavotte. In each arch the
panes formed a triptych through which the garden could be
seen in a tempest, in snow or in rain. That afternoon the October sun penetrated to the center of the room like the weary
spear of a warrior of old.

Concha was standing motionless in the arch of the doorway
looking out toward the road while doves circled above her

nead. Concha was vexed because I had heard with a smile her account of a celestial apparition accorded her as she slept in my arms. It was such a dream as might have come to one of the saints in those stories told me as a child by the devout and melancholy lady of the Palace. I recall the dream vaguely. . . . Concha was lost in the labyrinth. Seated at the foot of the fountain she wept disconsolately. Upon this, an angel appeared before her; he wore neither shield nor sword; he was pure and sorrowful as a lily. Concha understood that the angel was not come to contend with Satan. She smiled up at him through her tears and the Archangel, stretching above her his wings of light, guided her. . . . The labyrinth was the sin in which Concha was lost: the water of the fountain, the tears she must weep in purgatory—for, in spite of our guilty love, Concha would not condemn herself to an eternal punishment. The angel guided her through still-green myrtles to the arched gate where the two stone monsters faced each other. There he moved his wings as if to fly upward. Concha, on her knees, asked him if she should atone by entering a convent. The Archangel made no response. Concha, wringing her hands, asked if she should destroy the flower of our love and cast it to the winds. The Archangel made no response. Concha, dragging herself along the stones, asked if she were about to die. Again the Archangel made no response but Concha felt two tears fall upon her hand and roll like diamonds between her fingers. Then Concha had understood the mysterious significance of the dream. . . . When she had finished she sighed: "It is a notification from heaven, Xavier."

"Dreams are no more than dreams, Concha."

"I am going to die! . . . Have you no faith in visions?"

I smiled skeptically, for at that time I did not believe in them.

Concha moved slowly toward the door. The doves circling

above her seemed a happy augury. The moist green landscape smiled in the peace of afternoon. The scattered houses of the village and distant windmills stretched away beneath the trellised vines about the doorway to the blue mountains beyond, with the first snow of autumn on their peaks. The sun came blithely out between the showers. Village folk moved up and down the road; a shepherdess with a shawl of scarlet cloth about her shoulders was guiding her flock toward the Church of San Gundián; women came from the spring singing; a weary old man urged his cows as they stopped to nibble in a field; white mist seemed to rise between the fig trees. . . .

Don Juan Manuel appeared on the summit of the hill, splendidly magnificent, his rain cloak floating to the breeze. The major-domo stood at the foot of the stairs holding the reins of a thoughtful old white horse with a long venerable mane. The ancient nag was as grave and prudent-looking as an archbishop and had belonged to the Palace since time immemorial. He neighed in a truly noble manner and Concha, hearing it, dried the tears that were making her eyes more lovely.

"You will come back tomorrow, Xavier?"

"Yes."

"You promise me?"

"Yes."

"You are not going away vexed with me?"

"I am not going away vexed with you, Concha," I answered, with a lightly mocking smile.

We kissed with the romantic kiss of the times. I was the crusader departing for Jerusalem, and Concha the lady of the castle weeping in the moonlight. I confess that in the days when I wore Merovingian locks flowing on my shoulders, *à la* Espronceda and Zorrilla, I knew no other manner of leave-taking. Today, the years have imposed upon me the tonsure of an acolyte, which permits me only to murmur a sad good-bye.

Happy time, the time of youth! Yet who would be like the fountain in the labyrinth, ageless, soulless, laughing forever its crystal laughter?

XVII

From the glass-walled loggia Concha waved good-bye with her white hand. The sun was low and the moon's slim crescent just appearing in a sad autumnal sky. The Lantañón Palace was two leagues distant; a stony road that held great pools of water before which our Rosinantes hesitated, moving timorous ears. On the other side some peasant boy, quietly waiting while his oxen drank, would stand and watch us in silence. Shepherds driving their flocks back from the mountain halted at the turn of the road and herded their charges aside to let us pass. Don Juan Manuel went first. I could see him sway continually on his horse which seemed restless and unaccustomed to the saddle. It was a small mountain-bred dapple-gray with a wild eye and a hard mouth. It seemed his master had inflicted upon him a docked mane and tail as a chastisement for bad behavior. Don Juan Manuel used little judgment in managing him. He would punish him with the spurs and pull on the reins at the same time, which made the horse rear violently. It never managed to unseat the rider, however, for at such moments the old hidalgo displayed great skill. When we had gone about halfway, complete darkness came upon us. Although Don Juan Manuel swayed continually in his saddle, this did not prevent him from raising a powerful voice to warn me of the bad spots in the road. We came to a fork where three roads met. Some women, kneeling in prayer at a wayside shrine, rose to their feet as we approached. Don Juan Manuel's horse took fright, shied violently and threw his rider. The horse broke away through the screaming women and bolted off at a gallop, dragging the body of Don Juan Manuel, held fast by a foot in the stirrup. I could hear the dull swish of the body as it struck against the thorns that lined the road. In the blackness I saw sparks fly from the horse's hoofs as it dashed down the stony grade descending to the river. After a time I managed to ride ahead and turn my horse across the road. The runaway stopped, flanks quivering and covered with sweat. I jumped to the ground. Don Juan Manuel's body was a mass of blood and mire. As I bent over him he slowly opened his eyes. In pain and bewilderment he closed them again without uttering a complaint. I realized that he had fainted. Lifting him from the ground I laid him across my horse and started back. As we approached the Palace I was obliged to dismount; the body was slipping and I had to place it more securely across the saddle. The coldness of the lifeless hanging hands frightened me. My horse neighed as I took up the bridle again. We drew near the Palace. Through the darkness I made out three men mounted on mules coming through the garden gate to the road. I questioned them from a distance: "Are you hired mounts?"

"Yes, Señor," the three responded in chorus.

"Whom did you bring to the Palace?"

"A lady and two little girls. They arrived this afternoon on the boat from Flavia-Longa."

The three reined their mules to the edge of the road to make way for us. When they saw Don Juan Manuel's body lying across my saddle they muttered together in low tones but did not dare to question me. They undoubtedly thought that I had committed a murder, and I could swear that the three yokels were trembling as they sat their mules.

I dismounted in the middle of the road and ordered one of them to get down and hold my horse while I broke the news at the Palace. The youth jumped off without a word. As he took the reins he recognized Don Juan Manuel: "By Our Lady of Brandeso! His Excellency, Don Juan Manuel of Lantañón!"

Holding the bridle with a trembling hand, he asked in a low respectful tone: "An accident, Señor Marquis?"

"A fall from his horse."

"He seems to be dead."

"Yes, he does seem so."

At that moment Don Juan Manuel painfully raised himself from the saddle: "Only half dead, cousin," he said with a groan that he courageously changed to a sigh.

He directed a questioning glance at the yokels and then turned to me: "What men are these?"

"The hirelings that came with Isabel and the children."

"Where are we then?"

"Back at the Palace."

I took up the bridle and entered the ancient avenue. The yokels took leave of us: "Good night. A safe journey to you."

Don Juan Manuel turned, groaning, and raised himself with a hand on either side of the saddle. He called after them into the distance, his voice as arrogant as ever: "If you find my horse, take it to Viana del Prior. El Berbes will keep him for me."

At the words of the old hidalgo a voice lost in the silence of the night came faintly back on the breeze: "It will be done, Señor padrino."

In the familiar darkness of the chestnut avenue my horse, scenting the stable, neighed again. Ahead of us, close to the Palace, two servants passed talking together in rustic accents. The first one carried a lantern which swung slowly and measuredly as he walked. The smoky oil flame came through the damp-obscured glass with a flickering light that fell upon the wet ground and the wooden shoes of the peasants. They stopped in front of the stairs a moment talking together in low tones. When they saw us they came forward holding the lantern high to throw the light far along the road. They were sheep-tenders who had just been distributing the nightly portion of fresh grass among the stalls. They came up, stupidly frightened, and by the light of the lantern, which they fastened to the balustrade of the staircase, deferentially lowered Don Juan Manuel from the saddle. The old hidalgo walked up the stairs leaning on the servants' shoulders. I went ahead to break the news to Concha. Poor child, she was so good that she seemed always awaiting a fitting occasion to be frightened.

XVIII

I found Concha in the morning room with her daughters, amusing herself in combing the long golden curls of the younger child. The other one was seated beside her mother on the Louis XV sofa. The two children resembled one another closely; blonde with the color of gold in their eyes, like two young princesses in Titian's later manner. The elder was named María Fernanda and the younger María Isabel. They both talked at once, recounting the tale of their journey, while their mother listened, enchanted and happy, her pale fingers lost in the child's golden hair. When I entered she started slightly but controlled herself. The children gazed wide-eyed at me as their mother exclaimed in a voice which trembled a little: "How nice! Did you come from Lantañón? You must have known the children were here."

"I heard of it in the Palace. It is to Don Juan Manuel that I am indebted for the pleasure of seeing you. He fell from his horse going down the Brandeso Hill."

The children questioned their mother: "Is that our uncle from Lantañón?"

"Yes, children."

Leaving the ivory comb imprisoned in the child's curls, Concha drew a pale hand from among the threads of gold and silently extended it to me. The children's innocent eyes never moved from us.

"Merciful heaven!" their mother murmured. "A fall at his age? Where were you coming from?"

"From Viana del Prior."

"How was it that you did not meet Isabel and the children on the road?"

"We took the short cut over the mountain."

Concha looked away, so as not to laugh, and went on combing her daughter's curls, the waving, golden mass of a Venetian matron spread over the shoulders of a child. Isabel came in soon afterwards. "I knew that you were here, cousin," she said.

"How did you know?"

"Because I have seen my Uncle Don Juan Manuel. It was really a miracle that he wasn't killed."

Concha stood up, a child on either side smilingly supporting her, as if it were a game. "Poor man! Let's go and see him, little ones."

"Wait until tomorrow, Concha," I said.

Isabel went over and made her sit down: "It is better for him that he should rest. We have just bound him up in wet vinegar cloths and Candelaria and Florisel have put him to bed."

We all sat down. Concha told the elder child to call Candelaria. The little girl was running to the door when her mother stopped her: "Where are you going, María Fernanda?"

"I thought you told me . . . ?"

"Yes, my child, but it is enough to touch the gong by the dressing table."

María Fernanda flitted shyly over to obey. Her mother kissed her tenderly, then, smiling, kissed the little one who was gazing at her mother with big topaz eyes. Candelaria entered pulling threads for lint from a square of white linen.

"Did you ring?"

María Fernanda stepped forward: "I rang, Candela. Mamma told me to."

The child ran to the old servant and, taking the kerchief from her hands, began to pull the threads. María Isabel, seated upon the floor with her cheek against her mother's knee, lifted her head coaxingly: "Give it to me, Candela. I want to pull the threads."

"Another came first, my dove." And Candelaria, with the loyal smile of an old family servant, showed her wrinkled hands empty. María Fernanda sat down again upon the sofa. My cousin Isabel, who had a partiality for the little one, took the sweet white linen and tore it in two: "Here, darling, take this."

After a moment, María Fernanda, placing thread after thread on her lap, exclaimed with the gravity of a grandmother: "There's a spoiled child for you!"

Candelaria awaited orders in the middle of the room, her hands crossed over her starched, fluted apron. Concha questioned her about Don Juan Manuel: "Have you left him alone?"

"Yes, Señorita. He is asleep."

"In which room did you put him?"

"In the garden room."

"You will prepare a room for the Señor Marquis also. . . . It would never do to allow him to go back to Lantañón alone."

And Concha turned on me her lovely, delicate smile. The old nurse's wrinkled forehead took on a tinge of red. She looked at the children with tenderness; then, with the stark severity of a duenna: "The Bishop's apartments are prepared for the Señor Marquis." And she silently withdrew.

The children applied themselves diligently to fraying the linen, with now and then a furtive glance to see which was getting on the faster. Concha and Isabel talked impenetrable secrets together in undertones. A clock struck ten. In the children's laps the linen threads grew slowly into snowy nosegays.

XIX

I sat down by the fire and entertained myself moving the logs about with the antique tongs of bronze, lavishly ornamented in the traditional manner. The two children had fallen asleep; the elder with her head on her mother's shoulder, the younger in my cousin Isabel's arms. Outside, the rain beat against the windowpanes, and the wind passed in gusts over the dark, mysterious garden. The embers on the hearth shone like rubies; from time to time a gay flame ran lightly over them. Concha and Isabel continued to talk in low voices so as not to waken the children. Seeing each other after such a long time, they turned their eyes to the past, endlessly recalling things that happened long ago; a lengthy whispered exposition of distant relationships long since forgotten; of pious delicate old aunts and pale cousins who pined for lovers; of the unfortunate Countess de Cela, wildly in love with a young student; of Amelia Camarasa who died of consumption; of the Marquis of Tor, known to have had twenty-seven bastards. They talked of our venerable uncle, the noble Bishop of Mondoñedo, who, with the saintly spirit of charity, sheltered in his palace the widow of a Carlist general. I took little notice of what Isabel and Concha were murmuring. From time to time, always at great intervals, they directed a question at me: "Perhaps you know, Xavier. How old is our uncle, the Bishop?"

"He must be seventy."

"Just what I said."

"I thought he was more."

And once again the smooth, warm murmur of feminine conversation resumed its flow until they turned to direct another question at me:

"Do you remember when it was my sisters took their final vows?"

Concha and Isabel seemed to look upon me as the family chronicle. So the evening passed.

About midnight the conversation, like the fire on the hearth, died down. After a long silence, Concha sat up, sighing with weariness, and tried to waken María Fernanda, who was sleeping peacefully on her shoulder.

"Ah, darling child, I can't hold you any longer."

María Fernanda opened eyes heavy with the adorable sleep of childhood. Her mother leaned over to reach for her watch which lay in a jewel box with her rings and her rosary: "Twelve o'clock and these children still up! Don't go to sleep again, precious."

And she tried to lift María Fernanda who had dropped her head to the arm of the sofa.

"You must be put to bed at once."

With her pale lips curved to a faint smile, she regarded her youngest asleep in Isabel's arms with hair spread out around her, a child-angel sepulchered in waves of gold.

"Poor little mite, it hurts me to waken her. Will you ring, Xavier?" she added, turning to me.

At the same time Isabel tried to get up with the child in her arms.

"I can't, she is too heavy."

She gave up, vanquished, and smiled into my eyes. I went to her and took the little one carefully in my arms without waking her; the flood of gold streamed over my shoulder. At that moment we heard, in the corridor, the slow footsteps of Candelaria coming for the children to put them to bed. When she saw me with María Isabel in my arms, she approached respectfully: "I will take her, Señor Marquis. Don't trouble yourself any more."

And she smiled the kindly tranquil smile that one often sees on the lips of toothless grandmothers. Quietly, so as not to waken the child, I stopped her with a gesture. My cousin Isabel got up and took the hand of María Fernanda, who began to cry for her mother to put her to bed. Concha kissed her, saying: "Do you want Isabel to feel hurt?" And then, looking uncertainly from one to the other of us, anxious to please the child: "You don't want her to feel hurt, do you?"

The child, still drowsy-eyed, turned to Isabel with a beseeching look: "Would you feel hurt?"

"So hurt that I wouldn't sleep here tonight."

María Fernanda felt a great curiosity: "Where would you go to sleep?"

"Where could I go? To the priest's house?"

But the child realized it was not fitting that a lady of the house of Bendaña should be lodged elsewhere than in the Brandeso Palace, so with mournful eyes she said good night to her mother. Concha remained in the sitting room alone. When we came back from the bedroom where the children slept we found her in tears.

"She grows more mad about you every day," Isabel said to me in an undertone.

Concha fancied she was murmuring something else, and she looked at us through her tears with jealous eyes. Isabel pretended not to notice it. Smiling, she entered the room in front of me and went over and sat on the sofa beside Concha.

"What is the matter, little cousin?"

Without answering, Concha brushed her handkerchief across her eyes and then ground it between her teeth. I looked at her with a smile of understanding and saw the red mount to her cheeks.

XX

As I was closing the door of my bedroom I saw, in the dark corridor, a white shadow moving slowly along the wall. It was Concha. She came to me without a sound. "Are you alone, Xavier?"

"Alone with my thoughts."

"What bad company!"

"You have the power of divination. I was thinking of you."

Concha stopped at the threshold. Her eyes had a frightened expression and she smiled weakly. She looked toward the dark hall and shuddered, utterly pale: "I have just seen a black spider. . . . It was running along the floor. . . . It was enormous. I don't know whether I am bringing it in with me. . . ."

She shook the train of her white gown in the air. We went in and softly closed the door. Concha stopped in the middle of the room, drew a letter from her breast and held it out to me: "From your mother."

"For you, or for me?"

"For me."

As she gave it to me she covered her eyes with her hand and I saw her bite her lips to keep back the tears. At last she burst into sobs: "Oh, God. . . . Oh, God!"

"What does she say?"

Concha clasped her hands over her forehead which was almost hidden under great waves of black hair that streamed out tragically like heavy smoke from a torch in the wind.

"Read! Read! Read! . . . That I am the wickedest woman in the world. . . . That I am leading a scandalous life. . . . That I am doomed to eternal punishment. . . . That I am robbing her son!"

With great calmness I held the letter to the candle flame.

"But I wanted you to read it," Concha moaned.

"No, my dear, the handwriting is too impossible."

Seeing the letter fly away in ashes, Concha dried her tears:
"How could Aunt Soledad write to me like that when I love
her and respect her so! Why should she hate me? Why should
she curse me when nothing would give me greater joy than to
care for her and wait upon her, like a daughter. Oh God, I am
well punished. . . . To tell me that I am making you unhappy . . ."

Without having read my mother's letter I could imagine it.
Frenzied outcries—the angry anathemas of a sibyl—Biblical
citations! I had received so many letters like it. The poor lady
was a saint. She was not in a saint's niche only because, having
been born head of a noble house, she felt it her duty to per-
petuate an escutcheon as illustrious as that of Don Juan Manuel
himself. But for the obligation of assuring male succession to
the entail, with all its illustrious privileges and revenues, she
would have been a saint in the Spanish manner, abbess of a
convent, fanatical seer of visions, militant bride of Christ.

For many years now, my mother, María Soledad Carlota
Elena Agar y Bendaña, had led a devout retired life in her
Palace of Bradomín. She was a tall, gray-haired woman, very
charitable, but credulous and despotic. I used to visit her every
autumn. Although frail in health, the sight of her first-born
always seemed to put new life into her. She passed her days
seated at a great window in a chair of crimson velvet studded
with silver nails, spinning for her servants. In the afternoons
the sun reached to the depths of the room and marked a golden
path like the stele of light in the saintly visions of María
Soledad's childhood. In the silence, she heard day and night
the distant murmur of the river as it fell over the milldam. My
mother passed hours and hours at her spinning wheel with its
distaff of blessed aromatic wood; a prayer forever trembled on
her faded lips.

All my misdeeds she blamed upon Concha, holding her in horror for them. She remembered, and looked upon it as an affront to her white hairs, that our love affair had begun in the Bradomín Palace one summer that Concha had spent there to be a companion for her. My mother was Concha's godmother and, up to that time, had been extremely fond of her. After that she never saw her again. One day when I was away hunting, Concha left the Palace forever. She went alone, weeping, with covered head, like a heretic expelled by the Inquisition from a Spanish city of old. My mother's curse followed her from the door. Beside my mother stood a white-faced servant, the informer who told of our love. Perhaps the same lips had told her now that the Marquis of Bradomín was staying in the Brandeso Palace.

Concha continued to lament: "I am well punished. . . . I am well punished. . . ."

The round tears slid slowly down her cheeks, pure and clear as unset diamonds. My lips drank the tears on her eyes, on her cheeks, at the corners of her mouth. Concha laid her head upon my shoulder and shivered: "She will write to you too," she sighed. "What will you do then?"

"Whatever you wish," I whispered in her ear.

She was silent a moment, with closed eyes. When she opened them I saw intense love and the sorrow of renunciation. "If your mother writes, you must obey her."

She started to leave me. I stopped her. "You are not saying what you mean, Concha."

"Yes, I am saying what I mean. You know what injury I am doing my husband, day after day. Well, I swear that, in the hour of my death, I would rather have your mother's pardon than my husband's."

"You will have everybody's pardon, Concha—and the papal benediction as well."

"Ah, if God should hear you! But no, God cannot hear us—neither you nor me."

"We'll tell it to Don Juan Manuel, then. He has a more powerful voice."

Concha was in the doorway gathering up her white draperies. She shook her head reprovingly: "Xavier, Xavier!"

"You are not going?" I said, drawing near to her.

"Yes. I'll come again tomorrow."

"Tomorrow you'll do as today."

"No. . . . I promise."

She was in the corridor now. I heard her call in a low tone: "Come with me. I am afraid of the spiders. Don't talk loud. Isabel sleeps in there."

And her hand, ghostlike in the darkness, waved toward a closed door, from under which a pale gleam spread along the black floor.

"She sleeps with a light."

"Yes."

I stood still and drew her head to my shoulder. "You see . . . even Isabel cannot sleep alone. Let us follow her example."

She laughed silently. I lifted her in my arms, carried her as if she were a child down the long corridors to her room, and put her down before the door which stood open to the dark beyond.

XXI

I went to my bed exhausted and lay the whole morning, hearing between dreams the laughter and cries and racing of the two children. They were playing in the loggia upon which the three doors of my bedroom opened. I slept but little, in a miserable state of semiconsciousness. I noticed it when the children stopped in front of one of the doors and when they raised their voices. The green gadfly, nightmare, circled about me ceaselessly like the spindle of a spinning witch. All at once it seemed to me that the children were going away. A voice called them from the garden and they passed running before the three doors. The loggia was left deserted. I lay in a lethargy which in the most painful way destroyed all my volition. My thoughts, in a grotesque rhythm, wandered through an intricate maze and searched the baleful nest in which are born bad dreams and hideous ideas and torturing fancies.

The silence was broken by the lively barking of dogs and the music of bells. A grave ecclesiastical voice which seemed to come from far off called: "Here, Capitán! . . . Here, Carabel!"

It was the parish priest of Brandeso who had come to the Palace after Mass to pay his respects to my noble cousins. "Here, Capitán! . . . Here, Carabel!"

Concha and Isabel were taking leave of the priest from the terrace: "Good-bye, Don Benicio."

"Good-bye, Señoritas," the priest replied, descending the stairs. "Retire inside, for the air is cool. Here, Capitán! . . . Here, Carabel!"

I could hear distinctly the frolicsome racing of the dogs. After a moment's silence Concha's voice was raised languidly: "Don Benicio, you celebrate Mass in the chapel tomorrow. You won't forget?"

And the grave ecclesiastical voice replied: "I shall not forget. . . . I shall not forget."

It ascended from the garden like a Gregorian chant, accompanied by the jingling of the dogs' bells. The two ladies said good-bye once more and the grave ecclesiastical voice repeated: "Here, Capitán! . . . Here, Carabel! Tell the Marquis de Bradomín that a few days ago I was hunting with the Chamberlain and we flushed a covey of partridges. Ask him

when he will come out with me to shoot them. But don't tell
the Chamberlain when he comes. He charged me to keep it
secret."

Concha and Isabel passed before the three doors. Their
voices were a soft, sweet murmur. The terrace regained its
silence and in that silence I awoke completely and could not
induce sleep to return. I rang a silver bell which, in the dimness of the bedroom, shone with ecclesiastical splendor on the
crimson velvet cover of an antique table. Florisel came to serve
me while I dressed. Time passed and I heard the children's
voices again. They were coming from the pigeon-house with
Candelaria. They carried a pair of young doves and were talking about them excitedly. The old servant was saying, as if it
were a fairy tale, that if they clipped the dove's wings they
could let them free in the Palace.

"When mother was little, like us, she loved to play with
pigeons too."

Florisel threw open the three doors that opened on the
loggia. I walked out and called to the children who ran to kiss
me—each with a white dove in her hands. They made me think
of the celestial gifts accorded the young princesses who, like
irises of cerulean blue, perfume the pages of the golden legend.

"Did you know that our uncle of Lantañón went off at daybreak on his horse?" the children asked me.

"Who told you so?"

"We went to his room to see him and found everything
open, doors and windows, and the bed all tumbled. Candelaria
says she saw him go—and Florisel too."

I could only laugh. "Does your mother know?" I asked.

"Yes."

"And what does she say?"

The children looked at each other and hesitated. Then, with

an exchange of smiles, they cried both together: "Mother says he's crazy."

Candelaria called them and they ran off to clip the wings of the young pigeons and free them in the rooms of the Palace— the game that Concha, as a child, had loved so much.

XXII

In the shining laziness of afternoon, with all the windows of the loggia gilded by the sun and doves flying overhead, Isabel and the children talked of going with me to Lantañón to inquire how our uncle, Don Juan Manuel, had reached home.

"How far is it, Xavier?" Isabel asked.

"About two leagues."

"Then we can go on foot."

"Won't the children get tired?"

"They're used to walking."

The children rushed forward exclaiming radiantly in unison: "No, no! We climbed Pico Sagro last year without getting tired."

Isabel looked out toward the garden: "I think the weather will be fine."

"Who can tell! Those clouds carry water."

"Yes, but they are going the other way." Isabel trusted to the gallantry of the clouds.

We two were at the window, close together, talking and studying the sky and the landscape. The children were clapping their hands and screaming at the doves to frighten them into flying. I turned and saw Concha standing in the doorway. She was very pale, her lips were quivering and her eyes had a strange expression as she looked at me. There was anger in them and longing and supplication. She raised both hands to her forehead. "Florisel told me that you were in the garden," she murmured.

"We have been."

"You were hiding from me, it seems."

"Yes. We were conspiring," Isabel answered smiling.

Taking the two children by the hand, she left the room with them. Concha and I were alone. She moved languidly over to her chair and sat down. She sighed heavily, as she often did, and told me she was dying. I went up to her laughing and she became indignant. "Laugh! You do well to leave me alone. Go with Isabel."

I took up one of her hands, bunched the fingers into a pale little rose, and with closed eyes kissed them.

"Don't make me suffer, Concha."

She dropped her lids over tear-filled eyes and said, in a low penitent voice: "Why do you want to leave me alone? It's not your fault, I know. It is she who is mad about you and runs after you."

I dried her tears: "Concha dear, it is you who are mad and nobody else, but it is such a charming madness that I would never wish to see it cured."

"I am not mad."

"Indeed you are—mad about me."

"No, no, no!" she repeated in pretty vexation.

"Yes."

"Conceited!"

"Why then do you want to keep me beside you?"

Concha threw her arms about my neck, kissed me and exclaimed laughing: "The truth is, if you are so vain of my affection, it must be because it is so valuable."

"Of priceless value."

Concha passed her hands over my hair in a lingering caress: "Let them go without you, Xavier. You see, I care more for you than for my own children."

Yielding like a submissive child, I pressed my head against

her breast and closed my eyes. With rapturous ecstasy that yet was sorrow I breathed the perfume of that drooping flower.

"I will do whatever you wish. You know that."

Looking me in the eyes and lowering her voice, Concha murmured: "Then you won't go to Lantañón?"

"No."

"Are you annoyed?"

"No. I am only sorry on the children's account. They were told they could go."

"They can go with Isabel—the major-domo can accompany them."

At that moment a sudden shower lashed the windowpanes and deluged the green garden; clouds obscured the sun; and the October afternoon took on a soft, sad light that seemed the very spirit of autumn.

María Fernanda entered much distressed: "Have you seen what bad luck we are having, Xavier? It is raining."

Then María Isabel came in: "May we go if it clears, Mamma?"

"Yes, if it clears," Concha answered.

The two children stationed themselves at the window and with faces glued against the glass watched the rain. Dark, lead-colored clouds were gathering over La Sierra de Céltigos on a watery horizon; shepherds, calling their sheep, hurried down the road enveloped in capes of frieze; a rainbow spanned the garden; the dark cypress trees and rain-washed myrtle trembled in rays of orange light. Candelaria, with skirts tucked up above clumping wooden shoes, went about, under a big blue umbrella, gathering roses for the chapel altar.

XXIII

The chapel was dark, damp, resounding. Above the altar hung a shield of sixteen quarterings, enameled in color, gules and

azure, sable and sinople, gold and silver—the arms granted
by writ of Their Catholic Majesties to Captain Alonzo Bendaña, founder of the house of Brandeso.

There is a wild legend recounted of this same Captain in
the nobiliary accounts of Galicia. The tale goes that having
taken prisoner his enemy, the Abbot of Mos, while on a hunting party, he dressed the abbot in a wolfskin and turned him
loose on the mountain, where his enemy was torn to pieces by
the teeth of the dogs. Candelaria, Concha's old nurse, like all
ancient servants, was intimately familiar with the history and
genealogy of the house she served. And in the old days, she
used to relate to us this legend of Captain Alonzo Bendaña, as
it is given in those old accounts which no one now reads. But
Candelaria knew furthermore that two black dwarfs had carried the Captain's body to hell. It was a tradition of the house
of Bradomín that the men of the race were cruel and the
women pious. I well remember the time when there was a chap-
lain attached to the Palace and my Aunt Agueda, following a
noble old custom, used to hear Mass from a small gallery near
the pulpit, surrounded by all her daughters. In this gallery
was a bench of crimson velvet, its high back crowned with two
escutcheons, but only my Aunt Agueda, because of her age and
failing health, enjoyed the privilege of being seated there.

At the right of the altar was interred Captain Alonzo Bendaña with other caballeros of his line. A statue of a praying
warrior guarded the sepulcher. At the left of the altar was
interred Doña Beatriz de Montenegro with other ladies of various lineage. The sepulcher was adorned by the statue of a
praying nun, robed in the white habit of the Comendadoras de
Santiago. The chancel lamp burned day and night before an
altarpiece as finely wrought as the jewel of a queen. An evan-
gelic vine laden with golden fruit framed the guardian saint,
pious King Mago, as he offered myrrh to the Infant Jesus. His

gold-embroidered, silken tunic shone with the splendor of an oriental miracle. The light of the lamp, between silver chains, had the timid flutter of a prisoned bird struggling to fly upward to the Saint.

That afternoon Concha desired to place with her own hands the rose-laden vases at the feet of King Mago as an offering of her devout spirit. Afterwards, accompanied by the children, she knelt before the altar. To me, in the gallery, Concha's voice was only a murmur as she recited the Ave Marias, but when it came to the children to respond I could hear every word of the ritual. At the end of the prayer, Concha kissed the rosary, got up and traversed the chancel, making the sign of the cross. She called the children to pray before the sepulcher of the warrior, where Don Miguel Bendaña, Concha's grandfather, was also buried. This Señor of Brandeso was in the act of dying at the time when my mother brought me to the Palace for the first time. Don Miguel Bendaña was an aristocrat, despotic, generous, faithful to the traditions of his house. Upright as a lance, he passed through the world with no unbending to the common touch. Beautiful and noble eccentricity! When he died, at eighty years, his spirit was still valiant, proud and finely tempered as an ancient sword. For five days he lay at the point of death refusing to confess himself. My mother asseverated that she had never seen the like. That old hidalgo was a heretic. One night, a short while after his death, I heard it related, in a hollow whisper, that Don Miguel Bendaña had murdered one of his own servants. Well might Concha pray for his soul!

The afternoon was dying; the prayers reverberated through the quiet dark of the chapel, solemnly sad like an echo of the Passion. I drowsed in the gallery. The children seated themselves on the steps before the altar. Their dresses were as purely white as the liturgic linen. I could just distinguish a shadow that prayed under the chancel lamp. It was Concha. She had an open book between her hands and read with head devoutly bent. Now and then, as the wind stirred the draperies of the great, high window, I could see the moon's pale, supernatural face gazing from the now darkened sky, like some goddess looking to her altars in wood and lake.

Concha closed the book with a sigh and called again to the children. I saw their white shadows flit across the chancel and I knew that they knelt beside their mother. The trembling lamplight shed a pale glory over Concha's hands as they supported the open book. In the silence her voice read slowly and devoutly. The children listened. I divined their bright hair flowing over the pure whiteness of their garments. Concha read.

XXIV

It was the middle of the night. I was writing when Concha softly entered my room, wrapped in her nunlike gown. "To whom are you writing?" she asked.

"To Doña Margarita's secretary."

"What are you saying to him?"

"Giving an account of a donation for missions which I have made in the Queen's name."

There was a moment of silence. Concha stood, leaning her hands on my shoulders. As she bent over me her hair brushed my forehead. "Are you writing to her secretary or are you writing to the Queen herself?"

I turned with deliberate coldness: "I am writing to the secretary. Surely you are not jealous of the Queen?"

"No, no," she protested eagerly.

I took her upon my knee and said, caressing her: "Doña Margarita is not like the other, you know. . . ."

"A great many things that were said of the other were calumny. My mother, who was her lady-in-waiting, always maintained so."

Seeing that I smiled, poor Concha dropped her eyes in adorable embarrassment.

"Men always believe the evil that is spoken of women. . . . And a queen has so many enemies!"

She saw the smile still on my lips and twisted my black mustache with her white fingers: "Naughty mouth!"

She stood up with the intention of going. With one hand, I detained her.

"Stay, Concha."

"It cannot be, Xavier. You know that."

"Stay," I repeated.

"No, no. . . . I want to confess tomorrow. . . . It frightens me to offend God like this."

I stood up, courteously, icily disdainful. "It appears, then, that I have a rival?"

Concha looked at me with supplication in her eyes: "Xavier, don't hurt me so."

"I have no wish to hurt you. I leave the Palace tomorrow."

Tearful, angry, she exclaimed: "You shall not leave tomorrow!"

Almost tearing off the clinging white gown, she stood naked, trembling.

I held out my arms: "My poor love!"

She looked at me through her tears, pale and changed: "How cruel you are. . . . Now I cannot confess tomorrow?"

I kissed her and said to console her: "We will both confess the day I leave."

I saw a fugitive smile pass in her eyes: "If you hope to gain your liberty with that promise you will not succeed."

"Why?"

"Because you are my prisoner for life."

Circling my neck with her arms she laughed. The black knot of her hair came down; she lifted the dusky perfumed flood in her white hands and whipped me with it.

"The lash of God!" I sighed, with eyes half closed.

"Be still, heretic!"

"Do you remember how this used to make me all but swoon?"

"I remember every bit of your mad behavior."

"Whip me now, Concha. . . . Whip me as though I were the Divine Nazarene. . . . Whip me to death. . . ."

"Be still, be still."

With wild eyes and hands that trembled, she commenced to gather up the dark, perfumed mass. "You fill me with terror when you say such impious things. Yes, terror . . . because it is not you who speaks. It is Satan. Even to your voice you are different. It is Satan."

In extreme agitation she closed her eyes as my arms sheltered her lovingly. It seemed to me that a prayer strayed on her lips. Laughing, I sealed the lips with mine. "Amen. . . . Amen. . . . Amen!" I murmured.

There was a silence. Suddenly I felt her mouth moan under my mouth. "I am dying."

Her body, clasped in my arms, trembled as if shaken by a mortal chill. Her livid head rolled on the pillow in a faint. Her eyelids half opened, sluggishly; I saw her eyes, dulled, anguished.

"Concha. . . . Concha. . . ."

I sat up against the pillow. Instantly cool and prudent I freed the hands that were still clasped around my neck. They were like wax.

I stood irresolute, not daring to move.

"Concha. . . . Concha. . . ."

Far off, I heard the howl of a dog. I slid to the floor without a sound. Seizing the light I gazed at the changed face. I touched the forehead with a trembling hand. The chill repose of death appalled me. No, I could not depend upon myself. I thought of fleeing and cautiously opened a window. With my hair standing on end I gazed out into the blackness, while inside the room the curtains of my bed fluttered and the flames of the candles in the silver stands wavered sickeningly. The dog's howl still came from very far away; the wind went through the labyrinth complaining like a soul in pain; clouds passed over the moon and quenched the burning stars as death snuffs out poor human lives.

XXV

I left the window open and, moving without a sound, as if I feared my footsteps might waken the pallid specter on the bed, I crossed to the door which, but a moment before, had been closed by hands tremulous with passion that now were motionless. Fearfully I looked down the black corridor and adventured into its dark. Everything in the Palace seemed to sleep. My footsteps scarcely made a sound, but they rang in my imagination with a fearful resonance. Far ahead, in the antechamber, a pale light trembled from the lamp that burned before the image of Jesus of Nazareth. That holy face, livid and discomposed, inspired a greater fear than the dead face of Concha. With trembling limbs I reached Concha's bedroom and stopped at the door to watch a streak of light, far down the corridor, which marked on the blackness of the floor the bedroom where my cousin Isabel was sleeping. I feared to see her appear, aghast and terrified at the sound of my footsteps. I feared her cries would alarm the Palace. I resolved to go in to her and tell her everything. I moved stealthily to her door.

Opening it softly, I called in a muffled voice: "Isabel. . . . Isabel. . . ."

I waited. Nothing disturbed the silence. I took a few steps forward and called again: "Isabel. . . . Isabel. . . ."

Still no response. My voice died away in the vast chamber, as if too terrified to sound. Isabel was asleep. In the faint glow of the night light that flickered in a crystal vase, my eyes made out the wooden bed. In the silence, my cousin Isabel's breathing rose and fell with a slow regular rhythm. Beneath the damask coverlet her body showed softly indefinite; her loose hair lay like a dark veil spread over the white pillows. I called again: "Isabel. . . . Isabel. . . ."

I had reached the bedside and stretched out my hand. By chance it rested on my cousin's bare, warm shoulder. I felt a quiver. In a low voice I spoke again: "Isabel. . . . Isabel. . . ."

Isabel sat up with a start: "Don't call. Concha can hear you."

My eyes filled with tears. Bending down I murmured: "Poor Concha cannot hear us."

One of Isabel's soft tempting curls touched my lips. I believe I kissed it. As with the saints, my heart is at its tenderest when touched with grief. Concha in heaven will have pardoned my weakness, for here on earth she knew it well. Isabel, breathing excitedly, whispered: "Had I suspected this I would have turned the key."

"Which way, Isabel?"

"To lock you out, bandit. To lock you out!"

I had not the heart to contravert my cousin Isabel's suspicions. To prove her mistaken would have been so ungallant and so painful. Isabel was pious and the knowledge that she had calumniated me would have caused her suffering. Ah me!

All the saintly martyrs gone before me, monks, and patriarchs and holy fathers, were in better case than I to triumph over sin. The lovely women who tempted them were not their cousins. Life plays some cruel jests. When destiny smiles on me, it is always as it was that night, with the leering grimace of a bowlegged dwarf capering on castle chimney tops by moonlight.

Suffocated by my kisses, Isabel stammered: "I'm afraid Concha may come."

A shudder of horror ran through my body. Isabel thought it was the ecstasy of love. She never knew why I had gone to her.

XXVI

When my mortal eyes again beheld Concha's yellow disfigured face, when my feverish hands again touched her stiff hands, the terror that I felt was such that I began to pray, and again the temptation came to flee by the window which stood open to the dark, mysterious garden. The silent breeze of night fluttered the curtains and lifted the hair on my head. The stars were paling in the livid sky and the wind had visited the silver candelabra, extinguishing the flames till only one remained. The ancient cypresses, standing erect below the window, slowly bowed their melancholy tops and the moon passed fugitive and white between them like a soul in torment. In the silence the distant crow of a cock announced the imminent dawn. A shudder passed through my frame and I gazed with horror at the inanimate body of Concha stretched upon my bed. Then, suddenly recovering my senses, I lighted all the candles of the branching candlestick and placed it in the doorway to illuminate the corridor. I went back; my arms grasped with terror the ghastly phantom that had so often slept in them. I walked

out with the funereal burden. As we crossed the threshold, an
inert hand swung itself slowly through the burning candle
flames and knocked over the candelabrum. On the floor the
candles continued to burn where they fell with a sickly, flickering light. For an instant I stood petrified and listened. All
that I heard was the murmur of the fountain in the labyrinth.
I went on. Ahead of me, in the vast antechamber, shone the
lamp of the Nazarene; I was afraid to pass before that livid,
disheveled image. I feared its dead gaze. I went back.

To reach Concha's bedroom without going through the antechamber it was necessary to traverse the entire Palace. I did
not hesitate. One after the other I passed through huge salons
and shadowy corridors. At times the light of the moon reached
into the deserted depths of the apartments. I moved like a
shadow before the long succession of gloomy, leaded windows
standing somberly closed, in crumbling, blackened frames.
When I crossed before a mirror I closed my eyes so as not to
see myself. Cold sweat stood on my forehead. At times the
darkness was so dense that I went astray and was forced to
adventure at random—rigid, anguished—supporting the body
with only one arm, the other stretched out before me to prevent a stumble. As we passed through a doorway, a waving
strand of the tragic hair caught and held fast. I groped about
in the blackness trying to loosen it. I could not. It became more
entangled every moment. My hand, stupid with terror, trembled over it and the door pulled slowly open and closed, creaking lengthily. To my horror, I saw that day was dawning. Giddiness seized me and I pulled . . . the body seemed trying to
escape my arms. In desperation, I clasped it more tightly. Under the forehead, tight-drawn and dark, the waxen eyelids
slowly opened. I pressed them shut and pulled brutally until
the beloved, perfumed hair broke. . . . With the body grap-
pled in my arms I fled.

I reached the open door of Concha's bedroom. The warm perfumed dark beyond breathed mystery as if it still guarded the tender secret of our amorous hours. What a tragic secret it must guard henceforth!

Carefully, cautiously, I left Concha's body stretched upon the bed and moved away without a sound. At the door I stopped, irresolute, and drew a long breath. I was uncertain whether to go back and place a last kiss upon those icy lips. I resisted the temptation. An almost religious scruple constrained me. I feared there might be something sacrilegious in the sensuous grief that possessed me. The warm fragrance of the bedroom kindled voluptuous memories of the senses that were a torture to me. I fervently desired to feel pure and sweet, but could not control my wild imaginings. It has happened at times even to the mystics that sacred things have suggested to them monstrous diabolisms. To this day there is a touch of subtle depravity in the sorrow that the memory of Concha's death brings to me. It claws at my heart like a lean cat with glittering eyes. It twists my heart till it bleeds in agony, yet all the while, deep down, the devil in me, who can change all grief to glee, laughs and laughs.

My memories, lost glories of my soul, are like burning music, cruel and sad, to whose strange rhythm dances the weeping phantom that was my love. Poor white phantom! Worms have eaten the eyes; tears roll from the sockets as it dances in the ring of my youthful memories; never touching earth, it floats upward on a wave of perfume, the scent of her sweet hair which lives on after she has gone. Poor Concha! Her passage through the world left behind no more than a wake of perfumes. But it may be that she, the whitest and chastest of my loves, was never more than an exquisite incarnation of the sensuous perfumes of Aphrodite.

XXVII

María Isabel and María Fernanda first announced themselves by knocking with childish hands upon my door. Then came their fresh voices, crystal clear, like the voice of a mountain spring as it talks with the birds and the flowers. "May we come in, Xavier?"

"Yes, children, come in."

The morning was well advanced and they had come to inquire, in Isabel's name, how I had passed the night—a gentle question that filled my heart with remorse. The children stood beside me, in the window, looking out into the garden. The frowning green branches of a yew tree brushed mournfully against the panes. Under the wind from the mountains the yew felt shiverings of cold, and the touch of its green branches on the panes seemed like an appeal from the dark old garden for the children to come out and play. Deep in the labyrinth, a band of doves circled about close to the ground, and from the cold blue sky above a keen-eyed hawk swooped down on long, black wings. "Oh, Xavier, kill it! . . . Kill it!" the children cried.

I went for the gun which slept, dust-covered, in a corner of my room and came back to the balcony. The children clapped their hands: "Kill it! Kill it!"

At that moment the hawk fell upon the doves which flew about terror-stricken. I put the gun to my cheek and, when an opening came, fired. Some dogs barked in the fields near by. The doves wheeled about in the smoke and the hawk, with wings outstretched, fell dead. The children ran down and picked it up by the tips of the wings. Bright blood trickled from the plumage of the breast. They started off carrying the hawk triumphantly between them. A new anxiety awoke in me.

"Where are you going?" I called to them.

They turned in the doorway, smiling delightedly. "Wait and see how we will frighten mother when she wakes up."

"No, no, no!"

"Oh, just a make-believe fright."

I did not dare to stop them. I stayed and waited, sick at heart. Bitter suspense! Waiting on that radiant morning of sunlight for the fatal moment when the cries of the innocent should ring through the chambers of the Palace! Heartbroken moans and violent sobbings. . . .

I felt the dull anguish of despair in the presence of that mute, cold phantom, Death, who reaped the dreams in the garden of my heart . . . beautiful dreams conjured up by the magic of love! An extraordinary sadness fell upon me; as if the twilight were closing in upon my life; as if my life like a dreary day of winter were drawing to a close, to begin anew, tomorrow, with a sunless dawn. Poor Concha was dead! Dead, that flower of my dreams to whom all my words seemed beautiful! That flower of my dreams to whom my every gesture seemed sublime! . . . Would I ever again encounter a pale princess with enchanting, sorrowful eyes who would see me always magnificent? In the face of this doubt I wept. Wept like an outworn god of antiquity, lamenting the extinction of his cult.

Prometheus

RAMÓN PÉREZ DE AYALA

I Rhapsody by Way of Prologue

How the Modern Odysseus Met with
the Modern Nausicaa

Why leave the land of unhappy hours
In search of fresh adventure
If these lost hours are your companions,
If the dust of the day's journey
On sandal and vestment
Goes with you?

Whatever way you travel . . .
Footpath . . . byway . . . highroad . . .
Always in eyes and mouth
The bitterness of the dust
Of a strange land!
You will never reach the longed-for
Destination.

Your hand will not relinquish the staff.
Doomed to wander

You will know yourself in the deeps of the heart
Forever an exile.

Do not travel by land!
Make your way across the sea.
Set foot upon shores of mystery,
As if born to a new life.

On an unknown course
The sea-chariot goes flying,
Giving its canvas sails
To the wind.
No dust arises on its journey:
And the bough of an oak tree
Glories at the prow.

Govern your own soul: be self-sufficient.
Make of your life a colossal dream
Ceaselessly renewed.
Cling to the floating spar,
Strike out across the sea.

The adventure befell more or less as it is related by the bard Homer, him of the eyes without light. The events, as frequently fortunate as ill-fated, which preceded the adventure, likewise the accompanying circumstances, reproduce the ancient fable, even though changed times have introduced slight variations. Events, circumstances and variations afford more than sufficient material for a preliminary rhapsody, and therefore the narrator finds himself forced into a summary account. Thus, what in epic ages was an heroic chant, to the sound of the cither, is today a mute and graphic voice, that is to say, the written word, with no other accompaniment than the

languid stridency of the metallic pen over the perishable paper.
The bard has degenerated into a novelist.

Sing, oh meddlesome goddess of these plebeian days; goddess of impertinent curiosity and prying boredom, who hast
no joy unless it be in raking over the ashes of thy neighbor's
hearth! Sing, I tell thee, the rare emprises of love and fortune
of the modern Odysseus, a man magnanimous, astute when
occasion required, like to the Immortals in his eminence, in his
corpulence, in the breadth of his shoulders, and in his predilection for ambrosial beverages, in common speech, alcoholic
drinks, which delightfully cloud the brain, and cause one to
break forth into Olympic laughter, and other follies, wholly
useless: for the Immortals, guests of the limitless Ouranos,
differ from poor mortals in that, having in their own hands
the dominion of incalculable time, they are not enslaved by
minute practical endeavors, and act always in a fashion that to
us seems inconsistent and nonsensical. Sing, or relate, oh tattle-
tale, gossiping goddess! how the divine Odysseus, born in the
city where Ares was dashed down by the Baptist, set out for
sacred Ilios, the citadel of which he took by virtue of his
genius; how, later, he visited the land of the lotus eaters, whose
fare is a flower which causes loss of memory, and grants the
sweet gift of forgetfulness; how, fleeing from them, he suffered ills without number, and fell at length into the arms of
the revered and enchanting Circe, of the abundant tresses;
how, thanks to Hermes, god of the golden wand, who in every
respect preserves his youthful beauty, he escaped from the
malignant, ardent Circe and descended to the dwellings of
Hades, a sorrowful land, blooming with asphodel, through
which wander the empty phantoms of those who have ceased
to live, and how he there questioned about the inscrutable
future the Theban Tiresias, seer of far-reaching fame in mythic
antiquity, and how, hearing him, and finding himself sur-

rounded by incorporeal shades, the illustrious and subtle Odysseus, in spite of his immutable soul, felt in his limbs the pallid
terror; how his companions slaughtered and ate the flocks of
Helios, who beholds all things, and moved the Immortals to
vengeance; how the excellent Odysseus, in like fashion as other
less excellent and not at all excellent mortals, moved between
Scylla and Charybdis, or, as we say, went from Herod to
Pilate; and how he idled in his own despite in the pleasant
lair of the caressing nymph Calypso; sing or narrate above all,
oh goddess who presumest to a wisdom thou dost not possess!
how the modern Odysseus met Nausicaa of the snowy arms,
because this is the only thing that truly interests us at this
point.

Perhaps more than one reader may take a fancy to this invocation, as prolix as it is mysterious. Let us add an observa-
tion: the many allusions with which it is interwoven will have
later their exact interpretation or explanation. And now we
begin the story.

The magnificent Odysseus had now to his credit forty days
in the power of the wheedlesome nymph Calypso; forty days
which he imagined as many years. The modern nymph did
not dwell in a cave, but in a country house, distant from town
by as far as a shout can be heard, to employ the system of
topographical measurement of Homer himself; a system somewhat elastic, because if the house be near the sea, the loud
murmur of the waves drowns the human voice before it has
reached half its distance. It is meant by this that even though
the house stood out in isolation, all neat and spotless in the
midst of a garden, the surrounding region abounded in groups
of laborers' houses, and in mariners' cottages. Farmhouses and
cottages did not crowd one another, nor did they lean one
upon the other forming a hamlet, much less a town, but each
one went off in its own direction, scattered hither and yon, in

the shelter of a hillock, or in the shadow of a fig tree. The
garden of the nymph was of great pleasantness. There grew
the willow, the poplar, and the odorous cypress, where the
birds who fly afar come to build their nests; the hawk, and the
garrulous sea raven which is always made uneasy by the whispering of the foliage. Four rivulets ran along, withdrawing or
joining together, in the fashion of a net, with the limpid waters
of which the gentle fields grew green, and violets and very
many other flowers in every kind blossomed forth. Over the
front of the house a virgin grapevine clung tremulous with
unripe clusters. Such was the mansion of Calypso, who, it
must be said in passing, and in honor of the truth, was not
called Calypso, because she was named Frederica Gómez, and
was the childless widow of a colonist who had returned,
wealthy and enervated, from South America. Nor was Odysseus
named Odysseus either, but his true name shall be disclosed
when the opportune moment presents itself.

Frederica and Odysseus were living together, imperfectly
united by unrequited affection, for Odysseus did not respond
to the passion of Frederica. Odysseus was desirous of departing; but whenever he found out a way of escape, Frederica
held him back with tears, wails, and commotion. To try to
forget his anguish, and under pretext that he was very fond of
swimming, Odysseus spent almost all the day in the sea. He
swam like a Triton. He would go out into the open sea, and
spend four or five hours swimming continuously. And when
he was not in his bath, he sought shelter in the aloofness of a
wood, where he sighed deeply for his lost liberty, until he
determined in his mind to escape. And thus it befell. In odd
moments he began to cut down trunks of trees which then he
bound one to another, tying them with hempen ropes in the
form of a raft. Of all this industry nobody had a suspicion,
and least of all Frederica. When the contrivance was ready,

Odysseus paid some laborers to take it down to the beach, at dusk. After supper, Odysseus said he was going into the garden to smoke a cigarette. He went out one door, and entered by another stealthily; he went upstairs to steal a sheet, and again went out with as much rapidity as if Hermes, god of perennial youth, who has wings on his ankles, were carrying him suspended in air. . . . Nevertheless he stopped at a tavern to buy sundry bottles of red nectar and crystalline ambrosia, which the tavern keeper, a layman in matters mythological, denominated wine and whisky. Odysseus reached the shore, bared his legs, and pushed the raft into the water with great difficulty and delay. In the meantime, Frederica, lashed by impatience, also went into the garden, and as she did not run across Odysseus, and the latter replied not to plaintive solicitations, she felt in her heart a foreboding of serious disaster. She left the garden, scoured various farmhouses, and passed by the tavern where they informed her that Odysseus had gone beachward. In that direction, then, ran the afflicted nymph; at the very moment when the fugitive had succeeded at last in floating his contrivance. With oars manufactured for the occasion, Odysseus was rowing rapidly towards the somber sea.

"Man alive! What are you up to?" asked Frederica.

"Fleeing, my friend, as you see. I have broken the irksome bond in which you held me. I am going at random, I know not where. What matter! Any servitude or punishment whatever will be better than the yoke of your roly-poly arms, because, convince yourself, oh estimable friend! you are now somewhat past your prime. Ah! I am carrying off a sheet of heavy linen which belongs to you, but in exchange I leave you two suits of fine woolen; all my underclothes, which are in good condition; some patent leather shoes; some dull calfskin boots; and some espadrilles. You come out winner."

Frederica first tore her hair; then broke forth into impre-

cations and sorrowful supplications; and finally, giving up all
for lost, she screamed, "Wicked devils take you!" and stretched
out her clenched hands towards the sea, as if invoking the
furies of Poseidon, him who rules the waters and makes the
earth tremble when it so pleases him. Meanwhile Odysseus had
been lost to view.

It was an August night, diaphanous, and seething with
golden constellations. Odysseus, resourceful in devices, erected
a mast in the center of the raft, and with another stick as
crossbeam, and with the sheet, set up a sail as one does a
banner. He drank unhurriedly a bottle of crimson nectar, and
threw himself down to sleep. And thus he went sailing, beneath the sentinel stars, over the swelling and gentle sea. He
awoke late in the morning. The sun was shining almost per-
pendicularly. Odysseus stretched himself, and breathed as
deeply as if he wanted to drink up the firmament. He breakfasted off white ambrosia, and cold meats which he had in his
pocket. He looked about him. A promontory rose from the
neighboring coast, with reefs at its base amid foam. On its
summit, a lighthouse. And the huge mass was like the prow of
a vessel painted scarlet. On either side, the land fell away
toward the horizon, silvery green in color like the olive. The
gulls were soaring, giving forth long cries, and from time to
time appeared a wild duck with burnished throat extended,
like a work of the ceramic arts. Out at sea could be seen a line
of barks for tunny fishing, the sails of yellowish ocher. And
Odysseus experienced a marvelous expansion, as if he were
lord of heaven and earth.

"That must be Cape Roquedeira," he murmured. "In any
case, be it what it may, what does it matter?"

He drew in the sail, put off all attire, and cast himself into
the water. He swam several hours, now putting off from the
raft, now resting against it. And when he got out of the water,

the sun was already shining low. He let the air dry him, and, having dressed, once more hoisted sail and left the course of the raft to the will of the gods. And the raft followed the outline of the gloomy shore. Now Odysseus perceived the mouth of a large river, which melted into the sea with mournful plaint. And before the moon could peep out on the horizon, the wrathful Poseidon, as if he showed himself propitious to the prayers of Frederica, drew himself erect in all his members. The great waves, full of violence, heaved the raft from side to side. In the same fashion as autumnal Boreas drives over the plain the dried leaves, so the winds drove the raft from one side to another. Now Euros gave place, that Zephyros might pull it; now Notos gave in to Boreas. And the raft was broken into shivers. Odysseus bestrode one of the tree trunks as if it were an unbroken horse, but to no purpose; and at last he had to fight hand to hand with the innumerable raging waves. He was giving himself up for lost, when the sea spat him out upon the sand. By dragging himself along, he reached a meadow in which were fragrant shrubs. He was naked and exhausted. Darkness enveloped him. And there, beneath a shrub, he fell asleep.

While the patient Odysseus lay sleeping, vanquished by sleep and fatigue, not far from the bush which served him as shelter in a house furnished with unusual lavishness slumbered also the virgin Nausicaa, of the alabaster arms, like to the immortal goddesses for her loveliness and grace. She slept and dreamed. She dreamed she heard a voice saying to her:

"Nausicaa, why were you born so neglectful? Why don't you take pains to dress yourself in the best and most becoming things that you possess? Your beautiful clothes lie forgotten. Prepare yourself, for the hour of your betrothal draws nigh, and now you will not be a maiden much longer."

When Nausicaa awoke, she said to herself:

"What a droll dream! If I believed in omens——"

But as you never can tell, she put on her loveliest garments, and, having breakfasted, in company with several other maidens, two of them her sisters, and two her friends, she went down to a meadow adorned here and there with flowering shrubs, at the farthest boundary of the estate, close to the shore. They rode in a vehicle half cart, half carriage, drawn by a donkey named Agamemnon, and they carried sheets for the bath, and rackets with which to play battledore and shuttlecock. Their hair flying, they began the game with a great hubbub, so that they awoke the crafty Odysseus, who, seeing the maids, knew not what to do. Hunger gnawed his entrails, and impelled him to show himself; but he dared not for fear of frightening the damsels. But it befell that a shuttlecock lighted where Odysseus was. And the girl who ran up to recover it cried out frightened:

"A man, and naked!"

Before a prospect so horrifying, the maidens fled. Only Nausicaa remained, because her heart was strong and fearless, and she divined some misfortune.

Odysseus tore off a great leafy branch with which to cover his nakedness, and walking on his knees, he approached Nausicaa, and spoke as follows:

"I beg a favor of thee, be thou goddess or mortal. If thou art a goddess, of those who inhabit the boundless Ouranos, thou seemest to me Artemis, daughter of the great Zeus, for thy beauty, thy stature, and thy comeliness. If thou art a mortal, of those who inhabit earth, thrice blessed thy venerable parents, thrice blessed thy brothers and sisters; but happier than all he who, lavishing upon thee marriage gifts, shall lead thee to his home. I have been shipwrecked——"

Nausicaa, at the same moment that she regarded Odysseus

as the handsomest man she had ever seen in her life, murmured in an undertone:

"Poor wretch! He has lost his mind——"

And Odysseus, who heard her:

"No, I haven't lost it yet, though I fear to do so if I contemplate you much longer."

And then, with a sudden change:

"Help me. See to providing me with something which will make me presentable. I am an honorable man and of gentle birth. I have suffered many evils, and, last of all, shipwreck. Besides, I am fainting with hunger. Later I shall relate to you my life and miracles. Grace!"

Nausicaa, turning to the other maidens, shouted:

"Come back! Don't be silly. Bring one of the bath sheets for this man to cover himself."

And then, addressing herself to the subtle and magnanimous Odysseus:

"Come home with us, and there you shall eat something, and we shall see if my brothers' clothes fit you."

II   Odysseus

Odysseus, vagabond king,
The gods of the blue Ouranos
Already have delayed for many years
Your home-coming:
When out of exile
You return
Home to sweet Ithaca,
Will your thanes know you?

The king turned beggar,
Who will say it is the king of old?
Who now recalls

His face?
But Odysseus has a bow so mighty
No other living man,
Odysseus and no other,
May set the arrow free.

Heaven is the target
Toward which the king aims.
Bow in hand
The king aims at heaven itself.
Will the arrow attain such height?
The arrow lost itself
In the sky.

You, like myself,
All of us, Brother,
We are as Odysseus:
Each possesses a bow
Useless to other men,
To one man only
Alive and responsive:
Each aims at the sky.
If anyone fail . . . coward!

Odysseus was professor of Greek language and literature in
the University of Letters of Pilares. It is not to be wondered
at that, granted his profession, he should be much given to
employing Homeric locutions. This false Odysseus was a great
friend of ours. Hence it is that recalling, as we recall, very
vividly his manners and character, having felt ourselves, for
a moment, beneath the spell of that powerful personality, we
have begun to relate his true history in a style allegoric, epic,

and obedient to no rules. In his ecstasies of Bacchic enthusiasm, which were sufficiently frequent, he used to say he was
Odysseus. Because in him the heroic was mingled with the
humorous, Odysseus was the hero of antiquity whom most he
loved and admired. Whenever he read the Odyssey, he wept
bitter tears, not of exaltation, but of sadness, as an exile in
time who had been born thirty centuries too late.

The modern Odysseus figured on the payroll under the name
of Mark de Setiñano. But this was not his true name either.
He was really called John Pérez Setignano.

He was born in Florence, a city which in ages of paganism
had for its tutelary divinity the god Ares, according to the
Greeks, or Mars, according to the Latins, and later, when the
new law of Christ prevailed, placed itself under the patronage
of the Baptist. His father was a Spaniard; his mother an
Italian, of aristocratic lineage. His father had been a handsome youth, distinguished for his handsome face and his indo-
lence, a quality by which, according to some authorities, one
can see that man is of divine origin. The idleness of this great
man, who was called Antonio Pérez Fillol, was, I need not say,
more than godlike; for never did he do aught else than eat,
sleep, and make love to women, or rather better, let himself be
made love to. He was the son of Antonio Pérez Novella, a
mediocre painter, born in Murcia, who had established himself
permanently in Florence, and is there buried. He also was a
fine-looking fellow, for beauty, distinction, and proud bearing
were the only heritage of the family. With the attractive qualities of Antonio Pérez Fillol, and his splendid presence, Bea-
trice de Setignano became enamored. She was a young Florentine, winsome, discreet, of noble blood, and not ill-provided for
as regards fortune. They married and had a son, John; the
wife died at the end of seven or eight years, and when the
fine-looking youth, now widowed, had consumed the money his

wife had left, he took himself out of the way by throwing himself into the Arno. The son was then somewhere about sixteen. Some maternal uncles took him in charge until he finished college. He had turned out like his father and grandfather: of unusual stature, vigorous, his features clearly cut, regular, and manly. From childhood he had been taciturn and haughty. He took no part in childish games, but went about solitary, imagining unheard-of emprises. His mind was tortured with dreams and formless chimeras. In the crisis of adolescence, and at the death of his father, his temperament changed. It seemed to him he already felt himself a man, wholly free, master of himself and the future. He mingled in the youthful society of other students, and while he attended with delight his university courses, he devoted himself noticeably to developing strength and agility of body. He early contracted the vice of drink. The very day he took his degree of doctor of letters, his uncle took him aside, and addressed him as follows:

"I suppose you know that your father ran through your mother's fortune, all of it except sixty thousand lire which he could not get his hands on because I had them safely put by. These sixty thousand lire are at your disposal. On these, as you will understand, one cannot live, but I consider them no trifling help to enable you to see, thinking the matter over thoroughly and calmly, what you are to do, and over what road you are going to travel. You have in your favor all that a man could desire at the beginning of life. If you fail, on you will be the blame. While you are picking out your path, my house is yours."

After the interview, John locked himself up to meditate. He did not know what to decide upon. He scrutinized the future, and all horizons seemed to him too limited for his ambition. He had an heroic soul, and knew not what he wished, what to resolve. If he had been asked, "Should you like to be king?"

he would have replied, "Pshaw!" and made a wry face. He wanted to be himself, his very self, but in a manner he could not as yet define; he wanted his own glorification to a maximum degree, like a great dike raised in the middle of the stream of time, which gathers and restrains the waters of the past in a quiet and deep lake, and then casts them over into the future in an imposing and impetuous cataract. In a word, so vague were his aspirations that he decided to wait until they should grow clearer and become more concrete. From that moment he withdrew from social intercourse, and applied himself to reading and studying. Most of the hours of the day and night he spent at his books. And the hours of rest he devoted to exercising himself in gallant and violent activities; swimming, horseback riding. Whenever his uncle asked him, "Are you considering something?" he would reply, "I don't know yet. I am studying. I am thinking deeply. In any case, I shall not have lost time, for my studies will help me to win a professorship."

"But are you going to turn teacher? What are you seeking in books?"

"Wisdom."

"Wisdom does not lead to success. To attain it, intelligence coupled with natural aptitude suffices, without further training, and even instinct is sufficient on condition that upon one or the other will power is grafted. To will is to accomplish. But in order to will one needs a plain object, looked at from only one point of view. And wisdom presents to us objects in all their aspects, prevents us from going in a direct line towards our aim, and forces us to circle about one point, like the butterfly around the light by which it is dazzled or consumed. Wisdom does not lead to success. Or are you seeking wisdom for itself?"

"For itself. I am endeavoring to know things in all their

phases, and more than in all their phases in all their recondite meanings and correspondences."

"But the fact is that books do not serve the purpose either. Wisdom is acquired by the direct study of nature and of men, not by the study of the dead letter; it is granted by the slow and unhurried experience of a life which has known how to employ itself well, not by the gracious and delightful experience of books. The experience of one has never been of benefit to the other. And when wisdom at last has been attained, in extreme old age, when strength is lacking us to make use of it, tell me: for what do we want it?"

"It does not matter to me that plenary wisdom is not gained except when one is grown old. I find no way to conjecture how great a joy it will be to know completely, because I cannot conceive that it can be greater than to learn little by little, and step by step."

"In short, you wish to be a man of thought."

"Yes."

"I should prefer your being a man of action."

"That too."

"One does not fit in with the other. Thought is a hindrance to action."

"On the contrary, I am convinced that it is a stimulus, a motive force. The dove can believe that it would fly more swiftly without the weight of the air, but it is certain that unless it rested its wings upon the dense air, it would fall to the earth."

"I know the metaphor. The disadvantage, dear John, is that I do not understand you."

"I do not understand myself either."

"Then let us wait until you understand yourself, and we understand each other."

"Let us wait."

The fact was that John felt himself passionately drawn towards books and towards drink by a power of attraction superior to his will. He did not read carelessly and at random, with silent and stupefying voracity like a pedantic and unsystematic reader. He read methodically the most select works, in the classics as well as in cultured modern tongues. He imbibed with ecstasy the most noble, the most ancient, the most rarefied essences of the human heart and intellect throughout the centuries, and he assimilated them into the blood and marrow of his soul. He read as he drank: with a relish, and in such wise that his pulses quickened, his mind grew keener, and he put on as it were a new life. And so, in his spirit were becoming amalgamated countless seething inquietudes, presumptions, eager longings, glimpses, impulses and terrors, which flowed together in him, proceeding from remote zones, from the cardinal points of the soul of humanity, scattered over divers ages and over divers lands. But in him had engraved itself that sentence of his uncle's: "Only action leads to success." Success, that is, the perfect realization of one's own destiny. John had confidence in his destiny. He said to himself one day: "I want to find my norms of action." And he left Florence on a journey of apprenticeship over all Italy. He visited the cities, mingled with many classes of men, high and low, sought intercourse with women, scrutinized, meditated, passed whole nights with his light burning, the bottle within reach of his hand, elbows on the table, and forehead in his hands; but he could not succeed in solving the great problem: that of putting himself in harmony with himself, of discovering the ideal which befits one. "A man of action, yes," he would say to himself, "but where are the noble and unheard-of acts in which to engage oneself?" Italy seemed to him a country too much subject to rule and measure, like a work of art already fashioned, a piece of sculpture minutely modeled. All was petrified; all had a finished, final shape; over everything was reflected the golden dusk of tradition. And it was a deficient tradition, broken up into various traditions, unfused, without connection, and without fertility; the tradition of Rome, force without grace or sagacity, and the tradition of the Renaissance, grace and subtlety without strength. For John, the living tradition, the true tradition, must be one of trinity in unity, eternally renewed; vigor, grace, and subtlety, understanding by subtlety the active intelligence. One night in Naples, face to face with the Tyrrhenian sea, John inhaled the fragrance of the orange trees. He thought: "I seem to be in Spain—Why? Why?" And he did not quickly hit upon the answer. He had never been in Spain, and in that crisis, he felt homesick for Spain. "Oh, beloved fatherland," he sighed. And why? He had a sudden revelation. "The tradition of Italy moves me not because I am not an Italian. I am a Spaniard. Italy is a statue. Spain is as yet youthful flesh, not a tradition, but blind inheritance. It is the country of possibilities. It is the virgin country, almost a child, for men of action, and men of thought. Why? I know not, but so it is." It was a revelation. It is true that that night he had drunk more than usual. But that night was in his life like a signpost which marks the parting of the ways. He wrote to his uncle to say good-bye, and took the first boat for Spain, an English vessel going to New York, which would stop at Gibraltar. The short crossing from Italy to Spain gave him an opportunity to know at close range the Anglo-Saxon. He mixed with Englishmen and North Americans. In them he found something which approached the archetype of hero towards which he was guiding himself, in which are merged strength, grace, and subtlety, so proportioned as to produce a perfect equilibrium. Then he thought that perhaps the naïve and adventurous heart of the legendary Argonaut pulsed again in the English explorer, and that the Argonaut's inordinate love for wealth, more successful in gaining its ends than the Englishman's, was re-embodied in the Yankee financier. But both types, even though heroic, within actual times, John judged as too paltry for his ambition. He aspired to the type of the demigod, to Prometheus; and if he himself could not be Prometheus, at least he aspired to apprehend, to understand, to divine him, and to aid in his conception.

John reached Spain, and first went to Seville. There he lengthened out his stay to two months, awaiting the Fair. The bullfights impressed him profoundly. He thought for a few days that bullfighting was his vocation. The great feast fascinated him with two powerful charms: first, the attraction of naked tragedy, a struggle with the blind and hostile forces of nature, with death; and then the immediate sanction of success before the intoxicated and delirious multitude. So much to heart did he take it that he hastened to attempt the first rudiments of the art, passes with the cloak and the decoying of the bull, and he was obliged to cut his beard and hair which had lent to his head a Capitoline aspect. Very soon he found out that the art of bullfighting did not embrace technical difficulties, nor require great courage or skill. Its essence was grace, a gift which the gods bestow at their caprice, and not strength, a quality which man can acquire or develop. Consequently, like any art which is the outcome of the gift of grace, it was decadent. He renounced bullfighting, but remained in Seville, his senses overcome by gentle languor, and once more he let his beard grow. And this stay in Seville constitutes one of the adventures referred to in the invocation of this story, which John designated as: "Sojourn in the land of the lotus eaters, who feed upon a flower which causes loss of memory, and which grants oblivion." And in order to flee from that forgetfulness which threatened everything, John fell into the arms of a fascinating Sevillian, Lolita the Fleshy, so nicknamed in spite of her slenderness, because she had been born by the Gate of the Flesh. And she is the Circe of the invocation, from whom John liberated himself through the good offices of Hermes, who is also called Mercury, the god who presides over the distribution of wealth and property; and this we state in order to make plain that we have not hinted at anything malicious, but simply mean that as Lolita's fondness for him was costing John an eye, and the sixty thousand lire had dwindled to a half, John reminded himself to remind himself no longer of his beloved, and to abandon Seville. He traveled over the greater portion of Spain in search of the living triune tradition, with the following result: that in the South, grace and subtlety lacked strength; in the East, strength and subtlety lacked grace; and in the North, strength and grace lacked subtlety. And finally he wound up in an ancient city, dead from time immemorial, the name of which we have no reason for divulging. And this adventure is the one John described as "Descent into the dwellings of remembrance, peopled by the empty phantoms of those who have ceased to exist"; because the city, although it abounded in self-propelling figures that resembled men, held only phantoms. And there he consulted Tiresias, who was a seer and had the visage of an owl. And the seer with the owl's face said to John: "Wretch, you have come to regions where one cannot arrive without having forfeited one's humanity. No longer are you a man, nor can you recover man's estate. Henceforth you shall be but the recollection of a man." And John felt in his innermost being pallid and penetrating terror. And from that city of silence John departed for Madrid. Unholy Madrid captured him with its sinister spell. Very quickly he acquired innumerable friends, and became an out-and-out son of Madrid. It was then that he became naturalized as a Spaniard, adopting the name of Mark de Setiñano, because he still maintained an heroic spirit, and John Pérez seemed to him a passionate adjuration to a plebeian Nemesis. His stay in Madrid, Mark entitled: "Episode in which my companions made slaughter of the flocks of Helios, inciting the gods to vengeance"; and by this heading he gave to understand in allegorical fashion that in Madrid night is turned into day, and the penalty is to accomplish nothing worth-while. Money was now becoming scarce; or, what amounts to the same thing, John was moving between Scylla and Charybdis, and from Herod to Pilate. As Odysseus clung to the fig tree, so Mark clung to a professorship of Greek in the University of Pilares, which it was announced was open to competitive examination. He revalidated his diploma in Spain, and obtained the chair without any difficulty. Once more he acquired a love for books, and applied himself to the ordering of his thoughts, and moralizing on his experiences. From his love for ambrosial libations he had not fallen away one whit. When he won his professorship and went to establish himself in Pilares, he was thirty-three, and in the prime of his manhood. Discriminating and clear-sighted in his judgments, he immediately comprehended Pilares and its inhabitants, and the lot that the future held for him there. Nothing more appropriate than to limit ourselves to his own words. After holding his professorship a few months, he wrote as follows to his uncle.

"Dear Uncle: I am a schoolteacher in a Spanish province. I came to Spain thinking it the country of possibilities. Now I look upon it as the country of impossibilities. This so far as I am concerned, for I have forsworn success, and acknowledged myself a defeated man. I am a failure because I have had no father, or have only half had one, for the function of a father is not merely to beget. My father transmitted to me one element of success: vigor. Grace I owe to my mother. The rest I have acquired for myself. I believe I am a perfect man, as will be proved to you by the naturalness with which I speak of my perfection. This explains, moreover, why I am a defeated man; because in order to make of myself a man, I have needed time, and upon reaching the period of perfect maturity, I see that it coincides with the period of decline of the elements that make for success. The result of my journeyings and studies may be synthesized into a few brief postulates: Happiness is reserved for the man of action; but the man of action does not invent activity, he realizes it. The man of thought conceives action, therefore the man of thought should precede the man of action. The man of thought begins by thinking himself happy in the fruition of knowing purely for the sake of knowing; until the sorrow comes of realizing that felicity resides solely in action; and finally from this grief ascends the sublime joy of recognizing that for him also is reserved the most noble mode of action, that of begetting a man of action, and this happiness is increased when the man of thought is at the same time a defeated man of action, when he knows that he himself might have been a man of action. In other words: if indeed I have relinquished personal success, it is because I aspire to the vicarious success of paternity. What I wish I might have been, that my son Prometheus will be, a demigod, a redeemer—for now more than ever humanity has need of him—a living bond, and a link between earth and heaven. For behold how I imagine humanity. What to us, looking upwards from the earth, is heaven, is from the other side, to the gods who gaze down upon it and walk upon it, earth. And humanity is as it were a garland which hangs from this ceiling, forming large and diversified festoons from one point to another of the vault from which it is suspended. Very well then, each point of contact through which at distant intervals it meets heaven, is such a man as I call Prometheus. When from one point to another the historic distance is too greatly prolonged, the festoon drops so low that humanity wallows in the slime. This being so, I dream of my Prometheus. My spirit and my flesh are imbued with this meaning of the future, and make prophecy of it to me. I suppose you will say that all this is because I am in love, and want to marry. No, sir. Not yet have I met the woman whom I am destined to marry. I am going to seek her with all deliberation and serenity. She shall be strong, as I am strong; she shall be beautiful, as I am beautiful; she shall be intelligent, as I am intelligent. I shall marry with due consciousness of my responsibility, with the clear perception that I am the providential and beloved instrument of the genius of the race."

To this his uncle replied:

"Dear Nephew: I am very feeble. Soon I shall die. In my will I leave you an inheritance of one hundred thousand lire. Your letter has greatly pleased me. I always considered you crazy, and this it is that gratifies me. Your father was more than circumspect, and was very uncongenial to me. I do not believe, like you, that humanity is an ornament attached to heaven by the semidivine nature of some exceptional men. These men touch the heavens with their foreheads because other men boost them. It is no merit in the top of the tree that it is the top, that merit belongs to the trunk and the roots. It is not to the credit of the apex of the pyramid that it is the apex, that credit is due to the base. Let humanity sink as far as possible in the mire until it gains a foothold. Afterwards, in his good time, Prometheus will arrive. And from this point on you are right: Prometheus is born of men like you, men impelled by yearning desire to soar, and vanquished by that very aspiration. These defeated men, dear John, I think are the leaven of humanity."

On receiving this letter, Mark commented: "My uncle is in his second childhood; nevertheless he is not far off the track."

Mark fulfilled systematically the duties of his professorship, but he lived above all delivered over to the obsession of being father to a hero. Consequently he was to be assailed by reiterated erotic attacks which grew more frequent with spring. And this was the reason why he began to make advances to Frederica Gómez, a sentimental, violent, portly woman, and a widow besides. Frederica conceived a passion for Mark, and Mark, for pastime, let himself be led whither she would lead him, which was to a lovely country house, at the beginning of summer, but unfortunately, with the beginning of summer, boredom set in for Mark.

III   Nausicaa

Naked my mother bore me,
Beautiful as an Immortal.
I rule my destiny;
Adversity flees before me.
I am Man. Man am I,
King of the floating world;
I am the salt of the earth;
With me History ends,
With me History begins.
Utterly naked I am
As a primeval dawn.
So the sea cast me up
Where its curved margin flowers.
I come from mystery that sings:
I come from depths of the past.
Just at the future's door
I find you, Nausicaa,
White-armed, slim, strong,

Nausicaa, beautiful!
Fold me in your white arms;
Claim me in nuptial joy.
We are the pillars of Hercules
On which the globe is poised;
About us like a garland
Is wreathed Eternity.

Nausicaa was called Perpetua Meana. When Mark found out
her baptismal and surname, he praised the first, considering
it lovely and significant, but the second disgusted him for its
lack of euphony, and for other reasons. Perpetua was a handsome girl, her figure well-filled out, but sober in its curves
according to the Greek canon, very rosy and very fair, her skin
covered with a silvery bloom, her eyes black. As one born in
Andalusia, and as the daughter of an Andalusian, she was naturally attractive, without running into extremes of vivacious-
ness, and she was simple and frank without being bold. She
was the essence of femininity in her loveliness, and in her freshness like to that of a rose; somewhat virile in her character
and expression. The mother had died, and as the elder sister
she ruled the house. She was full twenty-five years old when
Mark met her, as has been related. Her two sisters were pretty
too, but they had turned out puny. She had three brothers
who were so many barbarians. One of them had taken a notion
to play the accordion; another, to paint; and the third, to
hunt. The father had been named delegate of the Treasury in
Pilares that very spring when Mark was seized with his fancy
for Frederica. Don Tesifonte Meana (a name that Mark es-
teemed both beautiful and melodious) was a native of Extremadura, and doubtless was descended from a race of con-
querors, because the hours he was not in his office he devoted
exclusively to the conquest of maidservants. Within a month

of his abiding in Pilares, he was the idol of the guild of serving maids because of his generosity, the nightmare of the barracks, and famous throughout the town. Although elderly, he was still tall and erect, firm in his step, and not ill-looking. Don Tesifonte, and his offspring as well, were persons with something angelic in their make-up. They rejoiced in the gift of attracting sympathy; they captivated the affections.

Soon after their arrival in Pilares, the Meana family established very close, almost fraternal friendship with an indigenous family, that of the widowed Marchioness of San Albano. The Marchioness showered all manner of attentions on Don Tesifonte, and the latter conducted himself with signal good breeding towards the Marchioness. The two sons of the Marchioness of San Albano, Donatín and Fidelín, did not conceal their inclination for the two younger daughters of Don Tesifonte, Cachito and Pujito, appellatives derived, contrary to every law of linguistics, from Concepción and Paula. Perpetua was left over. Let it be said in passing that Perpetua never had enjoyed great favor with the youth of the opposite sex, doubtless because of a certain majesty and air of command for which they reproached her as very unwomanly, indeed as somewhat masculine. Finally, the two sons of Don Tesifonte, Ferdinand and Alfonso, divided their affections equally between the accordion and painting on the one hand, and on the other, the two daughters of the Marchioness, Mary Cleophas and Anuncia. Edward, the last offshoot of Don Tesifonte, was left over. He it was who took delight in the exercise of the chase, in tramping cross-country up hill and down dale, and in pursuing and killing wild animals. In short: the two families were so united by powerful affinities that they threatened to blend into only one. When summer came, the Marchioness of San Albana invited the Meanas to a sumptuous estate, with a medieval castle and rich inheritance, which she possessed by the seaside, in San Albano, for there it was that the title was situate, by grace of his Holiness, Leo XIII. The Meanas accepted with alacrity. Don Tesifonte remained in Pilares because the Delegation of the Treasury held him to service as attached to the soil. On the beach of San Albano it was that Mark, fleeing from Frederica, after suffering shipwreck, found himself like Odysseus: naked, hungry and exhausted.

IV Mark and Perpetua

Sing we the beauty of life,
Thrilling the vigorous body!
Supreme glory of earth!
Joy of the senses, mouth
Of woman to quench man's thirst,
Bosom erect and soft
Made for his eyes and touch,
Voice cool like a stream
Refreshing his arid soul!
Song of the nightingale
In the willows by the brook,
Roses, roses and jasmine
Woven in flowing hair!
Then . . . sea, and ruddy shore,
Meadows, woods, mountains,
Stars above them all . . .
These exist for the sake
Of man and woman made one.
Nature were deaf and blind
Bereft of human desire;
Mute, chaotic, dead,
Apart from two youthful lovers.
Oh ecstasy of the senses!
Oh body, temple of Beauty!

The Marchioness was given over to the cosmetic arts. She was in the hands of a maid who was combing her hair with great skill and deliberation in such wise as to make her skimpy locks simulate the hirsute luxuriance of a merino sheep. In spite of her capillary penury, the Marchioness bore with distinction, decorum and dissimulation the limping superstructure of her beauty. She had been very beautiful. Now if she was not, she seemed to be. Her skin was still smooth and rosy; her teeth were perfect, and her limbs agile to a certain point. She stood out among the other matrons for her youthfulness of face, her erectness of figure, and her imposing gestures. She was in her dressing room, next to the balcony and facing the garden, with her eyes half closed, as if the tickling of the nape of her neck provoked in her delightful daydreams. She heard steps.

"Who is coming in without my permission?" she asked astonished, for she did not wish any one to penetrate into the mysteries of her toilette.

"It is I, Marchioness," replied Perpetua, advancing with decision.

"But were you not on the beach with the other girls?"

"You shall see. Something serious has happened."

The Marchioness would have liked to strike a statuesque attitude of patrician composure, indicating that she was ready to receive the most tragic of news, but the hairdresser held her condemned to a motionless and ridiculous attitude.

"Has anyone been drowned?"

"Drowned, no. But if not drowned, it has been by a miracle."

"Tell me the truth; don't waste time in circumlocutions. Who has been drowned?"

"Nobody. Last night, apparently, there was a wreck near the shore."

"I heard the storm. I couldn't sleep the whole night."

"I always sleep like a log. Now for it. This morning we found on the beach a castaway. He is a man, a youth, about thirty. He was naked, hungry, and exhausted. We brought him along, and he is waiting in the orchard."

"But, my child, did he come with you so, in that state—of innocence?"

"No, ma'am. None of us saw him because he covered himself with branches. That is to say, I saw his arms and the upper part of his chest. Then we gave him some sheets. And so he came. He looks like a Moor. He is very tall, very strong, and very handsome."

"Handsome he has to be in order to look well to you in such attire. And what do you want me to do?"

"Help him. Offer him something."

"Very well thought out. See here, have them make him a cup of mallows tea, piping hot, for surely he must have caught cold."

"It isn't that. I mean that he remain here, in the house. That he stay for dinner——"

"At the table with us?"

"Yes, ma'am."

"Have you gone crazy, my child? A man enveloped in a sheet, seated at table with us?"

"But by dinnertime he will be dressed, of course. My plan is as follows: that he put on a suit of Ferdinand's. Then let him dine here, rest, sleep in the house tonight. And tomorrow will be time enough to decide. He will tell us his story, which must be very interesting."

"God knows what such a man can be."

"He is a gentleman, a great gentleman; it is only necessary to see him."

"Thanks to you, I am now eager to make the castaway's

acquaintance. All right, darling; act and manage as if this house were yours."

"Everything is already arranged. Neither your sons nor my brothers are up yet, except Edward, who went out hunting early. I have already begged clothes of the four for Mark to try on. I had forgotten, the castaway told us his name was Mark Setiñano."

"The name sounds familiar, but I can't place it. Now leave me to finish fixing myself and then I will go down and offer hospitality to this stranger who has fallen from heaven, or issued from the sea."

They had accommodated Mark in a bedroom of the house, where a servant brought him, shortly afterwards, a great armful of clothes. None of them fitted him.

"Tell the young lady that it is impossible, physically and metaphysically, for me to enclose myself in these insignificant garments, under penalty of bursting them and continuing as Edenic as before. What's the matter, friend? By the idiotic look upon your countenance and your gaping mouth, I gather that you do not understand elegant language. See here, the best thing is for you to tell your young lady to locate herself on the other side of that door for me to explain to her what is happening."

Perpetua on the outside of the room, and Mark within, held the following conversation:

"Madam, these clothes are of no use to me."

"I suspected it already, but you say whatever you have in mind."

"Various solutions. First: that I may be provided with a carpenter's chisel to reduce my dimensions and accommodate them to the capacity of the garments. Approved?"

"Rejected."

"Second: to call in a shirtmaker, shoemaker, and tailor to take my measure for shirts, shoes, and suit. Approved?"

"In San Albano there are no shirtmakers or shoemakers, nor any tailors."

"Third: to dress myself as a woman, although I declare I abhor all trickery, particularly of this kind. Approved?"

"Promptly rejected."

"Fourth: that a messenger be sent to Pilares on horseback, and at breakneck speed, with a letter of mine to bring me clothes and money, for I find myself with empty pockets. Approved?"

"Approved. But while he is going and coming, which is a whole day, what are you going to do?"

"Send me a deck of cards and I'll play solitaire."

"Nonsense! You must come out."

"I'll come out in the sheet."

"The Marchioness won't have it."

"I'll fix it up as a tunic, adopting Hellenic lines."

"Hardly!"

"Well then, there's no help for it. Scour the surrounding country for a man of my size."

"Oh! I have it!" exclaimed Perpetua, clapping her hands. "Pepón the gardener's son. He's a monster."

"Well, let's try if his monstrosity coincides with mine."

"I did not want to hurt your feelings."

"I know it. They are not hurt."

"The worst is that his clothes are very coarse."

"No matter."

"I'll be back in a minute."

"One moment, before you go——"

"Out with it."

"Have you ever heard anything of Prometheus?"

"Of Prometheus?"

"Have you not dreamed something out of the ordinary?"

"Yes, sir; as luck would have it, last night I dreamed very queer things; but I do not remember anything about Prometheus."

"All right. Thank you."

"I'll hurry."

Mark dressed up in Pepón's clothes: cotton trousers, slashed in the seat, and with decorations of green material, a flannel shirt, espadrilles, and some socks of Ferdinand's. In such attire he presented himself before the Marchioness, to make salaams to her, and offer her voluble demonstrations of gratitude for hospitality so generous. The Marchioness observed immediately the unusual appearance of Mark, as well as the distinction and elegance of his manners. The matron, with frank cordiality, offered him her house for as long as he liked; and the castaway replied that he accepted only until they fetched him clothes and money from Pilares. Then the Marchioness, accompanied by Perpetua and the other girls, showed Mark the various rooms of the house, the outbuildings and the gardens, until it was time for dinner. By that time, the anything but diligent young men, Donatín and Fidelín, Ferdinand, and Alfonso, were up and had been presented to the mysterious guest, the San Albanos receiving him with undisguised frigidity. All sat down to table.

"You say, sir, that your Christian name and surname——" insinuated the Marchioness, looking with her mother-of-pearl lorgnette into the soup tureen which a servant placed beside her, as if she were looking for the name in the soup, which had alphabet noodles.

"Mark de Setiñano."

"Oh, yes, I know. I say that the name is not a Spanish one."

"No, madam. Although naturalized a Spaniard, I was born in Italy. Setiñano is a Florentine name, a family of dukes."

"In Italy, everyone is a prince and an adventurer. It is a great country for rogues," interpolated Donatín, who was much puffed up on account of the splendor of his title, and forgot it came from Rome.

"Young man, you have uttered a piece of impertinence," replied Mark with Olympian and annihilating calmness, not deigning to look at Donatín, who, somewhat taken aback, corrected himself.

"I did not mean to refer to you. You will understand that I am accustomed to move in the society of dukes."

"And I in that of lackeys and upstarts," replied Mark, contemplating Donatín with such absolute disdain that the handful of letters the latter had in his mouth was converted into a choking mass of cacophonies.

Perpetua felt her heart swell in her bosom with joy. The Marchioness said within herself, "He is a prince in disguise." She admonished her first-born:

"Donatín, you are a troublesome and inexperienced youth. You should avail yourself of the lesson this gentleman has given you, and in future be more heedful of the obligations which hospitality imposes upon well-bred people. And you, Mr. Setiñano, will know how to overlook the folly of his few years. Let us go on talking about yourself, of your shipwreck. The *yacht,* was it yours?"

"What yacht, Marchioness?"

"The yacht on which you were sailing."

"Madam, I was not sailing on a yacht, but on a raft."

And he commenced to tell the story of his wreck, suppressing its causes, in order not to scandalize the ladies. He spoke with peculiar eloquence and color, so that he held all spellbound. Then they questioned him about Italy, and again he spoke beautifully and with feeling. At the end of dinner appeared the younger one of the Meanas, Edward, back from hunting.

He was beginning his college course in Philosophy and Letters, and as soon as he saw Setiñano, he advanced to greet him.

"Why, do you know Mr. Setiñano?" the Marchioness and Perpetua questioned at the same time.

"He is professor of Greek in the University."

The Marchioness suffered disillusionment.

"Misfortune obliged me to take up teaching," Mark explained.

The Marchioness brooded. She muttered, as if meditating aloud:

"Greek. But does Greek exist?"

"It exists and it does not exist," replied Setiñano. "Classic Greek is a dead language."

"A dead language!" repeated the Marchioness. "Well, I imagined it had no existence. As we say, when a thing is unintelligible, it is in Greek. But so it is: what more utter nonexistence than to be dead! And how can one study or learn a dead language? I don't take that in."

"Because, if indeed it is not actually spoken, there are preserved written works and memorials of a time when it was spoken."

"Ah, now I see! But what most surprises me is how a duke can set himself to study these queer things."

"Madam, there has existed in Italy since the Renaissance the tradition that noblemen should be doctors in the humanities."

"Yes, yes; you are right. I had not understood. It is perfectly clear."

The Marchioness, even though she had not understood, approved emphatically, not wishing to display anew her simplicity and ignorance.

After dinner, all withdrew to their rooms, and Mark remained alone in the one assigned him. In the late afternoon, the families went out for a walk in the country. They went in couples, a Mr. San Albano with a Miss Meana, and a Mr. Meana with a Miss San Albano; in the rear, the Marchioness leaning on the arm of Mark, whom she accepted as a magnificent paladin in spite of the coarse material of his attire, and on the other side of the Marchioness, Perpetua, who smiled constantly to herself, but said not a word.

That night, before retiring, the Marchioness said to Perpetua:

"You were right, my child; the castaway is the handsomest man I have ever seen. Besides, how learned he is! Have you ever known anyone who knows so much?"

Perpetua did not reply. She went out, saying good night; she undressed quickly, buried herself between her sheets, put out the light, and questioned eagerly the nebulous divinity of dreams, on whose lap the future is held.

On the following day, a little before dinner, arrived Don Tesifonte, and the emissary with some clothes of Mark's and some papers.

"A hearty welcome, Don Tesifonte," said the Marchioness.

And then, scrutinizing him with her lorgnette:

"I find you very much deteriorated, and grown very old."

"Confounded, meddlesome old woman," thought Don Tesifonte. "Probably it is that stuck-up, mischievous imp, Manuela, who is to blame for my deterioration." Manuela was a cook who was keeping Don Tesifonte's head in a whirl.

He added aloud:

"It is due to overwork, and the heat, my dear and respected friend."

"Why, I find father as usual——"

Mark, in the meantime, had opened the papers, and was glancing through them.

"Heavens!" he exclaimed. "My uncle, the Duke of Setiñano, is dead."

"Do you inherit the title?" inquired the Marchioness, tremulous with solicitude.

"No, Madam, he had children."

"God's will be done; neither title nor money."

"Money, yes, a mere trifle; about twenty thousand dollars."

"Well then, congratulations," said the Marchioness with too much readiness.

"Marchioness——" reproached Perpetua.

"The Marchioness has spoken correctly," interrupted Mark. "My uncle died a natural death, in extreme old age. Before a life so full and harmonious, one so lengthy and ended in its appointed time, like a perfect circle which is completed, there is no reason for a lachrymose attitude. His was a great intelligence and a great heart. All that he lacked was Prometheus. His son Vittorio will certainly not be Prometheus."

Mark looked into the eyes of Perpetua, and Perpetua, who had not dreamed the night before, thought at that moment she was dreaming, and the vistas of her dream were infinite.

During the afternoon's walk, Don Tesifonte gave his arm to the Marchioness. Mark walked beside Perpetua.

"In short," said Mark, "now I am dressed like a human being. Don't you think I am another man?"

"Yes, indeed you are; but I am going to tell you my opinion. In peasant's clothes you look better than in those of a gentleman. In the sheet, you looked better than in peasant's clothes. And when you appeared to me on your knees in the midst of the cinnamon bush, I liked you even better than in the sheet."

"You have spoken with peculiar circumspection, and with words weighty with meaning. In phrases so brief, you have said everything. Would you like our conversation to be an interpretation and explanation of what you have said?"

"Very well."

"A needless question. As far as my short experience goes, I am of the opinion that no Spanish girl would have dared to speak as you have spoken. Your words have been crystal."

"If my sisters, or the San Albano girls, had heard me, they would have been scandalized as if it were a question of cynical and immodest expressions."

The face of Perpetua revealed a marmoreal gravity and a pallid chastity.

"I am satisfied," said Mark, his expression serious and tender. "Let us begin the commentary to your first words. It might be understood that in the rapid lapse of a few hours, and in process of the four phases into which I have been transformed before your eyes, I have been decreasingly to your taste."

"It is not that exactly. For me you continue the same, and not only have you not deteriorated in other respects, but you have gained."

"Will you permit me to speak to you with words absolutely clean and truthful, avoiding all euphemism, hypocrisy or falsehood, and giving to the feelings the name that befits them?"

"That is the way I should like us to talk."

"You said a moment ago that for you I continue to be the same. I suppose you meant the same man, the same individual, the same essential personality, that appeared to you behind that shrub." Perpetua assented. "In fact, that was I in my most concrete individuality. Presently you came to know little by little, gradually, my social entity, that complexity of usages, customs, costumes, conventionalisms, and other externalities that compose the social entity, and which, in the majority of cases, serve only to conceal the paltriness of the concrete individuality. Do I make myself clear?" Perpetua assented. "Let us take a leap in our ideas. Let us imagine the procedure of a

Spanish girl who marries. She makes the acquaintance of her
betrothed at a ball or on a walk, that is to say, she becomes
acquainted with the most external externality of the individual
who one day is to be her husband. Gradually, as intimacy and
confidence become more closely established, it is possible that
she comes to see her sweetheart in his shirtsleeves, in a bath-
sheet. . . . What is certain is that she will not see him as you
saw me until they are married." Mark made a very thoughtful
pause. "We have begun at the end." Mark made another pause,
and prolonged it until Perpetua spoke.

"And how would you have matters arranged?" asked Perpetua, taking the colloquy in a festive sense. "I hope you don't
expect people to go to balls and promenades as they came into
the world, with some foliage as their only garment. That would
be a sight!" she ended with a strained laugh.

"Yes, that would be a sight. But do not be untrue to yourself. We have agreed to employ transparent, truthful words,"
said Mark gravely. "Granted what the human race has ended
in, it is certainly impossible for marriages to be arranged, the
contracting parties having previously made each other's acquaintance in their concrete individualities. Do you understand
me?"

"Too well."

"But that it cannot be does not mean that it ought not to
be. Marriage should be a matter of the selection of the species.
And what is forbidden the generality of people is granted to
others selected by providential means. An ancient philosopher
did not want unions to take place except between individuals
perfect and suited to each other. And he desired even more:
that the fruit of these unions, should it be born defective, should
not be allowed to live." A pause. Perpetua walked with thoughtful head. "Do you not find something providential in our meeting?"

"Yes."

"And, upon seeing me, did you experience some feeling of a distinctly different kind from any you had experienced up to that time?"

"I do not know how to explain myself, and not appear immodest."

"Speak sincerely."

"I will tell you that of all the men I have known, not one has inspired me with any other feeling than calm and natural friendship. I could not see in them beings different from myself—how shall I put it?—men. They seemed to me rather more girl friends than men friends; not very intimate girl friends, either, and, therefore, tiresome to have to do with very frequently. Perhaps the fact that no one has made love to me has helped to bring this about. Many times I have questioned myself, what is love? When I see pairs of sweethearts, or my friends tell me their love affairs, they produce on me the effect of people full of pretense, affected, fond of make believe and exaggeration; and within themselves empty or untrue. When I saw you——. I am going to be honest, my first thought was: How handsome that man is! It was the first time that my thought spelled out the word man. Afterwards, during the hours we have spent together, I have thought frequently: I could spend my whole life at Mark's side without growing weary. I cannot tell you more now."

For a long time they did not speak. Suddenly Mark said:

"When should you like us to be married?"

"Whenever you please."

"Well, then, next month."

They continued in silence all afternoon. On their way back from their walk, it was night and the moon was shining.

"One thing I should like you to explain to me, Mark. You have been speaking of marriage as if it were a matter of breeding horses, dogs, or thoroughbred pigs. If it is only that—I do not want to marry."

"That it must be; but besides, it is love."

Mark took Perpetua's hand and gazed into her eyes, filled with the moonlight. Perpetua tried to repeat the last word, but her throat was voiceless.

The Meanas were reputed, among their acquaintances, a clan of cave dwellers. Their voracity was phenomenal. The Marchioness said it was heavenly to see them eat. The one who ate and drank the most was Don Tesifonte. But his off-spring, masculine as well as feminine, scarcely yielded him the advantage.

That night, after supper, Don Tesifonte said, addressing Mark:

"I am fifty." (He dropped off seven.) "Never have I run across anyone who rivaled me in eating and drinking, unless it be my children. But tonight, Mr. Setiñano, you have humbled my vanity. I did not think anyone could surpass me. You can beat me twice over."

"Excellent Don Tesifonte," replied Mark, "I eat thus be-cause I am in love, and the same thing happens to me as to the Immortals who inhabit the immeasurable Ouranos. Love does not take away my appetite; it fortifies it. Because love needs sustenance to attain the plenitude of its fruition and I am the father of the future Prometheus."

"I must retract my words, Mr. Setiñano. Now I do not ac-knowledge your superiority, because drink does not lead me into any aberrations."

"Oh, excellent father-in-law!" concluded Mark, before the stupefied company. "The fact is you have not understood me." And he gave vent to a shout of laughter veritably Olympic.

V   *Prometheus*

Oh human body, temple of Beauty,
Poor pagan temple,
The lamp of the soul was without oil,
Was lifeless.
Dawnlight has left the temple;
It has fallen into dark ruin.
The gods have lost their followers,
Have fled like drifting shadows,
Have fled to hide them, weeping,
Behind the scriptural fig trees.
Thither they are pursued
By wavering shapes of victims.
Dim, faraway,
Odysseus passes,
Wailing for wrath and sorrow.
Odysseus, bow slung on shoulder,
The bow of his misdeeds.
A voice unknown
Speaks with a benign music:
"Odysseus, man of might,
Whose gaze was fixed so high,
Whose arrow was loosed
Against the very heavens
That brood over all,
If again you aim at the sky,
Take care to tip the arrow with your soul
Securely caught,
With your own soul of grief:
Then with determined will
Send it flying into the sky."

Spring was on the point of merging into summer, as if it obeyed the behest of a joyous myth, when Perpetua announced to Mark that they were going to have a child. Mark, who was in dressing gown, working up some notes for his class, raised the skirt, and with it covered his head.

"What are you doing?"

"Shedding tears of joy, and as manly decorum prevents my showing my face with tears on it, I cover it over with my dressing gown, which I wish indeed were a tunic or peplos."

Immediately he rose, held his wife in a close embrace, and broke forth into cries of enthusiasm.

In the tender nights of spring, husband and wife leaned out of their sun parlor, their hands lovingly enlaced. She felt within her being, crowned with happiness, the throb of the great coming life, and he also thought he felt its harmonious pulsation communicated to him through the sweet and diligent hands of his wife. Before the gallery rose a hill, and on its summit a cemetery set with solemn trees. Pale flashes of lightning at times lighted up the horizon, like the sudden wink of an enormous pupil. And Mark invoked Prometheus, who stole the living fire and gave it for the use of man. Occasionally they pressed each other's hands with greater force, as if making a silent compact of mutual confidence in destiny, and they sobbed, their hearts almost leaping from their breasts.

The moment arrived in which the prophecies must be fulfilled, and the eagerly desired hero emerge from nebulous omens into the turmoil of terrestrial struggles: the throes of childbirth.

"Are you casting me from the gynaeceum?" sighed Mark when they banished him from the sufferer's room.

Excited and frowning, he paced the passage with great strides. Heavy silence brooded over the house. The mother accepted the agony of her trial with mute energy.

The midwife went in, a wizened, expectorating old woman, with horn-rimmed glasses, and her sleeves rolled up.

Mark went into one of the rooms. Lolling in an armchair, the doctor was reading a newspaper.

"Not yet?" asked Mark.

"Not yet."

Mark escaped into the passage, and then into the sun parlor. A sinister idea suddenly insinuated itself into his brain. Suppose a deformed child were born to him! He began to quiver. His heart rose to God: "Who can make clean a creature conceived in corruption unless it be Thou alone, oh God?" He raised his hands to his temples as if on the point of swooning. Immediately, something like a resplendent smile suffused his heart, and rose to his lips. Something mysterious and hidden sang in his soul, giving promise of a sturdy flower of his own familiar garden.

From the depths of the nuptial chamber began to rise various hushed noises; panting, steps, hoarseness, sobs.

Mark had refused to inform Perpetua's family. He was alone, and he was like a man distraught.

The physician, tapping his shoulder, said to him:

"You can go in now."

"All right?"

"Yes, a boy."

Mark rushed into the bedroom. The midwife was bathing the newborn child. It was a repulsive, sickly creature, with distended cranium and crooked back. Prometheus! The mother, with scarcely audible voice, murmured:

"What is he like? Kiss him."

And as Mark, stupefied, stirred neither hand nor foot, she insisted:

"Kiss him."

Half-crazed with grief, Mark put his lips to that wretched,

pitiful flesh, which held such great and heroic dreams. Then he approached Perpetua's bed, sank on his knees, and put his head on her pillow. There, by the sweet, feverish face, wax-colored, and made translucent by the mystery of motherhood, he cried hopelessly, with utter abandon, like a child.

A dog was howling in the street. A bell tolled a death knell.

The mother suckled the child. He grew up rickety, and the sinuosity of his back defined itself as a round hump. He was exceptionally precocious. At six, such audacity was displayed by his face, fine-drawn and sharp as a blade, so penetratingly would he stare older people through and through, and so morosely would his eyes flash, that one could only say that in him was lodged some malevolent sprite. Mark translated the expression of his child in these words: "Why did you bring me into the world?" His parents surrounded him constantly with almost tearful loving kindness. But Prometheus was churlish, and rejected with coldness the fondling of those at home. With outsiders, on the contrary, and with visitors to the house, sisters and friends of Perpetua's, he was caressing and tiresome. The youngster snuggled between the knees of the women, resting his head on their laps. They stroked him with negligent gloved hands while they gabbled nothings. At times, Prometheus would seize a gloved feminine hand, breathe in its odor, and kiss it. Whenever he noticed that any lady looked at him pity-ingly, he would leap to his feet, and run out of the room un-sociably. He would hide in a corner and cry, and then refuse to eat.

Mark confined his agony within a wall of silence. His wife, gentle and faithful, divined the gloomy course of his thoughts, and tried to placate them by softly kissing his brow on which the hair had turned white.

At seven, Prometheus went to school. His father took him the first day. He implored from the master leniency for the pupil. He was taking him to school above all for him to entertain himself with the friendship and games of the other boys, not for him to learn, for there was more than enough time for learning, granted indeed that knowledge was of any use. More than sufficiently meditative on his own account was Prometheus. The master promised to be indulgent. And he was.

The professor's child enjoyed privileges and immunities which the unruly mob of pupils coveted. They revenged themselves during the recesses by mocking the little hunchback and calling him nicknames. When Prometheus caught the insults, his lower lip, prominent and with a premature down, would take on a ghastly yellowishness. Then, beside himself, and in a frenzy, he would charge like a gigantic spider upon the insulter, and bite and scratch him. He made himself feared.

Years were passing. The tall young boys went forth to grammar and high school; new pupils entered. And Prometheus was still in primary.

Prometheus protested daily, with outbursts of furious anger, against his sailor suits. He tore them to tatters. He wanted to dress like a man. He was now fourteen. They ordered a young man's clothes for him. Prometheus was eager to put them on, and look at himself in the glass. Seeing himself in such attire more humpbacked than ever, he rushed against the mirror, giving howls of pain. His mother wanted to take him in her arms, and he struck her. Again he put on sailor suits, with large blue collars which covered over the hump.

In the school, he came to be a petty king, consecrated by his age, and by the tolerance of the master. He had his favorites and his gloomy hatreds, which he satisfied with abnormal rancor.

Through a whim which his mother failed to understand, and although the school was but a few steps away, Prometheus refused to go unless accompanied by the maid, who also went for him when school was over, and the two would go walking in the park. There came a time when Prometheus refused to return to the public promenades. He hated frequented places where he saw his former companions now gallivanting in incipient love affairs.

The maid, Louise by name, and Prometheus began to go out every afternoon into the outskirts of the town, and into the adjacent villages. They traversed in silence gentle fields, leafy woods. The cows grazed to the sound of the drowsy copper bells. On the farms they would take warm milk, in the shelter of the barns.

One day Louise announced to her mistress her intention of leaving. No one was able to find out why.

Prometheus received the news of Louise's departure with stolid countenance. On the day following, he went to school alone. When school was out, he went in the direction of the environs of the city as usual. He penetrated into a shady lane bordered by the high wall of a convent. The vesper voice of the organ could be heard. He came to a sloping meadow, of disagreeable color, with a red path furrowing it, and by this path Prometheus descended. Behind some fig trees a blue smoke ascended to the heavens. Prometheus walked an hour cross-country, at random. He sat down on a white, polished stone on the edge of a road. It was nightfall. A milkmaid came along, with much swishing of skirts, her arms akimbo, her jug on her head. When she was near, Prometheus came out to meet her.

"Will you give me a little milk? I'll pay you well. I'm thirsty," he said.

His voice had choked. He stretched out his convulsed, bony hands towards the peasant.

The milkmaid, not as yet recovered from her amazement, was gazing at Prometheus from top to toe. She crossed herself.

"Heaven defend me: it is the devil."

And letting fall her jug, she fled, impelled by terror. And Prometheus ran after her.

"Why are you running away? Why are you running away?"

He could not reach her. He threw stones after her.

He stamped his feet, and foamed at the mouth.

And by that time it was deep night.

Very early in the morning, Telva de Nola left the farmhouse to milk the cows, humming an old ditty as she went. She stopped, speechless. She made an effort, and shouted:

"Nolo! Nolo! By the souls of the blessed!"

Nolo, dazed with sleep, peeped out of an excuse for a window, framed in by a wild grapevine.

"What's that thing swinging in the fig tree?" said Telva.

Nolo came down to make a closer examination. At the extremity of the place, dangling from a fig tree, the body of Prometheus danced in the breeze, misshapen and unsubstantial, like an untimely fruit.

Saint Manuel Bueno, Martyr

If with this life only in view we have had hope in Christ, we are of all men the most to be pitied.

I Corinthians 15:19.

MIGUEL DE UNAMUNO

Now that the bishop of the diocese of Renada, to which this my beloved village of Valverde de Lucerna belongs, is seeking (according to rumor), to initiate the process of beatification of our Don Manuel, or more correctly, Saint Manuel Bueno, who was parish priest here, I want to state in writing, by way of confession (although to what end only God, and not I, can say), all that I can vouch for and remember of that matriarchal man who pervaded the most secret life of my soul, who was my true spiritual father, the father of my spirit, the spirit of myself, Angela Carballino.

The other, my flesh-and-blood temporal father, I scarcely knew, for he died when I was still a very young girl. I know that he came to Valverde de Lucerna from the outside world— that he was a stranger—and that he settled here when he married my mother. He had brought a number of books with him: *Don Quixote*, some plays from the classic theater, some novels, a few histories, the *Bertoldo*, everything all mixed together. From these books (practically the only ones in the entire vilîage), I nurtured dreams from girlhood. My good mother gave me very little account either of the words or the deeds of my father. For the words and deeds of Don Manuel, whom she worshipped, of whom she was enamored, in common with all the rest of the village—in an exquisitely chaste manner, of course—had obliterated the memory of the words and deeds of her husband; him she commended to God, with full fervor, as she said her daily rosary.

Don Manuel I remember as if it were yesterday, from the time when I was a girl of ten, just before I was taken to the convent school in the cathedral city of Renada. At that time Don Manuel, our saint, must have been about thirty-seven years old. He was tall, slender, erect; he carried himself the way our Vulture Peak carries its crest, and his eyes had all the blue depth of our lake. As he walked he commanded all eyes, and not only all eyes but all hearts; gazing round at us he seemed to look through our flesh, as through glass, and penetrate our hearts. We all loved him, especially the children. And the things he said to us! Not words, things! The villagers breathed in the odor of his sanctity, they were intoxicated by it.

It was at this time that my brother Lazarus, who was in America, whence he regularly sent us money with which we lived in decent leisure, had my mother send me to the convent school, so that my education might be completed outside the village; he suggested this move despite the fact that he had no special fondness for the nuns. "But since, as far as I know," he wrote us, "there are no lay schools there yet—certainly not for young ladies—we will have to make use of the ones that do exist. The important thing is for Angelita to receive some polish and not be forced to continue among village girls." And so I entered the convent school. At one point I even thought I would become a teacher, but pedagogy soon palled upon me.

At school I met girls from the city and I made friends with some of them. But I still kept in touch with people in our village, and I received frequent reports and sometimes a visit.

And the fame of the parish priest reached as far as the school, for he was beginning to be talked of in the cathedral city. The nuns never tired of asking me about him.

Ever since early youth I was subject, I really don't know why, to great curiosity and restlessness, due at least in part to that jumble of books which my father had collected, and these qualities were stimulated at school, especially in the course of a relationship which I developed with a girl friend who grew excessively attached to me. At times she proposed that we enter the same convent together, swearing an everlasting "sisterhood"—and she even suggested that we seal the oath in blood. At other times she talked to me, with eyes half closed, of sweethearts and marriage. Strangely enough, I have never heard of her since, or of what became of her, despite the fact that whenever our Don Manuel was spoken of, or when my mother wrote me something about him in her letters—which happened in almost every letter—and I read it to her, this girl would exclaim, as if in rapture: "What luck, my dear, to be able to live near a saint like that, a live saint, of flesh and blood, and to be able to kiss his hand; when you go back to your village write me everything, everything, and tell me about him."

Five years passed at school, five years which now have faded in memory like a dream at dawn, and when I reached fifteen I returned to my own Valverde de Lucerna. By now everything revolved around Don Manuel: Don Manuel, the lake and the mountain. I arrived home anxious to know him, to place myself under his protection, and hopeful he would set me on my path in life.

It was rumored that he had entered the seminary to become a priest so that he might look after the children of a sister recently widowed and provide for them in place of their father; that in the seminary his keen mind and his talents had distinguished him and that he had subsequently turned down opportunities for a brilliant career in the church because he wanted to remain exclusively a part of his Valverde de Lucerna, of his remote village which lay like a brooch between the lake and the mountain reflected in it.

How he did love his people! His life consisted in salvaging wrecked marriages, in forcing unruly children to obey their parents, or reconciling parents to their children, and, above all, in consoling the embittered and the weary in spirit and helping everyone to die well.

I recall, among other incidents, the time when old Aunt Rabona's unhappy daughter returned to our town. She had gone to the city and lost her virtue there; now she returned unmarried and castoff, and brought back a little son. Don Manuel did not rest until he had persuaded her old sweetheart, Perote by name, to marry the poor girl and, moreover, to legitimize the little creature with his own name. Don Manuel told Perote:

"Come, give this poor waif a father, for the only Father he has is the one in Heaven."

"But, Don Manuel, I am not to blame——"

"Who knows, my son, who knows . . . ! And besides, it's not a question of blame."

And now poor Perote, inspired on that occasion to saintliness by Don Manuel, is a paralytic and an invalid, has as the staff and consolation of his life the boy he acknowledged as his son without believing it.

On Midsummer's Night, the shortest night of the year, it was a local custom here (and still is) for all the old crones, and a few old men, who thought they were possessed or bewitched (hysterics they were, for the most part, or in some cases epileptics) to flock to the lake. Don Manuel undertook to fulfill the same function as the lake, to serve as a healing pool, to treat his charges and even, if possible, to cure them. And such was the effect of his presence, of his gaze, and above all of his voice—the miracle of his voice!—and the infinitely sweet authority of his words, that he actually did achieve some remarkable cures. Whereupon his fame increased, drawing all the sick of the neighborhood to our lake and our priest. And yet once when a mother came to ask for a miracle in behalf of her son, he answered her with a sad smile:

"Ah, but I don't have my bishop's permission to perform miracles."

He was particularly interested in seeing that all the villagers kept themselves clean. If he chanced upon someone with a torn garment he would send him to the church: "Go and see the sacristan, and let him mend that tear." The sacristan was a tailor, and when, on the first day of the year, everyone went to congratulate the priest on his saint's day—his holy patron was Our Lord Jesus himself—it was by Don Manuel's wish that everyone appeared in a new shirt, and those that had none received the present of a new one from Don Manuel himself.

. He treated everyone with the greatest kindness; if he favored anyone, it was the most unfortunate, and especially those who rebelled. There was a congenital idiot in the village, the fool Blasillo, and it was toward him that Don Manuel chose to show the greatest love and concern; as a consequence he succeeded in miraculously teaching him things which had appeared beyond the idiot's comprehension. The fact was that the embers of understanding feebly glowing in the idiot were kindled whenever, like a pitiable monkey, he imitated his Don Manuel.

The marvel of the man was his voice; a divine voice which

brought one close to weeping. Whenever he officiated at Solemn High Mass and intoned the prelude, a tremor ran through the congregation and all within sound of his voice were moved to the depths of their being. The sound of his chanting, overflowing the church, went on to float over the lake and settle at the foot of the mountain. And when on Good Friday he intoned "My God, my God, why hast thou forsaken me?" a profound shudder swept through the multitude, like the lash of a northeaster across the waters of the lake. It was as if these people heard the Lord Jesus Christ himself, as if the voice sprang from the ancient crucifix, at the foot of which generations of mothers had offered up their sorrows. And it happened that on one occasion his mother heard him and was unable to contain herself, and cried out to him right in the church, "My son!" calling her child. And the entire congregation was visibly shaken. It was as if the mother's cry had issued from the half-open lips of the Mater Dolorosa—her heart transfixed by seven swords—which stood in one of the chapels of the nave. Afterwards, the fool Blasillo went about piteously repeating, as if he were an echo, "My God, my God, why hast thou forsaken me?" with such effect that everyone who heard him was moved to tears, to the great satisfaction of the fool, who prided himself on this triumph of imitation.

The priest's effect on people was such that no one ever dared to tell him a lie, and everyone confessed himself to him without need of a confessional. So true was this that on one occasion, when a revolting crime had been committed in a neighboring village, the judge—a dull fellow who did not know Don Manuel well—called on the priest and said:

"Let us see, Don Manuel, if you can get this bandit to admit the truth."

"So that afterwards you may punish him?" asked the saintly

man. "No, Judge, no; I will not extract from any man a truth which could be the death of him. That is a matter between him and his God. . . . Human justice is none of my affair. 'Judge not that ye be not judged,' said our Lord."

"But the fact is, Father, that I, a judge . . ."

"I understand. You, Judge, must render unto Caesar that which is Caesar's, while I shall render unto God that which is God's."

And, as Don Manuel departed, he gazed at the suspected criminal and said:

"Make sure that God forgives you, for that is all that matters."

Everyone went to Mass in the village, even if it were only to hear him and see him at the altar, where he appeared to be transfigured, his countenance lit from within. He introduced one holy practice to the popular cult; it consisted in assembling the whole town inside the church, men and women, old and young, some thousand persons; there we recited the Creed, in unison, so that it sounded like a single voice: "I believe in God, the Almighty Father, Creator of heaven and earth . . ." and all the rest. It was not a chorus, but a single voice, a simple united voice, all the voices based on one and piling up like a mountain, whose peak, lost at times in the clouds, was Don Manuel. As we reached the section "I believe in the resurrection of the flesh and life everlasting," the voice of Don Manuel was submerged, drowned in the voice of the populace as in a lake. In truth, he was silent. And I could hear the bells of that city which is said hereabouts to be at the bottom of the lake —bells which are also said to be audible on Midsummer Night —the bells of the city which is submerged in the spiritual lake of our populace; I was hearing the voice of our dead, resurrected in us by the communion of saints. Later, when I had learned the secret of our saint, I understood that it was as if a caravan crossing the desert lost its leader as they approached the goal of their journey, whereupon the people lifted him on their shoulders and brought his lifeless body into the promised land.

When the end of life drew near, most of the villagers refused to die unless they were holding on to Don Manuel's hand, as if to an anchor chain.

In his sermons he never inveighed against unbelievers, freemasons, liberals or heretics. What for, when there were none in the village? Nor did it occur to him to speak against the wickedness of the press. On the other hand, one of his most frequent themes was gossip, against which he lashed out.

"Envy," he liked to repeat, "envy is nurtured by those who prefer to think they are envied, and most persecutions are the result of a persecution mania rather than of an impulse to persecute."

"But Don Manuel, just listen to what that fellow was trying to tell me——"

"We should concern ourselves less with what people are trying to tell us than with what they tell us without trying. . . ."

His life was active rather than contemplative, and he constantly fled from idleness, even from leisure. Whenever he heard it said that idleness was the mother of all the vices, he added: "And also of the greatest vice of them all, which is to think idly." Once I asked him what he meant and he answered: "Thinking idly is a substitute for doing; or it is thinking too much about what is already done instead of what must be done. What's done is done and over with, and one must go on to something else, for there is nothing worse than remorse without possible relief." Action! Action! Even in those early days I had already begun to realize that Don Manuel fled from being left to think in solitude, and I guessed that some obsession haunted him.

And so it was that he was always occupied, sometimes even occupied in searching for occupations. He wrote very little on his own, so that he scarcely left us anything in writing, not even notes; on the other hand, he acted as scrivener for everyone else, especially mothers, for whom he composed letters to their absent children.

He also worked with his hands, pitching in to help with some of the village tasks. At threshing time he reported to the threshing floor to flail and winnow, meanwhile teaching and entertaining the workers by turn. Sometimes he took the place of a worker who had fallen sick. One day in the dead of winter he came upon a child, shivering with the bitter cold. The child's father had sent him into the woods to bring back a stray calf.

"Listen," he said to the child, "you go home and get warm, and tell your father that I am bringing back the calf." On the way back with the animal he ran into the father, who had come out to meet him, thoroughly ashamed of himself.

In winter he chopped wood for the poor. When a certain magnificent walnut tree died—"that matriarchal walnut," he called it, a tree under whose shade he had played as a boy and whose fruit he had eaten for so many years—he asked for the trunk, carried it to his house and, after he had cut six planks from it, which he put away at the foot of his bed, he made firewood of the rest to warm the poor. He was also in the habit of making balls for the boys to play with and a goodly number of toys for the younger children.

Often he used to accompany the doctor on his rounds, adding his presence and prestige to the doctor's prescriptions. Most of all he was interested in maternity cases and the care of children; it was his opinion that the old wives' saying "from the breast to heaven" and the other one about "little angels belong in heaven" were the greatest blasphemy. The death of a child moved him deeply.

"A child stillborn," I once heard him say, "or one who dies soon after birth, is the most terrible of mysteries to me. It's as if it were a suicide. Or as if the child were crucified."

And once, when a man had taken his own life and the father of the suicide came from another town and asked Don Manuel if his son could be buried in consecrated ground, the priest answered:

"Most certainly, for at the last moment, in the very last throes, he must certainly have repented. There is no doubt of it in my mind."

From time to time he would visit the local school to help the teacher, to teach alongside him—and not only the catechism. The simple truth was that he fled relentlessly from idleness and from solitude. He went so far in this desire of his to mingle with the villagers, especially adolescents and children, that he even attended the village dances. And more than once he played the drum to keep time for the young men and women dancing; this kind of activity, which in another priest would have seemed like a grotesque mockery of his calling, in him somehow took on the appearance of a holy, religious exercise. When the Angelus rang out, he would put down the drum and sticks, take off his hat (all the others doing the same) and pray: "The angel of the Lord declared unto Mary: Hail Mary . . ." And afterwards: "Now, let us rest until tomorrow."

"First of all," he would say, "the village must be happy; everyone must be happy to be alive. To be satisfied with life is of first importance. No one should want to die until it is God's will."

"I want to die now," a recently widowed woman once told him, "I want to be with my husband. . . ."

"And why now?" he asked. "Stay here and pray God for his soul."

One of his well-loved remarks was made at a wedding: "Ah, if I could only change all the water in our lake into wine, into a dear little wine which, no matter how much of it one drank, would always make one joyful without intoxicating . . . or, if intoxicating, would make one joyfully drunk."

Once upon a time a band of poor acrobats came through the village. The leader—who arrived on the scene with a gravely ill and pregnant wife and three sons to help him—played the clown. While he was in the village square making all the children, and even some of the adults, laugh with glee, his wife was suddenly taken with dreadful pains and had to leave; she went off accompanied by a look of anguish from the clown and a howl of laughter from the children. Don Manuel hurried after, and, a little later, in a corner of the stable of the inn, he helped her give up her soul in a state of grace. When the performance was over and the villagers and the clown learned of the tragedy, they came to the inn, and there the poor bereaved clown, in a voice choked with tears, said to Don Manuel, as he took his hand and kissed it: "They are quite right, Father, when they say you are a saint." Don Manuel took the clown's hand in his and replied before everyone:

"It is you who are the saint, good clown. I watched you at your work and understood that you do it not only to provide bread for your children, but also to give joy to the children of others. And I tell you now that your wife, the mother of your children, whom I sent to God while you worked to give joy, is at rest in the Lord, and that you will join her there, and that the angels, whom you will make laugh with happiness in heaven, will reward you with their laughter."

And everyone present wept, children and elders alike, as much from sorrow as from a mysterious joy in which all sorrow was drowned. Later, recalling that solemn hour, I came to realize that the imperturbable joyousness of Don Manuel was merely the temporal, earthly form of an infinite, eternal sadness that the priest concealed from the eyes and ears of the world with heroic saintliness.

His constant activity, his ceaseless intervention in the tasks and diversions of his parishioners, seemed, in short, a flight from himself, a flight from solitude. He confirmed this suspicion: "I have a dread of solitude," he would say. And still, from time to time he would go off by himself, along the shores of the lake, to the ruins of the abbey, where the souls of pious Cistercians seem still to repose, although history has long since buried them in oblivion. There, the cell of the so-called Father-Captain can still be found, and it is said that the drops of blood spattered on the walls as he flagellated himself can still be seen. What thoughts occupied our Dan Manuel as he walked there? I remember a conversation we held once in which I asked him, as he was speaking of the abbey, why it had never occurred to him to enter a monastery, and he answered me:

"It is not at all because of the fact that my sister is a widow and I have her children and herself to support—for God looks after the poor—but rather because I simply was not born to be a hermit, an anchorite; the solitude would crush my soul; and, as far as a monastery is concerned, my monastery is Valverde de Lucerna. I was not meant to live alone, or die alone. I was meant to live for my village, and die for it too. How should I save my soul if I were not to save the soul of my village as well?"

"But there have been saints who were hermits, solitaries," I said.

"Yes, the Lord gave them the grace of solitude which He

has denied me, and I must resign myself. I must not throw away my village to win my soul. God made me that way. I would not be able to resist the temptations of the desert. I would not be able, alone, to carry the cross of birth."

I have summoned up all these recollections, from which my faith was fed, in order to portray our Don Manuel as he was when I, a young girl of sixteen, returned from the convent of Renada to our "monastery of Valverde de Lucerna," once more to kneel at the feet of our "abbot."

"Well, here is Simona's daughter," he said as soon as he saw me; "you are a grown woman now, you probably know French, and how to play the piano, and embroider, and heaven knows what else besides! Now you must get ready to give us a family. And your brother Lazarus; when does he return? Is he still in the New World?"

"Yes, Father, he is still in the New World."

"The New World! And we in the Old. Well then, when you write him, tell him for me, the parish priest, that I should like to know when he is returning from the New World to the Old, to bring us the latest from over there. And tell him that he will find the lake and the mountain as he left them."

When I first went to him for confession, I became so confused that I could not enunciate a word. I recited the "Forgive me, Father, for I have sinned," in a stammer, almost a sob. And he, observing this, said:

"Good heavens, my dear, what are you afraid of, or of whom are you afraid? Certainly you're not trembling now under the weight of your sins, nor in fear of God. No, you're trembling because of me, isn't that so?"

At this point I burst into tears.

"What have they been telling you about me? What fairy tales? Was it your mother, perhaps? Come, come, please be calm; you must imagine you are talking to your brother . . ."

At this I plucked up courage and began to tell him of my anxieties, doubts and sorrows.

"Bah! Where did you read all this, Miss Intellectual. All this is literary nonsense. Don't succumb to everything you read just yet, not even to Saint Theresa. If you need to amuse yourself, read the *Bertoldo,* as your father before you did."

I came away from my first confession to that holy man, deeply consoled. The initial fear—fear more than respect— with which I had approached him, turned into a profound pity. I was at that time a very young woman, almost a girl still; and yet I was beginning to be a woman, in my innermost being I felt the juice and stirrings of maternity, and when I found myself in the confessional at the side of the saintly priest, I sensed a kind of unspoken confession on his part in the soft murmur of his voice. And I remembered how when he had intoned in the church the words of Jesus Christ: "My God, my God, why hast thou forsaken me?" his own mother had cried out in the congregation: "My son!"; and I could hear the cry that had rent the silence of the temple. And I went to him again for confession—and to comfort him.

Another time in the confessional I told him of a doubt which assailed me, and he responded:

"As to that, you know what the catechism says: That question you must not ask me, for I am ignorant; in Holy Mother Church there are learned doctors of theology who will know how to answer you."

"But you are the learned doctor here."

"Me? A learned doctor? Not at all. I, my little know-it-all, am only a poor country priest. And these questions . . . do you know who whispers them into your ear? . . . the Devil does!"

Then, making bold, I asked him point-blank:

"And suppose he were to whisper these questions to you?"

"Who? To me? The Devil? No, we don't even know each other, my daughter, we have never met."

"But suppose he did whisper them? . . ."

"I wouldn't pay any attention. And that's enough of that; let's get on, for there are some people, really sick people, waiting for me."

I went away thinking, I don't know why, that our Don Manuel, so famous for curing the bedeviled, didn't really even believe in the Devil. As I started home, I ran into the fool Blasillo, who had probably been hovering about outside; as soon as he saw me, and by way of treating me to a display of his virtuosity, he began the business of repeating—and in what a manner!—"My God, my God, why hast thou forsaken me?" I arrived home utterly saddened and locked myself in my room to cry, until finally my mother interfered.

"With all these confessions, Angelita, you will end by going off to a nunnery."

"Don't worry, Mother," I answered her. "I have plenty to do here, in the village, and it will be my only convent."

"Until you marry."

"I don't intend to," I rejoined.

The next time I saw Don Manuel I asked him, looking straight into his eyes:

"Is there really a hell, Don Manuel?"

And he, without any change of expression, answered:

"For you, my daughter, no."

"For others, then?"

"Does it matter to you, if you are not to go there?"

"It matters for the others, in any case. Is there a hell?"

"Believe in heaven, the heaven we can see. Look at it there"

—and he pointed to the heavens above the mountain, and then down into the lake, to the reflection.

"But we are supposed to believe in hell as well as in heaven," I said.

"That's true. We must believe everything believed and taught by our Holy Mother Church, Catholic, Apostolic, and Roman. And now, that will do!"

I thought I read a deep unknown sadness in his eyes, eyes which were as blue as the waters of the lake.

Those years passed as if in a dream. Within me, a reflected image of Don Manuel was unconsciously taking form. He was an ordinary enough man in many ways; we were as accustomed to him as the daily bread we asked for in our Pater Noster. I helped him whenever I could with his tasks, visiting the sick, his sick, the girls at school, and helping, too, with the church linen and the vestments; I was, he said, his deaconess. Once I was invited to the city for a few days by a school friend, but I had to hurry home, for the city stifled me—something was missing, I was thirsty for a sight of the waters of the lake, hungry for a sight of the peaks of the mountain; and, even more, I missed my Don Manuel, as if his absence called to me, as if he were endangered by my being so far away, as if he were in need of me. I began to feel a kind of maternal affection for my spiritual father; I longed to help him bear the cross of birth.

Thus I was going on my twenty-fourth birthday when my brother Lazarus came back from America with the small fortune he had saved up. He came back to Valverde de Lucerna with the intention of taking me and my mother to live in a city, perhaps even Madrid.

"In the country," he said, "in these villages, a person becomes stupefied, brutalized and spiritually impoverished." And he added: "Civilization is the very opposite of everything countryfied. The idiocy of village life! No, that's not for us; I didn't have you sent to school so that later you might degenerate here, among these ignorant peasants."

I said nothing, though I was ready to take a firm stand against moving away. But our mother, already past sixty, was adamant from the start: "Change pastures at my age?" she demanded at once. A little later she made it quite clear that she could not live out of sight of her lake, her mountain, and, above all, of her Don Manuel.

"The two of you are like cats that get attached to their homes," my brother muttered.

When he realized the complete sway exercised over the entire village—especially over my mother and myself—by the saintly priest, my brother began to resent him. He saw in this situation an example of the obscurantist theocracy which, according to him, smothered Spain. And he commenced to spout the old anticlerical commonplaces, to which he added antireligious and "progressive" propaganda brought back from the New World.

"In the Spain of sloth and flabby useless men, the priests dominate the women, and the women dominate the men. And the countryside! this feudal countryside!"

"Feudal," to him, meant something frightful. "Feudal" and "medieval" were the epithets he employed to condemn anything completely.

The failure of his diatribes to move us and their total lack of effect upon the village—where they were listened to with respectful indifference—disconcerted him no end. "The man does not exist who could move these clods." But he soon began to understand—for he was a good man as well as intelligent— the kind of influence exercised over the village by Don Manuel, and he came to appreciate the effect of the priest's work in the village.

"This priest is not like the others," he announced. "He is, in fact, a saint."

"How do you know what the others are like?" I asked. To which he answered:

"I can imagine."

In any case, he did not set foot inside the church nor did he miss an opportunity to parade his unbelief—though he always exempted Don Manuel from his scornful accusations. In the village, an unconscious expectancy began to build up, the anticipation of a kind of duel between my brother Lazarus and Don Manuel—in short, it was expected that Don Manuel would convert my brother. No one doubted but that in the end the priest would bring him into the fold. On his side, Lazarus was eager (he told me so himself, later) to go and hear Don Manuel, to see and hear him in the church, to get to know him and to talk with him, so that he might learn the secret of his spiritual hold over our souls. And he let himself be coaxed to this end, so that finally—"out of curiosity," as he said—he went to hear the preacher.

"Now, this is something else again," he told me as soon as he came from hearing Don Manuel for the first time. "He's not like the others; still, he doesn't fool me, he's too intelligent to believe everything he must teach."

"You mean you think he's a hypocrite?"

"A hypocrite . . . no! But he has a job by which he must live."

As for me, my brother undertook to see that I read the books he brought me, and others which he urged me to buy.

"So your brother Lazarus wants you to read?" Don Manuel queried. "Well, read, my daughter, read and make him happy by doing so. I know you will read only worthy books. You may even read novels; they are as good as so-called "history" books. You are better off reading than concerning yourself with village gossip and old wives' tales. Above all, you will do well to read devotional books, which will bring you contentment in life, a quiet, gentle contentment, and peace."

And he, did he enjoy such contentment?

It was about this time that our mother fell mortally sick and died. In her last days her one wish was that Dan Manuel should convert Lazarus, whom she expected to see again in heaven, in some little corner among the stars from where they could look down upon the lake and the mountain of Valverde de Lucerna. She felt she was going there now, to see God.

"You are not going anywhere," Don Manuel would tell her; "you will stay right here. Your body will remain here, in this land, and your soul also, in this house, watching and listening to your children though they do not see or hear you."

"But, Father," she said, "I am going to see God."

"God, my daughter, is all around us, and you will see Him from here, from right here. And all of us in Him, and He in all of us."

"God bless you," I whispered to him.

"The peace in which your mother dies will be her eternal life," he told me.

And, turning to my brother Lazarus: "Her heaven is to go on seeing you, and it is at this moment that she must be saved. Tell her you will pray for her."

"But——"

"But what? Tell her you will pray for her, to whom you owe your life. And I know that once you promise her, you *will* pray, and I know that once you pray . . ."

My brother, his eyes filled with tears, drew near our dying mother and gave her his solemn promise to pray for her.

"And I, in heaven, will pray for you, for all of you," my mother replied. And then, kissing the crucifix and fixing her eyes on Don Manuel, she gave up her soul to God.

"Into Thy hands I commend my spirit," prayed the priest.

My brother and I stayed on in the house alone. What had happened at the time of my mother's death had established a bond between Lazarus and Don Manuel. The latter seemed even to neglect some of his charges, his patients and the other needy, to look after my brother. In the afternoons, they would go for a stroll together, walking along the lake or toward the ruins, overgrown with ivy, of the old Cistercian abbey.

"He's an extraordinary man," Lazarus told me. "You know the story they tell of how there is a city at the bottom of our lake, submerged beneath the water, and that on Midsummer's Night at midnight the sound of the church bells can be heard . . ."

"Yes, a 'feudal and medieval' city . . ."

"And I believe," he went on, "that at the bottom of Don Manuel's soul there is a city, submerged and flooded, and that sometimes the sound of its bells can be heard."

"Yes. And the city submerged in Don Manuel's soul, and perhaps—why not?—in yours as well, is certainly the cemetery of the souls of our ancestors, the ancestors of our Valverde de Lucerna . . . 'feudal and medieval'!"

In the end, my brother began going to Mass. He went regularly to hear Don Manuel. When it became known that he was prepared to comply with his annual duty of receiving Communion, and would do so along with the other parishioners, a deep joy ran through the town, for we all felt that by this act he was restored to his people. The rejoicing was of such nature, moreover, so openhanded and honest, that Lazarus never did feel that he had been "vanquished" or "overcome."

The day of his Communion arrived; of Communion before the entire village, with the entire village. When it came time for my brother's turn, I saw Don Manuel—white as January snow on the mountain, and moving like the surface of the lake when it is stirred by the northeasterly wind—come up to him with the holy wafer in his hand, which trembled violently as it reached out to Lazarus's mouth; at that moment the priest had an instant of faintness and the wafer dropped to the ground. My brother himself recovered it and placed it in his mouth. The people saw the tears on Don Manuel's face, and everyone wept, saying: "What a great love he bears for him!" And then, because it was dawn, a cock crowed.

On returning home I locked myself in with my brother, and I put my arms around his neck and kissed him.

"Lazarus, Lazarus, what joy you have given us all today; the entire village, the living and the dead, and especially our mother. Did you see how Don Manuel wept for joy? What joy you have given us all!"

"It was for that reason that I did what I did," he answered me.

"Just to give us pleasure? Surely you did it for your own sake, first of all; because of your conversion."

And then Lazarus, my brother, grown as pale and tremulous as Don Manuel when he was giving Communion, bade me sit down, in the very chair where our mother used to sit. He took a deep breath, and, in the low tones of confession, he told me:

"Angelita, the time has come when I must tell you the

truth, the absolute truth, and I shall tell it to you because I must, because I cannot, I ought not, conceal it from you, and because, sooner or later, you are bound to sense it anyway, if only halfway—which would be worse."

Thereupon, serenely and tranquilly, in a subdued voice, he recounted a tale that drowned me in a lake of sorrow. He told how Don Manuel had appealed to him, particularly during the walks to the ruins of the old Cistercian abbey, to set a good example, to avoid scandalizing the townspeople, to take part in the religious life of the community, to feign belief even if he did not feel any, to conceal his own ideas—all this without attempting in any way to catechize him, to instruct him in religion, or to effect a true conversion.

"But is it possible?" I asked in consternation.

"Possible and true. When I said to him: 'Is this you, the priest, who suggests I pretend?' he replied, hesitatingly: 'Pretend? Not at all! That is not pretense. "Dip your fingers in holy water, and you will end by believing," as someone said.' And I, gazing into his eyes, asked him: 'And you, celebrating the Mass, have you ended by believing?' He looked away and stared out at the lake, until his eyes filled with tears. And it was in this way that I came to understand his secret."

"Lazarus!" I cried out, incapable of another word.

At that moment the fool Blasillo came along our street, crying out his: "My God, my God, why hast thou forsaken me?" And Lazarus shuddered, as if he had heard the voice of Don Manuel, or of Christ.

"It was then," my brother at length continued, "that I really understood his motives and his saintliness; for a saint he is, sister, a true saint. In trying to convert me to his holy cause—for it is a holy cause, a most holy cause—he was not attempting to score a triumph, but rather was doing it to protect the peace, the happiness, the illusions, perhaps, of his charges. I understood that if he thus deceives them—if it *is* deceit—it is not for his own advantage. I submitted to his logic—and that was my conversion.

"I shall never forget the day on which I said to him: 'But, Don Manuel, the truth, the truth, above all!'; and he, trembling, whispered in my ear—though we were all alone in the fields—'The truth? The truth, Lazarus, is perhaps something so unbearable, so terrible, something so deadly, that simple people could not live with it!'

" 'And why do you show me a glimpse of it now, here, as if we were in the confessional?' I asked. And he said: 'Because if I did not, I would be so tormented by it, so tormented, that I would finally shout it in the middle of the public square, which I must never, never, never do . . . I was put here to give life to the souls of my charges, to make them happy, to make them dream they are immortal—and not to destroy them. The important thing is that they should live in health, and concord with each other—and with the truth, with my truth, they could not live at all. Let them live. That is what the Church does, it lets them live. As for true religion, all religions are true as long as they give spiritual life to the people who profess them, as long as they console them for having been born only to die. And for each people the truest religion is their own, the religion that made them. . . . And mine? Mine consists in consoling myself by consoling others, even though the consolation I give them is never mine.' I shall never forget his words."

"But then this Communion of yours has been a sacrilege," I dared interrupt, regretting my words as soon as I said them.

"Sacrilege? What about the priest who gave it to me? And his Masses?"

"What martyrdom!" I exclaimed.

"And now," said my brother, "there is one more person to console the people."

"To deceive them, you mean?" I said.

"Not at all," he replied, "but rather to confirm them in their faith."

"And they, the people, do they really believe, do you think?"

"About that, I know nothing! . . . They probably believe without trying, from force of habit, tradition. The important thing is not to stir them up. To let them live with their untroubled feelings to protect them from the torments of doubt. Blessed are the poor in spirit!"

"That then is what you have learned from Don Manuel. And tell me, do you feel you have carried out your promise to our mother on her deathbed, when you promised to pray for her?"

"Do you think I *could* fail her? What do you take me for, sister? Do you think I would go back on my word, on a solemn promise made at the hour of death to a mother?"

"I don't know. . . . You might have wanted to deceive her so she could die in peace."

"The fact is, though, that if I had not lived up to my promise, I would be totally miserable."

"And . . . ?"

"I carried out my promise and I have not neglected for a single day to pray for her."

"Only for her?"

"Well, now, for whom else?"

"For yourself! And now, for Don Manuel."

We parted and went to our separate rooms. I to weep through the night, praying for the conversion of my brother and of Don Manuel. And Lazarus, to what purpose I know not.

From that day on I was afraid of finding myself alone with Don Manuel, whom I continued to aid in his pious works. And he seemed to sense my inner turmoil and to guess at its cause. When at last I came to him in the penitent's box—(who was the judge, and who the offender?)—the two of us, he and I, bowed our heads in silence and began to cry. It was he, finally, Don Manuel, who broke the terrible silence, with a voice which seemed to issue from the tomb:

"Angelita, you have the same faith you had when you were ten, don't you? You believe, don't you?"

"I believe, Father."

"Then go on believing. And if doubts come to torment you, suppress them utterly, even to yourself. The main thing is to live. . . ."

I summoned up courage, and dared to ask, trembling:

"But Father, do you believe?"

For a brief moment he hesitated, and then, mastering himself, he said:

"I believe!"

"In what, Father, in what? Do you believe in the after life? Do you believe that when we die, we do not die utterly? Do you believe that we will see each other again, that we will love each other in a world to come? Do you believe in another life?"

The poor saint was sobbing.

"My child, leave off, leave off!"

Now, when I come to write this account, I ask myself: Why did he not deceive me? Why did he not deceive me as he deceived the others? Why could he not deceive himself, or why could he not deceive me? And I want to believe that he was afflicted because he could not deceive himself into deceiving me.

"And now," he said, "pray for me, for your brother, and for yourself—for all of us. We must go on living. And giving life."

And, after a pause:

"Angelita, why don't you marry?"

"You know why."

"No, no; you must marry. Lazarus and I will find you a suitor. For it would be good for you to marry, and rid yourself of these obsessions."

"Obsessions, Don Manuel?"

"I know well enough what I am saying. You should not torment yourself for the sake of others, for each of us has more than enough to do answering for himself."

"That it should be you, Don Manuel, who says this! That you should advise me to marry and answer for myself alone and not suffer over others! That it should be you!"

"Yes, you are right, Angelita. I am no longer sure of what I say. I am no longer sure of what I say since I began to confess to you. Only, one must go on living. Yes! One must live!"

And when I rose to leave the church, he asked me:

"Now, Angelita, in the name of the people, do you absolve me?"

I felt pierced by a mysterious and priestly prompting and said:

"In the name of the Father, the Son and the Holy Ghost, I absolve you, Father."

And we went out from the church, and as I went out I felt the quickening of maternity within me.

My brother, now totally devoted to the work of Don Manuel, had become his closest and most zealous collaborator and companion. They were bound together, moreover, by their common secret. Lazarus accompanied the priest on his visits to the sick, and to the schools, and he placed his resources at the disposal of the saintly man. A little more zeal, and he would have helped at Mass. All the while he was sounding deeper into the unfathomable soul of the priest.

"What courage!" he exclaimed to me once. "Yesterday, as we walked along the lake he said: 'There lies my direst temptation.' When I questioned him with my eyes, he went on: 'My poor father, who was close to ninety when he died, was tormented all his life, as he himself confessed to me, by a temptation to commit suicide, by an instinct to self-destruction which had come to him from time immemorial—from birth, from his race, as he said—and was forced to struggle against it always. And this struggle grew to be his life. So as not to succumb to this temptation he was forced to take precautions, to keep watch over himself. He told me of terrible episodes. His urge was a form of madness—and I have inherited it. How that water beckons to me from its deep silence! . . . an apparent silence reflecting the sky like a mirror—and beneath it the hidden current! My life, Lazarus, is a kind of continual suicide, or a struggle against suicide, which is the same thing. . . . Just so long as our people go on living!' And then he added: 'Here the river eddies to form a lake, so that later, flowing down the plateau, it may form cascades, waterfalls, and torrents, hurling itself through gorges and chasms. Thus does life eddy in the village; and the temptation to suicide is greater beside the still waters which at night reflect the stars, than it is beside the crashing falls which drive one back in fear. Listen, Lazarus, I have helped poor villagers to die well, ignorant, illiterate villagers, who had scarcely ever been out of their village, and I have learned from their own lips, or divined it when they were silent, the real cause of their sickness unto death, and there at the head of their deathbed I have been able to look into the black abyss of their life-weariness. A weariness a thousand times worse than hunger! For our part, Lazarus, let us go on with our kind of suicide: working for the people, and let them dream their lives as the lake dreams the heavens.'

"Another time," said my brother, "as we were coming back, we saw a country girl, a goatherd, standing erect on a height of the mountain slope overlooking the lake, and she was singing in a voice fresher than its waters. Don Manuel took hold of me, and pointing to her said: 'Look, it's as though time had stopped, as though this country girl had always been there just as she is, singing in the way she is, and as though she would always be there, as she was before my consciousness began, as she will be when it is past. That girl is a part of nature—not of history—along with the rocks, the clouds, the trees, and the waters.' He has such a subtle feeling for nature, he infuses it with spirit!

"I shall not forget the day when snow was falling and he asked me: 'Have you ever seen a greater mystery, Lazarus, than the snow falling, and dying, in the lake, while a hood is laid upon the mountain?' "

Don Manuel had to moderate and temper my brother's zeal and his neophyte's crudeness. As soon as he heard that Lazarus was going about inveighing against some of the popular superstitions he told him forcefully:

"Leave them alone! It's difficult enough making them understand where orthodox belief leaves off and where superstition begins. It's hard enough, especially for us. Leave them alone, then, as long as they get some comfort. . . . It's better for them to believe everything, even things that contradict one another, than to believe nothing. The idea that someone who believes too much ends by not believing in anything is a Protestant notion. Let us not protest! Protestation destroys contentment and peace."

My brother told me, too, about one moonlit night when they were returning to town along the lake (whose surface a mountain breeze was stirring, so that the moonbeams topped the whitecaps), Don Manuel turned to him and said:

"Look, the water is reciting the litany and saying: *ianua caeli, ora pro nobis;* gate of heaven, pray for us."

Two tears fell from his lashes to the grass, where the light of the full moon shone upon them like dew.

And time went hurrying by, and my brother and I began to notice that Don Manuel's spirits were failing, that he could no longer control completely the deep-rooted sadness which consumed him; perhaps some treacherous illness was undermining his body and soul. In an effort to rouse his interest, Lazarus spoke to him of the good effect the organizing of a sort of Catholic agrarian syndicate would have.

"A syndicate?" Don Manuel repeated sadly. "A syndicate? And what is that? The Church is the only syndicate I know. And you have certainly heard 'My kingdom is not of this world.' Our kingdom, Lazarus, is not of this world. . . ."

"And of the other?"

Don Manuel bowed his head:

"The other is here. Two kingdoms exist in this world. Or rather, the other world . . . Ah, I don't really know what I'm saying. But as for the syndicate, that's a vestige from your days of 'progressivism.' No, Lazarus, no; religion does not exist to resolve the economic or political conflicts of this world, which God has left for men to argue over. Let men think and act as they will, let them console themselves for having been born, let them live as happily as possible in the illusion that all this has a purpose. I don't propose to advise the poor to submit to the rich, nor to suggest to the rich that they give in to the poor; but rather to preach resignation in everyone, and charity toward everyone. For even the rich man must resign himself—to his riches, and to life; and the poor man must show charity—even to the rich. The Social Question? Ignore it, for it is none of our business. So, a new society is on the way, in which there will be neither rich nor poor, in which wealth will be justly divided, in which everything will belong to everyone—and so, what then? Won't this general well-being and comfort lead to even greater tedium and weariness of life? I know well enough that one of the leaders of the so-called Social Revolution has already said that religion is the opium of the people. Opium . . . Opium . . . Yes, opium it is. We should give them opium, and help them sleep, and dream. I myself, with my ceaseless activity, give myself opium. And still I don't manage to sleep well, let alone dream well. . . . What a fearful nightmare! . . . I, too, can say, with the Divine Master: 'My soul is weary unto death.' No, Lazarus, no; no syndicates for us. If *they* organize them, well and good—they would be distracting themselves in that way. Let them play at syndicates, if that makes them happy."

The entire village began to realize that Don Manuel's spirit was weakening, that his strength was waning. His voice—that miracle of a voice—began to shake. Tears came into his eyes for any reason whatever—or for no reason. Whenever he spoke to people about the other world, about the other life, he was compelled to pause at frequent intervals, and he would close his eyes. "It is a vision," people would say, "he is having a vision of what lies ahead." At such moments the fool Blasillo was the first to break into tears. He wept copiously these days; he wept more than he laughed, and even his laughter had the sound of tears.

The last Easter Week which Don Manuel was to celebrate among us, in this world, in this village of ours, arrived, and everyone sensed the impending end of the tragedy. And how Don Manuel's words moved us when for the last time he cried out: "My God, my God, why hast thou forsaken me?" And when he repeated the words of the Lord to the Good Thief ("All thieves are good," Don Manuel used to tell us): "Tomorrow shalt thou be with me in Paradise." And then, the last general Communion which our saint was to give! When he came to my brother to give him the Host—his hand was steady this time—just after the liturgical ". . . *in vitam aeternam,*" he bent down and whispered to him: "There is no other life but this, no life more eternal . . . let them dream it is eternal . . . let it be eternal for a few years. . . ."

And when he came to me he said: "Pray, my child, pray for us all." And then, something so extraordinary happened that I carry it now in my heart as the greatest of mysteries: he bent over and said, in a voice which seemed to belong to the other world: ". . . and pray, too, for our Lord Jesus Christ."

All my strength had drained from me, and I stood up like a somnambulist. Everything around me seemed dreamlike. And I thought: "Am I to pray, too, for the lake and the mountain?" And next: "Am I bewitched, then?" Home at last, I took up the crucifix my mother had held in her hands when she had given up her soul to God, and, gazing at it through my tears and recalling the "My God, my God, why hast thou forsaken me?" of our two Christs, the one of this earth and the other of this village, I prayed: "Thy will be done on earth as it is in heaven," and then, "And lead us not into temptation. Amen." After this I turned to the statue of the Mater Dolorosa—her heart transfixed by seven swords—which had been my poor mother's most sorrowful comfort, and I prayed again: "Holy Mary, Mother of God, pray for us sinners, now and in the hour of our death. Amen." I had scarcely finished the prayer, when I asked myself: "Sinners? Sinners are we? And what is our sin, what is it?" And all day I brooded over the question.

The next day I went to Don Manuel—Don Manuel now like a Biblical figure facing death—and I said to him:

"Do you remember, Father, years ago when I asked you a certain question you answered: 'That question you must not ask me, for I am ignorant; there are learned doctors of the Holy Mother Church who will know how to answer you'?"

"Do I remember? . . . Of course. And I remember I told you those were questions put to you by the Devil."

"Well, then, Father, I have come again, bedeviled, to ask you another question put to me by my Guardian Devil."

"Ask it."

"Yesterday, when you gave me Communion, you asked me to pray for all of us, and even for——"

"That's enough! . . . Go on."

"I arrived home and began to pray; when I came to the part 'Pray for us sinners, now and in the hour of our death,' a voice in me asked: 'Sinners? Sinners are we? And what is our sin?' What is our sin, Father?"

"Our sin?" he replied. "A great doctor of the Spanish Catholic Apostolic Church has already explained it; the great doctor of *Life Is a Dream* has written 'The greatest sin of man is to have been born.' That, my child, is our sin; to have been born."

"Can it be atoned, Father?"

"Go and pray again. Pray once more for us sinners, now and in the hour of our death. . . . Yes, at length the dream is atoned . . . at length life is atoned . . . at length the cross of birth is expiated and atoned, and the drama comes to an end. . . . And as Calderón said, to have done good, to have feigned good, even in dreams, is something which is not lost."

The hour of his death arrived at last. The entire village saw it come. And he made it his finest lesson. For he would not die alone or at rest. He died preaching to his people in the church. But first, before being carried to the church (his paralysis made it impossible for him to move), he summoned Lazarus and me to his bedside. Alone there, the three of us together, he said:

"Listen to me: watch over these poor sheep; find some comfort for them in living, and let them believe what I could not. And Lazarus, when your hour comes, die as I die, as Angela will die, in the bosom of the Holy Mother Church, Catholic, Apostolic, and Roman; that is to say, of the Holy Mother Church of Valverde de Lucerna. And now, farewell; until we never meet again, for this dream of life is coming to an end. . . ."

"Father, Father," I cried out.

"Do not grieve, Angela, only go on praying for all sinners, for all who have been born. Let them dream, let them dream. . . . Oh, what a longing I have to sleep, to sleep, sleep without end, sleep for all an eternity, and never dream! Forgetting this dream! . . . When they bury me, let it be in a box made from the six planks I cut from the old walnut tree—poor old tree!—in whose shade I played as a child, when I began the dream. . . . In those days, I did really believe in life everlasting. That is to say, it seems to me now that I believed. For a child, to believe is the same as to dream. And for a people, too. . . . You'll find those six planks I cut at the foot of the bed."

He was seized by a sudden fit of choking, and then, composing himself once more, he went on:

"You will recall that when we prayed together, animated by a common sentiment, a community of spirit, and we came to the final verse of the Creed, you will remember that I would fall silent. . . . When the Israelites were coming to the end of their wandering in the desert, the Lord told Aaron and Moses that because they had not believed in Him they would not set foot in the Promised Land with their people; and he bade them climb the heights of Mount Hor, where Moses ordered Aaron stripped of his garments, so that Aaron died there, and then Moses went up from the plains of Moab to Mount Nebo, to the top of Pisgah, looking into Jericho, and the Lord showed him all of the land promised to His people, but said to him: 'You will not go there.' And there Moses died, and no one knew his grave. And he left Joshua to be chief in his place. You, Lazarus, must be my Joshua, and if you can make the sun stand still, do so, and never mind progress. Like Moses, I have seen the face of God—our supreme dream—face to face, and as you already know, and as the Scripture says, he who sees God's face, he who sees the eyes of the dream, the eyes with which He looks at us, will die inexorably and forever. And therefore, do not let our people, so long as they live, look into the face of God. Once dead, it will no longer matter, for then they will see nothing. . . ."

"Father, Father, Father," I cried again.

And he said:

"Angela, you must pray always, so that all sinners may go on dreaming, until they die, of the resurrection of the flesh and the life everlasting. . . ."

I was expecting "and who knows, it might be . . ." But instead, Don Manuel had another attack of coughing.

"And now," he finally went on, "and now, in the hour of

my death, it is high time to have me carried, in this very chair, to the church, so that I may take leave there of my people, who await me."

He was carried to the church and brought, in his armchair, into the chancel, to the foot of the altar. In his hands he held a crucifix. My brother and I stood close to him, but the fool Blasillo wanted to stand even closer. He wanted to grasp Don Manuel by the hand, so that he could kiss it. When some of the people near by tried to stop him, Don Manuel rebuked them and said:

"Let him come closer. . . . Come, Blasillo, give me your hand."

The fool cried for joy. And then Don Manuel spoke:

"I have very few words left, my children; I scarcely feel I have strength enough left to die. And then, I have nothing new to tell you, either. I have already said everything I have to say. Live with each other in peace and contentment, in the hope that we will all see each other again some day, in that other Valverde de Lucerna up there among the evening stars, the stars which the lake reflects over the image of the reflected mountain. And pray, pray to the Most Blessed Mary, and to Our Lord. Be good . . . that is enough. Forgive me whatever wrong I may have done you inadvertently or unknowingly. After I give you my blessing, let us pray together, let us say the Pater Noster, the Ave Maria, the Salve, and the Creed."

Then he gave his blessing to the whole village, with the crucifix in his hand, while the women and children cried and even some of the men wept softly. Almost at once the prayers were begun. Don Manuel listened to them in silence, his hand in the hand of Blasillo the fool, who began to fall asleep to the sound of the praying. First the Pater Noster, with its "Thy will be done on earth as it is in heaven"; then the Ave Maria, with its "Pray for us sinners, now and in the hour of our death"; followed by the Salve, with its "mourning and weeping in this vale of tears"; and finally, the Creed. On reaching "The resurrection of the flesh and life everlasting" the people sensed that their saint had yielded up his soul to God. It was not necessary to close his eyes even, for he died with them closed. When an attempt was made to wake Blasillo, it was found that he too, had fallen asleep in the Lord forever. So that later there were two bodies to be buried.

The village immediately repaired en masse to the house of the saint to carry away holy relics, to divide up pieces of his garments among themselves, to carry off whatever they could find as a memento of the blessed martyr. My brother preserved his breviary, between the pages of which he discovered a carnation, dried as in a herbarium and mounted on a piece of paper, and upon the paper a cross and a certain date.

No one in the village seemed able to believe that Don Manuel was dead; everyone expected to see him—perhaps some of them did—taking his daily walk along the side of the lake, his figure mirrored in the water, or silhouetted against the background of the mountain. They continued to hear his voice, and they all visited his grave, around which a veritable cult sprang up; old women "possessed by devils" came to touch the cross of walnut, made with his own hands from the tree which had yielded the six planks of his casket.

Those who least believed in his death were my brother and I. Lazarus carried on the tradition of the saint, and he began to compile a record of the priest's words. Some of the conversations in this account of mine were made possible by his notes.

"It was he," said my brother, "who made me into a new man. I was a true Lazarus whom he raised from the dead. He gave me faith."

"Ah, faith . . ."

"Yes, faith, faith in the charity of life, in life's joy. It was he who cured me of my delusion of 'progress,' of my belief in its political implications. For there are, Angela, two types of dangerous and harmful men: those who, convinced of life beyond the grave, of the resurrection of the flesh, torment other people—like the inquisitors they are—into despising this life as a transitory thing and working only for the other life; and then, there are those who, believing only in this life——"

"Like you, perhaps."

"Yes, and like Don Manuel. Believing only in this world, this second group looks forward to some vague future society and exerts every effort to prevent the populace from finding consoling joy in belief in another world. . . ."

"And so . . ."

"The people should be allowed to live with their illusion."

The poor priest who came to the parish to replace Don Manuel found himself overwhelmed in Valverde de Lucerna by the memory of the saint, and he put himself in my brother's hands and mine for guidance. He wanted only to follow in the footsteps of the saint. And my brother told him: "Very little theology, Father, very little theology. Religion, religion, religion." Listening to him, I smiled to myself, wondering if this was not a kind of theology, too.

I had by now begun to fear for my poor brother. From the time Don Manuel died it could scarcely be said that he lived. Daily he went to the priest's tomb; for hours on end he stood gazing into the lake. He was filled with yearning for deep, abiding peace.

"Don't stare into the lake so much," I begged him.

"Don't worry. It's not this lake which draws me, nor the mountain. Only, I cannot live without his help."

"And the joy of living, Lazarus, what about the joy of living?"

"That's for others. Not for those of us who have seen God's face, those of us on whom the dream of life has gazed with its eyes."

"What; are you preparing to go and see Don Manuel?"

"No, sister, no. Here at home now, between the two of us, the whole truth—bitter as it may be, bitter as the sea into which the sweet waters of our lake flow—the whole truth for you, who are so set against it. . . ."

"No, no, Lazarus. You are wrong. Your truth is not the truth."

"It's my truth."

"Yours, perhaps, but surely not . . ."

"His, too."

"No, Lazarus. It is not so any longer. Now, he certainly believes otherwise; now he must believe——"

"Listen, Angela, once Don Manuel told me that there are truths which, though one reveals them to oneself, must be kept from others; and I told him that telling me was the same as telling himself. And then he said, he confessed to me, that he thought that more than one of the great saints, perhaps the very greatest himself, had died without believing in the other life."

"Is it possible?"

"All too possible! And now, sister, you must be careful that here, among the people, no one even suspects our secret——"

"Suspect it?" I cried in amazement. "Why even if I were to try, in a fit of madness, to explain it to them, they wouldn't understand it. The people do not understand words, they un-

derstand only works. To try and explain all this to them would
be like reading some pages from Saint Thomas Aquinas to
eight-year-old children—in Latin."

"All the better. In any case, when I am gone, pray for me
and for him and for all of us."

At length, his own time came. A sickness which had been
eating away at his robust frame seemed to flare up with the
death of Don Manuel.

"I don't so much mind dying," he said to me in his last days,
"as the fact that with me another part of Don Manuel dies
too. The remainder of him must live on with you. Until, one
day, even the dead will die forever."

When he lay in the throes of death, the people of the village
came in to bid him farewell (as is customary in our towns)
and they commended his soul to the care of Don Manuel the
Good, Martyr. My brother said nothing to them; he had nothing more to say. He had already said everything there was to
say. He had become a link between the two Valverde de Lu-
cernas—the one at the bottom of the lake and the one reflected
on its surface. He was already one more of those who had
died to life, and, in his way, one more of our saints.

I was left desolate, more than desolate; but I was, at least,
among my own people, in my own village. Now, having lost
my Saint Manuel, the father of my soul, and my own Lazarus,
my more than corporeal brother, my spiritual brother, now it is
I realize that I have aged. But, have I really lost them then?
Have I grown old? Is my death approaching?

I must live! And he taught me to live, he taught us to live,
to feel life, to feel the meaning of life, to merge with the soul
of the mountain, with the soul of the lake, with the soul of
the village, to lose ourselves in them so as to remain in them

forever. By the example of his own life he taught me to lose myself in the life of the people of my village, and I no longer felt the passing of the hours, and the days, and the years, any more than I felt the passage of the water in the lake. It began to seem that my life would always be thus. I no longer felt myself growing old. I no longer lived in myself, but in my people, and my people lived in me. I tried to speak as they spoke, as they spoke without trying. I went into the street— it was the one highway—and, since I knew everyone, I lived in them and forgot myself (while, on the other hand, in Madrid, where I went once with my brother, I had felt a terrible loneliness, since I knew no one, and had been tortured by the sight of so many unknown people).

Now, as I write this account, this confession of my experience with saintliness, with a saint, I am of the opinion that Don Manuel the Good, my Don Manuel, and my brother, too, died believing they did not believe, but that, without believing in their belief, they actually believed, with resignation and in desolation.

But why, I have asked myself repeatedly, did not Don Manuel attempt to convert my brother deceitfully, with a lie, by pretending to be a believer himself? And I have finally come to think that Don Manuel realized he would not be able to delude him, that with him a fraud would not do, that only through the truth, with his truth, would he be able to convert him; that he knew he would accomplish nothing if he attempted to enact the comedy—the tragedy, rather—which he played out for the benefit of the people. And thus did he win him over, in effect, to his pious fraud; thus did he win him over to the cause of life with the truth of death. And thus did he win me, who never permitted anyone to see through his divine, his most saintly, game. For I believed then, and I believe now, that God—as part of I know-not-what sacred and

inscrutable purpose—caused them to believe they were unbelievers. And that at the moment of their passing, perhaps,
the blindfold was removed.

And I, do I believe?

As I write this—here in my mother's old house, and beyond
my fiftieth year, with my memories growing as dim and
blanched as my hair—outside it is snowing, snowing upon the
lake, snowing upon the mountain, upon the memory of my
father, the stranger, upon the memory of my mother, my
brother Lazarus, my people, upon the memory of my Saint
Manuel, and even on the memory of the poor fool Blasillo, my
Saint Blasillo—and may he help me in heaven! The snow
effaces corners and blots out shadows, for even in the night it
shines and illuminates. Truly, I do not know what is true and
what is false, nor what I saw and what I merely dreamt—or
rather, what I dreamt and what I merely saw—nor what I
really knew or what I merely believed to be true. And neither
do I know whether or not I am transferring onto this paper,
as white as the snow outside, my consciousness, so that it might
remain written, independent of me. For why cling to it any
further?

Do I really understand any of it? Do I really believe in
any of it? What I have recorded here, did it actually take
place, and did it take place in just the way I tell it? Is it
possible for such things to happen? Is it possible that all this
is more than a dream dreamed within another dream? Can it
be that I, Angela Carballino, a woman in her fifties, am the
only one in this village to be assailed by farfetched thoughts,
thoughts unknown to everyone else? And the others, those
around me, do they believe? And what does it mean, to believe? At least they go on living. And now they believe in

Saint Manuel the Good, Martyr, who, with no hope of immortality for himself, preserved their hope in it.

It appears that our most illustrious bishop, who set in motion the process for beatifying our saint from Valverde de Lucerna, is intent on writing an account of Don Manuel's life, something which would serve as a guide for the perfect parish priest, and with this end in mind he is gathering information of every sort. He has repeatedly solicited information from me; more than once he has come to see me; and I have supplied him with all sorts of facts. But I have never revealed the tragic secret of Don Manuel and my brother. And it is curious that he has never suspected. I trust that what I have set down here will never come to his knowledge. For, all temporal authorities are to be avoided; I fear all authorities on this earth—even when they are church authorities.

But this is the end. Let its fate be what it will. . . .

How, you ask, did this document, this memoir of Angela Carballino, fall into my hands? That, reader, is something I must keep secret. I have transcribed it for you just as it was written, just as it came to me, with only a few, a very few editorial emendations. It reminds you of other things I have written? This fact does not gainsay its objectivity, its originality. Moreover, for all I know, perhaps I created real, actual beings, independent of me, beyond my control, characters with immortal souls. For all I know, Augusto Pérez, in my novel *Mist,** was right when he claimed to be more real, more objective, than I myself, who had thought to have invented him. As for the reality of this Saint Manuel the Good, Martyr—as he is re-

---

* In the denouement of *Mist,* the protagonist Augusto Pérez turns on Unamuno and tells him that he, a creation of human thought and genius, is more real than his author, a product of blind animality.

vealed to me by his disciple and spiritual daughter Angela Carballino—it has not occurred to me to doubt it. I believe in it more than the saint himself did. I believe in it more than I do in my own reality.

And now, before I bring this epilogue to a close, I wish to recall to your mind, patient reader, the ninth verse of the Epistle of the forgotten Apostle, Saint Jude—what power in a name!—where we are told how my heavenly patron, St. Michael Archangel (Michael means "Who such as God?", and arch-angel means archmessenger) disputed with the Devil (Devil means accuser, prosecutor) over the body of Moses, and would not allow him to carry it off as a prize, to damnation. Instead, he told the Devil: "May the Lord rebuke thee." And may he who wishes to understand, understand!

I would like also, since Angela Carballino injected her own feelings into her narrative—I don't know how it could have been otherwise—to comment on her statement to the effect that if Don Manuel and his disciple Lazarus had confessed their convictions to the people, they, the people, would not have understood. Nor, I should like to add, would they have be-lieved the pair. They would have believed in their works and not their words. And works stand by themselves, and need no words to support them. In a village like Valverde de Lucerna one makes one's confession by one's conduct.

And as for faith, the people scarcely know what it is, and care less.

I am well aware of the fact that no action takes place in this narrative, this *novelistic* narrative, if you will—the novel is, after all, the most intimate, the truest history, so that I scarcely understand why some people are outraged to have the Bible called a novel, when such a designation actually sets it above some mere chronicle or other. In short, nothing hap-pens. But I hope that this is because everything that takes place happens, and, instead of coming to pass, and passing away, remains forever, like the lakes and the mountains and the blessed simple souls fixed firmly beyond faith and despair, the blessed souls who take refuge in the lakes and the mountains, outside history, in their divine novel.

Saint Alexis

BENJAMÍN JARNÉS

The Cradle

Gods and saints are habitually slow in coming on the scene.
Hierarchy—on earth as in heaven—is gauged by the number
of anterooms.

"Art thou He who is to come, or are we to wait for someone
else?" the Jews used to ask the Baptist; for Jews have always
preferred to spend their time in passive activity—except at
the Stock Exchange. And they bequeathed this posture of the
spirit to the Christians, who in turn elevated hope to the lofty
category of the theological virtues. Writs of virginity and pre-
ordained sterility existed in abundance so as to foster this
virtue. And saints and gods have been virgin and sterile from
the beginning of time. Their first and foremost concern has
always consisted in procuring for themselves a most extraordinary birth.

Aglae was childless. Her husband, Euphemianus, illustrious
senator of Rome, confidant of the ruler Theodosius, and pillar

of the new Imperial faith, dreamed of the perpetuation of his name, his titles, and his wealth. He yearned for a son, and awaited him in hope as the Hebrews awaited water from a stony cliff, or quails in the desert sands. He did not realize that God does not work miracles to assure offspring to a Roman citizen, and that no soul is created out of turn merely to animate the body of a future life-senator.

All of Rome knew and shared Euphemianus's hopes. He kept open house for widows, orphans, beggars, starving vagabonds— for everyone willing to wait in hope of somebody, be it man, saint, or god. With money, bread, and handfuls of dried figs the household shared its own pressing anxiety with all unfortunates. All that was requested of them was a prayer offered for the coming of a son.

From daybreak on, the palace swarmed with clients who came regularly to inquire about Aglae's womb—a whole small world of idlers and vagabonds depended upon the womb of that sterile matron. But in vain was the ass's head consecrated to Vesta removed from the marriage bed and replaced by a golden net in which a fish symbolized the Christ! In vain did the spinning women weave infant clothes of dubious destiny, adorning the loom with prayers as though with jasmine! In vain did Euphemianus ban from the dining hall Falernian wine and salmon, spreading his table only with flasks of vinegartainted water and handfuls of carrots! Laughter and music were displaced by silence and fasting, the delightful siesta by group recital of the Eighty-sixth Psalm.

Days, months, years. A plan for an original saint was being incubated in heaven; there was a shortage of new models. The brief path of rapid access to saintliness was not for these times. Constantine had locked up the torture chamber where bold young men, tender maidens, the old, and the adolescent had cast off their robes to sleep in complete immortality. The monumental gridirons on which deacons could be roasted whole, the stocks and the racks, were now for sale in the reliquary shops. The axe had rusted in its long wait for a victim. The bonfire had gone out in default of anyone illuminated enough to make a torch of himself.

Heaven's "voices" were soon to inspire not hymns and writs of piety, but lawsuits. The Church was being born at the point where religion was dying. The Cross was no longer a gallows but a throne, or a trinket on a bare bosom. The Church had exchanged her halo of stars for a crown of dust. She had reigned over souls; now she preferred to dominate bodies. Now she herself could erect scaffolds.

Constantine was dead. This catechumen—the arbiter of the new faith, who was slow to embrace it and received baptism in his final hour, by way of extreme unction—had dealt the death blow to the heroic age, to the epic of Christianity. Now, for many, the persecuted religion was a statute of the Imperial code. The Church decked herself in sumptuous brocades, laying aside her heroic hair shirt. Those illusory treasures of Laurentius which aroused the cupidity of the tyrant were now in the coffers of the Pontiff.

It was also possible to love Christ in silk and jasper. The bishops mutilated during the most recent inquisition concealed their stumps under purple tunics and their cropped ears under ruby miters. Quick paths to glory were closed. Mass canonization, like that of Sebasta or Caesarea Augusta, had been canceled. The standardization of saintliness was gradually eliminated; it was very hazardous to turn eleven thousand virgins all at once into eleven thousand tenants of Paradise.

In fact, the saint in the singular was now coming into existence—one who was not to be granted the privilege of a halo (as Theresa was), and in any case not merely by the simple process of decapitation. Only a few faithful to the old system, like Savonarola, were to cry out publicly against this change of spirit or to take refuge in the desert, like Jerome. The reign of sterile passivity was commencing in the country of divine adventure. The season of heroes was over; the time of bureaucrats had come. Rome had already witnessed a painful sight: the first tourist had come to visit the catacombs.

But the preparation was finished for the launching into the world of two new models of saints—Augustine and Alexis. One night Euphemianus heard from Aglae the sweet revelation. Fasting was over. He must be a robust baby! Hallelujah! He would be rich! (Heaven smiled.) He would have the lustiest maid in Rome to wife, a palace on the highest hill, and a life-senatorship! (Heaven's loud guffaws of laughter.)

Falernian and salmon returned to the table of Euphemianus. Hallelujah! Hangers-on, friends, spinning women, tramps, vagabonds, broke into a hymn of praise to the Virgin Mary. (It was the ancient hymn to Priapus Invictus, with only its words changed; for the tune belonged to a language which could hymn all gods. Esperanto will never be as successful as Orpheus.)

The boy was to be named Alexis, that is, Defender: defender of the Creed of Nicaea which Osius had just inaugurated. Thus Euphemianus paid homage to the author of *Meropis and the Parasites*, Menander's uncle; for this Alexis, the castigator of Sophocles, was his favorite author. (This was another pleasant example of hope. He died at the age of a hundred and six, after making his debut by winning the contest arranged by all the cities of the ancient world to award a prize to an uncle of Menander's.)

Thus ends the prehistory of Alexis.

The Vocation

In the sea of the Divine Will the activities of men hardly raise a ripple. Children's doings do not ruffle its surface at all. In every human life there is a subterranean phase, a phase of growth, from which only some infant prodigy is exempt. Luke himself, the chronicler of Jesus, takes account of this truth, and is careful to mystify the infancy, the adolescence, and a large part of Christ's youth. We barely know that Jesus was lost one weekday and was found debating with the Rabbis. All else, from Bethlehem onwards, is summed up in a single word: *He grew.*

Alexis also passed through these domestic, vegetal, years of growth; and, like Christ, he grew "in wisdom and in years." We find him again among the rosebushes in his garden, with his tutor, repeating his rhetoric lesson. His long adolescent locks are already cut; he has abandoned the tunic edged with purple, taking on the *toga virilis.* His personal life has begun.

Aglae and Euphemianus were already seeking out of the Roman families of noble blood a virgin worthy of Alexis. Adriana, Tulia, Sabina. . . . They would have to eliminate virgins whose names recalled shameful myths—Leda, Julia, Phryne. . . . And Dido, Paula, Crisogona—rich girls capable of plotting against his sanctity, who would come delighted to share his bed . . . Eulalia, Justina, Marcela. . . . Proffering him an inescapable vital machine, they would draw him away from any heroism and turn him into a normal, ordinary citizen —an indefatigable spectator at the Colosseum, a devout reader of Pope Damasus. . . . Julia, Faustina, Inez. . . . He will attend mass with the Emperor. He will buy books by Meletius and Amphilochius and avoid the contamination of infidels, since many illustrious Roman families still hide the books of the pedantic Julian and keep an ass's head on their conjugal couch, scorning Theodosius and retaining their lares. An army of goddesses and young men are hiding in pleasure houses scattered through the countryside, biding the chance of ex-

hibiting their obscene marbles at the very porticoes of Rome!
And what is even worse, the Manichaean poison is already
seeping into many feeble spirits; it penetrates through any
crevice or flaw of faith! Alexis will remain a most upright
senator, barricaded from any new opinion or new-fangled
notion! Alexis will be a senator without pores!

One must choose discreetly to find out the last redoubt of
the heretical microbe, for among Euphemianus's own friends
Getulius is an Apotactite, Claudius a Sacophorite, Manlius an
Encratite—three poisonous subsects of Mani, the other cruci-
fied One, threatening to corrupt the tender soul. And among
Aglae's friends, Lydia is a Marcionite, Diana a Hydroparastite,
Dido a Cataphrygian. The old errors always blossom forth
again.

Rome was inaugurating in the West the reign of the gentle
institution which was to renovate the face of the earth: the
pious hearth. Rome's power might decline, but the new structure
—the family—would continue unscathed. Alexis would be an
irreproachable pillar of it! They must dismiss the tutor. Alexis
was now capable of organizing his own life and ideas.

"My son! . . ."

George, Sebastian, Maurice . . . another, and a parallel
rosary of heroes. The absorbed Alexis was not listening to his
parents. Stephen, Paul, Irenaeus. . . . Alexis knew the history
of these men and of their triumphs over fire and ice. He had
read their blazing speeches delivered in the presence of the
awful caldron of boiling pitch. They emerged from torture
with their tongues cut off but with a new language: the signs
of stars in their eyes. The fever of those hearts burned within
him. His whole body was a little thing quivering before such
hard-won victories.

"My son! . . ."

He saw the body of the virgin Tabula, sawn off at the
waist; the breasts of Agueda on the ground, like broken pieces
of armor, which left her bosom bare and her heart wide open;
the feet of George thrust into shoes of red-hot iron; and
Blandina split in halves. . . . Alexis dreamed of adding his
own arms and legs to that bloody pyramid by which one scales
to heaven. But saintliness was now no longer a sudden palm
borne by an angel but a diadem forged hour by hour, day by
day, on the anvils of the world.

"My son! . . ."

Getulia, Cristeta, Lais. . . . Let them go on casting names
on the roulette board where the saintliness of Alexis was at
stake. The tutor, being neutral, had fallen asleep. Alexis un-
rolled a manuscript of the Acts of the Apostles. One culture
was crumbling; he must hurriedly acquire another. All Greece
was shadows and all Rome slime! The intellectual past was
drowned in darkness; new stars must be lit with the greatest
speed!

Youth, eager to know its true heritage, could not resign itself to having come into the world with hands empty or filled
with scorpions. A new mental orb had swum into ken, not after
slow conception, but born all at once in the sky. The Church,
in those first years of striving, without the leisure in which
genius ferments, had produced hasty and inadequate works.
Paul's Epistles were not enough. It was hard to acquire the
books by Ambrose, Cyril, Hilary, Eusebius and Clement. The
tyrants had destroyed many manuscripts. Copies full of errors
were in circulation. There was scarcely anybody sufficiently
learned to throw light upon them. . . .

There were always the Scriptures, but the hard style of the
prophets would confuse Augustine himself; and besides, copies
were scarce. Hebrew was almost unknown, and not everybody
knew Greek. Latin versions had not been published. To the rich

classical heritage there could be opposed merely a few parchments blazing with polemical zeal. . . .

"My son, Alexis! . . ."

He would read no more books. The old ones frightened him. Bishop Irenaeus had called Plato the fountainhead of all heresies. The new books saddened Alexis, for he believed he could preserve his faith better by reading Plato than the opuscules of that holy man Pinitus; and there were many gesturing Pinituses.

But Plato was banned by the inflexible authority of the popes, just as later, in Paris, Aristotle was to be repudiated and burned, then admired and annotated. For, apart from dogma, the Church has preserved the gift of opportune flexibility. If one pope condemns Vergil, another one lovingly translates him.

"Think, my son! . . ."

Alexis was obedient. He rejected everything that the Pontificate rejected. He went where he was told. . . . He had been born in a time of implacable revenge. Christ had conquered Jupiter. The zero hour had struck. The world applauded a new Divine champion. Alexis followed Him, dazzled.

He was rid of his tutor, that furtive smuggler of ideas. The tutor went away with a heavy heart, not so much because he had lost his salary as because he had lost a satellite. Being secretly an anthropomorphist, he believed he had found an original aspect of anthropomorphism, a new subsect. This was an incubating time for religions, and he had expected Alexis to be his first disciple.

But Alexis did not learn from his tutor the cult of the plastic and the free play of ideas. He rejected all deceptive forms, all display, all irradiation. He reread Clement's treatise, "Of the Rich Man Who Would Be Saved." It brought him to contempt for the world and disdain for things charming but inane. He hid his contempt and disdain beneath the accustomed velvets, beneath smiles and perfumes. But under his soft *toga virilis* a hair shirt was concealed.

"My son, Alexis! . . ."

First Hair Shirt

"Lord, a hair shirt is nothing! Its rebellious pricks begin to forget their pious mission of mortification and take pleasure in provoking a delicious tickling which ends in being a pure delight. The ultimate secrets of voluptuous pleasure are never revealed. The flesh is as much inflamed by the rubbing of silk as by the rubbing of brutal hemp hair.

"A hair shirt, Lord, is nothing! Once its first ardor is assuaged the weft coyly accommodates itself to the back, falls into definite furrows, slowly toughening the skin—the bruised skin which gradually disdains its injuries. The flesh is very docile, Lord! Only the spirit lives in ceaseless rebellion. Lord, a hair shirt for the soul!

"There is hemp, and thin thongs that make weals in the flesh, fine wires searing the flesh, deforming and breaking up the Apollo-complex. . . . But everything ends by making truce with matter. One can use iron spikes, but they must be used discreetly. They pierce the flesh, cutting into its depths; but they cause sores impossible to cure clandestinely. They affect one's gait and reveal the haughty apprentice-anchorite. Iron spikes cannot preserve their incognito. And a hair shirt that betrays its incognito is much more glamorous than an ermine cloak.

"To destroy the smoothness of the skin, to stripe and deface it, to cloud the vain mirror wherein the spirit founders, hemp and hair may suffice. But the body must keep erect as a mast on the winding seas of the world. Let nothing disturb the rhythm of the motor muscles; let nothing reveal that slowly acquired treasure of saintliness accumulated grain by grain, that apportioned modicum of grace. . . .

"Lord, a hair shirt is nothing," Alexis thought, "but if my friends suspected this hidden ostentation of mine all Rome would joke about it and my little act of penitence would be rudely interrupted. A hair shirt goes well with darkness. In the light of day it would cause me awkward blushes. Oh, but to find a hair shirt for the soul!"

Alexis was the very opposite of the Stylite, of whom he was unaware. Simon climbed up a pillar where he staged a spectacle of showy saintliness. Alexis went about it the other way. He would be a saint through peaceful means, not through wrangling opposition or warlike deeds. Indeed, the haranguing scaler-of-pillars does not give us a very clear example of the Divine Will, which has always preferred catacombs to pyramids.

Alexis did not make himself conspicuous; he preferred to creep by unobserved. Real originality, perhaps, consisted in surrendering oneself to unknown forces . . . not to put obstacles in their way, but to turn oneself into fine clay and clear water so as to become an amphora of God.

Silently Alexis followed his three friends, Lampius, Sedulius, and Dictinus—sons of illustrious patricians and perhaps the future counsellors of the Emperor. They were talking of the latest adventure of Lavinia, the dissolute wife of Jovianus, who danced naked on a table before the seamen of Ostia. Alexis hung behind, fearing lest he should fall into temptation. The three friends gossiped without paying attention to Alexis, who kept with them merely out of courtesy.

As they passed by a church dedicated to Mary, which had formerly been a temple to Diana, Sedulius began a risqué topic of conversation: the virginity of the Mother of Christ. He was a Coliridian. Of the two schools of the disciples of Apollinarius, now sternly persecuted by the Pope Damasus, the Antidicomarists denied Her virginity, but the Coliridians only mystified it. They transformed her into a new goddess, and offered her golden cakes, like Cybele.

Dictinus was a Sachophorite, but he did not dare to wear the picturesque uniform of his heresy except in private. Lampius was a bibliomaniac. He had read the treatise of Julius Firmicus, "Of the Error and Falsity of the Pagan Religions," and compared it with the "Treatise on Spiritual Perfection" of Diadocus of Photicia. In his process of comparing, collating, and compiling, error—like truth—passed him by.

"They say that Epiphanius, Bishop of Salamis, has written a fine book, the *Panarium.* I have ordered it to be copied for me. It refutes all the heresies; it is a regular medicine chest of antidotes. But there is nobody like Ambrose, or Gregory Nazianzus, or Ephraem."

Timidly Sedulius defended the verses of Apollinarius the elder, the first poet in the world to versify the Bible. He had got as far as Saul's she-ass. And then there was his son, a disciple of Plato, who had written his own *Dialogues.* Sedulius, like the two Apollinarii, felt homesick for the letters of antiquity. Like Jerome in his first phase, he read Plautus to console himself for his sins.

Alexis followed them automatically, with his eyes straying into an invisible world. The men reached the baths. A poet, nicknamed "Chrisologos" by way of a joke, was to recite his hexameters there today. Dictinus knew this and had carefully guided his three friends there. "Chrisologos" amused some of the bathers and exasperated others; but being undressed, none of them could escape him. Dictinus had conceived a diabolically ingenious idea. . . .

When Alexis returned to the consciousness of space and time he had already given over his valuables to the *capsarius* and entered the anteroom of the *tepidarium*. It was impossible for him to draw back. Lamius was already stripped and the other two were slowly and lazily following his example. On other evenings Alexis had succeeded in changing his path, but this time he was trapped.

His three friends were now naked, and their gleaming bodies, scented with mint, young and restless, moved with the fine agility of a faun or a gladiator in training. . . . Alexis hesitated. Sedulius and Dictinus eyed him quizzically. Never had they seen him naked. Sedulius thought that he might be marked by some shameful disease. Lampius remembered Thersites. Dictinus, a connoisseur of fine figures, looked and looked at the body still covered in its toga.

"Aren't you going to undress?"

It was premature for Alexis to reveal his saintliness to men. His hair shirt rustled under his scarlet-bordered linen. It ought not to sound a clarion-trumpet denouncing such a strange way of life. Saintliness is something mysterious; like virginity, it has such subtle fibers, so deeply hidden, that the mere suggestion of deflowering is a torture. Saintliness has its own taboo, whose secret is known only by the gods.

Saintliness, like a picturesque landscape, is often the enemy of hygiene. The spirit of blessedness and the spirit of the picturesque prefer not to be despoiled of their humility, of the forgetfulness enveloping them. They are enemies of the body—and of pruning. Hair shirt and tunic, like ivy and moss, may hide mutilations, ulcers, shameful stripes—all of these being small steps towards sanctity.

Finally Alexis found himself cornered by his three comrades. Escape was impossible and he was reluctant to carry resistance

too far. Holiness, he thought, is hardly a thing to be defended
with fists. And so he resigned himself, letting his toga be
stripped off.

His friends would be horrified at the sight of a body gray as
a camel's hide, wrinkled like the face of an old man. They
would see a waist marked by a coarse rope girdle, a breast
and back covered with the stripes of flagellation, a network of
red weals. They would be shocked; they would flee from him.
And he would be left alone.

The last of his garments was removed. Alexis stood naked at
last. Three astonished voices cried in chorus:

"Apollo!"

"Sebastian!"

"Alcibiades!"

A man, a saint, a god—Alexis's nakedness stood like a lily.
His legs were pillars of ivory, waist slender, thighs muscular;
the broad shoulders looked capable of supporting the frieze of
some temple of Diana, and the strong hips of bearing un-
flinchingly the weight of two drunken Vestals. His blue eyes
and trembling hands vainly sought any trace of the hair shirt,
or the shirt itself, which had disappeared from his body sub-
jected to the regime of sanctity.

Of his sanctity nothing was left but the odor, a subtle odor
foolishly mistaken by his comrades for spikenard: an odor of
sanctity which spread through the baths and was wafted over
Rome, to be languorously inhaled by the patrician girls, the
expectant virgins, numbered in Aglae's rosary. Soon all of
them heard of the magnificence of Alexis's youth. He became
a pagan spectacle, the object of all those soft maiden eyes. The
hard regime of sanctity was miraculously transformed into a
carnal perfume which was a gentle but insistent goad to virgins
and widows alike.

But the sanctity of Alexis preserved its incognito.

The Bridal Couch

By this time marriage in Rome was something divine: a sacrament instead of a social occasion, as solemn as a funeral. Adriana, the bride chosen for Alexis—or "Adriatica" as she was called by a thirteenth-century writer—did not wear the flame-colored veil of the earlier patrician girls, but the modest white veil of the Christian virgins whose company she was now to abandon. The flame had taken refuge in her eyes, impatient to close beneath the lips of Alexis—soft, longing, yearning eyes.

Nor would Adriana be borne across the threshold of the house of Euphemianus, like her illustrious ancestors. That was a pagan custom, now abolished. Christ had been resurrected. Constantine had beheld the fiery Cross. The old rites were gone; new ones were spreading over the world. The bride would not be wounded by the glances of the pretty little slave, her companion in the nuptial chamber, the licensed jester of the bridal ceremony!

Adriana was now already in Euphemianus's house. Alexis, permitting himself to be ordered about like a puppet, muttered "Yes" before the Pope. He had gravely walked the streets from the church to his house, surrounded by friends and followed by inquisitive children and girls. He had listened to twelve epithalamia in verse and seven in prose imitated from Ovid and Seneca but less subtle and piquant. He had listened to the counsels of nine old senators and three dried-up widows.

Alexis docilely submitted. With Adriana at his side, he presided over the banquet—a banquet attended by St. Paul and not by the pagan Alcibiades. The flute girls, formerly half-naked, were now dressed in red woolens trailing down to their feet. Dancing girls, formerly naked, now wore tunics of ankle length; and they crowned their foreheads not with myrtles but white lilies. Only the rose withstood the change, triumphantly remaining at the altars of both Christ and Aphrodite.

Adriana was the bride of Alexis! Hallelujah! On with the feast! The wine jugs were empty already! Petals of jasmine and violets shook to the floor. Corpses of roses mingled with lobster shells. The guests whispered Martial's epigrams to one another. Girls repeated the rosy hexameters of Ovid. Matrons with dreaming eyes recalled the anecdote of Alexis at the baths with all the embellishments added by Sedulius.

Cybele had returned to earth. Whenever the flesh, which needs very little coaxing, enters the easy region of delight it needs must seek some complacent god to share its joy with. In such transition seasons one forgets to listen to St. Paul but turns an ear again to the voice of Juno in her majesty. Minds become a battleground between two armies of gods, and as libation succeeds libation they tend to confuse Minerva with Origen, and Ganymede with the gentle Apostle John.

Alexis gave himself up to the urgings of invisible hands. All the pomp of Rome encompassed him. The Emperor had deigned to give him the kiss of peace, and the Pope his blessing. A chorus of senators applauded him, a chorus of maidens smiled at him, a chorus of matrons desired him, a chorus of little girls lowered their eyes in the presence of his radiant youth. . . .

Alexis trembled under his hair shirt. He began to doubt his guardian angel; for surely the hour had come for him to hear some celestial voice. But all day long, all this critical day, no voice had come to him. He had allowed himself to be carried along by his parents, by Adriana, by the Pope, and the Emperor; and he had felt no nudge from the angel. But he must not be impatient. He repeated to himself his favorite Psalm: *In Te, Domine, speravi; non confundar in aeternum.*

A little later a virginal body lay trembling in its full nakedness. . . . (*"Qui en son lit estoit couchie toute nue. . . ."*
Your chronicler of the twentieth century would like to spare
your blushes, adorable Adriana; but after all he must be faithful to his dear colleagues of the eleventh century, of the twelfth
century, of the thirteenth century, of the fourteenth century.)

Through force of example, the drunken guests were strolling
through the streets of Rome in search of a temporary couch
on which to wind up the festivities. The priest had crossed the
threshold, repeating the *Benedicite*. The maidens had stolen
away silently, with ardent eyes, trembling bosoms, and throbbing pulses—*Adolescentulae dilexerunt te nimis*, Alexis. The
matrons had taken their leave, with the air of people going
away from a spectacle just as the curtain rises. Aglae and
Euphemianus had kissed Adriana as she lay stretched out on
her couch, as though on an operating table.

The bridal couch! Alexis's ears were still ringing with the
great news which he had just heard from his friends. The
marvel of the century had risen: Augustine, Augustine! In
Ostia he had just lost his mother, the sainted widow Monica.
Augustine—and Adriana naked on her bridal couch!

St. Paul had been resurrected! The Church had received
from Christ her periodical allotment of fresh troops. A new
leader would bring new light to the lands! Adriana naked,
white, trembling! Augustine would make new the Christian
world! The bridal couch: mysterious as a sepulcher, sacred as
a cradle—the gallows for dream! The bureaucratic spirit of
the Imperial Court would be swept away by the thrust of
Augustine's genius! . . .

Adriana naked! Augustine had come down to earth. The
bridal couch—a noose, a contract, a duty! You are the source
of the tares and traps into which a man stumbles. Augustine—

and naked Adriana! From you crime is born, hierarchy, and all those things that nourish the pride of spiritual emptiness. Augustine had come down to earth! For him had Ambrose sung the first *Te Deum*.

Adriana was waiting. The Church had found her true spouse, her highest leader. Augustine—and Adriana naked! Knowledge and love, equally balanced in a single man. Hallelujah! Poor quivering dove! Augustine, the champion! Augustine, general of the Pauline hosts! And Adriana naked! The Church had found her true pulse—a leader and not merely another soldier.

The bridal couch! Paul reborn—with more vigor, with a clearer mind and a keener conscience. Adriana was waiting! The couch: a fetter, a pigeonhole, a vigilant sentinel over life; a man cut in two and his voice chained to a hearth. . . . The voice of Augustine would resound throughout the world. Augustine, scourge of heresies! And bridals meant birth. Augustine, the architect-genius of the City of God! Alexis, lord of a hearth and a small land, playing Providence to a few vagabonds!

Augustine, the intimate confessor of all the world! Adriana, naked, receiving the confession of Alexis in a tiny corner of the world! Burying in a shared couch all his original ardor of heroism, selling his saintliness for a little mess of delight! Augustine had made a thorough reckoning of all his pleasures. Underlining them with his tears, he flung them to the winds with all the might of David, with all the consummate ease of that divine slinger.

Adriana naked on her bridal couch! There would always be a woman intervening in his life. A weak spirit seeking only to be the instrument of God, he would never be more than a woman's plaything. *Mulierem fortem, quis inveniet? Procul.* . . . Yes, very far, to the last outpost. There was one strong woman, Monica, who had just wept her last tear in Ostia. And there was another strong woman who would never die—Mary.

Alexis would go in search of her, of that woman who, at the feet of the Divine Condemned, *stabat*. Who appreciates the force of that *stabat*, of that *she stood?* There was a truly strong woman: Mary. There was a steady will: Augustine. And Adriana naked! Poor eyes awaiting the spectacle of the baths! Poor flesh yearning to feel the contact of a palpitating bit of nothingness! St. Paul had arisen! Hallelujah!

The voices of his intimate friends who had stayed behind stumbled over their words. Euphemianus, himself a trifle unsteady, went on vaunting the marvels of his wine.

"This is twenty years old. Real Cecuba! The banks of the Volturnus yield no better. Twenty years old! There is no purer Falernian. Dry, with a little honey of Hymettus. Another glass?"

"Well, this must be the last one!"

Alexis trembled. The last one! They drank it and took their leave, laughing and staggering. And what about the voices? Alexis, the plaything of God, forsaken and anguished, detained Sedulius and Dictinius for a moment—but at last they too left tipsily. Lampius was asleep in the vestibule. The dog licked his face, waking him, and Lampius also disappeared. And so did Euphemianus, after stammering a litany. The whimpering Aglae led him away.

But what of the voices—what of the voices that should now tell him the way? Alexis was left alone in the desert. The voice of Saul, of Augustine! Adriana was there in the midst of the way, stretched across it, naked, a white abyss. Alexis set out on his way. He rapped his knuckles on the door and a low, trembling voice answered him.

He was submerged in a shining stream, shining with the whiteness of virgin linen, of walls and roses and silks. And in the midst of all that whiteness was something rosy, with black lashes flickering over violet eyes. Alexis drew near. Silently, with trembling hands, he handed the maiden a scarlet girdle sparkling with diamonds, and a gold ring set with a ruby that shone like a star, wrapped together in a rich crimson cloth.

Adriana hesitated, stammered a few broken words, then finally dared to take the gift. She stretched out her bare arm, for she was naked. Alexis *"mout la vit blanche et tendre, bien faite et parcreüe. . . ."*

But Adriana had to obey a legend, just as Alexis had to obey the voice of God which already announced itself faintly in the distance, like a subtle thread of sound piercing his temples. Something of Venus had once risen from the foam of the sea—an arm, rounded, warm, enticing one to set sail in the barque of Aphrodite. The enclosed garden sent forth a tendril of myrtle like a challenge. A trembling jet issued from the sealed fountain—a sweet summons to break the seven seals. The voice grew louder, nearer, more insistent. . . .

Alexis felt the warm touch of the myrtle. For a moment that quivering tendril held him earthbound. He kissed the tips of that conductor silently flowing with the pent-up eagerness of his bride. Her arm remained outstretched—seductive, enticing.

"I must go and undress," he murmured; and he went out quickly. He must take off the hair shirt encasing his breast, waist, and thighs and break those strands of hemp and wire—all those things that made a plowed field of his body. He must hide his sinner's garments. Adriana was awaiting a man, not a saint. Oh, for a hair shirt of the spirit to replace that ugly hair shirt of the flesh!

Alexis passed through the house like a sleepwalker. He reached his room. Taking off his bridal robe mechanically, he put on a dark cloak which he always wore when going through the city's suburbs distributing alms. He picked up some money and jewelry. . . . Impatiently Adriana murmured The Song of Songs: "His eyes are as the eyes of doves by the rivers of waters . . . his lips like lilies, dropping sweet smelling myrrh. . . ."

As he left his room Alexis stumbled over a sleeping servant. Then he met another who swayed drunkenly from side to side, bumping against the walls with hair disheveled. Some others lay asleep in the laps of Adriana's women. Only the dog was awake to recognize him, as on any other night; for the dog cared nothing for wine or the marriage bed. Alexis slipped on his sandals and crossed the threshold. . . .

Adriana still murmured The Song of Songs: "His hands are as gold rings set with the beryl: his belly is as bright ivory. . . ." Dark and silent, the city took Alexis into its entrails, swallowing up the son of Euphemianus forever. It made of him a shadow slipping hesitantly, stealthily, listeningly as it went. . . .

Augustine, Augustine! In Ostia there was a window framing the faces of both mother and son—Ostia, the port of Ostia, the window on the world. Boats were coming and going on the Tiber. Alexis sank to the bottom of one of them, covering his eyes with his hands. The freshness of the water enveloped him and caressed him, brushing away phantoms. . . . "His legs are as pillars of marble, set upon sockets of fine gold: his countenance is as Lebanon, excellent as the cedars. . . ."

The husky boatman stretched out his hand and received money and a name: Ostia. The boat slipped down the river, down the river. . . . "His mouth is most sweet: yea, he is altogether lovely. This is my beloved, and this is my friend, O daughters of Jerusalem. . . ."

Rome was no more than a dark quay where red snakes writhed, the sinuous torches of homecomers from some orgy.

"Whither is thy beloved gone, O thou fairest among women?"
. . . Alexis felt his heart tighten. A hair shirt, a hair shirt for
the soul! The river passed its hands across his brows, soothing
him and calming his fever. . . . Adriana in her nakedness!
Augustine! . . . "My beloved is gone down into his garden,
to the beds of spices . . . to gather lilies. . . ."

Rome was blotted out. There was only the river and the
clear sky and a life that had found its way, and Alexis asleep,
lulled by his voices. . . . "The voice of my beloved! behold,
he cometh leaping upon the mountains, skipping upon the
hills. . . ."

Round-Trip Voyage

Ostia—the port, the warehouse, the permanent fair of Rome:
arrival point for wanderings, departure point for escapes.
Alexis's boat was lost among the bellied galleys loaded with oil,
wheat, fruit, and perfumes. There were droves of bronzed slaves
and clusters of blonde slave girls. Here Paris at any moment
might surrender his apple. There were men from Greece, Spain,
Carthage, from the whole world that flowed to Rome the Siren,
or fled from Rome the Sovereign.

Alexis peeped out at this great highway that retains nothing
of footprints. He was not fleeing from Rome nor from the
world: he was fleeing from himself. A salt wave refreshed his
temples. The boatman saluted him and left. Alexis was alone,
with all the paths of the world spread out like a fan before him
—alone at last.

But his people were not far away. They would follow him,
harry him! A ship, a ship! Gangs of half-naked slaves bent
under chests and gear were tumbling into lighters. Alexis
hoisted a forgotten roll of carpets on his back, joined one of

the gangs, went forward furtively, and tumbled in along with them. Boarding a ship, he hid himself in the hold. Whither bound?

He felt the movement of being borne along as the ship was leaving port. Half-suffocated he awaited nightfall before daring to make his way to the deck in fear. Everyone was asleep. Alexis fell on his knees under the moon, that cold skylight in the heavens.

And the moon smiled down at him like a courtesan. She stretched out an arm to him—an arm rounded, warm, enticing; a fresh reminder of the mutilated trunk of Diana; a magic rope seeking to draw the fugitive to some couch among the stars. Suddenly Adriana looked down through that skylight— naked Adriana, anguished, swooning, sobbing. The startled Alexis turned his eyes away from the sky that mocked and betrayed him. A brusque buffet of wind forced the moon to withdraw her arm under the draping clouds. The sea, like the Tiber, passed a sponge across the fugitive's brow.

Alexis lay down on the deck. When he opened his eyes again they saw the rather unsociable sea lashing the ship with relays of scourges for daring to dance on its back like a child; but it was with a whip of roses, like the whip of the angry Venus. The fugitive saw surging towards him a skirmishing party of spray, a troop of naked girls. A white band of breasts, a girdle of Anadyomene, threatened to board the vessel.

Here were all those whose image made Ulysses tremble, with only Penelope, now weeping in Rome, missing from the cast. A manuscript of Homer, read in the garden, slowly opened at the passage about Circe; and another of Vergil, at the passage about Dido.

Aghast and desperate, Alexis tried to close his eyes again, but fingertips sharp as daggers pried them open. An arm, rounded, warm, enticing, had risen out of the sea, from amid the garland of breasts. It sought to drag Alexis to the coral palace where the Enchantress awaited him.

A catching of the breath, a sense of suffocation, a desire for tears or even death, overwhelmed the fugitive. Once more the waves passed their briny sponge across his brow. When he opened his eyes again a giant hand had passed over the troubled surface, sweeping away that white emergence. Dido had withdrawn her arm into her mantle of spray.

But Alexis kept on praying. Sky and sea whispered together, took counsel of each other, and finally decided to spare the fugitive. They reached out to him ladders of stars and stairways of spray so that his poor, tortured sight might rise to plumb the region of the unfathomable and beat upon the gates of eternity. All this was now cleansed of the old gods.

He found rest, at length, and slept. His head lay on a coil of rope; his feet against some hazy, moving object. He dreaded. Sky and sea had pardoned him; but in the land of dreams Dido invoked a frightful tumult. A legion of arms cut through the air: a barrier of ivory arms, rounded, warm, enticing, hemming him in and suffocating him. The boldest clung around his neck. The fugitive cried aloud and opened his eyes.

A slave girl—that hazy moving object at his feet—smiled and implored a caress. From among the piled baggage her arm was stretched out, begging that charity—her arm, rounded, warm, enticing. Alexis fled terrified to the hold. The slave girl, thinking him mad, laughed and stretched herself stark naked on the chests, reaching out her hands to the moon, offering herself as a brazen bell for the festal tunic of Tanit.

One morning the ship called at a port and Alexis was thrown out like a bale of merchandise. He did not ask where he was, but he had heard someone uttering the word Laodicea. He strolled through the streets, far from the port, far from the human turmoil. He slept against the doorposts of a temple. A later morning he resumed his wanderings. He did not know whither he was bound.

One evening he saw another city in the distance. He entered it; someone had referred to it as Edessa. He strolled about haphazardly. Seeing an open temple, he went inside and there, at last, found the Woman he was seeking. She also reached out Her arm towards him, but an Infant was resting upon it. It was not a naked arm but modestly covered in blue woolen. Alexis knelt down and prayed.

Days, months, years. All his jewels were now sold and he had given away his clothes and money to the poor. He was reduced to tatters and beggary. If anyone gave him bread, he ate only a piece of it, offering the rest to another beggar. He had changed—in face, voice, complexion. Gentility had dwindled away from him; he was a walking bundle of rags. Already he was become almost ripe for eternity.

One day he met Calpurnius in a square, Calpurnius, his father's jovial butler together with Lepidus, son of his tutor, his boyhood comrade. They did not recognize him, but asked about Adriana's husband, the wandering son of Euphemianus. Alexis gave no answer. Calpurnius gave him alms and, thinking him dumb, questioned no further. They went their way and Alexis followed them.

Thus he found out about the grief of his parents, the despair of Adriana, and the amazement of the Emperor and his friends. Euphemianus had dispatched his servants all over the Empire. They had picked up traces of Alexis at Ostia and Laodicea; then they had come to Edessa. Aglae had covered her head with ashes and was fasting until the fugitive's return. Mourning Adriana wept—a disconsolate Penelope, a woman scorned whose desire despaired within her, a hound weary of howling.

Alexis sought refuge before the Virgin Mary, whose awful

arm was concealed in its woolen sheath. Docile Alexis humbled by Mary went on begging in the streets of Edessa, giving away all his alms beyond what he needed to keep his skeleton self on its feet.

But the Virgin Mary herself betrayed him. She spoke, as to so many of her faithful, in that plain language heard by Bernardita and Joan of Arc. One night the acolyte—my medieval comrades, bear me witness!—heard himself called by his own name. Mary appeared to him.

"Alexis is a saint," she said simply.

The next day he was famous—as famous as that illustrious champion of the heights, Simon the Stylite. Nobody could oppose his consecration. Now the Church had two favorites—Augustine for the select minority, Alexis for the general public.

A swarm of beggars threatened to pull the new saint to pieces. One vagabond suggested that they tear his sackcloth covering to bits and sell the fragments to the silly bourgeois. Others would content themselves with pieces of his hair shirt. Alexis was a martyr to the fervor of the multitude. A hundred arms, still supplicating though this time inoffensive, were outstretched about him, begging a prayer, a crumb of his bread, a shred of his rags.

He fled in bewilderment. Mary had been too generous. Alexis as a reader of Plato had feared popularity; now as a reader of Ambrose he was a lover of chastity, and the people were threatening to strip him naked.

One day they brought him a dying child, but Alexis refused to touch him. Another day they brought a young girl whose soul was possessed by the devil. She shouted blasphemies at the Virgin Mary and threatened to bite Alexis. He made the sign of the Cross over that fiendish spirit lodged in the delicious body. The girl quieted. She fell on her knees, raising a suppliant arm, a round, warm, enticing arm.

Terrified, Alexis ran away, leaving his spectators amazed. He was the eternal fugitive. Now he would go to Cilicia, to Tarsus, to meditate on the words of the Apostle. He bade farewell in tears to the Virgin Mary without reproaching Her for so generous an indiscretion.

And once again he went down to the sea. One night he hid between two barrels of oil. Once more the moon, once more the sea, but a sea now without smooth billows, without breasts and naked white shoulders. Once more the female slaves on deck, but this time black-skinned and covered in ashen burnooses. One of them was snatched away by a wave. Alexis prayed for her and for all the passengers. A furious storm began to bandy the ship about, but thanks to Alexis's prayers the storm abated, and the passengers acclaimed the beggar-saint. But the fickle winds soon forgot the divine narcotic, turning their fiercest hounds on the waves. And the passengers, also fickle, threatened to throw Alexis into the sea.

The ship was foundering, the faith was foundering, as on the sea at Galilee. Alexis redoubled his prayers and the ship withstood the storm, but the rudder was washed away. The vessel drifted on, lost, mysterious. Nobody knew its destination. Hunger intensified, thirst became agonizing. . . . One morning the crew burst into the legendary cry, "Land!"

Ostia—the port, the warehouse, the permanent fair of Rome: arrival point for wanderings, departure point for escapes. Alexis flung his popularity into the sea, like a shoe that pinched him, and with it his appearance, his voice, the remnants of his gentility. It was the specter of the fugitive that returned.

A boat bore him up the Tiber. Rome was now enriched by a strange beggar and the wretched had a new comrade. A tattered cloak hung from his bent shoulders; he leaned on a stick; his head and feet were bare. He had neither change of linen nor beggar's pouch. The Evangelists would have found him irreproachable. In all things he followed the model of the great days of Christianity. Black locks of hair tumbled over his eyes, half-hiding his face, now dry and wrinkled as a raisin. He was tortured by the obsession to preserve his incognito.

He did not join the ranks of the beggars. Alone, jostled by passers-by, he sought refuge in a church of the Virgin Mary, as at Edessa. Rome, which had seen him born, must hide him very carefully, as the mothers of Bethlehem hid their children from the executions of Herod. Popularity, that irrational tyrant, everywhere threatened to smother him in her greasy arms.

All through Rome were scattered fragments of the youth of Alexis. Now he could set about making a selection of them and out of the most painful shreds weave himself a hair shirt. Like Augustine, he would bind about his body his own earlier life: an implacable, wounding mesh: each sin would be a sting. Thus would the spirit find its true prison. Memories, like walls of mist, would block flight at every turn. The delights over which he had shed all too few tears would twine themselves around him like so many serpents. He would spend the rest of his days on earth flagellating himself with his own past.

Alexis found his church. There were many of them in Rome, for paganism has found haven in the countryside. He need no longer fear to meet the shameless arm of the Capitoline Venus, for the Christians had shattered the temples of Love—bright, gay, coquettish temples that had invaded all seven hills of the city; small and hardly large enough to hold the priest, victim, and altar. The faithful sat outside on the grass, the sexes intermingled, making all the surroundings parties to the happy ritual. Prayer was an enjoyable sport then.

Now high roofs rose above the heads of the new faithful, walls hemmed them in, and the sexes were scrupulously segregated, for carnal love was Satan's favorite weapon. The churches were high, the windows were very high; the frontier between the realms of the spirit and matter were very well defined, for trees, fountains, sun and moon, dawn and dusk, were still tainted with paganism. Even current speech did not contain metaphors merging the elements into dogma.

The new spirit had been able to light its tiny lantern only in the darkness of secret congregations. The catacombs still imposed their enshadowed model. But by this time there had disappeared that multitude which, for four centuries, had regarded the church as an anteroom to the torture chamber—the tremulous flock expecting to hear at any moment the footsteps of the Imperial detectives.

Sadly, dejectedly, the beggar emerged from the church, as though from a garden whose perfume had vanished. Being hungry, he peered into an open doorway, then knocked timidly. Nobody answered. From inside he could hear music and the voices of a wedding feast, risqué verses and voluptuous epigrams. Alexis fled to knock at other doors.

He paraded his withered face through the streets of Rome. The city failed to recognize her Apollo. He passed by groups of gossipers, some of his old friends lounging in the sunlight. He enjoyed the sense of being completely unknown; and with lowered eyes he continued begging for a crust of bread.

At one door somebody offered him a whole loaf. He raised his eyes to see that generous hand. It was Adriana's: a small, rosy, dimpled hand, fitting termination of an arm rounded, warm, and enticing. Adriana looked compassionately at the stranger. Taking the bread, Alexis murmured a prayer . . . and stood motionless, unable to resume his slow mendicant's rhythm. He had fled from an arm and he had returned to it. Life converged at that point. . . .

Second Hair Shirt

An idea suddenly and tumultuously came to Alexis. He had traveled the world, he had blotted out his youth, he had purged himself of everything, he had regained himself. Penance, fasting, and vigil had erased his own appearance. . . . Now he saw it clearly. Here was the hair shirt he had been seeking: the hair shirt of the soul!

His own house should be his exacting torture chamber, and that arm his merciless lash. He would watch it lose its fragrance till it finally withered to a stick; he would watch it gradually aging and decaying until it crumbled into dust. Lord, that other hair shirt was nothing at all—merely a bit of hemp hair, a few strands of esparto grass that soon tired of gnawing the flesh, and ended by making truce with the senses!

Alexis walked firmly into the entrance hall. Adriana watched him enter with surprise. Euphemianus and Aglae came forward. This beggar wanted to stay here, like a lost dog straying in from the street. Alexis continued, crossing the garden and penetrating to the very heart of his home like a sleepwalker following a phantom. He stopped at the foot of the stair-case. . . .

Euphemianus granted his request, but in the name of Alexis, of his son who one night for some mysterious reason had fled from his home, leaving behind nothing of himself but his name. The boon was granted in the name of Alexis in return for prayer for Alexis. The beggar was to pray for himself, to shrink into humility before his own name, that reliquary in the home. Here Alexis was everything, and the beggar was nothing, nameless, homeless, countryless.

Yes, the hair shirt was very well concealed! The beggar was nothing, just a ragged piece of humanity which was to wear itself away and smash itself into a hundred fragments so as to liberate the soul; a spark of divine light in a cubbyhole under the stairs.

Henceforth he could use that murderous arm as a tarred rope for flaying himself. All the sorrowful intimacy of his frustrate home rasped him like a shirt of Nessus. An opulent household turned itself inside out to present him with its interior drama, like an old courtesan offering herself bare of make-up, in the nakedness of her decay.

For this entire household consumed itself in tears—silent and secret tears. Euphemianus dragged his years like a tattered cloak. Aglae sought consolation in the church, returning home every day with a new line on her face and a new ulcer on her soul. She was not granted the gift of forgetfulness. Sometimes in the dead of night a wailing voice could be heard crying: "Where are you, my Alexis? How could you be so cruel? What could we have done to hurt you?"

And another voice, Adriana's younger voice, echoed from her never-shared bed: "If you had intended to abandon me, why did you bring me here? Am I to go on waiting all my life? Could you not even send me a message?"

The double lamentation drove arrow after arrow into the heart of the every-praying beggar. Adriana writhed in despair on her abandoned couch. Aglae watched from her window for the coming of some new stranger. Melancholy and bent, Euphemianus dragged on his back the burden of his years.

The beggar toughened his heart in silence under the brutal punishment of grim, inimical time that stood still every other moment, as a torturer stops his rack at every turn of the screw to gloat sadistically over the wild agony of his victim.

So you achieved your desire, O beggar of genius! You had found the cruelest kind of hair shirt, woven of the tough fibers of time, steeped in tears, and dyed with the shadows of endless vigil. How admirably designed was your factory of sorrows, how well you organized its output from your cubbyhole under the stairs!

You overlooked nothing, beggar! Young servants tormented you, mocked you, and sometimes granted you the Evangelical boon of a buffet. For you each slap was one more stairway climbed towards your dreamed City of God. And you had other torments as well. Calicrates and Calpurnius, those two old servants laughing up their sleeves at the new faith, and pouring libations to frenzied Bacchus one night. . . .

The beggar watched them shamelessly stroking the curves of an empty amphora, as though they were stroking the limbs of Leda. How easily these apostate folk relapsed, in their hours of sincerity, into the old ways of life! Smiling Aphrodite still excited their hearts even though they had been washed in the blood of the Lamb. Ceres still crowned with ears of corn even though they had been crumbled into the Bread of Life, like Victor the martyr between the millstones. Antinous fascinated them, even though they had known Sebastian.

No, a religion was not a good thing to be changed by Imperial decree. Where Symphora, hanging by her hair, had confessed Christ, there would also remain the altar to Hercules—Hercules, the boxing champion of the world, old Uranus included. And Adriana, that intact virgin whose breasts grew dry and hard as pointed stones, thwarted in their destiny of nourishing the future strength of an illustrious offspring; Adriana with her urgent womb capable of bestowing on Rome a score of warriors, patricians, and poets—today she writhed like an eleventh Wise Virgin admitted without a place to the bed of the Heavenly Spouse—and watched the oil of her lamp wasting away.

Already those tiny workers who begin by furrowing foreheads were creeping around her eyes, gathering about her mouth, overrunning her entire face, preparing it for the yellow seed of autumn. The little spirits of grief pinched Adriana's cheeks, sucking their juices, and climbed over her breasts, sapping them and probing them until they were but wan specters of those "two young roes that are twins, which feed among the lilies."

All the fine edifice of her was cruelly tormented by those somber gnomes. Those "pillars of ivory," her legs, were now no better than stucco. Her drooping shoulders overshadowed that "belly as bright ivory." Adriana wasted away until she was no more than a thread strung with the phantoms of herself. Day by day, as she brought food to his cubbyhole, she added sharp points to the beggar's hair shirt.

The longed-for hair shirt! There it was, fashioned with elaborate cruelty by the hands of the unconscious torturer of his life—those hands that day by day lost more of their silken smoothness, as her voice day by day lost something of its sweetness. Oh genius of a beggar, who knew how to invent the most torturing hair shirt the world has ever known!

Apotheosis

One morning Pope Innocent celebrated the Holy Sacrifice in the presence of Honorius and his court. The faithful watched in silence as a fragment white as snow was lifted in the hands of the Pontiff.

The moment had come to reveal to the people the new model of saint, the latest and now fully achieved creation. The Virgin Mother had been somewhat precipitate at Edessa, as at Cana; but Jesus always forgives the soft-heartedness of mothers. The beggar was to be transformed into a saint—to become the comrade in heroism of Roland, of the Cid, of Charlemagne, of Iseult, of Mary of Egypt, of the Magi. An archangel was about to rise up from a rubbish heap.

A Voice was heard on high, the same voice that halted Saul, that incited Joan, that ever halts and incites the puppets of God.

"Seek ye the Divine Kingdom, and the Saint shall pray for Rome! On Friday he departs from this world!"

The news ran through Rome. A Saint! On Friday the whole city hurried to church to witness the spectacle . . . Innocent, Honorius, Euphemianus, bishops, senators, tribunes, deacons, centurions, virgins, poets, dancers, players, and plebeians.

Again the Voice was heard: "Seek the servant of God in the house of Euphemianus!"

All eyes turned toward the old senator. Innocent and Honorius reproached him:

"Why have you kept silent?"

"My lord, I knew nothing of this!"

"To your house!"—and Pope, Emperor, bishops, senators, tribunes, deacons, centurions, virgins, poets, players, and plebeians made their way to the house of Euphemianus. Servants hurried on ahead so as to tidy up the house. There was hustle and bustle, carpets and tapestries, festoons of foliage, roses and perfumes.

Everything was adorned and perfumed except the cubbyhole under the stairs. There Alexis lay dead, behind a barricade of furniture which had been cleared out of the great hall where the Pontiff was to be received. Euphemianus inquired in all directions.

"My lord," said Adriana, "might it not be this poor man who lived under the stairs? He died today."

"What?"

"Yes, and yesterday he asked me for a parchment, which he wrote on. They tried to snatch it away from him as a joke, but the poor man resisted—he who was always so docile."

Euphemianus hastened to the den. There, serene and solemn as his own recumbent statue, the beggar reposed. In his right hand he clasped the parchment. They tried in vain to take it from his grasp. The majesty of his attitude was so great that Euphemianus, as though in a trance, fell upon his knees. Little by little the beggar's rags were transformed into purple, the ashen-colored face into amber, the hands into ivory. His mouth glowed and his whole body exhaled an aroma of spikenard. Euphemianus ran to the Pontiff.

"I have seen the Saint!"

Neither Pontiff nor Emperor went to the den. Their majestic paraphernalia prevented them from stooping so low despite all their prayers. The body had to be carried away on a stretcher, to be installed in the great hall. There Innocent went down on his knees and humbly asked Alexis for the parchment. The Saint suffered it to be taken. Innocent handed the parchment to his chamberlain.

And so this true story was told for the first time—the story of Adriana, Euphemianus, Aglae, Ostia, Laodicea, Edessa, the Virgin Mary . . . the hair shirt of the flesh, and the hair shirt of the soul. . . .

The saintliness of Alexis was uncorked like a bottle of champagne. Euphemianus screamed aloud, Aglae wept, Adriana fainted. Honorius and the Pope looked at each other. What a success for the Empire and the Papacy! the faithful applauding, the actors weeping with Aglae!

"Chamberlain," ordered Innocent, "make a note to add to the calendar of Saints, Alexis, confessor. His tomb in St. Boniface; his festival today, June 17th. Ritual, twofold; color, white. The hymn of Ambrose and Augustine to be sung in all the churches. Broadcast these instructions throughout Christendom!"

"And let the bells be rung throughout the Roman empire," added Honorius.

"My lord, that is impossible. Bells have not yet been invented. If they had been, they would have rung of their own accord."

The Village Idiot

CAMILO JOSÉ CELA

The name of the village idiot was Blas. Blas Herrero Martínez. Before the death of Perejilondo, the previous village idiot who had managed to forget that Hermenegildo was his real name, Blas was a rather dull boy who stole pears, and who served as the victim of everyone's useless blows and ill-temper. He was a pale boy, long-legged, solitary, and tremulous. The village did not warrant more than one idiot; it was too small to accommodate more than one, and Blas Herrero Martínez, who was aware of this and had a high regard for tradition, was content to roam about the pine groves and meadows stealing whatever he could, without ever coming too close. In this way he patiently waited for the now aged Perejilondo to be taken away in a wooden box with his feet in front of him and the priests behind. Custom was custom and had to be respected; there was a saying in the town to the effect that custom was more important than the king and no less important than the law. Blas Herrero Martínez, who understood life intuitively and with the same accuracy as a well-trained hound following a scent, knew that his time had not yet come, and courageously resigned himself to waiting. Even though the contrary may appear to be true, in this life there is always time for everything.

Blas Herrero Martínez had a small, bald, pointed head, a narrow chest, spindly legs, freckles, and buck teeth; he was cross-eyed and he drooled. The lad was an obvious sort of idiot, with every requirement scrupulously fulfilled; considered carefully, as one should consider him, Blas played the role of village idiot to perfection. He was unmistakably an idiot and not just a run-of-the-mill type whose idiocy could not be established without a doctor's diagnosis.

He was good-natured and gentle, and always smiled like a sick calf even when he had just been hit with a stone, a frequent occurrence, since the villagers were not exactly what one might call sensitive. Blas Herrero Martínez of the little ferret face would wiggle his ears—one of his talents—and nurse his latest wound, which bled a watery pale pink, smiling all the while in a manner hard to describe: perhaps he was imploring his tormentors not to hit him with the second stone on the sore made by the first.

In the time of Perejilondo, on Sundays, which were the only days when Blas felt he had some right to walk through the village streets, our village idiot would sit down after Mass at the door of Louise's café and wait the two or three hours required for the customers to finish their aperitifs and go home to dinner. When Louise's café was entirely empty or nearly so, Blas would go in smiling and slip under the tables to pick up the cigarette butts. Sometimes there were very good days; two years before, for example, there had been a very gay party and Blas had managed to fill his tin with about seven hundred cigarette stubs. The pride and joy of Blas Herrero Martínez was this deep, beautiful, shiny yellow tin on which were painted a shell and some words in English.

When Blas finished his task he ran breathlessly to see Perejilondo, who by this time was very old and scarcely able to move. He said to him: "Perejilondo, look what I've brought. Are you satisfied?"

Perejilondo answered in his best falsetto: "Yes. . . . Yes. . . ."

Then he gloated over the butts with a miserly smile, and, seizing half a dozen in a haphazard way, gave them to Blas.

"Did I do the right thing? Are you satisfied?"

"Yes. . . . Yes. . . ."

Blas Herrero Martínez took his stubs and, unrolling them, made whatever kind of cigarette happened to come out. Sometimes the result was a rather thick cigarette but at other times it came out so thin that it was almost impossible to smoke, worse luck. Blas always gave the butts he found in Louise's café to Perejilondo, because Perejilondo was the rightful owner of all the butts in the village. After all, it was not for nothing that he was the ranking village idiot. Once it became Blas's turn to dispose of the butts at will, he would not allow any newcomer to cheat him either. That was hardly to be expected! Fundamentally, Blas was a conservative with a great regard for tradition, and he was aware of the fact that Perejilondo was the official village idiot.

Nonetheless, on the day of Perejilondo's death Blas could not restrain a spontaneous feeling of joy and began to jump and gambol about like a lamb in the meadow where he usually went to drink. Shortly thereafter he realized that he had done wrong and then he went to the cemetery to do penance and to weep over the mortal remains of Perejilondo, a man over whose grave nobody else had ever done penance, nor wept, nor was ever destined to weep. For a few weeks he brought the butts to the cemetery; after setting aside his half-dozen he carefully buried the rest over the grave of his mentor. Later on he gradually stopped doing this and finally did not even bother to collect all the butts; he merely picked up as many as he needed and left the rest for whoever came after him and wanted them. He forgot Perejilondo and observed that something strange was happening: it was an unfamiliar sensation to bend down to pick up a butt and not wonder whether or not it really belonged to him.

The Bewitched

FRANCISCO AYALA

After having presented his petition in vain at the Court, González Lobo—who had arrived in Spain from the Indies near the end of 1679 on one of a fleet of galleons bringing gold to celebrate the marriage of the king—retired to live in the city of Mérida, in a house with one of his father's sisters. Never once after that did González Lobo leave Mérida. He was received with rejoicing by his aunt Doña Luisa Alvarez, who had been alone since the death of her husband a little while before, and he helped her with the management of a small property to which, in later years, he was to be the heir. Here he lived out the rest of his life, dividing his time between his labors and his devotions, and, during the evenings, he was wont to write. He wrote, in addition to many papers, a long report of his voyage, which, after innumerable extraneous niceties, tells how he came to appear before the King, Charles the Bewitched. It is with this piece of writing that the present note is concerned.

The report in question does not presume to draft a memorial, nor anything of that nature. Neither does it appear to have been intended to institute or support any particular claim. It might better be said that it is a report of the disillusionment of the author's hopes. He composed it, no doubt, as a diversion in the vigils of an old age turned entirely towards the past and confined between the walls of memory. In this senility of his, even the echoes of the civil war then being waged over the crown of the unfortunate deceased Charles could arouse neither emotion nor curiosity.

Some day this notable manuscript must be published. I would reproduce the entire text were it not so exhaustive and so uneven. It is overloaded with tiresome data on the trade of the Indies, with critical appreciations which might perhaps be of interest to historians and economists today; it devotes excessive space to a rather farfetched comparison between the crops of Peru and agricultural conditions in Andalusia and Extremadura; it abounds in trivial details. The author lingers over incredible minutiae and takes pleasure in vague meanderings, while on the other hand he at times skips over with but a passing allusion some terrible atrocity or some great and noble deed which may have come to his attention. In any case, it would not seem wise to print so disorganized a piece of writing without retouching it a bit and relieving it of the many impertinent excrescences which make it painful and disagreeable to read.

It is worth noting that once the reader has finished this work, at a cost of no little effort, he is left with a feeling that, notwithstanding so much insistent detail, something has been concealed from him. Other people who are acquainted with the text have corroborated this impression of mine; and a friend whom I interested in the study of the manuscript, after thanking me, even added in his letter: "More than once, upon turning a page and raising my head, I thought I could see in the

murky depths of the tome the dark glance of González Lobo
as he shrouded his joke in the winking of half-closed eyes."
There can be no doubt that the writing is extremely disconcerting and poses many problems. For example: what purpose
does it serve? Why was it written? One may agree that it had
no other aim but to assuage the loneliness of an old man reduced to the solitary contemplation of his memories, but how
can one explain the fact that, even after many rereadings, one
can find no statement of the nature of the claim which the
author took to the Court, nor of its origin?

Furthermore, if the basis of this claim rested solely on merits
accruing to the writer from his father, it is rather surprising
that he does not mention this even once in the course of his
report. The conjecture that González Lobo was orphaned at
an early age and therefore had no particular memories of his
childhood might apply; however he omits even his name while
at the same time flooding us with tiresome observations about
climates and flora; he wearies us by cataloguing the riches to
be found in the cathedral church of Sigüenza. Say what you
will, what he reveals about his life before his voyage is summary in the extreme, and always introduced incidentally. We
learn something about him from the priest who gave him sacra-
ments and penances. In one episode, introduced as a warning
to youth, he tells us that one good friar was so exasperated at
the obstinacy and stubborn silence with which his pupil opposed his reprimands, that he threw his books to the ground,
and, making the sign of the cross over him, left him alone with
Plutarch and Vergil. This is brought in by way of expiation,
or, better, as a sort of moralizing lament, for the deficiencies
of style which marred his prose.

But this self-effacement is not the only inexplicable thing in
a report so full of wearisome explanations. Along with this
weighty and salient problem, other more subtle ones arise. The

laboriousness of the journey and its many setbacks, the increasing delays in the steps which brought him to the Court (González remained in Seville more than three years without his memory's offering any justification for such a prolonged stay in a city where nothing should have detained him) contrast with the swiftness with which he desisted from his aspirations and retired from Madrid, having scarcely looked at the King. This creates another minor enigma, and there are many others like it.

The report opens with the beginning of the voyage and concludes with the audience before King Charles II in a palace chamber. "His Majesty wanted to show me benevolence"—are his concluding words—"and gave me his hand to kiss. But before I could reach out to take it, there jumped onto it a curious little monkey which had been playing about, and which now distracted his royal attention by demanding caresses. Then did I recognize my opportunity, and withdrew in respectful silence."

Equally inexplicable is the opening section of the manuscript in which González takes leave of his mother. There are no explanations or admonitions, nor even tears. We see the two figures etched against the dawn sky, in a background of Andean peaks. González had to cover a long distance before morning; and mother and son walked side by side, without talking, to the church, an edifice a little larger, a little less poor, than the dwellings. Together they heard Mass. After this, González turned to descend through the footpaths of the cordilleras.

A little farther on, we find him in the middle of the bustle of port. Here his small figure can scarcely be discerned among the comings and goings of the people milling around him. Standing and waiting by the glittering, blinding ocean, he entertains himself by watching the preparations of the fleet. At his side, on the ground, he has a small chest. Everything whirls before his patient gaze; sailors, officials, stevedores, soldiers, cries, orders, blows. González Lobo remained quietly in the same place for two hours, and another two or three passed before the many oars of the first galley began to move in rhythm, dragging it over the turgid water of the harbor. Later, he embarked with his chest. To the long voyage his memoirs contain only this succinct reference: "The crossing was happy."

But, perhaps for lack of incidents to recount, perhaps to compensate for the unrealized anticipations, he fills folio after folio with descriptions of the many inconveniences, risks and dangers which beset the traveler by sea, and with methods of averting losses which the interests of the Crown suffer because of pirates. The reader might think that it was not a traveler writing, but a politician, or perhaps a schemer. And then we do not encounter him again until Seville.

In Seville we see him reappear, out of a labyrinth of moral, administrative and economic considerations, following behind a Negro who is carrying his chest on his shoulder and who is taking him to find a room, through a maze of little passage-ways and alleys.

He has left behind him the ship from which he disembarked. It is still there, rocking in the river; you can see, very near, its beflagged masts. But between González Lobo, who is now following the Negro with his chest, and the vessel which brought him from America, there is the Customs Office. Throughout the piece there is not a single expression of vehemence, not a hint of impatience, nor a complaining inflection. Nothing disturbs the tranquil course of the narrative. Nevertheless, the reader who has his finger on the pulse of this prose, and has learned to sense the throb concealed beneath the rhetoric then in vogue, can detect in the author's discussions of a better ordering of the trade of the Indies and of various standards of good government which it would be advisable to institute, all the boredom of interminable negotiations, capable of exasperating anyone with a less fine disposition.

It would transcend the purpose of these notes, intended only to call attention to this curious manuscript, to offer a complete summary of its content. Perhaps the day will come when it can be edited and annotated with the careful erudition it deserves, and prefaced by a philological study in which the many questions which its style provokes are discussed and elucidated. But even from a superficial glance, it is apparent that the prose as well as the ideas of the author are anachronistic; for incidents, customs, attitudes and phraseology belonging to several generations, including some preceding his own, are distinguishable here. This might possibly be explainable in terms of the personal idiosyncracies of González Lobo. At the same time, as is generally the case, this conglomeration reminds one of our contemporary sensibility.

Nevertheless some such study must still be made, and without its guidance it would not seem advisable to publish such a book, which would, moreover, need to be preceded by a geographic-chronological chart tracing the itinerary of the journey, in itself no easy task considering how great are the confusion and disorder with which the material is strewn through the pages, how dates are altered and trivial events are emphasized, and how facts are mixed with hearsay, the remote with the present, incidents with judgments, and the author's own opinion with that of others.

For the moment, I will confine myself to anticipating this chart, and to calling attention anew to the central problem which the work poses: to discover the true purpose of a journey whose motivations remain very obscure, if not entirely hidden, and the relation of this purpose to the subsequent wording of the report. I must confess that, preoccupied with this matter, I have toyed with various hypotheses, which, however, I have had to reject quickly as unsatisfactory. After thinking it over, it seemed to me much too fantastic to believe that González Lobo might have been concealing an identity in which he felt himself called to some high destiny as a descendant of noble blood. Actually, this would not clarify anything. It occurred to me also to wonder whether his work might not be a mere literary invention, calculated with painstaking care to symbolize in its apparent slovenliness the arduous and unpredictable course of human life, implicitly moralizing on the vanity of all the anxieties in which human existence is spent. For several weeks, I adhered obstinately and enthusiastically to this interpretation, and felt even that the protagonist might also be an imaginary person; but finally I had to resign myself to rejecting this theory, for it is certain that the literary conscience of the epoch would have plainly forbidden such an idea.

But this is not the time, of course, to digress on such questions, but merely to review the manuscript and give a brief outline of its contents.

There is one part, interminably long, in which González Lobo is lost in the labyrinth of the Court. He describes with unsparing rigor his struggle of the halls and the waiting rooms, where hope was lost and the passing of time found him no further in his quest. He vents his fury in noting down each one of his negotiations, which got him not one step higher. Pages and pages are full of tedious references and details which are of no importance and whose purpose is difficult to conjecture. Pages and more pages are filled with paragraphs like this: "I got in without any trouble this time, thanks to being well known already to the head doorkeeper; but at the foot of the great staircase which leads from the entrance hall [he is referring to the Palace of the Council of the Indies, where many of the negotiations took place] I found the guard changed. I had then to explain my entire business again as on previous days, and to wait until they sent for a page to ascertain whether my entry was to be permitted. While I waited, I entertained myself in watching those who went up and down the stairs, nobles and clergy, greeted each other, stopped to converse or moved ahead amid reverences. No little time did my good page delay in returning with the message that I might be received by the fifth assistant of the Third Secretariat, who was competent to hear my business. I proceeded according to directions, and took a seat in the waiting room of the fifth assistant. It was the same antechamber where I had had to wait the first day, and I seated myself on the same bench where I had waited more than an hour and a half that other time. Nor did it appear that this time the wait was to be any briefer: time dragged by; I saw the door open and close an infinite number of times, and various people went in and out to see the fifth assistant, who himself passed by me without any sign of recognition, frowning, with eyes straight ahead. Finally, tired of waiting, I approached the guard at the door to remind him of my case. The good man recommended patience to me, and, because I did not lose it, he had the kindness to conduct me a little farther, into the very office of the fifth assistant, who would not be long in returning to his desk. While waiting for him, I wondered if he would remember my business or would send me again to the secretariat of another section of the Royal Council where he had previously referred me. There was a mountain of files on his desk, and the walls of the room were lined with shelves, also piled high with documents. In the front part of the room, back of the assistant's chair, was a large and not very good portrait of the deceased king, Philip IV. On a chair, near the desk, another great heap of papers awaited their turn, and the inkwell, full of coagulated ink, also awaited the return of the fifth official of the Secretariat. . . . But that morning it turned out to be impossible for me to talk with him, because he finally came in, very upset, to hunt for a particular file, and asked me with all courtesy to excuse him for he had to confer with his Lordship and was not free to talk to me at this time."

Tirelessly, González dilutes his reports with such particulars, sparing not a day or even an hour, so that frequently he repeats two, three, and even more times, in almost parallel terms, the tale of identical negotiations, distinguished only by date; and when the reader believes that he has finally arrived at the end of a most painful business, he sees unfolding before his weary eyes another one just like it, which he will also have to pursue step by step, only to reach the next. The writer might very well have dispensed with all this labor and excused his readers from it by simply noting, if this was important to his intention, the number of visits which he had to make to such or such an office and on what dates. Why did he not do it thus? Did it afford him some peculiar pleasure to see the manuscript bulk up under his pen like a tumorous growth, to see how its increasing volume threatened to surpass the actual time elapsed? Of what worth is it to us to know that there were forty-six steps in the staircase of the Palace of the Holy Office, and the number of windows in each façade?

He who faithfully accomplishes the imposed task, boring through the entire manuscript from beginning to end, line by line, without omitting even a comma, feels not so much relief as true emotion when the course of the writing suddenly takes an unforeseen turn, promising new perspectives to a jaded attention. "The next day, Sunday," one reads suddenly, without any transition, "I went to confession with Doctor Curtius." The sentence leaps out from the mechanical reading, like something sparkling in deadened gray sand. . . . But if the tender throbbing evoked by the word "confession" gives rise for a moment to the hope that the narrative may now provide more intimate revelations, the mystery of his vicissitudes is, on the contrary, shrouded more than ever by the secrecy of the sacrament. Prodigious always in details, the author continues his silence on the subject of cardinal importance. The scene changes, but not the attitude. We see the small figure of González Lobo advance, mount slowly up the middle of the wide flight of steps, the approach to the portico of the church; we see him pause a moment at the side, to take out a little money from his pouch to succor a beggar. He even tells us with useless exactitude that this beggar was an old and blind paralytic, whose limbs were encased in shapeless bandages. Here González also adds a long digression, lamenting the fact that he has not means enough to alleviate the misery of the rest of the poor sitting there like a cordon of grief along the length of the ascent.

Finally, González's figure is again lost in the hollow atrium. He has lifted the heavy curtain, he has entered the nave, he genuflects before the high altar. Then he approaches the confessional. Near it, he waits on his knees for his turn. How many times did the beads of his rosary pass between his fingertips before a fat white hand finally signaled to him from the dark that he might approach the Sacred Tribunal? González Lobo notes down this fugitive gesture of the white hand in the shadow; equally has he retained over the span of years the impression of displeasing harshness with which the Teutonic inflections of his confessor sounded in his ears. But that is all. "I kissed his hand and then went to stand by a column and hear the Holy Mass."

It is disconcerting—disconcerting and more than a little irritating—to see how, after such overweening reserve, he goes on to describe extensively the solemnity of the Mass, the heart-rending purity of the young voices from the choir in their answers to the solemn Latin words issuing from the altar: "as if the skies had opened and angels sang the glories of the Resurrection." All of this, the phrases and liturgical chants, the glitter of silver and gold, the multitude of lights, the dense spirals of incense ascending in front of the altar between the twisted, ivy-covered pilasters up to the broken cupolas—all of this was of no greater novelty then than it is today; nor was it the occasion for such extensive description. It is difficult to convince ourselves that the author has not lingered over these obvious particulars to divert attention from the omission of what personally concerned him, at least to attempt to fill in by this means the hiatus between his confession—in which he would certainly have had to introduce some worldly or immodest ideas—and the visit which he made the following morning to the Dwelling of the Brotherhood of Jesus, in the name of Doctor Curtius. "I pulled the bell," he says when he has brought us as far as the door, "and I heard it ring nearer and louder than I had expected."

This is, again, only a reference to a petty fact. But through it the exhausted reader may discern a scene charged with tension; he pictures the melancholy and austere figure of González Lobo approaching the door of the Dwelling with his habitual parsimony, his sad, dull and listless countenance. On arriving there, González Lobo lifts his hand languidly up to the bellpull. But this hand, fine, long and deliberate, suddenly and unaccountably seizes it and pulls it violently, then drops it quickly. Now, while the bellpull is oscillating rapidly before his listless eyes, he observes that the bell is nearer and louder than one might think.

Actually, however, he mentions nothing of this. He says "I pulled the bell and I heard it ring nearer and louder than I had expected. Scarcely had its tumult died down when I heard the steps of the porter who was coming to open it for me, and who, after I had told him my name, let me enter without delay." In the author's company, the reader enters a room where González waits standing beside a table. There is nothing in the room besides this little table in the center, two chairs, and a piece of furniture against the wall with a great crucifix above it. The wait is long and the result is as follows: "I was not permitted to see the Grand Inquisitor in person. But, by his direction, I was sent to the house of the baroness of Berlips, nicknamed by the populace *The Partridge,* who, they assured me, would have all the information necessary in my case. Still, I soon discovered," he goes on, "that it was no easy thing to obtain a hearing with her. The power of influential people is measured by the number of favor seekers who knock at their doors, and here the whole patio of the house was a waiting room."

Thus the report conducts us from the Jesuit Dwelling—so silent that the ring of a bell in its vestibule is like the fall of a stone into a well—to an old palace in whose patio is gathered a boisterous multitude of petitioners, eager sycophants in the traffic of influence, soliciting exemptions, buying positions, demanding favors, or negotiating privileges. "I posted myself in a corner of the corridor and, while waiting, amused myself by contemplating the great variety of faces and conditions here congregated, when a soldier, putting his hand on my shoulder, asked me from whence I had come and for what. Before I could answer, he went on to ask forgiveness for his curiosity, stating that the long wait forced him to entertain himself somehow and that recollections of the old country are always pleasing material for conversation. He told me that he, for his part, was a native of Flanders, and that he was at present serving in the Royal Palace Guards in the hope of obtaining subsequently a post as gardener on the royal estate; that this hope was founded on and sustained by the influence of his wife, who was the King's dwarf, and who had already given more than one display of her knack for obtaining small favors. I wondered then while I was listening to him whether perhaps this might not be a good means of arriving sooner at the end of my desires; and so I told him how my wish was only to kiss the feet of His Majesty, but that, a stranger in the Court, and without friends, I could not find any means of getting an audience with his Royal Person. This incident, González adds, turned out happily, for the soldier, after having lengthily emphasized the extent of his sympathy for my helplessness, and his desire to serve me, drew near to my ear and concluded that perhaps his aforementioned wife—who was, according to what he had told me, the dwarf Doña Antoñita Núñez, of the King's Chamber—could devise a means of introducing me to his High Presence, and that without doubt she would be glad to do it, if I knew how to ingratiate myself and move her will with a gift of the ring which he saw on my little finger."

The pages which follow contain, in my judgment, the greatest literary interest of the entire manuscript. Not so much for their style, which unchangingly retains all of its characteristics: archaic lapses, sometimes clumsy haste, and always the elusive manner in which as soon as one believes he has straightened out the circumlocutions of the officialese prose, he is suddenly involved in the vague allusions of one who wrote for his own enjoyment without considering possible readers—not so much for the style, I say, as for the narrative, in which González Lobo appears to have outdone himself. The narrative eddies here, it loses its habitual dryness, and even seems to sparkle with unaccustomed good humor. González takes pleasure in describing the aspect and mannerisms of Doña Antoñita, her movements, gestures, attitudes, grimaces and smiles, her speech and her silences, throughout the curious negotiation.

If these pages had not already exceeded the limits of prudence, I would reproduce the passage in its entirety. But discretion obliges me to limit myself to this sample of its tenor: "Then," he writes, "she let fall her handkerchief and waited, watching me, until I should reach for it. As I stooped to pick it up, I saw her little eyes at the level of my head, laughing. She took the handkerchief which I handed to her and crushed it between the diminutive fingers of a hand already adorned with my little ring. She thanked me, and her laugh sounded like a flute; her eyes were lost in her face, and now, her luster quenched, the large forehead was hard and cold as stone."

This passage again displays the same vanity of petty detail, but do you not detect here an amusing inflection, giving, in such an apathetic writer, the effect of his joy when, finally and unexpectedly, the exit from the labyrinth where he had been lost is discovered to him? His perplexities have disappeared, and perhaps he even enjoys detaining himself in the same spot from which he hitherto had wanted so desperately to escape.

From here on the report loses its accustomed despondency, and, as if to keep pace with the rhythm of the writer's heart, speeds up without destroying the general effect. It carries forward the burden of the wearisome journey and in the countless folios which contain his peripetiae, from that remote mass in the Andean peaks up to this moment in which he goes to appear before His Catholic Majesty, there seems to be included all the trials of a lifetime.

And now we have González Lobo in the company of the dwarf Doña Antoñita, en route to the Palace. He describes as always the patios, doors, entrances, guards, corridors, and antechambers which they traversed. He has left behind the Square, where a squadron of horsemen were performing maneuvers; he has left behind the suave marble staircase; he has left behind the great hall, opening on the patio to the right, and with a mural of a famous battle on the left, which he did not linger to admire, but of which he nevertheless remembered and described a close-ranked regiment which, from a well-defined perspective, marched in echelon formation toward a high, closed, defended citadel. . . . And now the enormous door at the top of the staircase, whose two oak panels opened before them and shut again behind them. The rugs silenced their steps, counseling circumspection, and the mirrors anticipated their entrance to the interior of desolate rooms submerged in shadow.

The hand of Doña Antoñita crept to the opening of another gleaming door, and her soft fingers grasped the shining metal of the handle, turning it noiselessly. Then, suddenly, González Lobo found himself in the presence of the King.

"His Majesty," he tells us, "was seated on a great throne, on a dais, his feet resting on a tobacco-colored silk cushion, placed up on a bench. At his side reposed a little white dog." He describes—and it is amazing that in such a short space of time he could have observed and retained so much—everything from the King's flaccid, dangling legs to his languid, discolored head. He tells us how the Malines lace which adorned His Highness's breast was wet from the continuous drooling from his mouth. He informs us that the buckles of the King's shoes were of silver, and his clothes of black velvet. "The rich habit in which His Majesty was clothed," writes González, "emitted a strong odor of urine; later I learned of the incontinence which plagued him." With similar imperturbable simplicity he continues noting down, through three folios, all the details which his incredible memory retained about the chamber and the mode in which it was furnished. With respect to the visit itself, which must certainly have been the memorable thing for him, he gives only this description, with which he brings his bulky manuscript to a close: "Seeing a stranger enter, the little dog jumped up, and His Majesty seemed to be disturbed. But on perceiving the head of his dwarf, who went before me, he resumed his attitude of languor. Doña Antoñita approached him and whispered a few words in his ear. His Majesty wanted to show me benevolence, and gave me his hand to kiss. But before I could reach out to take it, there jumped onto it a curious little monkey which had been playing about, and which now distracted his royal attention by demanding caresses. Then did I recognize my opportunity, and withdrew in respectful silence."

Twilight in
Extremadura

ROSA CHACEL

After long reflection, I find that only by recounting a few concrete examples can one define or explain the distant impressions that persist in one's memory. In the capital of my province, when I was still very small, I was returning home one night in the company of two or three adults from our household and we were crossing a square in which there was a statue surrounded by a walled garden. I had hung back a few paces, and I kept rubbing against the lapel of my jacket a round, smooth stone which I had found in the park. Meanwhile, I sang a popular tune with words that did not belong to it; for no apparent reason and without the slightest attempt at improvisation, I murmured words which seemed automatically to adapt themselves to the music—words which nothing in the world could induce me to reproduce here.

After endless, countless years, that recollection periodically flashes into my mind, but I have been able to reveal those words to only one person. I will simply state now that any of the words, individually, can be said anywhere at all and that taken all together they cannot be considered either evil or obscene, but their childish incongruity still fills me with terror.

The residue of that moment of solitude is, in reality, a mixture of delight and terror. I was only three yards away from my companions, but when I recall the deserted square, the fence against which my shoulder brushed, the contact of the smooth stone, and the melody of my song with its impenetrable words, I am enveloped in an atmosphere of intimacy which time has been powerless to diminish.

I think that the foregoing may serve as an example of what is usually called an indelible memory, although I do not know why I have given it as an example when the story I have to tell is quite different. Many people think that small, subsidiary events detract from the core of a story, but that is not always so; when there emerges from the lengthy narration of real events one brilliant point which transcends but does not abandon reality, other similar incidents cluster about it to form a constellation which serves to corroborate its truth, to testify to its authenticity, proving that its brilliance is not merely an accidental spark.

Even further: I believe so firmly in the mystery inherent in these events that not only have I no fear of accumulating and analyzing them, but I even manage to classify them and go so far as to foresee and to produce them.

For example, not too long ago when I was walking alone at dusk along a wide avenue, I crossed a side street and saw, in the house on the corner, the window of a fruit store with the light already on; a white cat was sitting on the sidewalk in front of the door; in the window an electric bulb hung suspended over the fruit, shedding its rays on the street where it flickered faintly like a memory of the fading daylight. I turned my head and looked, and without stopping I thought: I shall never forget this, and I have not.

Now, the recollection that I shall try to relate is not, like the first, a fixed orbit that keeps reappearing in all the darkness of its atmosphere, nor is it, like the second, a cleanly stamped image that persists in flowering occasionally; it is more like a culmination or apotheosis, and I have succeeded in reconstructing the drama which preceded it only by means of the most painstaking introspection.

A thousand years ago a day dawned that was different from all the others. Getting out of bed, eating a hurried breakfast, going to school—all those things which had always seemed disagreeable—seemed quick and effortless. And it wasn't that I was looking forward to anything at all extraordinary. I was obliged to get up a half hour before my usual time and I didn't mind, despite the fact that the only novelty was that I had to have a letter registered before going to school. Moreover, even before remembering the letter I felt more contented than on other days. When I began to be awakened by the rays of light filtering through the cracks, I tried, as on other occasions, to shade my face with the bedclothes. I thought: here comes the light, because I felt it strike my eyelids; then I opened my eyes and saw the letter on the night table, propped against a vase.

As I went to the post office, I kept on looking at the envelope, in a corner of which my mother had written in a very clear hand "sample without value," and it was very hard for me to understand how something which had required so much effort to make could be sent in so casual a manner. But I was told that those words sufficed, and I could not contradict them. When I caught sight of the almond trees stretching their bare branches over a wall I remembered that my mother had begun that piece of work in the dead of winter. Every afternoon she would sit next to the fire with a ball of yarn and do something incomprehensible, until finally one day I asked her "What are you doing?" and she answered *"Frivolité."* "And," I inquired, "what is *frivolité?*" "Why," she answered, "as you see, it's a bit of lace work." But I didn't see any lace: all I saw was that she worked a shuttle in and out of the yarn that was stretched between her fingers and that from them were suspended some white hoops. She spent her afternoons in that way and, on some days, even her mornings. When I returned from school and my father had not as yet come home, a special sort of silence seemed suddenly to descend upon the house and it was all because my mother was seated at the window working at her *frivolité*. At such times I sat down at the door and I felt that time had come to a stop.

Opposite our house the road began to dip down toward the fields. The only part of the village that was visible was some massive walls on the right, into the shade of which crowded a flock of sheep seeking its afternoon nap. Their bells tinkled constantly because the ewes were not still for a moment, moving about in a vain attempt to find a comfortable position in which to rest, and the males, apparently out of ill-temper, did the same. It seemed to me that the milling of the sheep near the wall, my hunger, and the midday light could last forever, so long as my mother did not stop casting the yarn.

All of this went into the letter that was to be registered as a sample without value, and I saw through the envelope all the phases through which it had passed. I also remembered the moment when, after having been sewn all around a piece of material, it was being ironed between damp cloths which emitted clouds of steam. When it finally emerged, it turned out to be a handkerchief with all the little hoops placed next to each other on the edges, forming stars in each corner. Then, after being folded in fours, it was inserted between two post cards which we all had inscribed for Grandma, and it was to arrive just in time for St. Joseph's Day.

I went along slowly, thinking of all these things, and I wanted very much to tell it all to the man in the post office so that he would be very careful, but I knew that such a thing couldn't be done. As I was approaching—the post office was on the other side of town, toward the main road and away from the houses—I saw four boys from school walking almost surreptitiously along a path. "Hey!" I called, "where are you going?" Three of them hurried on but one turned around and I ran to catch up. When they saw that I was going to reach them they stopped and said, "Are you coming?" I asked them what special reason they had for not going to school, but they wouldn't answer me; they simply told me to go with them. I replied that if they would wait a minute I would register a letter and then I could accompany them. The boy who was more friendly with me than the others because we shared the same bench observed that the letter was unusually thick and taking it out of my hand he asked, "What's inside? There's something in it." I nodded assent but my only thought was to get hold of it again without having to pull it away because I was afraid that it might get wrinkled. The other three withdrew a little, saying, "Are you coming or not?" One of them was leading a dog by a rope and the animal kept jumping at his side as if it too were impatient. In order to distract the boy from the letter I again asked him what they were going to do and, pointing to the dog that was with the others he said, "We're going to hang him." I saw at once that it was not a joke; moreover, the boy kept repeating with insistent curiosity, "What's inside?" I could barely answer but I was afraid to keep silent because then they would notice it and so I said,

"It's a handkerchief." It seemed like an evasion. "A handkerchief? Nonsense!" And he didn't give me back the letter; I
couldn't decide whether to hit him or to burst into tears, but
above all else I didn't want them to notice anything. I wanted
desperately to get the letter back and I realized that I would
have to say something to convince him to return it to me, so
then I said: "All right. It's not just an ordinary handkerchief,
like all the others; it's a hanky of *frivolité*." The riot that
ensued! They were convulsed with laughter, they laughed as
pigs would laugh if they could. And between peals of laughter
each one repeated constantly, in his own way *"Frivolité . . ."*
One of them assumed the falsetto of a pansy, another dragged
out the final syllable "té, té, té, tarateté . . ." And it was all
so revolting! I couldn't recover from my astonishment. Why
did that word reduce them to that state? And the most extraordinary thing was that I myself, sure as I was that the
word indicated nothing more than the name of some lace edg-
ing, understood precisely what they were thinking and I saw
what they were doing with the word because I knew that they
were capable only of obscenities. The fact is that I realized
that what I had said had made the situation worse rather than
better. Then, with a tremendous effort, because my voice
seemed stuck in my throat, I managed to say to the boy,
"Well, if you're all going to just stand there saying idiotic
things I won't be able to have it registered and then I won't
have time to go with you." The boy gave me the letter almost
without noticing it because he was still laughing. I was off
like a shot to the post office.

I went up to the window, I paid and put the stamps on, and
here my memory fails me. I feel somehow as if in connection
with the stamps I had planned something beforehand and I
don't know if at that moment I lacked the will to do it or if I
had already forgotten it or if it is just that I am forgetting it

now. I don't know, but there is some point there that is not clear. What is clear is that when I finished I ran, half unconsciously, to join the others.

It seemed impossible that I was going to tolerate all that, but it was necessary. I knew that only by participating in that bestial act, that filthy and stupid deed, would I be left in peace afterwards, and that if at some time they should mention that little word to me I would be able to assert myself.

I caught up with them before they reached the brook. They were going around Nicasio's garden. I suddenly had an idea and I said, "Why don't we go in and ask Nicasio to let us catch some crabs? There are lots of them near the sluice." The boy who was leading the dog and who was the eldest— he must have been more than twelve—turned around to look at me and he stared because he suspected my intentions. I withstood his gaze with such an innocent face that I convinced him that he had made a mistake, but I had to control myself for a while as if I were engaged in a tremendous struggle, because when he had turned around he was sure that he was right. When he saw that I looked perfectly natural he said "All right, on the way back." And we went on.

We went along the highway to Jerez and there in a ravine near the road the commons began. There were various trees spaced fairly wide apart and all the boys headed for a fig tree. No, I said to myself, not on the fig tree, because I will never be able to stop myself from looking at a fig tree; let it be on another tree. And I don't know how I had the calm to tell them: "Don't go near the fig tree because the owner will raise a rumpus." They answered "But these trees don't belong to anyone!" And I, with great aplomb, assured them, "Fig trees always belong to somebody." I don't know why they believed it, but they went to an ash tree that grew in the lowest part of the field bent over as if at the water's edge. But there wasn't any water; there was only a tangle of thistles and nettles.

They began to argue about the procedure to be followed. At first they said that the best thing to do would be to tie the rope around the longest branch and then pull hard on the end. They thought that he would go up like a miller's sack on a pulley, but the rope wasn't long enough. Then they decided that two of them would climb up the tree, attach the rope and then suddenly let go. I didn't want to have anything to do with the preparations.

By this time the sun was very high and the cicadas chirped wildly about us, out from a grove of cork trees which stretched in the distance toward Jerez I heard the doves cooing with a greater sadness, with a more intense despair than ever before. I looked in that direction because I didn't want to see what they were doing, but the oldest one, who gave the orders, realized that I was trying to slip away, and, pretending to need my help, called out, "Hey you, what are you doing there?" I repeated my previous gambit and remarked as if I hadn't even heard his question: "Do you hear the dove? . . ." His inability to decide whether I was a fool or merely pretending to be one made him so angry that he turned his back on me without replying, unwilling to have anything further to do with me. What I had in mind was to seem to be there but without really noticing what was going on, and it seemed best to show by some word or action that I was watching in order to have again the opportunity to escape. Nevertheless, it turned out that I really began to pay attention to what was happening because I perceived that the dog was the most alert observer of all.

The boys were arguing, pointing alternately to him and to the tree, and the dog followed their movements as if he were accustomed to having them throw stones for him to fetch. He watched their hands when they pointed upwards and barked as a sign that he was ready to run, forgetting that he was tied up; he wagged his tail and sometimes panted a bit, showing his teeth in the semblance of a smile. They continued to argue without coming to an agreement and now and then the dog emitted a sound like "wow," just once, as if he were asking a question or saying: Come on, make up your minds.

Suddenly they lifted him up. One of them was already up in the tree and among the three of them they lifted him as high as they could. The dog continued to smile, but feeling uncomfortable and off balance, kept looking at the ground and struggling to jump. The one who was up in the branch couldn't manage to tie the knot, and declared that the rope was partly worn at the tip and that it would break with the weight. He didn't want to be to blame if they were not successful and he kept explaining all the difficulties that he found up there as if it were a very delicate job. It lasted forever. The branch couldn't have been more than three yards above the ground but the boy's voice seemed to come from very high while the cooing of the doves appeared to get louder and louder; the cork trees were far away, but the doves sounded very close to us, as if they were coming nearer. I looked, I couldn't help looking, but I did not see; I mean, I saw just their faces: everyone's and the dog's. What I had no way of knowing was whether they were beginning or finishing; whether they were going through with it or going to give it up for one reason or another; whether it was difficult, impossible, or already accomplished.

The fact is that they let go of him. Everyone stepped back. I did too, and I think I turned my back; I do know that I bent down and picked up a stick that was lying on the ground and with it struck some dry thistle, releasing a cloud of burrs. Nevertheless I saw everything. I saw that he kicked a minute when he felt himself unsupported, and with that agility that animals possess in escaping from under the wheels of a car he made a tremendous effort, trying every possible position in a matter of seconds, moving to the right, the left, up and down as if looking for something. Suddenly, he gave up the struggle and became something indefinable: he ceased to be a dog. His body looked like a sack with four sticks protruding from it and his head became the head of a monster; his smile had widened and he had opened his mouth in a kind of frenzy, as if he had finally understood.

I can't remember what the others said; I kept on hitting the weeds and the stones along the way. I could hear them making comments, but I couldn't understand them. The only thing I heard clearly was the clicking of the stones against each other when I sent them flying.

We stopped near a brook. The water was so warm that we couldn't feel it on our feet, and in the stagnant pools there was a little mud that scarcely felt solid underfoot: for a moment it seemed that I had no feet. The water came up to the middle of my calf and it was as if the part of my leg that was in the water had ceased to exist. I remained standing in the water for a long time, pretending to look for crabs. But I wasn't really looking: I was trying to think. I tried to understand why the others had done it and why I had allowed myself to become involved. Could I have said that I had not done it? Further, did I want the others to say it or didn't I? And if I had refused to go, what would they have said about me? It is certain that I would not have gone on any other day. If I had not told them about the handkerchief I would have had the courage to refuse: basically, I had gone along to defend something. . . . And at the same time it was completely idiotic to try to excuse myself as if one could make reparation for one act of cowardice by committing another.

We waited there until about noon before returning home in order to give the impression that we had just come from school. I was unconcerned when we saw some men who were coming from Jerez with some mules. One was an old man who sold grape syrup and who went through the villages accompanied by his son. They said something when they passed and the boys remarked, "We're in for it; they must have seen us and they'll tell everybody about it as soon as they can." But I didn't care: I kept sinking my feet into the mud and then I dried them on the bank and tried to put on my shoes and socks, but I couldn't get my socks on, and the sand between my toes which I had not felt before now seemed like sandpaper inside my shoes. I had to cross the village that way because my house was on the other side.

I had planned to come in as usual and at the same time I kept saying to myself: I'll put my books down in normal fashion and I won't speak until they say something to me. But I never came home that way: I always made a lot of noise and began calling my mother even before I entered the house. I arrived quietly and went in: there wasn't a soul in the dining room, and the silence was as absolute as if the house were empty. It would have been natural to go to see where my parents were, but I didn't; I simply listened for footsteps in order to be able to pretend that I had only just then come in, but when I heard them there wasn't enough time to pretend anything. I heard the steps from behind the door of my father's study and the door was opened immediately. They both emerged, one behind the other, but my mother, who came last, did not come all the way out but stayed in the doorway, holding on not to the doorframe but to the doorway itself; no: she was holding on to the air. I saw her come to an abrupt halt as if her refusal to take another step constituted a palpable barrier. My father, on the other hand, came head-on like a locomotive. He wasn't moving very fast but he appeared to be traveling along an immovable track and I was directly in his path. He didn't say a word but reached out his hand and gave me a slap which resounded exactly like a clap of thunder when lightning strikes the house. I can't say that it hurt much, I recall only the thunderous noise and the quivering of the muscles in my neck. I wasn't aware of the pain because my consciousness had diminished to the point where I imagined that I had died. It was only a second, but with the small degree of consciousness I had left I thought that I would never again return to life. It seemed that the blow had broken my spine, had severed my head from my neck, and that therefore I could not breathe. I don't know how long I remained in that state, I don't know how my feet, which no longer had any connection with my head, managed to get up the stairs and take me to my room. Nor do I remember how I dropped to the bed face down, but I do recall that my first clear thought was that the pillow still smelled of barber shop cologne. My hair had been cut two days before and the smell still persisted. When I inhaled that fragrance I regained consciousness, but only my memory returned; it was as if I had begun to remember myself, and I began to cry. I hadn't cried that way for a long time. I cried as if I were in the throes of an attack, unable to breathe as if in a fit of whooping cough; when the paroxysm was coming to an end I began to think about everything that had happened and I saw my father advance again; I buried my face in the pillow, once more starting to sob convulsively. This happened again and again. I think I cried for hours until I fell asleep. When I woke up I could tell by the light that it was late afternoon. I raised my head a little to see if I could hear anything, but there wasn't a sound; just the same enormous silence in the house as before. I listened for a while and I finally made out some footsteps that I recog-

nized at once: it was the maid coming to my room. I pretended
to be asleep; she came in and spoke to me, making it obvious
that she knew that I was awake. She leaned against the rail
of the bed and said, "Go downstairs . . . there's nobody
there." I shook my head and she continued: "Will you drink
this glass of milk?" I saw that she had left a glass on the
night table and I again began to shake my head, but she picked
up the glass and sat down on the edge of the bed. She shook
me a little saying: "Go on, drink it." I sat up and took a sip.
She asked, "Do you want me to bring you some bread?" I had
to make a tremendous effort to say no because that was exactly
what I had in mind. The milk was so good and so rich that
it left a white streak inside the glass, and I was extremely
fond of dipping bread into it—white bread, not rolls or anything sweet. Since my first sip I had been thinking constantly
of that crusty white bread that tastes so wonderful when
dipped in milk, just as it is, without sugar; but I had the
courage to say that I didn't want it and I drank the milk by
itself.

The girl made me get up and pushed me toward the door,
saying: "Go downstairs, because Mother is attending a no-
vena."

I went to the door and sat down on the stone stoop; I knew
that my father wouldn't come home until much later. I was
sitting in my usual place; the silence was immense, and in the
midst of it I thought I could distinguish the tinkle of cowbells.
The panorama that stretched before me was so extensive that
at first I couldn't see the flock, but finally I caught a glimpse
of it. By this time they were far off in the ravine and were
beginning to disappear between the hills, but when I managed
to see the last straggling lambs the cowbells became clearer
until they were swallowed up between the slopes.

It was growing dark and a dense layer of gray clouds lay

upon the horizon. At one point in the distance, however, there was a rift in the formation and the clouds above it shone luminous in the setting sun. They scarcely seemed to be moving closer and the slight changes in their configuration were very gradual; nevertheless one could not imagine them as having come into being except as the product of a spontaneous impulse; they burst forth in great puffs like steam escaping from a locomotive, and yet they were passive. They seemed full of latent power with their dynamic impulse undiminished by their tranquillity, with their brilliant crests and gray paunches, sliding evenly through space like swans gliding over the surface of the water. Then I looked about me almost without moving my head; I scrutinized everything within range, confirming the solitude of the countryside; I listened very carefully and I heard only silence, into which perhaps some sound had deposited its last trace like an almost imperceptible perfume. I remained motionless with my arms crossed and my hands hidden underneath them, understanding all of it. My only movement was to run my tongue softly over a sore on the inside of my lip, where the point of the eyetooth had broken the skin. My lip was still swollen and was bleeding a little, but the wound didn't taste only of blood, but as if new strength were coursing through my body to concentrate in that painful spot, to repair the damage. In the part of my lip directly beneath my left eyetooth I found a taste as pure as the smell of rain.

Was I thinking all this at that moment? I don't know, but what remains in my memory like a climax of clairvoyance, like a summit scaled under the influence of my quiescence and solitude, is a sort of revelation which made clear to me the clouds in their potent slowness, laden with thunderbolts; I mean that that moment still seems to me the moment when I understood pain and the taste that lightning and rain must leave on the earth.

And after having gone back with my analysis to the beginning of that disgraceful, abject day spent under the cruelty of the sun and the weeping of the doves, I realize that only that pain, that purifying thunderbolt, could have left in my mouth its springlike taste of renewal and redemption.

The Stuffed Parrot

RAFAEL DIESTE

In his Seamen's Supplies & Accessories Shop (the "accessories" included, among other things, espadrilles, overalls, fertilizers, and sulphate for vineyards), Don Ramón had a stuffed parrot. It was a forbidding looking bird, and clung by one claw to its perch, to which it was attached by a little chain as if it were a live parrot and might escape. So that those who saw it for the first time would go up to it and say:

"Polly want a cracker! . . ."

Or any of those special phrases that one must know in order to converse with a parrot.

But the bird never uttered a word. It was Don Ramón, if he was in good humor, who answered for it at times.

"What a queer bird!" the visitor or customer would then exclaim. "It talks without opening its mouth, and the sound seems to be coming from afar. It reminds me of that fellow with the top hat who came around with the circus."

"Yes, it's a ventriloquist," Don Ramón would explain.

At other times he would say:

"It's sleeping, don't bother it."

Or else:

"It just doesn't feel like talking. It's thinking, recollecting. . . . It has a right to be silent. Why don't *we* talk instead? What do you think of the new mayor?"

"Sir," a farmer who had gone in for sulphate once answered him, "I have a right to be silent."

"All right," replied Don Ramón, "then I know what you think. We agree, we agree."

One day there came in a lady who was very much like a magpie, but not a stuffed one—rather a very lively, active, and loquacious specimen. She was the mother of the new schoolmistress, and very friendly with the new mayor, as she was later with all his successors as long as she breathed. She had come to buy some cord in order to make a little net purse, to hold what we would see after a while. Thicker. No, thinner. A little thicker, please. Not *so* thick. A little thinner. And then she began to talk to the parrot. But not a word out of it.

"He's a bit sad," Don Ramón said. "Keep trying, ma'am Let's see if you can snap him out of it."

And the lady persisted:

"Darling, open your beak. The King of Portugal . . ."

Finally, Don Ramón went over to the parrot, examined it with the air of a doctor, and said, without shaking his head:

"Madam, you have come on a rather mournful occasion. Poor thing! Yes, his discourtesy was beginning to surprise me."

"What's the matter?"

"He is dead."

"Dead?"

"Dead!"

"Horrors!" shrieked the lady. "I've been talking to a dead parrot!" And she went away crossing herself.

These and other things were recounted at home. Rather, my father told them, and of course much better than I.

On certain evenings, a small social gathering would be held in the Seamen's Supplies Store. Don Ramón had been first mate of a large sailing vessel, and till the end of his sea ventures had remained loyal to sails.

"More than once I was offered the helm of an enormous luxury liner, but I didn't accept. I'm not opposed to progress, but I didn't accept."

"A luxury liner! . . . Why, there are magnificent ones, Don Ramón, real previews of the floating palaces of the year 2000. Have you seen the latest issue of *La Ilustración?*"

"I have every respect for the year 2000, but I belong to a different era. In short, I refused. And besides," he concluded, with the tone of one who is confiding halfway, but still keeping the ultimate secret to himself, "besides, in time sails will come back. I know what I'm talking about. *Sails will come back!* Huge frigates that will be able to carry one of those luxury liners we have now (though I admit they're good for rivers) in the hold of their prows without even bending their nose, or in their stern, without settling at all. Sails will still give plenty to talk about."

"I should say so!" a young pharmacy student on vacation remarked.

"Just recently I saw a very interesting study on that subject in *Alrededor del Mundo.*"

"Don't tell me about it . . ."

"Just hear what the article said. . . . It's a strange article, and yet, if one reads it carefully, one finds it's scientific. . . . It seems that now, by means of——"

"No, no, please, dear Lisardito! I've sailed for a good many years! No, really. I'm not talking nonsense. Please! I'm not talking about freaks. About toys for sailing in washbowls——"

"Nevertheless," argued Lisardito, "there are things that begin in washbowls and you should see where they end up!"

"Where do they end up? Be specific. Come on, come on, my future Doctor in Pharmacy. Where do they wind up?"

"Let's take it step by step. They begin in a washbowl . . . well, granted, there's nothing wrong with that. Now, once they begin——"

"Don't get worked up, it's useless. They begin there . . . All right, agreed, let's not repeat . . . and they never move out of there! Don't doubt it for a moment, they don't leave there. It seems as though they do, but no siree! What happens is that *we* are put *inside*. How pretty! What a world! And that's the outcome? You must have read that also in *Alrededor del Mundo*. For now they're beginning to say that the world has gotten too small for man. Oh yes, I read that article. By a Mr. _____, well, some philosopher from Chicago. One has a right to be deaf, gentlemen."

"Things are warming up here," put in a third party. "What do you have to say to that, Lisardo?"

"Well, I say that that philosopher, who incidentally is not from Chicago, but a friend of mine from La Estrada who signs his name W. T. Smith, so that he'll be published, is right to a certain extent. Naturally, he read half of what he says somewhere else, and the other half——"

"What about the other half?"

"Oh, what difference does it make?—I told him."

"Well, well, what do you know! Then *you* are the horrible philosopher? I was very eager to meet him!" shouted Don Ramón, going to get one of the oars he had for sale, and brandishing it like a lance against Lisardo. "You have put yourself in the washbowl and now you say that the world is too small. . . . Overboard, overboard with him!"

A great uproar of laughter greeted this, and suddenly some

time later there appeared another article by the same W. T. Smith, entitled "The World Is Not So Small As They Say."

"This is fine now. These fellows should be hit on the head with a yardstick. Now it turns out that I am smaller than a mosquito, a nothing, a little speck in that immensity of W.T.S.'s. Don't puff yourself up so much to say that, Mr. W.T.S. Or were *you* the cause of this, Lisardo?"

"I was to some extent, and so were you. After listening to you that night, I gave the matter some thought, and since I exchange letters with Smith, something probably filtered through."

"All right then, keep on reflecting. Do you have a sweetheart? No? Well, get one, anyone at all, without reflecting. She'll give you a rough time of it, but what of it? Who has ever heard of a philosopher without a sweetheart?"

"I'm studying pharmacy."

"Pharmacy without philosophy, philosophy without a sweetheart . . . That's the way the world goes. And you shrinking and stretching it through Smith, as you feel like inflating or deflating yourself. But I wanted to tell you the story of this parrot. It's a slight yarn but it may have depth. . . . Who would have said so when it was just an egg in the wood!"

"I see, it has a story? Let's hear!"

"Oh I don't know, I was only fooling," Don Ramón said after a brief pause, with a somewhat ambiguous gesture. "I bought it already stuffed at a country fair."

Since Don Ramón had a son of my age, named Rodrigo, who had taught me how to play checkers, on a board of his own handicraft and with equally crude cardboard men, I was allowed to attend those sessions on certain nights. There still remains in my memory the sound of gay discussions and bits of stories whose beginning and end I can't make out, though I have never given up the hope of finding out, should my old bones still chance upon some witnesses of the events, or their heirs—for they dealt with matters long past, to judge from echoes like these: At that time one had to go through the wood . . . When the High Court of the Admiralty was located here . . . Some of the castle walls were still standing . . . He went to his grave with the secret, but if you ask *me* . . . Not one remained of the family. It was a miserly estate. If it had been prosperous, some heirs would have turned up already. But there it is, without a roof, buried in brambles . . . The deceased had said so, and he was right . . .

On one of those nights on which I accompanied my father, he did not seem at all in a hurry to leave, although his cronies had departed. Rodrigo, contrary to custom, had lost at checkers. So he was terribly bored and sleepy. He and I had already run in the nearby streets and alleys, shouting in the darkened halls or frightening the cats; we had climbed to the room upstairs to take a look at the miniature brigantine that his father kept in a bell glass; the arms of the clock were approaching that hour which children generally do not see, except by daylight. And so there was no reason whatever for little Rodrigo not to go to sleep. However, he must have been very ashamed to yawn and rub his eyes while *I* was still there, on that pedestal that the late hours of night create for adults, because suddenly he imbued his retreat with a certain acrobatic, burlesque splendor, as if his adventure in departing were quite as important as mine in remaining, or perhaps even more so. His plan was perfect. First, "good night," with a farcical air. Then a deep bow. And finally a pirouette and flight, with a noisy display of speed upon entering the hallway and climbing the stairs. I smiled as if I were an accomplice.

"Don't you have any volumes of *The Customs of Mankind* around, so that Félix can entertain himself?" my father asked Don Ramón.

Our host looked under the counter and got out a volume of *The Customs of Mankind, The Arabs in Spain, Edible and Poisonous Mushrooms,* and a novel by Mayne Reid.

"Thanks, that's fine. Don't trouble any more; these are plenty," said my father.

But Don Ramón pulled out still another book and said, slapping it: "This one is *very* good. *Nautical Guide.* Let him look at the chapter on knots and hitches. A lad should know how to tie and untie. . . . Anyway, read whatever you like, Félix. That book by Mayne Reid is good too, though at times he tangles things up and unwinds them at will."

I thanked him for his advice and began to look at the pictures of *Edible and Poisonous Mushrooms,* feeling a very peculiar uneasiness before the beautiful disguise of certain poisonous ones—just look at that *Hypholoma fasciculari!*—and the harmless look of some edible ones: like that awful *Periza amantia.*

The street was silent and dark. The howl of a dog was heard from various directions and distances, and finally ceased. I had passed from mushrooms to the customs of mankind, to head hunters. And as I left the Court of the Lions, I realized that it was not the gurgle of a fountain that I was hearing, but rather what my father and Don Ramón were saying in low tones. I raised my eyes and saw that they had gone to sit out in the open, near the door. I remained in my place, trying not to listen and even muttering the captions of the illustrations in order to maintain inviolable the zone of my attention. Perhaps that is why I heard it all with such amazing clarity. . . .

"No, no, Manuel. How could you think that I would confide any secret to Lisardito? I was just tempted to open up a path through which he could see how difficult it is to measure the world. And besides, when a man has kept certain things within him for a long time, they begin to bother him. And in my case, even more, because I'm so open naturally. But that wasn't the right time. Lisardo is a good, wholesome fellow, but that type can't be trusted in certain matters. They would give him the chills; he would make some benevolent comment; but I would then become a character from his nightmares."

"You don't distrust his discretion, do you?"

"What I distrust is his fortitude. He can hold but a very light load, Manuel. Just put some more on him, and you'll see. . . . Before he capsizes, he throws everything overboard."

"Is the matter so weighty?"

"How should I know? Up till now I have withstood it and kept it to myself, without asking anyone to lend a hand."

"Not even Rosa?"

"Rosa? I generally don't tell my wife any more truth than she can stand. If you throw that weight on her, it will knock her down, and then see what help it is: the load is intact, and you have *her* on top to carry on your back. No, no . . . I offer her the best room in my house. There's no doubt about it, she has it easy with me and can go about with full confidence. And everything else, hushed up. Naturally, at times there are blind alleys, walls that sound hollow to her. And that stuffed parrot fascinates her; I see that it intrigues her because she doesn't ask. . . . And she does well there: she protects herself."

"To tell the truth, Don Ramón," my father said, "I don't protect myself, but neither do I ask any questions. I thought it was merely something picturesque, one of those many sea yarns that you tell. But why talk about it any more? If you feel that it will do you good to tell me, I'm listening. And if not . . ."

"How old is your boy?" Don Ramón asked, lowering his voice.

"Twelve, like yours, I think; a few months difference more or less. He's very fond of reading, and quite intelligent, but he's not at all clever."

"And his memory?"

"He says that he remembers when he was baptized. Nonsense. Nevertheless, at times he tells of things that seem impossible for him to be able to recall; and when I look back, I realize that they did happen. But he is very bad on errands. He goes for camphor and brings back sugar. He goes for sugar and brings back a stamped envelope. Fortunately, one always needs those things."

"Are you amusing yourself?" Don Ramón asked me suddenly, raising his voice.

"Very much!" I answered, terrified.

They must have deduced from my start that I was very absorbed. The fact is that Don Ramón then peered cautiously onto the street, as if with my presence disregarded as being too innocent, he suspected some possible espionage; but he apparently did not discover any old woman lurking near the wall, for he sat down again with the utmost tranquillity. But then, as if it were unbecoming or embarrassing to tell it seated, he stood up again, and so did my father. The story continued on out to the sidewalk; paused in the middle of the store, was submerged a bit in the shadow of the hallway, and finally settled down at the climax of the tale, since both were once more seated—this time not on chairs, but on bales, and whether by chance or by involuntary gravitation, under the presidency of the dead parrot.

I remember very well what Don Ramón related then; and, told as far as possible in his words, it was the following:

"After that we changed our route, and for two years I didn't touch at Antwerp again. So I couldn't fulfill my promise. It wasn't easy to write to her, and I hadn't left any mediator between us. It isn't in my nature, and even less under those circumstances. In short, she didn't hear from me during all that time, nor I from her, although I'm sure she remembered me. And that's not boasting. I'm too old and hardened now to let vanity matter. I remembered her too, and I still remember her, although she doesn't hold a candle to my wife. No, sir, not at all. I can say so truthfully. If it were otherwise, I would say so also, my dear Manuel. To return to the story, and to finish up the background, I'll say only that he was still a tyrant."

"What do you mean?"

"Well, I don't understand it myself. . . . He frightened people. . . . They weren't married, but he kept her with him, and she served to attract guests. She was beautiful. And what a voice! Believe me, Manuel, just to see her and hear her, it was worth remaining there and finding the room satisfactory, even though it was a hole. One would say: 'Isn't there a higher room, with windows and slightly larger?' 'Perhaps tomorrow or the next day,' she would answer. . . . Well, you stayed, even if it meant sleeping on a couch, temporarily or the whole year. But don't get any wrong impressions. In the first place, *he* was there, with his small eyes and thin lips and his gray, cropped head, always smiling to the customers, even with certain indulgent winks, but fierce somber inside when giving orders, or even as soon as he turned his back. I noticed it for the first time in a mirror. He had just made me a bow, and when he turned around, his face was completely changed. But it was an interesting thing, because the moment he felt himself observed, he again bowed to me from the depths of the mirror. I don't know whether I read it in Mayne Reid, but he seemed like a skull that greets you from the depths of a well. Now, to the story: She was gorgeous, and you stayed on. But no illusions. As I said, he was there, vigilant and austere, but besides, *she* wasn't frivolous. She was waiting for love, that's all. And as soon as one looked at her with the air of a conqueror, she continued to be polite, but turned into marble. I'm sure that she was marble with *him,* too. No, he had no reason to fear phantoms. What he feared was a man. *the* man. What he feared was something serious and splendid: that there could develop a real love. That, I am sure, terrified him, reduced him to dust, to cobwebs. And I know I didn't read that anywhere. I saw it. I saw it just as clearly as he saw me and feared me, even though I didn't assume any conquering airs, nor any kind of insolence or studied gallantry at all. To a certain extent, *he* had been the conqueror, if deception is conquest. He had committed the fraud of wooing just to glory in a splendid 'catch.' And it was she who later refused to get married. He did want to, or rather, sometimes he did and sometimes he didn't. . . ."

"Why did she stay with him, then?"

"How should I know? It was a struggle. Perhaps it was a penance that she imposed on herself. Maybe it was fear. Oh, it probably was for no reason in particular. But I have also thought this at times: that she was waiting for the man, the true love that redeems one from fear, in order to tell the other, the ghost: 'So, now you see he exists. Here he is. Kill me if you wish. . . .' "

Don Ramón was silent for a moment. Then he began to say, hesitantly:

"I don't know exactly what I was saying. She doesn't compare with my wife, believe me. I know. Now then, the fact is that she was murdered. I'm losing the thread of the story. Well, I was saying that we changed course, and two years later . . . Don't worry, Manuel. It's nothing. When I recall these things and begin to think about them there always comes a point at which my mind runs away with itself. Anyway, it's all over. Now we have something to laugh about a little. But not much. We arrived at Antwerp. A friend of mine had gone ashore before me, and towards nightfall, as I was heading into that square, not far from the port, where the Cathedral is, I came across him, and he said: 'Something very odd just happened to me; it's really funny, although it certainly is weird. I was passing by a hotel which used to have a café and bar on the ground floor, and with which I was already familiar from other voyages; I remembered an extremely beautiful girl I had seen there and of whom I never could find out whether she was the proprietor's wife, maid, or sister—though I don't think she was his sister, because they didn't look at all alike—and it occurred to me to go inside. I pushed the French door open, the little bell rang, I closed it again, and found myself alone. Everything looked rather dilapidated. Dust on the tables, very few bottles in the showcases, very little light, and nobody there. But then I heard a woman's voice, and because of the sweet inflection and a certain singsong that were familiar to me, I said: this is she. The voice sounded somewhat deteriorated, but it said the usual thing: "Passez, messieurs et dames, passez." Actually I did go in, but no one appeared. And the voice persisted: "Messieurs et dames, passez. En avant, s'il vous plaît. Merci beaucoup. Au revoir." To whom was it saying good-bye? "En avant, s'il vous plaît." 'I kept on advancing,' said my companion, 'until I began to get uneasy and then I discovered something that almost made me burst out laughing: a parrot. And how well I knew that parrot! It must be a century old and surely is one of the founding fathers of the house! And almost at the same time, along comes the proprietor, in mourning, and a little yellower than usual, and he says to me: "Excuse me, sir, but we aren't serving. We haven't been for some time now." "Excuse *me*, sir, I didn't know. And do you still take guests?" "Oh, no sir, it isn't possible. Since my wife died, things started going badly. We couldn't attend to it ourselves. So we don't serve any more." "Oh, she died? I'm sorry. An excellent woman.

Well . . . wouldn't it be better to close the door and take the sign off? Otherwise you'll be bothered a great deal." "J'attends quelqu'un." And right away he smiled sweetly, with his mouth very sad and wide, and concluded: "Mais pas à vous, monsieur." '

"In view of the fact that *he* wasn't the one whom the proprietor was expecting, my companion went away, and the parrot still kept up its annoying repitition:

" 'Passez, messieurs et dames. En avant, s'il vous plaît.'

"Do you follow me, Manuel? What would you have done? But I'm talking nonsense. Anyone knows what *you* would have done. But not even I knew what I was going to do. I told my friend that, indeed, it was really funny and of course quite weird, and I continued on my way and he on his. I don't generally carry weapons. That one belonged, to a certain extent, to my job. A sailor's jacknife. I didn't intend to use it, but something told me to open it in my pocket. It comes in handy in certain situations, at least to give someone a scare, if need be. Since I was not thinking about anything, I can't say that my thoughts or any purpose brought me there. I shivered a little with surprise when the bell rang. It sounded just as before. And the door heaved a squeak from its rusty hinges, just as before. And what my shipmate had said was accurate in every detail.

" 'Passez, messieurs et mesdames, passez. En avant, s'il vous plaît.'

"That imitation made me furious. And each time it said 'passez' I moved forward with increasing rage. The proprietor appeared. He looked at me and said very quickly:

" 'Soyez le bienvenu, monsieur.'

"There was no doubt that it was I whom he was awaiting. And then, with a mournful air, his fingers entwined on his chest, he moaned:

" 'Elle est morte. Ma femme est morte.'

"How is it possible, Manuel? Do you understand? I am sure that he smiled.

" 'Elle est morte.'

"I understood him perfectly.

"He meant: I killed her. She is my exclusive possession. And now you are going to know me. (That's what that man wanted—to be known).

" 'Asseyez-vous, monsieur. Voulez-vous quelque chose? Depuis qu'elle est morte . . . Mais pour vous il y a toujours quelque chose. Un petit moment. Pardon.'

"And then he disappeared. I sat down, and he reappeared almost immediately. I saw a blade gleam behind his sleeve. I let him approach. I looked only at his face, and when his smile was sufficiently odious and significant, before he struck, I had already defended myself. . . . I remained seated as I was, with him at my feet. And then something unforgettable occurred—the most grotesque thing that ever happened in my life. The parrot had kept a respectful silence until that moment. But suddenly, when I raised my head, it said, as if it were choking:

" 'Merci beaucoup!' "

Don Ramón said this so well that I almost broke forth in a loud guffaw. . . . It took a tremendous effort to control myself, for I understood that it wasn't a laughing matter, and of course Don Ramón was livid.

"Then," he said, after a pause, "I got the wild notion of stealing the parrot. I put it into a little luncheon cloth that was on the table, and, tying the four ends well so that it couldn't move or mutter, I returned to the ship. We sailed on the following day. I deliberately avoided reading the newspapers. And now comes the second crime. How long do you think a man can stand a parrot that keeps repeating 'merci beaucoup'? So, one very calm, moonlit night, I took it out of my cabin, tied it to the mast of the prow, and shot it, using a small air rifle with which we used to amuse ourselves at target practice once in a while. If you look carefully, you can discover where the bullet went in and out. We were already very close to port, and so it could arrive intact, and I immediately had it stuffed. And there it is. . . ."

But suddenly Don Ramón looked at me; my mouth and eyes were wide open, and he asked my father, rather alarmed:

"Does the boy know French?"

"Very little, just a few words I taught him."

Don Ramón lowered his head, and I noticed that he looked at my father out of the corner of his eye.

Well, they finally took leave of each other. I remember that my father, who was not accustomed to such familiarities with anyone, placed his hand on his friend's shoulder, and said to him:

"See you tomorrow, Ramón."

Then, instead of walking towards home, he set off in the opposite direction. We walked a mile or so without uttering a word. We passed between great masses of pine trees, far from town, and for the first time he spoke, to ask me:

"Are you afraid?"

"Not with *you*."

"And alone?"

"We'll see."

We kept on walking in silence. In a large clearing I thought I saw the fleeting shadow of a fox.

"Were you listening to what Don Ramón said?"

"Somewhat, without meaning to."

"Well, did you understand?"

"Yes."

We began to walk again, this time homeward bound. Half-way along the road my father said:

"Don Ramón is my lifelong friend, since school days."

I answered simply:

"I won't say anything."

When we arrived at the door of our house Father offered me his hand, for the first time in his life, as to an adult. And I didn't know what to do at first. But then I clasped his too. Like Don Ramón.

The Return

CARMEN LAFORET

It was a bad idea, thought Julian as he pressed his forehead against the windowpane and felt the wet cold go right through to the bones that stood out so clearly under his transparent skin. It was a bad idea, sending him home for Christmas. Besides, they were sending him home for good; he was completely cured.

Julian was a tall man, encased in a nice black overcoat. He was blond, with prominent eyes and cheekbones that emphasized his thinness. But Julian was looking well these days. His wife marveled how well he looked every time she visited him. There was a time when Julian had been a handful of blue veins, legs like long sticks and big gnarled hands. That was two years ago when they committed him to the institution, which, strangely enough, he was reluctant to leave.

"Very impatient, aren't you? They'll be coming for you soon. The four o'clock train is due very shortly and you'll be able to take the five-thirty back. And tonight you will be home, celebrating Christmas Eve. . . . Julian, please do not forget to take your family to midnight Mass, as an act of grace. . . . If our House weren't so far away . . . It would be pleasant to have all of you here tonight. . . . Your children are very handsome, Julian, especially the youngest; he looks like a Christ Child, or a little Saint John, with his curls and blue eyes. I think he would make a fine acolyte, because he has a very bright face. . . ."

Julian listened to the nun's prattle in adoration. Julian loved Sister María de la Asunción very much, for she was fat and short with a smiling face and cheeks like apples. Waiting in that enormous forbidding visitors' room, ready for departure and plunged in thought, he had not heard her footsteps. . . . He had not heard her come in, because the nuns, despite their tiers of skirts and their wimples, have a tread as light and silent as a sailboat. But when he noticed her, his heart jumped with joy. The last joy he would derive from this stage of his life. His eyes filled with tears; he had always been inclined to sentimentality, but now it was almost a disease.

"Sister María de la Asunción . . . I should like to attend midnight Mass here with you this year. I think it would be all right if I stayed here until tomorrow. It would be enough to be with my family on Christmas Day. In a certain sense, you are also my family. I . . . I am very grateful to all of you."

"Don't be foolish; that is impossible. Your wife is waiting for you right now. As soon as you have rejoined your family and are working, you will forget all this; it will be like a dream. . . ."

Then Sister María de la Asunción left too, and Julian felt dejected again, for he did not like leaving the asylum. It was a place of death and despair, but for him it had been a place of refuge, of salvation. . . . And even the last few months, when the authorities felt he had fully recovered, it had been a place of happiness. They had even let him drive! And not just going through the motions. He had driven the Mother Superior herself and Sister María de la Asunción to the city to do some shopping. And Julian knew how brave these women had been, putting themselves like that into the hands of a lunatic . . . or a former lunatic: he had once been considered dangerous. But he did not disappoint them. The car had run perfectly under his expert control. The nuns had not even been shaken by the deep ruts in the road. When they got back, they congratulated him and he had felt himself blushing.

"Julian . . ."

Sister Rosa was standing in front of him, the nun with the round eyes and oval mouth. He did not like Sister Rosa very much; in fact, he did not like her at all. And he could not understand why. At the beginning, he was told, they had been obliged to put him into a strait jacket more than once for having tried to attack her. Sister Rosa always seemed frightened of Julian. Now, suddenly, as he gazed at her, he realized whom she resembled. She resembled poor Herminia, his wife whom he loved so much. Life was so full of puzzles. Sister Rosa looked like Herminia, and yet, perhaps because of that, Julian could not abide her.

"Julian, a call for you. Will you come to the phone? Mother asked me to tell you to answer it."

"Mother" was the Mother Superior herself. They all called her that. It was an honor for Julian to answer the telephone.

It was Herminia on the line, asking him in a shaky voice to take the train by himself, if he didn't mind.

"Your mother is not feeling well; no, nothing serious— another of her liver attacks. . . . But I didn't dare leave her alone with the children. I couldn't call you earlier; she was in too much pain and I couldn't go out. . . ."

Julian still held the phone in his hand, but he was no longer thinking about his family. All he could think of was that he would have an opportunity to stay here for the night; that he would help them light the lights before the shrine of the Nativity, he would have a wonderful Christmas Eve dinner and sing carols with the rest of them. It all meant so much to Julian.

"Then I'll probably come tomorrow. Don't be frightened. No, nothing wrong; but since you are not coming, I thought I would help the sisters a bit; they have so much to do at Christmas time. Yes, I'll be there for dinner sure. . . . Yes, I'll be home for Christmas Day."

Sister Rosa was at his side, staring at him with her round eyes and oval mouth. She was the only unpleasantness he was glad to be leaving forever. . . . Julian lowered his eyes and humbly requested an audience with "Mother"; he wanted to ask her a special favor.

The next day, Julian was riding in a train through a gray sleet on his way to the city. In a third-class coach he was wedged in between turkeys, chickens and their owners, all bursting with optimism. All of Julian's property that morning consisted of a battered suitcase and the good black-dyed overcoat that kept him pleasantly warm. As they approached the city, as its smell struck his nostrils and he looked out upon the enormous rows of depressing factories and workmen's flats, Julian began to feel he had had no right to enjoy himself so fully the evening before; he should not have eaten so much of so many choice things; he should not have sung in the voice which, during the war, had helped the other soldiers in the trenches through long hours of boredom and sadness.

Julian felt he should not have spent such a warm, cozy Christmas Eve, because for several years now they had had no such celebrations at home. Poor Herminia had probably managed some shapeless nougats made of sweet-potato paste and painted in gay colors, and the children had spent half an hour chewing on them eagerly after an everyday dinner. At least, that is what had happened the last Christmas Eve he had spent at home. He had been out of work for months. He had always been a good provider, but then came the gasoline shortage and things came to a standstill. Herminia scrubbed stairs. She scrubbed countless stairs every day until the poor thing couldn't talk of anything but stairs and the food she could not buy. At the time Herminia was pregnant again and her appetite was something terrific. She was a thin woman, as tall and blonde as Julian; she was easy-going and wore thick glasses despite her youth. . . . Julian could not swallow his own food as he watched her devour her watery soup and sweet potatoes. Watery soup and sweet potatoes: that was what they ate every day at Julian's house all that winter, morning and evening. Breakfast was only for the children. Herminia looked greedily at the hot bluish milk they drank before going off to school. . . . Julian, who, according to his family, had always been a glutton, left off eating entirely. . . . But that was much worse for everybody, because his mind started to go and he became aggressive. Then he began imagining that his poor flat was a garage and that the beds crammed into all the rooms were luxurious automobiles. And one day he tried to kill Herminia and his mother, and they had to drag him out in a strait jacket. . . . But all that was part of the past. The relatively recent past. Now he was going back, completely recovered. He had been fine for several months now. But the nuns had sympathized with him and let him linger on a little while longer, just a little while . . . until the Christmas holidays. Suddenly he realized what a coward he had been, putting it off. The streets leading home were full of brilliantly lighted shop windows. He stopped at a pastry shop and bought a tart. He had some money and spent it on that. He had eaten so many the last few days that it did not tempt him, but his family would not feel that way.

It was not easy, climbing the stairs to his flat, his suitcase in one hand, the sweet in the other. It was very high up and he was eager to see them all, to kiss his mother, the old lady who always smiled and pretended nothing was the matter so long as her pains were not too bad.

There were four doors, formerly green, now nondescript. One of them was his. He knocked.

He was in Herminia's skinny arms; the children were shouting. A pleasant smell wafted in from the kitchen. Something good was cooking.

"Papa, we've got turkey!"

That was the first thing they told him. He looked at his wife. He looked at his mother; she had aged greatly and was very pale from her last illness, but she had a nice new woolen shawl over her shoulders. The little dining room boasted a basket brimful of sweets, gewgaws and ribbons.

"Did you win the lottery?"

"No, Julian, when you went off, some ladies came. . . . From a welfare organization, you know. . . . They took good care of us; they found me work and they are going to get you a job too, in a garage."

In a garage? Of course, a former madman could not be a taxi driver. A mechanic, perhaps. Julian gazed at his mother again and saw her eyes were full of tears. . . . But she was smiling, smiling as always.

Suddenly Julian felt his shoulders sag again under a load of responsibilities and worries. He had come back to the large family standing around him and it was his business to rescue them from the clutches of Charity. They would go hungry again, of course. . . .

"But Julian, aren't you glad? . . . We're all together again, all together at Christmas. . . . And what a Christmas we're going to have! Look!"

And again they pointed to the gift basket, to the children eager and wide-eyed. They were doing it for his benefit as he stood there, a sad, thin man with bulging eyes and a black overcoat. And it was as if he had left childhood behind again that Christmas Day so that he might look once more upon life —with all the cruelty that, beneath those gifts, it would have forever.

In the Trenches

ANTONIO SÁNCHEZ BARBUDO

In Sector X, as in many others, the network of the trenches is a veritable labyrinth. You come first to a house in a grove, a hospitable looking house, clean, with flowers in pots around it; then you progress into a small square formed by thick-topped trees and the still erect walls of an old ruined building, walls which gape with empty windows. There is still a hall almost intact. Here you can see beds lined up, with soldiers sleeping in them. And in this same hall there is a great hole, a dark mouth opening down into the earth, through which you descend by a rude ladderway; this is the entrance to the trenches.

The network of trenches is a world in itself, a world apart, closed in and shadowed. A world in the earth, within and near danger, close to death and anguished in waiting, close to noise and silence. Here no one can forget. The war seeps into your pores. It is a threatening language of fire, a watchful waiting. *They* are there, they are very near; you can hear their steps and their voices. And we are here, comrades, together, united against them.

War is stark and unsheathed in the trenches. It is found in the smallest pulsations. It extends throughout the excavations, taking diverse forms and colors and adopting the strangest noises. War and death lurk behind embrasures or hide themselves in shadowy corners.

There are parts of the trenches that are covered, rigid and impregnable, and there are deep circular caves, illumined by a tenuous light; there are narrow communicating ditches and nooks in the sodden earth where silent ruddy lamps glow as in a corridor of fear. There are places where glory is overhead, open trenches protected by sandbags, very near to the flight of the birds, which fear the sudden shooting.

It is more agreeable, naturally, to stay in the open trenches; but nevertheless it is in the covered parts that one must stay most of the time; their loopholes dominate the dangerous areas.

In the trenches, glued to the earth, almost invisible, quiet as saints in their vaulted niches, are the soldiers; each one at his post, watchful, silent, vigilant. In the dimness the light from the opening glimmers over the sentinel with his gun, a green light of the savage forest, with its quiet branches, trunks, and leaves, and its mysteries. The spirit of the woods is in the light, the singing, imprisoned light, the pulsating light.

The sentinel scrutinizes once more the familiar details around him. He leans over to one side to see a piece of sky and waits, everlastingly waits. You pass by and salute him; he salutes you also with an earthy voice, the natural voice of a strange world. He himself seems to be earth, glued there. Who is he? It could be Mariano, someone, anyone. A few yards further on you see another sentry, also silent, who smokes calmly and watches. You salute him and he salutes you; then another, another, another. . . .

Joaquín García had been lucky, as luck went in this place. His sentry post was a better one than many others. Over on his left, the covered trench had some openings large enough for a little light to enter, light which, before coming to the trenches, first passed over a few small shrubs and grasses which grew in the crevices, a greenish, subtle, placid light, which gave to this portion of the crooked trench a poetic repose, the enchantment of a walled garden, a Velázquez-like mystery of enchanted space. The slender shoots and the leaves of the tender plants seen in this half-light of the sun had a sheen and a splendor which spoke of the open air and song. On the opposite side, the trench was darker.

To contemplate the lamp which was a few steps from him, with its frosted glass and its silent deadened light, produced in Joaquín a deep melancholy. In vain he tried to go on looking at the lamp, which, deadened as it was, yet had a heart of fire in the incandescent red filaments. He looked at the quiet green light outside to console himself.

A light crackling in the woods brought him out of his abstraction; he gripped his gun tightly and searched the familiar tangle with his eyes. His will was tense, his imagination did not wander; Joaquín was now an automaton, a man wholly given over to his duty. He was a machine. Still he did not shoot. He had learned to control himself, and this exercise in coolness pleased him. He heard nothing; the tension of his nerves, his fixed gaze, now relaxed again; he glanced at the fallen trees, the trunks, the intertwined branches, the high sun-lit leaves. The sun shone on some points, on others there was a river of shadows as it grew late in the evening; but the whole was alive, luminous as a great Impressionist painting transformed into reality and space, totality and life. It was the way his little window framed the countryside that led Joaquín to think of it as a picture. And this frame aided in understanding, in essence, the way that life is circumscribed. Of course this was only a manner of thinking, for you cannot shut life into a frame; but Joaquín, as we have seen, all alone with himself and his watching, was able to understand life better by imagining the frame and putting it there. He could ignore the rest of life for a moment, could limit reality to a certain defined plane, and could find it and identify it. The countryside thus confined was an indefinable marvel to him, and, although he was unaware of it, prayers and ballads rose from his closed lips and from his eyes, prayers and ballads which he sang to life, to beauty and to the mysterious force which animates living.

In the exact center of the scene, there was a scorched automobile riddled with bulletholes. In the interior of it were the remains of a rebel commandant who had died here months before in the days when the Madrid front was immobilized. Through the window of the car you could see the bald head and pieces of uniform covering the skeleton. The automobile, mired in the earth and almost covered by branches, was a symbol of fatality. It was in no man's land, and no man could retrieve it from there.

When Joaquín heard the noise in the little sector which was assigned to him to guard from his peephole, he looked instinctively and first of all at the automobile, for it seemed to him that it would be from there that whatever menaced him would come. At times, during his daydreams and meditations, half asleep, Joaquín had seen or imagined that he saw the commandant fully dressed in gold braid and ribbons; he saw him get up and, with an imperious command, threaten someone with his riding crop. Intimidated men followed him in black tricornes or black cassocks. The commandant yelled and the ends of his mustache quivered; and they all watched him in terror, hidden behind the trees. But Joaquín was there, aiming with his gun. And suddenly, like a great dream, a wind would blow over from the village, and they were routed; everything crumbled, the shadows disappeared, the soldiers would not obey, the fascists fell, and the commandant, whose color changed, dropped his crop, sank silently in the automobile and died there. There was his corpse still.

Joaquín felt a certain kinship with those human remains, shameful as it was to confess it. He would have killed the commandant without compunction a thousand times as if he were truly alive before him or had truly risen from the dead; but this skeleton, the death and silence fallen here, were part of Joaquín and belonged to him.

Again a sudden noise made him whirl around and fiercely scan the auto, the trunks of the trees, the ground around him. There was no doubt; someone had spoken, had seemed to call him. Someone was crawling over the ground. "No, not yet," he murmured; "let's wait and see who it is." His finger caressed the trigger and his knee pressed the box in which the hand grenades were kept. There was the noise again, yes, near the auto. Joaquín looked for a second time at the immobile head of the commandant, with its petrified laugh, its grimace of abandon.

Suddenly something happened. The noise became distinguishable and there appeared behind the automobile, back of a wheel, an arm and then a head, and then an entire trunk. Joaquín still held his shot, sure of himself, and waited; he could kill him as soon as he wished with a single shot at the head.

"It is the commandant," he thought; "the commandant has escaped and is crawling under the auto."

Then his will, always so firm and disciplined in action, became suddenly paralyzed. He wanted to shoot, but he could not. It was not the commandant; it was he himself, Joaquín, who was in front of him, coming towards him.

"Do not shoot," the figure cried, advancing, terror-stricken.

Joaquín was unable to understand. He looked at the man fixedly, without relaxing his aim.

It was himself, yes. It was his death-kin who was coming. . . . There was the uniform . . . but no, it was a living man who was approaching Joaquín.

"Comrade, do not shoot," the fugitive cried out; and he ran quickly, his eyes fearful and his arms upraised.

A shot from the other lines brought Joaquín out of his stupefaction.

"Here, over here," he called from the trenches of the Republicans.

The soldier, dazed and distraught, ran from one side to the other. Many shots rang out. "If this had happened in the dark of night I would have killed him," Joaquín told himself, aloud.

The soldier threw himself to the ground, and finally saw a hole newly blasted by dynamiters. He got there, crawling, and threw himself in, head first. Joaquín then heard voices and happy laughs around him in the trenches. The machine gun sounded in front of him. He shot his gun off too, responding happily.

"Ha! How mad they are!" he murmured between his teeth, smiling.

He thought that he must go over quickly to see the fugitive, the man who had escaped through the enemy lines, and embrace him. But now he was shooting, methodically. And at times he looked at the automobile and the branches of the trees, and it seemed that he could look at the skeleton plainly, as if freed of a nightmare. The dead man was there, but his brother in Death, his living comrade, had come. A phantom had flown.

The Launch

MAX AUB

He said he was born in Bermeo, but the truth was that he came
from a little town across the mouth of the Mundaca river, a
settlement which was known by no name, or by many names,
which is the same thing. The beaches and cliffs of this area
were all that he knew of the world. For him, the Machichaco,
Potorroari and Uguerriz marked Ultima Thule; for him, Sol-
lube was Olympus; Bermeo, Paris; and the Atalaya mall, the
Elysian Fields. The wide expanse of his world, his Sahara, was
the Laida, and the end of his world to the east was the steep,
flat-topped, reddish Ogoño. Beyond was Elanchove and the
gentlemen of Lequeitio, in hell. His mother was the daughter
of an overseer in an arms factory in Guernica. His father was
a miner from Matamoros: he did not live long. They called
him "El Chirto," perhaps because he was half crazy. When he
became ill he left the Franco-Belgian mines of Somorrostro,
and went to work in a sawmill factory. There, among the wood-

479

planing and dovetailing machines, Erramón Churrimendi grew up.

He was fond of the little steamboats, the tunny boats, the pretty little sardine fishing smacks; the fishing tackle: the trotlines, the sieves, the fish traps, the nets. The world was the sea, and the only living beings were the hake, the eels, the sea bass, and the tunny. And he loved to catch moving fish in the water with a deep fisherman's net, to fish for anchovies and sardines with a light, or at dusk; and to catch the bonito and tuna with a spinning tackle.

But he no sooner put his feet in a boat than he became sea-sick. And there was nothing he could do about it. He tried all the official medicines, and all the recondite ones, and all advice, spoken and whispered. He followed the advice of Don Pablo, of the drugstore, of Don Saturnio, of the City Council; of Cándida, Don Timoteo's maid; of the doctor from Zarauz, who was a native of Bermeo. To no avail. He had only to put one foot in a boat, and he became seasick. He tried a hundred stratagems: he would get aboard on an empty stomach, or after a good breakfast, sober, or drunk, or without having slept; he even tried the magic cures of Sebastiana, the woman from the edge of town; he tried crosses, lemons, the right foot, the left foot, at 7:00 A.M. on the dot, at low tide and at high tide, on the right day of the week. He went after Mass, after several "Our Fathers," and he tried pure will power and even in his sleep he heard: "I'll never be seasick again, I'll never be seasick again. . . ." But nothing helped. As soon as he put his foot on a moving plank, his insides turned round and round, he lost all sense of balance, and he was forced to huddle in the corner of the boat to keep out of the others' way, hoping to stay unnoticed. He spent some terrible moments. But he was not among those who despair, and for many years he repeatedly dared the adventure. Because, naturally, the people were laughing at him—not much, but they were laughing at him. He took to wine. What else could he do? Chacolí wine is a remedy. Erramón never married, the idea never even occurred to him. Who would marry him? He was a good man. Everyone admitted that. He was not even guilty of anything. But he got seasick. The sea made sport of him, and without any right.

He slept in a cabin by the estuary. It belonged to him. There was a beautiful oak there—if I say *there was,* it's for a good reason. It *was* really a splendid tree, with a tall trunk and high branches. A tree the likes of which there are not many. It was his tree, and every day, every morning, every evening, on passing by, the man would touch it as if it were a horse's croup or the side of a beautiful woman. Sometimes he even spoke to it. It seemed to him that the bark was warm and that the tree was grateful to him. The roughness of the tree perfectly matched the rough skin on the man's hand. There was a perfect understanding between him and the tree.

Erramón was a methodical man. So long as there was variety in his work he did whatever he was asked, willingly and tidily. He was asked to do a hundred odd chores: to repair nets, to dig, to help in the sawmill, which had been his father's; to him it was all the same whether he raised a thatch or calked, or earned his few pesetas by helping to bring in the fish. He never said no to anything. Erramón also sang, and sang well. He was greatly respected in the tavern. One of his Basque songs went something like this:

> *All the Basques are alike.*
> *All save one.*
> *And what's the matter with that one?*
> *That's Erramón.*
> *And he's like all the rest.*

One night Erramón dreamed that he was not seasick. He was alone in a little boat, far out on the sea. He could see the coastline clearly in the distance. Only the red Ogoño shone like a fake sun which was sinking in the middle of the earth. Erramón was happier than he had ever been in his life. He lay down in the bottom of the boat and began to watch the clouds. He could feel the incessant rocking motion of the sea. The clouds were flying swiftly by, pushed by a wind which greeted him without stopping; and the circling sea gulls were shouting his welcome:

"Erramón, Erramón!"

And again:

"Erramón, Erramón!"

The clouds were like lace doves. Erramón closed his eyes. He was on the water and he was not seasick. The waves rocked him in their hammock back and forth, back and forth, up and down, in a sweet cradling motion. All his youth was about his neck, and yet, at that moment, Erramón had no memories, no other desire than to continue forever just as he was. He caressed the sides of his boat. Suddenly his hands were speaking to him. Erramón raised his head in surprise. He was not mistaken! His boat was made of the wood of his oak tree!

So shocking was the effect that he woke up.

From that moment on, Erramón's life began to change completely. It entered his head that if he made a boat out of his tree he would never again become seasick. In order to prevent himself from committing this crime, he drank more chacolí than usual; but he could not sleep. He turned over and over in his bed, hounded by the stars. He listened to his dream. He tried to convince himself of the absurdity of all this:

"If I've always been seasick, I'll continue being seasick."

He turned over on his left side.

He got up to look at his tree, and caressed it.

"Will I end by winning or losing?"

But deep inside he knew he should not do it, that it would be a crime. Was it his tree's fault that he got seasick? But Erramón could not resist the temptation for long. One morning he himself, aided by Ignacio, the one from the sawmill, cut down the tree. When the tree fell, Erramón felt very sad and alone as if the most beloved member of his family had died. It was hard for him now to recognize his cabin, it was so lonely. Only with his back to it, facing the estuary, did he feel easy.

Every afternoon he went to see how his tree was changing into a boat. This took place on the beach where his friend Santiago, the boatwright, was building it. The whole thing was made of the trunk; the keel, the floor timbers, the frame, the stem, the beams, even the seats and the oars, and a mast, just in case.

And so it was that one August morning when the sea did not seem like one, it was so calm, Erramón plowed outward on it with his new boat. It was a marvelous boat, it flew at the slightest urging of the man; he dipped the oars gently, throwing back his shoulders before he slightly contracted his arms, which made the boat fly. For the first time Erramón felt drunk, ecstatic. He drew away from the shore. He dipped the right oar a few times to make a turn, then the other in order to zigzag through the water. Then he drew the oars in and began to caress the wood of his boat. Slowly, the boards were letting in a little water. Erramón raised his hands to his forehead to dampen it a little. The silence was absolute; not a cloud, not a breeze, not even a sea gull. The land had disappeared, submerged. Erramón put his hands on the gunwale to caress it. Again he removed his hands wet. He was a little surprised: splashes on the wood had long since dried in the sun. He glanced over the inside of the boat: from every part water was slowly seeping in. On the bottom there was already a small puddle. Erramón did not know what to do. Again he passed his hands over the sides of his boat. There was no question about it; the wood was gradually letting water in. Erramón looked around; a slight uneasiness was beginning to gnaw his stomach. He had himself helped in calking the boat and was sure that the work had been well done. He bent down to inspect the seams: they were dry. It was the wood that was letting the water in! Without thinking, he raised his hand to his mouth. The water was sweet!

Desperately, he began to row. But despite his frantic efforts the boat did not move. It seemed to him that his boat was caught among the branches of a giant underwater tree, held as if in a hand. He rowed as hard as he could, but the boat did not budge. And now he could see with his own eyes how the wood of his tree was exuding clean, fresh water! Erramón fell to his knees and began to bail with his hands, because he had no bucket.

But the hull continued to ooze more and more water. It was already a spring with a thousand holes. And the sea seemed to be sprouting branches.

Erramón crossed himself.

He was never seen again on the shores of Biscay. Some said that he had been seen around San Sebastian, others that he was seen in Bilbao. A sailor spoke of an enormous octopus which had been seen about that time. But no one could give any information about him with any certainty. The oak tree began to grow again. The people shrugged their shoulders. The rumor spread that he was in America. Then, nothing.

The Cathedral of Hearts

JOSÉ MARÍA GIRONELLA

One day it occurred to him that cathedrals should not have been constructed with stone but with human hearts; hearts one on top of the other, as though they were bricks.

"Why don't you build a cathedral like that?" suggested his daughter, a girl with long and slender legs "—a cathedral made of hearts."

"You are right," he answered; and, putting on his coat, he directed his steps toward the cemetery of the city.

The conversation with the gravedigger was short and to the point. He would pay him one duro for hearts of normal size and seven pesetas for all large ones in perfect condition.

"Agreed?"

"Agreed."

From that day on the man went to the cemetery every night after dinner, smoking a cigarette as he walked between the trees alongside the highway.

The gravedigger was waiting for him, his table piled high

with hearts. On some days he would have two, on others four, and on a particularly cold or lucky day six.

"This afternoon I found a magnificent one!" The gravedigger would say to him from time to time. "Look, what a beauty! This one is surely worth seven pesetas to you!" And he would show him the heart of a poor old servant, or of a poor shoemaker.

"This one here, on the other hand, I can give you for a real," he would add with sudden generosity, as he showed him the heart of an adulteress or a deserter.

They rented a large warehouse on the outskirts of the city, and proceeded to deposit their unusual bricks. On Saturdays they opened the windows to prevent the air from becoming stale.

The war, of course, was of great help to them. Material began coming in by the barrel. There were mornings when as many as forty or fifty pierced hearts reached the warehouse.

In '39, the man's daughter, who drew fairly well and had designed some sort of plan for the project, came to visit the warehouse. She glanced at the piles of hearts, made a rapid calculation, and concluded that only a few more would be required.

They transported the hearts to the mountain in mule carts. As the site of the temple, they had chosen a small barren plain, which the carts, moving up a wretched path, reached only with difficulty.

As soon as the gravedigger had made his last trip, father and daughter began to work like expert bricklayers. It was autumn, and they worked mostly by the light of the moon.

The seven-peseta hearts were used for the foundation. They had to support the entire structure. Those that cost one real would be utilized at points of lesser importance.

The cathedral grew little by little. On each side altar they put the heart of a child. When December arrived, they were beginning work on the curve of the apse; and on the main altar the man lined up the hearts of all his friends.

One day, before closing the apse, they took stock. They were short one heart.

"We will have to go down for it," said the father.

"No, no!" objected the daughter. "Impossible! It is for a place of vital importance." And she added: "It has to be a heart in which you can have full confidence." Upon which she smiled, and then, doubling over, as though struck by a thunderbolt, she offered her own to her father.

He uttered a cry of fear and surprise. Finding himself alone before his work on the top of the mountain, he walked around like a madman, jumping over rocks and weeping. At last he made up his mind and tore out the heart of his daughter. It was the only one that had not cost him anything. He placed it at the very top, over the center of the apse, thus completing his gigantic project.

For two years he remained on top of the mountain, purifying himself. He prayed in the interior of the cathedral night and day. With the sharp, cool winds blowing continuously on the mountain tops, no decomposition set in, not even in the summer.

From time to time, the gravedigger came up to visit him and to bring him clean linen. One day he said to him: "Do you remember the warehouse? It has been converted into a garage."

At Christmas time of the third year, the gravedigger brought a bottle of wine and sweets in addition to the linen. The man ate with appetite and drank, and then, when he was alone again, he lit up a pipe and sat near the fireplace which warmed him.

The fumes of the wine began to charm his spirit, and the

architect remembered the world. For a minute he closed his eyes. Is it then not possible to have a single desire? he murmured. Then he fell asleep on the floor with his legs drawn up.

He woke up a little later than usual with a bitter taste in his mouth and went to the cathedral to pray. He entered, and, as was his custom, went up to the main altar with his arms extended.

Hardly had he knelt, when from the center of the vault a drop of blood fell down at his side.

Heavens! He looked up and saw that the uppermost hearts were beginning to drip blood. It was like a fine and continuous rain that gradually stained the cathedral. A pool formed on the ground, and the apse itself, now viscous, reeled and cracked, and gave the impression that it was about to come apart.

The man ran out of the temple, pursued by little drops that struck his head and eyes. When he was twenty feet away, he heard a dull noise behind him, a mute and heavy thud.

He looked around, disconsolate, and grew pale. His creation had turned into a hecatomb. The hearts had all come down and were spread out here and there in formless heaps. Only, all the way on top, in its original place, like a small abandoned bird, his daughter's heart was still fluttering and bleeding.

He didn't even have time to break into tears. One of the hearts had suddenly begun to beat, and then to skip haltingly in the direction of the path that led down to the city.

Another heart followed, and then another, and another. Within five minutes the entire mass of hearts had begun to move. They were spread out over the entire mountain, and gradually covered the slopes and rocks. They were like large crabs or little red octopi marching in guerrilla formation to conquer the walled city that was visible at the bottom of the valley.

"Hey, hey there!" shouted the man, heading toward the octopi that led the way, and in whom he recognized the deserters. But no human power could hold back the formation.

After an exhausting five-hour march, the mass of hearts reached the gates of the city, and silently entered through the side streets. The inhabitants were immediately aware of the presence of this army of crawling, wriggling parasites.

"They are hearts!" murmured some women fearfully.

"They are hearts!" repeated two women from a window.

"They are hearts!" cried out the entire city, running out into the streets.

"There is my son's!" shouted an old woman all of a sudden, and stretched out her arms.

"That is my brother over there!" exclaimed the voice of a young girl, as she dropped the pail she was carrying.

"Father, mother, brother, son!" The entire city was filled with arms stretched out to receive the resuscitated hearts.

And the people found out the truth at last. For every heart immediately and without hesitation headed for a definite house or place to be near that which it had loved most during its lifetime. There were dozens of astonished husbands who watched the hearts of their wives climb unfamiliar staircases. It was the greatest confusion a city had ever witnessed. For every heart moved without secrecy. One small and unknown heart turned slowly toward the cemetery. Half a dozen entered the church and stretched out humbly before the first station of the cross. Two young and handsome ones, doubtless those of women, headed like arrows toward one of the movie theaters and clambered onto a seat where they sat expectantly. A number of old and wrinkled ones directed their steps toward the bank of Spain.

In the homes, the faithful hearts were received joyfully. The family would kneel around the heart with boundless tenderness.

Nobody spoke, and tears rolled to the ground. For its part, the heart sighed happily.

In one home, however, the reception was quite different. The heart of the head of the family entered the dining room at the moment when his widow and children were seated at the table with hardly anything to eat.

"Look, mother!" cried the smallest, "I want some, I want some! . . ."

At midafternoon, the architect who had built the cathedral and was responsible for this turmoil found himself alone at the center of the city, when all hearts had already arrived at their destinations.

Then, forlornly shaking his head, he began to climb the mountain, in search of his daughter's heart. As the shadows began to spread over the world, he arrived at the top, exhausted. He looked toward the place where the apse had been, and saw nothing. He experienced uneasiness and doubt. Where was his daughter? He heard the sound of footsteps behind him. He turned around, suddenly filled with hope, and clearly distinguished the silhouette of the gravedigger who fled down the mountain, with a little package in his hand.

MODERN LIBRARY GIANTS

*A series of full-sized library editions of books that formerly
were available only in cumbersome and expensive sets.*
THE MODERN LIBRARY GIANTS REPRESENT A
SELECTION OF THE WORLD'S GREATEST BOOKS

These volumes contain from 600 to 1,400 pages each